GREGORY BELL

INTEGRITY'S PLIGHT

The Lies That Bind

Gregory Bell

Published by Gregory Bell.

For information, send an email to info@integritysplight.com
http://www.integritysplight.com

ISBN-13: 978-0692593752
ISBN-10: 0692593756

DEDICATION

I would like to dedicate this, my first published novel, to my parents, Marcus and Doris Bell. Writing a book, trying to get it published while raising a family, and managing life in general make for unique and unusual adventures. I want to thank my parents for ensuring that my sister and brothers and I got the proper tools, education and, most importantly, the guidance to be able to navigate through both the smooth and the rough times.

We are taking the same light you shone on us to illuminate the paths of our children. If all goes as envisioned, they will go further than we have.

ACKNOWLEDGMENTS

There are so many people I would like to acknowledge that it is difficult to begin. But here goes.

To the four lovelies in the Bell household; my wife Victoria and my three daughters, Alice, Margaret and Marian. Thanks for keeping me well supplied in love, hugs, kisses and Haagen-Dazs.

I thought that this book was finished before I handed it to Sharon Reitman and Ruth Duncan Bell for editing. I was wrong. Thank you for the sharpened pencils, the adherence to grammar and punctuation and for putting up with someone who thought every word he had written served a purpose, even as you showed him that literally, thousands of them did not. I was too close to the project to edit it properly. They were too professional to do otherwise.

Thanks for all of those confidence-builders out there who read a portion of what I had written and provided comments/revisions or just plain positive reinforcement. You don't know how much that means to a first timer.

To my mom who thought that I would be a preacher, to the El Cerrito High School English teacher who got me the reading lists from the world's leading universities at a time when you had to send a stamped letter and research the addresses in encyclopedias; to the journalism professor at Hayward State who challenged me to always do my best; to the Air Force Wing Commander in England who told me that I was an excellent writer; to the CLEO program law professor from the University of Utah School of Law who told me that I would do something great. I don't know if I'll ever achieve or live up to those lofty platitudes, but thank you to all who believed that I might. I will always keep trying to be what each of you saw in me.

Special thanks to a forward thinking businessman named Jerry Bell who proved invaluable in getting this novel published. I don't know if it would have happened without him; but I can say that it did happen because of him.

TABLE OF CONTENTS

PREFACE

Integrity's Plight explores the role that ethics, morality and integrity have played, or failed to play, in the American experience. This novel also aims to understand the role that redemption and second chances play in driving our daily activities.

Are right and wrong the concepts that we live by to promote, create and ensure a peaceful and benevolent society, or are they just the difference between being caught or getting away with activities benefitting the individual to the detriment of society? How does promoting the individual's goals over society's needs benefit anyone? Should it have ever become acceptable to individuals, their elected officials and society as a whole to gain power and wealth, if we lose the one trait, morality, that allows us to best control that power and wealth? "Integrity's Plight," offers responses to these questions.

My time as a military officer taught me accountability, integrity and responsibility. I learned that you can delegate authority but you cannot delegate responsibility. Observing the corporate world for the last three decades has been eye-opening, to say the least. There are literally no rules in the corporate world, save capturing all and giving little of it back.

The difference between the military world and the corporate/government worlds was significant. Gone was a concern for the person next to you or the people behind you, All that exists is a clawing, ever-moving effort to get what someone else has- methods and manner be damned. I came back to a world where all that matter was more. Professionally, I chose not to live that way.

I have served in altruistic governmental/municipal positions since 1997, trying where I may to ensure that federal and state civil rights laws are adhered to. It is a never-ending, uphill struggle. You face constant confrontations from without, little to no support from within, all the while working for unknown, faceless souls who you hope will benefit, but who will never know your name, the efforts you made on their behalf or ultimately the sacrifices you made to help them. Helping others is your only reward-it is the only constant. I

1

will always dedicate my literary achievements to those who help and serve others. I can honestly say I know what they have gone through, or are in the process of going through. They will always garner my respect.

INTEGRITY'S PLIGHT

GREGORY BELL

CHAPTER 1

COLLISION

The sun had barely fallen beneath the horizon when the fog banks made their ominous appearance. Rolling over the coastal range and down into San Francisco, out onto the bay itself and finally covering the east bay, the fog assumed a mythical quality; an ethereal force whose purpose was to regain during the dead of night the area which it must always yield at sunrise. And throughout time, both past and present, these two forces have continued their pointless conflict, much to the dismay of those whose lives it interferes.

"The fog's not too thick tonight, is it sir?"

"No it isn't," replied Capt. Benjamin Marlowe, "but let's be careful nonetheless. Complacency in this soup will get us in serious trouble."

Marlowe was the captain of the `Benician Guardian', an 880 foot supertanker carrying a partial load of 50,000 tons of Alaskan crude oil to Los Angeles. The ship had just off-loaded 60,000 tons at the company refinery in Benicia and was just getting underway when the fog rolled in. Like every able-bodied seamen, Marlowe had been in fog before, in fact he'd been through worse here in the San Francisco Bay. But all in all, he would not have been adverse to avoiding it altogether.

"What's our speed?" Marlowe enquired.

"Eight knots, sir," replied the helmsman.

"Keep her there until we clear the Golden Gate, then proceed at twelve knots until we clear this fog. About how long until we approach the Golden Gate?"

"About an hour," came a voice from the back of the bridge." ...maybe less."

"Good," said Marlowe, .".keep your eyes open gentlemen, we wouldn't want to hit anything."

Twenty seven miles south of the Golden Gate, the Montgomery Oil Company tanker, `Pacific Patriarch' was running a course roughly parallel to the Pacific shoreline, about fifteen miles out. She was on her maiden voyage and seventy-two hours earlier had begun offloading her first 100,000 ton cargo of Alaskan crude into a tank farm in the Los Angeles harbor. She was on her way back to Alaska for another load, thus beginning the journey anew.

"Sir, tanks number one and two have been inspected and were found satisfactory."

"Thank you," said Roland Mathis, the first mate. "Two down and five to go." The `Pacific Patriarch' was a big ship, not as massive as the 200-525,000 ton ultra large tankers that ply the Persian Gulf to Europe routes, but considered good-sized for the Alaska-Los Angeles run. Her seven main cargo tanks each held over 25,000 tons of oil, and that was not her full cargo rating.

"I never did like this tank cleaning madness," the first mate confided to another of the bridge crew. "But mine is not to make reply, mine is not to reason why, mine is just to ..."

"Sir, it seems as though we're entering a fog bank of some size," came a voice from the back of the bridge.

"I see," the first mate replied. "Bring her down to half speed and make sure the collision avoidance system is operating properly. Also, amend the log to reflect our slowing."

"Capt. Marlowe, we've cleared the Golden Gate. Your orders, sir?"

Proceed at half speed until we clear the fog," Marlowe said. He slowly walked over to the port and then to the starboard side of the bridge and observation deck. It was an old seaman's quirk that he developed years ago. It unnerved the crew the first time they saw it, but that was countless voyages ago. They now knew that this nervous strolling was simply Marlowe's way of looking for the best vantage point to see what was in front of him. Marlowe learned long ago that there was always something out there, and to keep from finding it with the expensive bow of your ship, you had to avoid it. And you can't avoid what you couldn't see.

"The fog's getting thicker," Marlowe began. "Just twenty minutes ago you could see twice the length of the ship. Now you can hardly see the bow or..."

A piercing wail suddenly ripped through the hushed atmosphere that was the bridge. Almost as if on cue, from the back of the bridge, the collision avoidance system was sounding the alarm with its noise making attachments blaring as if all hell had broken loose.

"Radar, what have we got out there?" shouted Marlowe.

The radar operator was already hunched over his monitor, staring intently.

"Sir, I don't have anything on my radar," he yelled. The din from the collision avoidance system was such that Marlowe couldn't hear the answer. He quickly walked over and turned off the alarm.

"What do you have on your monitor?" Marlowe snapped.

"Nothing sir, come see for yourself."

"Damn, its malfunctioning again." Marlowe pivoted around and barked, "Helmsman, put her over fifteen degrees to port."

A mood of deep concern reigned on the bridge of the `Patriarch'. Knowing that all eyes of the bridge crew were on him, the first mate of the `Patriarch' calmly looked out into the wall of mist that had effectively cut his vision down to less than one length of his ship. Mathis, acknowledging that any sign of emotion could serve to unnerve the crew, slowly turned away from the fog-obscured Pacific and looked over to the radar specialists. In a tone that tried to hide its apprehension, he asked the radar specialists for the distance of the ship that had set off their collision avoidance system.

"About four miles sir, at about twelve knots. They have turned to port."

"Towards us?" Mathis replied quizzically. Then if we maintain our present heading, they should pass well behind us."

"Actually sir?" the radar specialist replied, "we've slowed up somewhat, so they should pass in front of us."

"Although not by any overwhelming distance," came another voice from the back of the bridge.

The concern in that voice was not lost on the first mate. He looked over to the radar operator and said, "Keep your eyes open, man. Not only on that one but any other ship that could cause us a problem."

"The rest of you," he was now addressing the entire bridge crew, "help the radar ops out. We could use all the eyes we've got and more tonight."

Mathis had been in this situation before. In his thirteen years on the sea he'd just about seen it all. But this was his first voyage as the first mate. Never before had he carried the responsibility that came with that rank. But as he was fond of saying, "You gotta be a first mate before you can be a captain." The trip down from Alaska was so uneventful that it was almost boring, serving no other purpose to Mathis than the transportation of oil. A fog bank, on the other hand, served as a sounding board; helping him learn what to do in this kind of situation. This, and similar examples like it, allowed Mathis to gain valuable experience. This would help him tremendously when he came up for his captain's boards.

As it was a new ship and its personality had not yet been defined, everyone on board was a little tentative. But all that it took was one glance at Mathis to see that, while everything wasn't as good as it could have been, at least it was under control.

For the next ten minutes the men on the bridge of both ships were tense. Capt. Marlowe and his crew were travelling blind, without radar coverage, and were keeping a lookout for the ship that activated their collision avoidance system. On the `Pacific Patriarch', the crew had stopped looking at the `Guardian', assuming that she would safely pass by them. Their attention was now being held by a small South American coffee freighter that had just set off their collision avoidance system. The freighter, an 28,000 tonner, had left the bay right behind the `Guardian' and followed her out. When the `Guardian' turned to port to avoid the `Patriarch', the little freighter, the `Juan Gormon', simply went full steam. Whatever the reason they accelerated for worked; they cleared the bow of the `Patriarch' by almost two miles and disappeared in the fog.

"This has been a busy night," said Mathis. "We haven't heard that collision device in a while and now, twice right off the bat."

Mathis looked back to the helmsman, then back to the foggy ocean in front of him. His last statement about the number of alarms made him wonder if the ship should be further away from shore.

"Maybe the further from shore, the less chance of one of these cowboys hitting me," he thought to himself.

"Helmsman, prepare for a course change."

"Whereabouts, sir?" replied the helmsman.

"I'm going to take her out further from shore. Out to about twenty five miles," said Mathis. "Navigator, please amend the log to show this action and..."

The first mate never finished his sentence.

For the third time in less than an hour the collision avoidance system let out its alarm.

Suddenly, with the shock of a recurring nightmare, the collision avoidance system went off again. Mathis experienced that dreaded half-feeling that something awful was about to happen.

"Get me a bearing on that other ship!" Mathis yelled while spinning around to face the radar operator,

The radar operator looked down at his screen and gasped. The radar's screen covered an area of over seventy nautical miles. The radar operator had looked down at his monitor just in time to see two white dots side by side at the very center of the screen. One dot represented the `Pacific Patriarch' the other was unknown. At the instant the radar operator recognized what was happening, the two white dots merged into one.

"Damn it man, where is the other ship." screamed Mathis.

The last time the collision avoidance system went off, the crew didn't worry much due to the calmness of the first mate. There was something different about the situation this time. Now there was a terror in his voice, one that they had never heard before. One that, they would soon find, was totally justified.

The radar operator stood up. His face was pale and ashen, and as he turned to the first mate, the rest of the bridge crew knew that they were suddenly, yet irrefutably, in danger.

The radar operator pointed to a spot in the fog forty five degrees to starboard. At that same time, at that same spot less than 200 yards ahead of them and about 180 yards off their starboard beam, the bow of the `Benician Guardian', moving at twelve knots, broke through a gap in the fog.

The collision avoidance system on the 'Guardian' went off at the same time as the one on the `Patriarch'. Capt. Marlowe, knowing that their own radar system was inoperative, or at least grossly inaccurate, immediately looked out across the front of his ship. Just off the port bow he saw several bright flashes of light dancing about 35 feet above the surface of the water.

Then they disappeared.

The captain turned to the helmsman and yelled again.

"HARD APORT, Man. NOW!"

"What is it, Sir--what did you see?"

"Running lights," Marlowe said. "There's a ship out there and judging from the height of the lights, she's either a big, empty tanker riding high or a real big freighter. And she's too close. Too damned close."

"Captain," came an urgent cry from the helmsman, "she's not responding to the wheel!"

Marlowe quickly looked back into the fog trying to relocate the running lights. He couldn't find them.

Marlowe turned and bounded the short distance between where he was standing and the wheel. He pushed the helmsman aside and grabbed the wheel, turning it furiously, hoping that it would respond to him as it refused to for the helmsman. It only took a few seconds for Marlowe to realize that the helmsman was right; the ship was not responding.

Marlowe looked over to the radio operator and signaled him to call the Coast Guard and issue a MAYDAY. Marlowe issued the order to reverse engines, but he knew that the massive propellers twenty five feet below the surface were still churning forward. The great momentum of those twenty seven ton screws would not be offset by the reverse steam on the turbines for several minutes. A 60,000 ton ship with 50,000 ton of oil takes two to four miles to stop. The distance that they had to react in was measured in yards, not miles. It was at this time that the bridge crew of the `Patriarch' saw the bow of the `Guardian' breaking through the fog.

On the `Patriarch', Mathis gave the order "hard abort" when he first saw the `Guardian," but he knew that the ship would have barely begun turning when they collided. He also ordered the engines into full reverse, not because he thought that he could avoid the imminent collision, but hopefully to control the amount of damage about to be inflicted on his ship. The captain was awake and on his way to the bridge, but Mathis knew that the collision would occur before he got there.

Mathis opened up the shipboard intercom and said, with the most authoritative voice he could muster, "ALL HANDS BRACE AND RIG FOR COLLISION."

Capt. Marlowe had given the order for the entire crew to be standing by their damage repair/control stations. Through the fog, though just barely, Marlowe caught a glimpse of the most sickening sight of his entire maritime career. The bow of the `Patriarch' had just crossed his, and equal to the Plimsoll line, that massive red band that runs the entire length of the bottom half of the ship, was the `Guardian's' bow. The `Patriarch' was empty, and that red band stood close to twenty feet high. When the ship was laden with cargo, that line would be submerged.

Whatever other thoughts that Marlowe had, he didn't have time to mull over them. Just seconds after the ships crossed bows, the `Guardian' slashed into the unprotected side of the `Patriarch'.

With a screeching, grinding crash, the `Guardian' ripped into the innards of the `Patriarch'. The impact was so great that everyone on both ships was knocked down and sent sprawling by the violent union of over 250,000 tons of steel and cargo.

Marlowe was the first one on the `Guardian' to get back on his feet. Without a doubt, the damage he saw from the collision was the worst he'd ever seen. The `Guardian' had caught the `Patriarch' right smack on the area between cargo tanks three and four. The `Guardian's' momentum pushed it through the double hulls of the `Patriarch' and into the major bulkheads separating tanks three and four. The bulkheads, a major component to the structural integrity of the ship, were destroyed. But before they collapsed, they caused tremendous damage to the bow of the `Guardian'.

The `Guardian's' bow was designed to smoothly slip through waves, not withstand heavy collisions with structurally reinforced areas of other ships. Had they hit fifteen feet in either direction, they would have sliced through steel plating which, while damaging their ship somewhat, would not have done the amount of damage that the bulkheads did.

The `Guardian's' bow was enmeshed over twenty-seven feet into the other ship and bent downward at an awkward angle. The tremendous punishment it had absorbed was too much, and it collapsed.

Marlowe feared the worst. His fears where confirmed when he aimed a searchlight over the edge and saw a black syrupy substance coming up from the side. His forward cargo tanks had been ruptured, which meant that the forward collision bulkhead in his own ship, the one that had taken the brunt of the crash, was either gone or failing.

Marlowe then felt the ship give a mild shudder beneath his feet. At that instant, he realized that the two ships were still moving. The two giants had been locked together since the instant of the crash and had stopped all forward motion. The momentum of the collision was expended in the crash, so they were no longer moving forward. But both ships had been in full reverse when the crash occurred and now, twenty-five feet below the surface, their massive propellers were turning in full reverse. This was pulling the two ships apart. Marlowe saw the crew of the `Patriarch' racing to the railing overlooking the huge hole in the side of their ship. He felt the vibrations as the `Guardian' was trying to pull herself out of the `Patriarch'.

He turned to the second mate and said, "Tell the engine room all stop! We can't try to separate."

At that same moment, the ship gave a mighty shudder. Marlowe looked forward to the bow and saw his ship starting to slide back out of the `Patriarch' and into the water. With that shudder came a shower of sparks that resembled a 4th of July fireworks display.

The ship gave another shudder. Marlowe saw the sparks and yelled at the top of his lungs, "NOOOOOO!"

The shifting of steel on steel had caused a display of millions of sparks flying in every direction. With the last attempt to separate, thousands of these sparks found their way into the ruptured cargo tanks. With Capt. Marlowe's orders to stop his ship just halfway to the engine room, and with the first twenty feet of the `Guardian's' bow still enmeshed in her side, the `Patriarch' blew up.

The entire complement of the `Guardian," minus the engine room crew, was on some part of the ship's deck watching the two ships try to separate. They had, for some reason unknown to them, stayed near the rear accommodation area. This action saved their lives.

While they were watching the shower of sparks rise from the first separation attempt, they heard an anguished scream from the bridge. Before they could even turn to see what was causing the scream, the sparks from the two ships entered the ruptured cargo holds and caused the fumes there to ignite.

A brilliant white flash, a loud crack and a tremendous concussion once again threw the crew to the deck. Millions of cubic feet of gas, touched off by the sparks entering the ruptured tanks, erupted into a massive explosion which sent a fireball 300 yards across rising from the spot where the center of the `Patriarch' used to be.

The thunderclap from the explosion was heard as far away as the cities of Pinole and Fremont, over 40 miles away in opposite directions.

The center of the `Patriarch' was gone. So was the bow of

the `Guardian'. In one searing instant thousands of tons of steel and oil were blown skyward in a tremendous blast. The crewmembers of the `Patriarch' had raced to the collision area just in time to be blown apart. On the bridge of the `Patriarch', First Mate Mathis, the just-arrived captain and the entire bridge crew were instantly incinerated by the fireball that smashed into the accommodations area before rising thousands of feet into the night.

The bow section of the `Patriarch' had drifted forward for a few hundred yards, but now, with its innards hopelessly wrecked, it took on water and quickly sank from view. The rearward accommodations area, where most of the ship's crew had been, was first wracked by flames during the explosion, and then sank almost immediately. The few crewmembers who survived the collision and the firestorm, were now being dragged down by the suction of the sinking vessels. It had taken almost a year to build the `Pacific Patriarch'. She and her crew died in less than two minutes.

It had been less than one minute since the explosion and no more than three since the collision, but it seemed like an eternity for the `Guardian's'crew. While they had watched the death of the `Patriarch' and her crew, they knew now was not the time to mourn. Capt. Marlowe looked to the front of his ship and he knew instantly that they were all in tremendous danger. What remained of his bow was down in the water. The concussion of the blast had rocketed unchecked though his ship, mainly though the cargo areas. It smashed through interior bulkheads that, while they were strong, weren't strong enough. The heavy collision bulkhead at the front of the ship was the only one on board that could have stopped the concussion from rupturing the cargo tanks. But it, and twenty-odd feet of the bow disappeared in the blast, leaving the sea to pour into the shattered tanks.

The oil leak of a few minutes ago was nothing compared to the torrent of oil escaping now. Marlowe knew that there was nothing that he or anyone else could do to stem the spillage. He scanned the deck in front of him to see what his next course of action would be when he noticed a peculiar rise almost halfway down the ship. He knew immediately what it was. The rise was caused by one of the ruptured bulkheads almost being blown through the roof of one of the cargo tanks. It spelled disaster for his ship, as there was now nothing to keep the ocean out of his ship except the rapidly spilling cargo.

An oil tanker with a load of crude oil has a lot in common with an ice berg; most of it is underwater. The `Guardian' was carrying 50,000 tons of oil when her bow was collapsed by the collision. This opened the first cargo tank to the sea, which poured in slowly at first. The explosion ripped apart the first cargo tanks and destroyed the interior structural integrity of the entire ship. The interior bulkheads failed and opened up the entire cargo to the sea. As the sea came into the ship, the oil obligingly left, thus making more space for more water to enter. As oil is lighter than water, the oil simply floated out of the gaping hole where the bow used to be. The Pacific Ocean was pouring into tank no. 1 and beginning to enter the remains of tank no. 2. Again looking off to the side, Marlowe could barely make out the expanding patch of oil that was emanating from his ship. An oil refinery would have taken half a day to empty this ship of its cargo. The ocean worked far quicker. Tank no. 1 was already 3/4 full and tank no. 2 was beginning to fill fast. Marlowe, as well as several other crewmembers, were now noticing that the bow was even lower than before.

In his mind's eye, Marlowe knew exactly everything that was happening to his ship. He also knew the inevitable outcome. They had just minutes to get off of the ship or they would share the same fate that befell the `Patriarch's' crew.

He looked over to one of the crewmembers who was staring at him and said, "The ship is dying."

And it was. An oil tanker like the `Guardian' can sail around the world with its cargo tanks full of oil. But filling those same cargo tanks full of seawater would sink her quicker than any torpedo could. In a fashion, this is what was happening to the `Guardian'. When the saltwater rushed into tank number one, it displaced the oil that was there. This oil spread out over the Pacific to become a monster oil slick. The water in tank number one, being heavier that the oil it displaced, pulled the rest of the bow area down into the water even more. This was allowing more water to rush into tank number two. This self-perpetuating situation was pushing the bow of the ship deeper and deeper into the water. Marlowe grasped this situation about the time that tank number two was half filled. He estimated that by the time tank number five filled up, the ship would sink. Time was not only his enemy now, but a precious resource that could, by no means, be wasted.

"All hands on deck! All hands on deck!" Marlowe growled into the intercom.

This is no drill! Abandon ship now! Repeat, abandon ship now!

No one on board faltered or questioned the authenticity of the abandon ship order. This was removed by the immediacy and terror in and of the captain's voice. His was the cry of a prophet; the cry of a man who knew what fate had in store for him yet still had the time and opportunity to change that fate. He called over to the first mate, asking if the life boats had been lowered. The mate hurriedly replied that they were in the process of lowering them now.

"Hurry it up, man," Marlowe snapped, "we've only got minutes left."

While the rest of the bridge crew ran to the nearest of two lifeboats, Marlowe quickly scanned the bridge and a portion of the accommodations area to ensure that no one would be left.

Proof of Marlowe's command over his crew was evident in the hurried evacuation. It wasn't an 'every man for himself' scramble but an orderly response to the captain's orders. To prevent confusion during an emergency, everyone on board was assigned to a lifeboat the day they came aboard the ship. Confusion in a situation like this could cost lives. As each life boat could safely carry twenty five crewmembers, and the `Guardian' had a complement of only 34, the knowledge that there was room for everyone went a long way in avoiding a rush for the boats. Marlowe knew this and made sure his crew did too.

As the first lifeboat was being lowered, the ship shook.

Everyone stood still, from the men still on board to those in the lifeboat, all experiencing a gnawing sensation in the pits of their stomachs. It was a feeling they all shared and none verbalized; a feeling that this shuddering was a harbinger of their own deaths.

The electric winches, however, performed flawlessly, paying out the line to lower the lifeboat into the water. At both ends of the lifeboat, crewmembers got up to unleash the winch cables.

The first crewmember had just set his hand on the cable release when the ship shuddered again. This time, the motion was so violent that it lifted the lifeboat, still attached to the winches, clear out of the water.

The `Guardian' had rolled to starboard, the opposite side of where the lifeboats were being lowered. The roll was only a few degrees, but it was enough to pull the lifeboat clear of the water. Only by tripping the emergency winch releases were the crew able to free themselves. The lifeboat plopped into the water, free from entanglement with the `Guardian'. But the problems were far from over for Marlowe and his men.

The `Guardian's' roll had now made it impossible for the other lifeboat to be launched. Marlowe looked up on the railing and saw eleven crewmembers whose escape was now threatened. The roll had shifted tons of equipment and debris onto the lifeboat winches and controls, and the lifeboat itself was now caught up in all sorts of cables and machinery. There was simply no time left to free the other lifeboat. Marlowe knew that they only had minutes, at the outside, to flee before the `Guardian' joined the `Patriarch'.

Marlowe looked up at the men on the railing. They were trying to figure out their next course of action, not realizing that their options were few. Marlowe knew that they wouldn't last long in this oil coated water, so a prolonged float was out. If they were too close to the ship when it went under, they would go down with it.

Marlowe had made his choice and ordered the lifeboat he was in closer to his stricken ship. He knew his lifeboat would be maxed out at twenty five, but he wasn't going to leave eleven of his men to die.

"Jump!," Marlowe yelled. "We'll put you in this lifeboat. Hurry, Damn it. We're out of time."

One by one the crewmembers quickly jumped into the water and swam to the waiting, and now overloaded, lifeboat. As soon as the last man was onboard, the lifeboat's motor roared to life. Although extremely overloaded, the lifeboat slowly but surely, made headway.

They were almost a mile away when they heard a gut-wrenching whine. It was a sound none of them would ever forget.

Almost in unison they looked back to their ship. Its tortured structures were giving way, and with each long drawn out groan, more oil was being released.

Suddenly, the ship lurched forward. The whole crew knew she was sinking.

The water around the front of the ship began to boil as if the ship were heated steel. The bubbling water presented a display of mystical coloration, boiling upward around the ship to break the surface in a phosphorescent rush. The reflection of the moon, which broke through certain spots of the fog, and the lightness of the fog against the tumbling water contributed to this effect. This phosphorescent fountain was only interrupted by black patches of oil, which seemed to absorb rather than reflect the light.

Fifteen minutes later all was quiet again. The fog had, yet again, reclaimed California's central coast and the neighboring Pacific with its ambivalent awning of mist and spray.

CHAPTER 2

CRISIS CONTROL

David Morris was at home, resting up after a proverbial 'hard day at the office'. His hard day had taken place at the Bennington Oil refinery in Benicia and not the company's air-conditioned tower in San Francisco. From eight o'clock that morning till just after nine in the evening, he had been engaged in, preparing for, hosting, and escorting a contingent of media members around the refinery.

Bennington Oil had just finished a $325 million dollar modification project at the refinery, and they wanted everyone to know it. As deputy director of public relations for Bennington, it was Morris' job to show them.

He spent the entire day with the media representatives, finishing at the refinery at five p.m. Following that, they adjourned to the company's headquarters building where the group was treated to dinner. With the exception of two film crews, who left early to try and prepare their footage for the ten o'clock news, the group dined in the company's fifteenth-floor restaurant.

Dinner, drinks and conversation weren't over until almost eight, and with all of the other loose ends that needed taking care of, Morris didn't get home till almost ten-thirty.

While the newspaper reporters stated that they wouldn't be running their features for another few days, two of the television correspondents had indicated that they would try and run their segments that night. Only one actually did.

Morris asked his lover Alice to videotape it. A lawyer with a small East bay firm, she worked more conventional hours and could easily record the segment. His plans for the rest of the evening were just to settle in with her and review his performance.

He had just pulled his evening chair around to face the television, and had started thinking to himself about his weekend plans when a sharp, loud roar rolled through the fog shrouded night and shattered the evening calm,

"What the hell was that?" Morris inquired.

Morris walked over to the window and looked out into the cold, misty fog. Ghostlike, the fog now hung thick and heavy all throughout the bay, like a suffocating blanket, hiding all of the nighttime activities. He turned away from the window and headed back into the living room. Alice was just coming back into the room when he returned.

"What was that?" she asked.

"I don't know, but it was loud," Morris said, emphasizing the word `loud'. Probably thunder over this damned fog."

It couldn't be thunder," said Alice. "Thunder is a slow rolling rumble...." while she was saying this she was gesturing with her hands, describing a rolling motion to highlight her point.

"Whereas what we just heard was a quick sudden bang." She stopped her rolling motion and smashed her right hand, now clenched into a list, into her flattened left hand. She timed the impact so that her hands came together on the word 'bang'.

"No," she said, "I don't think that was thunder."

Morris stood looking at her and added, "You Berkeley lawyers sure get dramatic."

"If it wasn't thunder," he challenged, "what was it?"

"That's easy," she said. "It's probably one of your stocks falling off the big board."

She started to laugh while Morris gave her a mock disparaging look.

"You think you're so damned funny, don't you?" he stated matter—of —factly.

She strolled over to the sofa, still laughing, and let herself fall into it. It took her almost half a minute to regain herself.

When she'd stopped laughing, she got up and walked over to Morris, took his hands and led him to the couch.

"C'mon, let's go look at the tape of David Morris, public relations professional unchained."

He looked over at her and in his best Ralph Cramden imitation said, "Oooh, one of these days, Alice, one of these days!"

For the next forty minutes they attended to the living room and its VCR. They viewed and reviewed his media performance at the refinery, critiquing it and coming up with several ideas as to how he could improve himself before he was next called upon to deal with the media.

He wouldn't have time to implement the suggested improvements.

The ringing phone in the kitchen interrupted their critique. Morris walked the fifteen feet to the phone and answered it. Alice was still on the sofa, but close enough to hear every word he said.

"Yes. When? How bad? Almost an hour ago. Any word on the crew? OK, as soon as I can."

Alice saw him hang up and slowly walk back over to the sofa.

"What's up, hon?"

"We've gotten a mayday from one of our tankers right outside the bay. It went down and it's spilling its load. I don't know much more," he added reluctantly, "except that I have to go back to the office."

"I thought so," she said. "Hon, I was tired and I was sort of hoping that we could go to bed." The alluring way she stated this obviously meant she was looking for more than just sleep.

"Aye comely wench," Morris said in a fairly mediocre pirate imitation," so it was sleep ye thought ye'd be getting from me, eh. Why I..."

The ringing phone cut him short. It was a reporter from one of the local all-news radio stations inquiring about the events outside the bay.

Morris quickly gave him the number to the office and directed him to call there. This call, coupled with the first one, brought to the forefront of his mind the awesome reality of what must have happened outside the bay. He began thinking about just how large this incident could get.

Morris looked over at Alice and didn't say a word. He didn't have to. Alice knew that no matter what Dave's heart wanted, his head needed to get to the office and prepare for the coming storm.

He walked over to her and wrapped his arms around her and said, "Sorry darling."

In a pouting fashion she said, "I know. Go on to the office."

Morris wasn't sure of what to expect when he got to the office. The forty six story building was dark except for the brightly lit top twelve floors. This part of the building belonged to Bennington Oil, the rest being leased out to a collection of smaller businesses and agencies.

The guards at the entrance checked his I.D. and approved his entry. The elevator smoothly ascended to the 40th floor, where all of the company's executives were marshaling. When the elevator doors opened, Morris was surprised by what he saw.

The boardroom at Bennington Oil was a flurry of activity. The crash had occurred over two hours ago and most of the staff had only been called within the past hour.

But now the office was fully manned and running. While the entire staff wasn't present, each functional agency that played a role in crisis management had representatives there.

During the day, the business suit is the company uniform. However, at almost 1:47 a.m., in the midst of a crisis, that rule gets somewhat bent. Morris noted the array of outfits his co-workers were wearing. The Bennington Oil staff was in everything from blue jeans to track suits. Sartorial integrity is generally waived when staff members were summoned to work as fast as possible. Morris looked at his watch and noticed that it was going on two a.m.

"This is just what I needed," he thought. "A long day followed by a long night."

He stepped into his office and saw that his staff was already working at full steam. They were monitoring the early news reports; calculating the potential damage in terms of credibility, corporate image, and oil pollution and possible repercussions from the public. They also began plotting the appropriate corporate move and planning the other necessary crisis control functions.

Three blocks away at the 48-story Montgomery Oil building, much of the same thing was occurring. While they were in fact, two separate companies, they were following the same fundamental course of action.

Both public relations offices were preparing initial releases for the media. Both were preparing media and community strategies for dealing with the massive oil slick heading for shore (as well as the tremendous media onslaught coming with it.) High level strategy meetings were planned by both companies to devise their companies' next step.

They also took the time to draft letters of condolences to the families of the crewmembers who died in the accident. Only one chief executive officer would need to forward the drafts for final copies.

Reports as to what was going on, as well as what had actually occurred, were filtering into the Bennington Oil headquarters. Public relations had been monitoring the news reports, and the maritime transportation department had been working closely with the Coast Guard to further determine what was happening. Their inputs had been drafted into a short briefing, which was to be given by the public relations department to the entire staff.

Noise and activity had begun to build up in the room, giving it the impression of an overcrowded pool hall instead of the board room of a Fortune 500 company.

Bill Martin, chief of public relations for Bennington Oil and Morris' immediate boss, stood up in the crowded conference room. Forty-two members of the company's staff were present and all of them were talking and illustrating their own plans of action when they noticed that Martin had stood up and begun walking towards the podium.

The droning of forty-two people talking simultaneously

eased, and was instantly replaced by silence. By the time Martin had reached the podium, the members of Bennington Oil's key staff were nervously waiting to see just what they were up against.

"I'm Bill Martin of the public relations staff, and I'll be filling you in on the accident that occurred a few hours ago." Martin's strong and confident voice permeated the crowd as if he were speaking to each of them on a one-to-one basis. He was being extra careful to speak slowly and clearly, so that he would only have to give this briefing once. Time was extremely valuable, now more so than ever, and he didn't want to spend any of it reiterating his presentation to someone who wasn't listening carefully.

"As all of you know," Martin continued, "one of our ships was involved in terrible accident. Unfortunately, I have to tell you that it's even worse than we originally thought. Our tanker was departing our Benicia refinery with 50,000 tons of crude oil on board, bound for Los Angeles. Somewhere offshore, but not far offshore, it collided with a tanker from Montgomery Oil. Our captain recognized the markings and saw the name of the tanker. It was the PACIFIC PATRIARCH and it was on the downhill side of its maiden journey. Between seventeen and twenty miles outside the Golden Gate they collided in heavy fog. Both ships sank within minutes."

Martin paused for a moment and added, "Actually ours sank...theirs blew up."

The members of the staff grew quiet with that last statement. Several of the staff stared at each other before one of them asked the question that they all had on their minds.

'How many men were killed?"

Martin scanned the room and then looked straight at the man who asked the question.

"Of ours," Martin said, "None. The captain must have done a great job because the Coast Guard said that all of our men were accounted for. They came ashore somewhere up on Muir Beach."

The insensitive way in which the death toll was broken down into an 'us' versus 'them' was not lost on the staff, least of all on Morris.

"How many of their crew was lost?"...came from the back of the room.

Martin looked down and scanned a note card on the podium, shook his head slowly and looked back up.

"It's bad," he said slowly, "Real bad. The Coast Guard reports that all hands, the entire complement of the PACIFIC PATRIARCH perished with the ship. We don't yet know the exact numbers, but the Coast Guard said it's over thirty five."

The entire staff was awestruck. They knew, from a. possible pollution aspect, that this could be a terrible incident. But none of them were prepared for such a high death toll.

One of the younger executives muttered, "That's almost as many people as we have in this room." Everyone, including the CEO, took a look around the room to see what thirty five people in one spot looked like. This action personalized the death toll, putting it in a perspective that they could all visualize and comprehend. Only when they saw the faces of each other and realized how many lives were extinguished in one cataclysmic instant, did the real effect of the tragedy start setting in.

Morris was miffed at the callous way that Martin had briefed the staff, but he let it go. The situation at hand was as bad as it could get. Over thirty-five men dead, two tankers destroyed and a massive oil slick was being released. This oil slick would soon be coming ashore on the beaches outside the bay as well as coming unchecked into the bay. This was not only one of the costliest tanker collisions in terms of life or money, but also the largest environmental threat to the area since two Chevron Oil tankers collided near the Golden Gate in the early seventies.

The question and answer segment of the briefing lasted another ten minutes, after which all of the staff members left, heading back to their respective departments. Morris was waiting by the door for Martin, to talk to him about his presentation, when he noticed Martin, the chief of strategic planning and the Chief Executive Officer leaving through the CEO'S private entrance. Morris walked over to Martin before he left and heard him tell the CEO, "I think that this plan will work. There will never be a time like this again!"

Morris, assuming that Martin was talking about a public relations plan for the accident, turned around and headed back to his office without waiting to speak to him.

Morris put his opinion of Martin's briefing aside while he walked down the corridor to his office. He was concentrating on the enormous job at hand.

The eyes and ears of the media never slept nor blinked, and they were now focusing their scrutiny on two oil companies in San Francisco.

Constantly utilized too late or never consulted with when it mattered, the public relations department was now carrying the ball for Bennington Oil. It was Morris' intention to see that it' didn't get dropped.

Morris spent the next two hours contacting each of the major department heads and seeing what they were planning on doing. Money to combat the spill and its poisonous effects was being allocated. Oil spill contingency plans, which were created exactly for this kind of occurrence, were being taken off of the shelves and reviewed

Morris had drafted the company's first statement to the media and had one of his subordinates take it to the CEO for approval. Twenty minutes later it came back endorsed and Morris had it released. Any press queries dealing specifically with the crash were referred to the Coast Guard.

Morris then had the staff start working on their second statement, which he was hoping to release to the media in two to three hours. His intention was to keep a steady flow of new information going out to the press.

The first statement to the press simply said that one of the company's tankers was involved in an accident and sank, that its cargo was spilling and the company would do all it could to battle the spill, and that further details about this disaster would be forthcoming as soon as possible. That release was sent to the media at four o'clock Friday morning.

This first statement was a simple informative note to the press explaining the situation. The next statement would have a greater purpose.

The second release would be deliberate, telling the public exactly what Bennington Oil was planning on doing. By illustrating in greater detail what the company was doing, this release would be the first in an effort to keep the public from being swayed against their'. It was scheduled to go out no later than midday Friday.

The best way to have the public behind you and sympathetic to your cause was to have the media on your side. As the gatekeepers, the media plays a large pan in the formation of public opinion. What they covered, or what they didn't cover, impacted greatly on how the public viewed the world.

No one was more aware of the importance of the media than Morris. He had already begun drawing up a list of media contacts that he wanted to take up in the company chopper and provide an aerial view of the slick, as well as to talk to selected company officials on the control efforts.

His first choice was Larry Nelson, a reporter from the East Bay Gazette-Journal. The Gazette was the largest paper on the east bay, with a circulation of over 300,000. The slick was slated to hit the east bay hard, and Nelson would be able to tell those affected most what Bennington Oil was doing to control the spill. Morris and Nelson went back a long ways, and they both had a healthy respect for each other's' abilities. It sometimes brought them against each other, but the ill-feelings never lasted for long. Morris was only inviting the radio and print media out for the chopper ride. The television stations owned their own choppers and the skies would be full of them at first light. He did, however, call their press desks and asked if they wanted company experts to go up with them. All four major television stations said yes, and Morris tasked one of his staff to assemble the experts. They would, in the next few hours, all come to Morris' office for a quick brief on what they could and couldn't say. No speculation on the cause of the accident or any statement or acceptance of responsibility could be mentioned. Morris gave each of them a two-page letter that detailed what would be done by the company, and told the group to keep their comments confined to the items listed.

It was closing in on five o'clock Friday morning, and Morris told them to be ready to go no later than seven. He turned them back over to his staff and went back to determining who would get the helicopter flights.

He had gone back into his office, sat down at his desk, and received the first pleasant surprise of the day. Typed on a sheet of bond were fifteen names of reporters, with their media affiliation and phone numbers attached. They represented the largest news organizations in the Bay Area that didn't own, or charter their own helicopters. The list read identical to the one that Morris would have prepared, given time.

At the bottom of the page were the initials A.R.

Morris walked over to the door and yelled across the hallway, "Alan Roth, the 2nd, thank you!"

Roth was the youngest member of the stall and as such, usually got the duties no one else wanted. As the current situation was one of controlled pandemonium, Roth helped out by being observant of what needed to be done, and picking up any duties that may have fallen in the cracks. As this was the first catastrophe to strike Bennington Oil while he was there, he was very eager to assist in any way he could.

Morris finished reading the list and handed it to a staff member to call the parties included. By six o'clock a.m. all of the media involved had voiced their acceptance.

Morris had done a quick walk through to see how his stall was doing when he noticed that Martin's desk was still empty. Morris thought for a second and then realized that not once during the whole time they were working on this catastrophe did Martin stick his head through the door. This absence was beginning to annoy Morris.

"Anyone seen Martin?" Morris inquired.

"Last I saw him, he was with the CEO." said one of the staffers.

Morris went back to his secretary's desk and called the CEO's office on the intercom. They told him that Martin had gone to see the chief of the strategic planning department and that he could probably be reached there.

Morris hung up and dialed the strategic planning office. He was getting upset.

"Let me speak with Bill Martin," Morris snapped.

The male voice at the other end of the phone simply said, "He's behind closed doors."

"You might want to open them," Morris shot back, "this is important."

The other end of the line went silent for a second before the unknown respondent answered back. "Just a minute, I'll get him."

After a few seconds Martin came to the intercom.

"Martin here, what's wrong?"

Morris was quick and to the point.

"You're in charge down here Bill. I've got a bunch of things finalizing and I need you to sign off on them."

"Dave," Martin said." I'm behind closed doors with Stan Jenkins, and when I leave from here I'm going to the hotel where we've got the crew sequestered and talk to them. Use your judgment and proceed as you see fit. Until I get back to you, you're in charge."

"What do you need to talk to the crew for," inquired Morris, "they..."

Martin cut him short. "Can't talk to you anymore Dave. I've got to go. I'll get back to you when I can. Until then, you're in charge there."

With that Martin hung up the phone.

Morris was stunned. He couldn't believe that during the greatest calamity ever to befall the company, the chiefs of public relations, strategic planning and the chief executive officer were "too busy" to be available.

'I hope they know what they're doing,' thought Morris.

Morris went back into his office and called the staff together for a meeting. He was about to lay down his plans for the rest of the day and he wanted to brainstorm it with them.

As he waited for his staff to assemble, he couldn't stop thinking about what the CEO, Stan Jenkins, and Martin might have to discuss that was so important. *What was so crucial that three senior corporate staff members would relinquish their responsibilities at a time like this?"*

The staff started arriving and Dave stopped his reverie. All of those thoughts were put into the back of his mind as he began discussing his plans for the next few days.

CHAPTER 3

THE SPILL

It was born on a dark, weather-obscured Pacific night. For over a week it had been held prisoner in the gray steel holds of the `BENICIAN GUARDIAN'. It had contracted when the ship was in the colder regions, and it had expanded when the ship neared the sun-kissed shores of California. It was intended to be refined into the myriad of products that could be derived from its hydrocarbon base.

A collision was not in the cards.

Its long, black tentacles were now in constant motion; reaching, stretching, yearning to touch land and impose its revenge. Free on the waves, there was only one malevolent function left to the freed petroleum. To destroy, to spoil, to rend useless and lifeless everything it touched.

The oil spilled for days from the ruptured holds of the `BENICIAN GUARDIAN' hundreds of feet beneath the surface of the Pacific, adding to the monstrous slick that began forming with the collision. The spillage was laying over the ocean's surface like an immense black awning; one that was several square miles large and continually growing.

When it was only four hours old, it had already covered more than twenty square miles. It's nine by two and a half mile shape was roughly elliptical, but it was spreading into a more triangular form, with its base heading towards the shore. It was a day older now, and several times larger than it was in its infancy.

The response agencies of the Bay Area deployed their fullest efforts, but luck was not with them. Their tasks were daunting enough: How does an agency protect hundreds of miles of shoreline from an oil slick with less than twenty four hours' notice. The answer was relatively simple—it can't be done. Booms and dispersants and numerous other spill response resources would be on airplanes and trucks within hours of the spill, but their full implementation would not take place by time the spill began touching land.

To compound the problems facing the response forces, the weather forecast was not promising. The seas were expected to start kicking up and higher waves were predicted. Higher waves would agitate the spill and defeat the deployed containment booms by forcing the oil over and under them.

By the time the source of the spill was located, the leading edges of the slick were less than fifteen miles from shore, pulsating towards the shore at two to three miles per hour.

The entire state of California was subjected to a slow, agonizing wait as the slick approached the shore. The slick moved almost in slow motion; as if it's slow, impending arrival could prolong the pain being felt

The next day's late-evening incoming tide grabbed the leading edge of the slick and started taking it under the Golden Gate and into the bay itself. In the morning, when countless commuters came over the Golden Gate, the Richmond-San Raphael and the Bay bridges, or drove along Interstate 80 on the east bay, they would witness a sight that would cause them heartburn, despair and rage.

By 4 a.m. the oil began entering the bay and had already begun smudging the shoreline around Ft. Baker and the Presidio. The slick had split into two large bodies, one, which was entering the Bay, and one that was assaulting the seaward side of the San Francisco peninsula.

It was still dark and foggy outside and no part of the slick could be seen from shore. The Coast Guard was out in force, but their prognosis was not encouraging. They had asked for all of the spill containment equipment that they could get their hands on, but it was a race against time that they knew they were going to lose.

The ships had collided barely a day ago just twenty miles out on an incoming tide, and while both ships had issued a `MAYDAY' warning, both ships were destroyed before they listed their positions. While the Coast Guard was resorting to vectoring their emergency forces to the last known radar plotting of the two ships, even this method had its shortcoming. Their spill response force would have to travel through the slick to try and find its source-which was not only obscured by evening's fog but several hundred feet of water.

By the time that the Coast Guard had discovered the location of where the two ships went down in the fog, the slick was already miles long. The Coast Guard was mobilizing everything they had in an effort to contain the spill, but it was closing in on the Bay before they could even deploy their fullest efforts. Over the next week the Coast Guard would provide a tremendous effort in the attempt to control the spill, and more than one Coast Guardsman would be heard to mutter. "If only those damn tankers were ten more miles out." Only providence knows if it would have made a difference.

Other agencies throughout the bay sprang into action to defend themselves against the- slick. Once upon a time at the Alameda Naval Station, hundreds of sailors would have been roused from their sleep and called to duty to place large booms around their vessels and piers in an effort to keep the oil out. But the Navy base was closed and there would be no forces available to prevent the oil from inundating the shore and the facilities of the once-proud military installation.

At the Steinhart Aquarium the large pipes that bring seawater from the Pacific into the aquarium were closed. For the next few days, until the tanker stopped leaking and the slicks either came ashore or dissipated, the pipes would stay shut to avoid allowing the poisonous oil from entering the aquarium's carefully controlled ecosystem. This efficiency would save the thousands of fish in the aquarium from a slow death. Unfortunately, in the open bay, the same could not be said.

Throughout the course of the day, the slick would

continue its onslaught into the bay and onto the miles of shoreline there. It hit primarily against the eastern side of the bay, coating shoreline from Pinole to Hayward with a thick layer of oil. Fears that the oil would travel through the Carquinez Straits and into the Sacramento River and Delta proved unfounded, as the slick spent itself against the east bay. However two tankers were sighted dumping oil into the bay the following night after cleaning their tanks. The Coast Guard frowned on this and promptly arrested the ship captains, both of who denied the charge and claimed that oil was from the slick.

The toll that the slick was taking on the wildlife of the bay would be evident by its first night. Thousands of birds that hunt or fish in the tides were diving into the slick looking for food. Only when they surfaced did they see the black gooey matter sticking to their feathers. Only then did they notice that the coat of oil that clung to them was affecting their ability to keep buoyant.

Birds in this state react the same way that a human being would--they panicked. An unimaginable horror and shock overcame the birds, as their unwelcome burden was not only weighing them down, but also destroying their natural ability to float.

Many of them tried to clean their wings by using their beaks to preen and cleanse themselves. The oil they swallowed in this manner ensured them of a slow and painful death. Other birds, recognizing the oil on the water as the culprit, tried to fly to get out of the water. But some of them were so coated with oil that all they succeeded in doing was exhausting themselves, and when their struggles ended, they sank like stones beneath the waves. By the second morning, thousands or birds would be laying on the beaches in various stages of life. Wildlife biologists estimated that for every bird that died on shore, at least ten died at sea. The birds, however, weren't the only victims.

Just across from Highway One in San Francisco, the Great Highway, lies Seal Rock. Seal Rock is just that, a large rock that juts upward just across from one of San Francisco's other landmarks, the Cliff House. It's appropriately named for the colonies of sea lions that inhabit it.

Miraculously the oil slick missed Seal Rock, bypassing it completely to come ashore almost a mile down the beach. Numerous sea lions, however, found themselves caught in the slick when they came up from feeding for air. By midday, twelve hours after the collision, an eleven person team of marine biologists from U.C. Berkeley was on their way to the island to see what they could do for the large numbers of sea lions that were seen to be just lying on the beach. It would later be revealed that the sea lions had their eyes coated with petroleum and try as they might, they couldn't remove it. Some of them had also ingested a great deal of oil arid their stomach linings were inflamed, as the oil attacks sensitive membranes and destroys the unprotected tissues. But these sea lions were lucky. The team was ready for this contingency and had begun measures to help them. By nightfall, 134 sea lions in all would require some sort of medical aid from the marine biologists. Twenty-eight would perish, and a further eleven that went blind from the petroleum would have to be destroyed. But, as the company experts would later testify, in a spill this size that low a number is considered extremely lucky.

Before it was thirty-six hours old, the spill had become the worst ecological nightmare the bay ever suffered. Fishes, crabs, clams, mussels and all other sea life in the bay would be affected. Some ecologists went as far to claim that chemical secretions by sea life, to signal the spawning processes, would be disrupted by petroleum. If true, then this would have an adverse effect on generations or wildlife to come. What was certain was that the oil contaminated miles of shoreline.

It would be another day before the oil stopped spewing out of the GUARDIAN. Most of the slick formed on the first night followed the tide into the bay and did its damage there. The outgoing tide actually pushed some of the oil away from the mouth of the bay and out into the open sea.

But when the tides came back in, the oil started coming ashore again. Diners, tourists, and the curious at the Cliff House would look down the beach from their seats and watch the slick come ashore in globules as small as basketballs to as large as flatbed trucks.

CHAPTER 4

EAST BAY PUBLIC RELATIONS

David Morris stood up and prepared to address the entire public relations staff. Yesterday, he had released them at six o'clock a.m. so that they could go home and freshen up; but with the caveat that they all be back in the office by nine. He'd also gone home and shaved, showered and put on a clean suit. None of them had gotten much rest this past night, and none of them were going to get too much of it over the course of the next few days. Now that they were all back in the office, he planned to inform them of the overall extent of the slick.

"This is about the worst possible thing that could have happened to us, to the bay, and to the industry," he began. "The damage likely to be caused by the oil is immense, and it isn't over yet. I talked the CEO's front office folks into letting me take the chopper for a quick ride around the bay and the peninsula about 90 minutes ago, and it's pretty grim out there."

He rifled through a small stack of three by five cards. "Listen to this."

"The oil has come ashore just south of the Seal Rock, and it's estimated that it will hit as far south as Montara State Beach. That's the most optimistic prediction I've heard. Some experts are hitting the airwaves saying that this spill could go as far south as Santa Cruz or Monterey. God only knows how many beaches and fishing grounds lay within that area."

"There's still a great deal of oil in the water," he added remorsefully. "However it's all very close to shore and our experts don't think it will come ashore on locations where it already isn't expected."

He put one of the cards down, picked up another and continued.

"Inside the bay doesn't look any better. Alcatraz, Treasure Island and Angel Island are going to get slimed big-time, if they haven't already by now. It looks as though the tides will take the oil to the east bay and coat their shoreline with it. The bay side of San Francisco may get out at this without too much harm if the tides and wind don't screw us. But none of our experts are counting on it."

Alan Roth, the youngest member of the staff spoke up. "This means that we should concentrate our efforts on the East bay media doesn't it? That area is much more populated than the ocean-facing side of the peninsula. Not to mention hardest-hit."

Morris looked over to Roth and replied.

"If you meant that we should give the east bay more effort because there are more newspapers located there than on the peninsula, you're correct. As far as who got hardest-hit by the oil slick, were going to treat all of the affected areas as if they were the hardest-hit. There's going to be a lot of ill-feelings over this and the last thing we need is to be accused of favoring one area over another."

Roth nodded his head and accepted the answer. He recognized, at about the same time he finished asking it, that he was asking a rookie question. Had Bill Martin been here he was certain to have received a snide reply as to the 'professional immaturity' of that question. But Morris wasn't like that. Morris had asked for Roth out of college and kept a close eye on him, serving as a sort of a guardian, or at least guiding, angel. Roth also noticed that the reply to his question was as diplomatic as it was didactic.

Morris continued his report on the effects of the spill.

"The oil has gotten as far inside the bay as Oakland. We flew over some salt pens in, I think it was Hayward but if not it was some part of the south east bay, and I don't think anything is going to keep the oil from totally inundating them. Actually they were salt pens when I last saw them as a kid, but I think now they are part of a wildlife park or something." Morris looked at the map he had brought with him and corrected himself. "It's part of the San Francisco Bay National Wildlife Refuge. I hope they come out of this without too much damage, but I doubt that they will. They are going to be in a very bad way by this time tomorrow."

"At the old Alameda Naval Station the slick has gotten into the pilings and under the piers, onto the shoreline-you get the picture. The Port of Oakland is a mess. There are a lot of container ships and freighters there that pull water from the Bay to cool their power plants. I don't know what happens when oil gets into a ship's cooling system- but I have a feeling that a hundred possible scenarios will be presenting themselves in the next few days--each attached to some sort of claims or billing statement from the ship owner's representatives. Also, it looks as though the Alameda channel is set to take a good hit. I didn't get a chance to take a look at that area, but if the oil gets into the channel, and there's no reason to believe it won't, it will affect Jack London Square and a lot of Oakland's waterfront, not to mention Alameda's entire waterfront. Alameda's beaches, some of the same ones that got coated in the seventies in the Chevron spill, will be getting it again. This time it'll be worse."

"If you have friends in Tiburon, Sausalito, Belvedere, Richmond, Emeryville, Albany and any other city inside the bay or along the peninsula, don't be surprised if they don't send you a Christmas card this year. Many of them are going to be unwilling participants in a maritime industrial accident and I guarantee you none of them are going to like it."

Morris went on.

"I have no idea how long it takes an oil-coated bird, or some marine mammal that ingested oil, to die from this exposure. But this I do know. Most of the wildlife victims of the spill are going to die in the water. This will lead to considerable speculation over how many animals actually died. I think the current equation is that for every one that is found dead on land, ten died in the water. Even those that we get to a rescue center, many are still not going to survive. We need to be very careful here. We plan to take care of all the animals we can. We're looking to set up a wildlife rescue and response center so we can treat those animals that we can find. The experts here in the company are working with the experts from some of the local universities to try and plot the exact parameters of the spill so that they can position the wildlife hospital closest to where it will be needed most. Look for ways of getting this information out. Right now, the most endangered animal in the San Francisco Bay Area is the flannel breasted, pinstriped Bennington Oil Public Relations staffer."

"Also, the oil rode the high tides right into the Emeryville mud-flats. For those of you who aren't familiar with the mud flats, that's an area that lies just off of the Interstate 80, at the intersection with the 580, the Nimitz and the Bay Bridge. It used to be known as a tremendous tourist spot because of the artistic people who would go out there and make designs and images with the driftwood, flotsam and jetsam that comes ashore there. Well a whole lot of oil has come ashore there, so you won't see many new visuals out there for a bit. Those that you do see will be ebony in hue."

"Finally," he paused for a second to catch his breath, "I don't know how many marinas there are in the Bay Area, but all of them from Golden Gate Park to Montara State Beach on the peninsula, and probably all marinas over on the East Bay will probably take one hell of a shot. In fact the CEO has already heard from his cronies at the St. Francis Yacht club. He's expecting to hear from many more. I can't imagine that straight petroleum on a ship's hull is a good thing. You folks get the drift. Frankly it's bad all over."

The staff members nodded their heads in silent approval. The damage had been as bad as they had expected, and it was nowhere close to being complete.

"I've talked to the CEO's number two and told him what I plan to do," Morris continued. "It's an obvious fact that the oil came from our tanker, and that the oil is fouling the bay. What we need to do is to let the world know what we're doing to control this problem and of our dedication to operating safely."

"This," Morris continued, "is what our company plans to do. So far, we've allocated twenty million dollars to be placed into an environmental contingency fund. I'm pretty sure more will come once the insurers get involved. This money will be used to purchase detergents to disperse the oil, straw to absorb it end to set up animal control areas to treat birds and animals that got involved in the slick. The money will also be used to place booms around sensitive areas that haven't, as of yet, been affected by the spill. Finally some of the money will be used to arrange for manpower to coordinate our spill control efforts. Both the feds and the state have coordinated spill response forces under their command and our efforts will most likely fall under their umbrella."

"However," he paused, "spills of this magnitude are never contained Everybody's actions will be part of a coordinated attempt to control, or mitigate, the damage."

Morris was about to begin his closing statements, but before doing that he asked his staff if they had any more questions. No one answered back.

"Then its unanimous," Morris joked. "You each understood every word I've said and you are now experts on this matter."

A light chuckle went around the room, the first such attempt at levity in quite a few hours.

On that positive note, Morris continued his briefing.

"It's imperative that we let the world know what we are doing to neutralize this problem, and let them know quickly. People whose livelihoods have been, or will be, affected by the slick are going to be looking for scapegoats. My goal is to make sure that when people mention Bennington Oil, it will be about our efforts to work, clean and control the slick, not as one of the companies that polluted the bay with 50,000 tons of oil."

"Now, all of you," he said while making a broad sweeping gesture towards the door, "back to the matter at hand."

The Bennington Oil public relations staff rose and headed

back towards their work areas. One staffer, Roth, stayed and waited until everyone had gone.

"Dave, I did some research on oil slicks and the control of same when I was in college. What I discovered was that there was no way to cleanup or control an oil slick. The technology still isn't there. Truthfully, are we doing anything more than window dressing?" Roth inquired.

Morris stared at Roth for a second before replying.

"Sometimes an event occurs that offers the participants nothing more than the opportunity to ride along. This is one of them. We'll never get that oil out of the water and we won't get it off of a hundred miles of shoreline either. But if we sit back and acknowledge that fact, and did nothing, we will encourage the wrath and the ire of the public. We may not be doing much, but we're doing something. As the public relations experts, it's our job to show the public what Bennington Oil is doing. The net results of this company's efforts will be forty acres of oil-soaked straw, the carcasses of thousands of birds and hundreds of tired volunteers. The public will see that and say. 'Well they didn't control it but they tried to." We'll know that we succeeded when the public considers us as much a victim as everyone else."

"At first, they won't," Dave continued. "But as time goes on, and they see our efforts, they'll switch over. Showing the frustration on the face of one volunteer who has worked for hours trying to keep the oil out of somewhere, only to watch it get in, will count more towards swinging the public over to our side than a hundred slanted newspaper articles. Remember that. Now back to work."

After Roth left, Morris started jotting down notes for the roughest part of his job. His staff would be calling all of the media in the Bay Area and telling them that Bennington Oil would be holding a press conference at three p.m. As the acting chief of public relations, it was Morris' responsibility to stand in front of the assembled group and reiterate the facts as they were, or as they would be, by the time the press conference commenced.

Yesterday he was on the news showing the local media about the new refinery upgrade in Benicia. That was totally forgotten now, overwhelmed by the events of last night.

The Bennington Oil story today would not be about their existing multi-billion dollar line of credit, or their new Benicia refinery modernization or their efforts to utilize new and unique technologies to coax more petroleum or petroleum equivalents out of their existing deposits and reservoirs. No, today's story would be about Bennington's part in the worst ecological nightmare ever to hit the Bay Area. Morris was certain that the media would play up the oil slick aspect of this accident. That was, after all major news. Bennington's efforts to combat the oil spill were big news too, but today, the biggest news story was the slick itself.

By the time the press conference would he held, the spilled oil would have hit a good portion of the East Bay. Morris closed the door to his office and started to think about what he planned on telling the assembled reporters. At one o'clock he scheduled a mock press conference with his staff to make sure everything was under control. The staff was currently divided into two groups. The first group was handling the incoming media inquiries, which had slowed down slightly after the press conference was announced. The second group was working on possible questions and answers for the mock press conference. Between the two, Morris was hoping to answer any questions generated by the media, either as they called in or as they inquired at the press conference.

He wasn't looking forward to the grilling in store for him from the combined local and national media. But getting the word out was very important right now, and it was his task to face the raging hoards and disseminate information. However the apprehension was still there.

Going in front of a press conference places one naked before the world. One thousand questions will be asked, and the one that causes the stumble will be the one that is remembered.

It was this stumbling block that Morris was trying to avoid, through foresight, preparation and skill. He was spending the time to build a suit of armor around himself, a suit made up of answers and qualified opinions. A lot of rhetoric, insults and innuendoes would soon spring up around this catastrophe; they almost always do in a disaster. Morris' plan was to be ready for anything and everything.

As he closed the door to his office, he once again looked into the darkened and empty office of Bill Martin.

"You lucky bastard" thought Morris, *"you should be the one getting thrown to the wolves, not me."*

Morris assumed that Martin was working some equally important issue, and as he had enough on his mind to worry about other than a missing leader, he turned his attentions back onto the press conference. Sitting down behind his desk, he began marshaling his train of thought on paper. Thoughts of his boss' whereabouts disappeared as he planned his next course of action.

Three o'clock came much too early. Sixty-eight members of the press responded to Bennington's telephonic invitations, and they were all taking their seats waiting for the conference to begin.

Morris looked around the room to see if he could spot any friendly faces in the pack. The first one he saw was that of Larry Nelson.

Nelson was one of the first media members that Morris met when he took his position at Bennington. Their rapport was instant, and they'd been good friends ever since. While they'd never been in a situation where one of them had to bail the other out of a problem, they shared a strong personal and professional bond and they both knew that they could count on the other not to play loose and fast with facts. Nelson had taken the helicopter orientation flight offered by Morris earlier in the day, and was now eagerly waiting for the press conference to begin. Morris knew Nelson to be a fair and objective reporter, and he felt that Bennington Oil would get a fair shake from him.

Morris saw a dozen faces that he knew or recognized, and with this added recognition came a lessened sense of apprehension. Just before he was to go out and brief the assembled press, he turned to one of his staffers and said that it looked like a pretty friendly crowd.

Morris had prepared himself for anything. He moved the press conference from the company's 46th floor briefing room to the one on the thirteenth floor. The one on the 46th floor belonged to Bennington and was right in the middle of their headquarters suites. A roaming reporter could find out a lot of sensitive items long before anyone could stop them. As Morris had anticipated on over fifty reporters attending the press conference, he thought it should he in an area where Bennington's already overtaxed corporate resources wouldn't have to also keep an eye out for intrepid members of the press. The conference room on the thirteenth floor was mainly utilized by the other tenants of the Bennington Building; its location would mean that there would be no security problems to the rest of the company.

Another big concern about the conference room on the 46th floor was the large corporate emblem emblazoned on the wall behind the podium. As the emblem was impossible to move, and impractical to cover, its presence would have been obvious during the press conference. Morris felt that some of his topics would be incriminating, especially when it came to the part about which ship actually carried the oil that was spilled. The last thing Morris wanted was Bennington Oil's corporate emblem, a large American bald eagle perched on an oil derrick with its wings outstretched, glaring over his shoulders and into the households of the millions of people who would either see the televised press conferences, or read about it online or in their newspapers.

Morris had also assembled a team of experts to help him, if necessary. They included the deputy chief executive officer and several company environmental specialists. They would serve as the executive validation; to reinforce, from an authoritative point of view, the information spoken by Morris.

Morris briefly looked over his notes once again and prepared to go out on stage. He looked over to where Roth was standing and gave him a confident "thumbs up." Roth smiled back and returned Morris' 'thumbs up'. With that, Morris walked out onto the stage and took his place behind the podium.

"Hello, I'm. David Morris, Deputy Chief of Public Relations for Bennington Oil and I'm going to discuss the cause and effects of this terrible oil slick that entered the bay today."

Following his introduction, he relayed to the assembled press the same information he had passed on to his staff earlier in the day. He added the names and locations of all of the East Bay cities where the oil had, or was, coming ashore. He stressed the steps that his company was taking, and pointed out that everything Bennington could possibly do, was being done to control this slick. He ended his presentation by adding that they had taken every foreseeable precaution to prevent this kind of thing from happening.

"But," as he ended his statement. "Sometimes, even the best efforts can prove to be insufficient."

The part of the press conference that he could have done without had now arrived.

"Do any of you have any questions for me to address?" said Morris. This was the part where, after riling up the media's interest with a statement, one throws aside their shield and asks for questions.

Morris had been sitting in his office almost the entire hour since the press conference had ended. His briefing to the press was short, no more than 20 minutes. Responding to their questions took only another forty-five minutes.

Everyone attending the press conference on Bennington's behalf, from the CEO's representative on down, thought that he had handled himself in the most professional manner. Compliments were quick to come on how well he performed both under the media's' lights and in setting up this short-noticed conference. Not a single word of dissatisfaction was uttered and seemingly, all the right people were happy with how it came off.

Except Morris.

Thirty seven questions had been asked after the press briefing was finished. Most of them were the updated repetitions of the questions asked right after the collision. Some, however, were original and Morris deftly answered them. Then, just when his confidences were at their highest and he was riding a crest of professional euphoria, he got blindsided.

In anticipation of this press conference, Morris had

prepared himself on all aspects of the collision and was ready to answer any questions. But there was one area he was planning on avoiding; one area of the company's performance that could cause a problem if discovered. He studied it and hoped that no one would ask about it. It was question number twenty-three that blasted Morris' confidence and put him on the defensive. He was now faced with extemporaneously having to defend the worst part of the company's operational record.

The whole scene had been replaying itself in Morris' head ever since the press conference ended. He remembered how the entire staff that he had brought with him as professional and technical experts held their breath while he weathered the questions. They were not trained in understanding the media, but they all instinctively knew when they were under fire.

Morris had let his mind wander back to the press conference; back to the only time during the entire event where he felt himself losing control. No matter which part he tried to review, his mind always went to that point where he turned to a nattily dressed, bearded gentleman and said "Yes sir, I believe you had the next question.

"Mr. Morris, I am Jan Taylor of the California Environmentalist Press Agency."

Morris felt a funny churning in his stomach. Talking to an environmentalist from his position during an oil slick is analogous to a Christian asking a Roman what sort of foods their lions had a preference for. He was particularly wary of these people and had every right to be.

"We are all aware of the high cost of the two tankers involved in the crash as well as the value of their cargo," said Taylor. "My question, however, takes a different tack. Last year, according to your annual statement, your company had revenues in the billions, and profits in the hundreds of millions, if not more. How much of that did Bennington spend on oil cleanup procedures, on training for this type of contingency and on spill unique equipment?"

Morris listened carefully to the questions. This was the one major area that Bennington was deficient. He knew this reporter would have a field day with his answer.

"I am sorry," said Morris tentatively, "I don't have those figures with me."

Morris took a look over to where the other Bennington members were. They gave him a look of support, as if with his reply the question was answered. For Jan Taylor, however, it was far from answered.

Taylor had made his name by being tough on oil and chemical companies. He knew how they operated, and he used that knowledge to keep from getting snowed by company P. R. specialists. Unless they had done their homework and they were as thoroughly familiar with their subjects as he was, Taylor usually humbled and embarrassed company spokesmen. Such was his intent now, only reinforced by Morris' reluctant stall attempt.

"As you don't have the answer then," said Taylor, "would you at least say that the amount was substantial?"

"Again," started Morris," as I don't have those figures it would be speculative at best if I were to try to quote figures that I am not familiar with."

Morris felt a major barrage coming. This reporter was playing upon the company's weakest point; their oil cleanup capabilities and assets dedicated for oil spill cleanup.

Unfortunately, this long neglected area was now coming back to haunt Bennington Oil. Almost all oil companies had developed large research and developmental testing facilities for this type of occurrence. As oil companies transport large quantities of oil, it is in their own best interest to be able to combat spills and other catastrophes. Bennington Oil however had not, and while this shortcoming would haunt the company collectively, on their thirteenth floor conference room it was affecting one Bennington Oil employee specifically.

Morris knew that however weak his company was in this area, a major press conference was not the place to discuss it. He silently steeled himself to take the offensive and lead this reporter away from this area. He knew it wouldn't be easy and the next question confirmed his thoughts.

"I've had the opportunity to review your company's stockholder statements," said Taylor.

"Mr. Taylor," Morris abruptly interjected "May I ask you to clarify your question, or inferences, as the case may be?"

Taylor stared hard at Morris. The eyes of the room were all fixed on these two men, and it was now Taylor's turn to move.

Proving that his nigh-sinister glare was no act, Taylor put away any attempt of congeniality that he was employing and in a very matter-of-fact tone phrased his question to Morris.

"Mr. Morris, does your company put all of its efforts and resources only into the profit producing side of the petroleum business?"

"No," Morris shot back, "We train and practice cleaning up oil spills, but there's no way to train for the size problem that we have now. What we do is formulate theoretical responses, test them as empirically as we possibly can and trust that they will work when we need them."

"The question," Taylor said forcefully, "was put to you as whether your company spends enough of its resources on oil pollution protection? Does your company take an amount commensurate to the threat potential of oil spillage and actively seek ways to first, prevent and second, control oil spills?"

The hostility of Taylor's tone was evident to everyone, but especially to Morris. The entire room was quiet except for the two men, one at the podium and the other amongst the assembled group. Morris eyed the journalist and again stated that he didn't have the figures that Taylor was looking for. That was the truth. Earlier in the afternoon he had seen exactly how much Bennington had spent on oil spill recovery technology. The low figure almost depressed him, so he left them on his desk.

Bennington had billions of dollars in revenues last year, and yet less than four million dollars was allocated to the problem of spilled petroleum. Most of that went to the recovering and re-utilization of spilled petroleum during tanker loading and unloading operations. The intent here was to try and recover the value of the oil spilled overboard more so than trying to prevent an ecological hazard.

The simple truth was that Bennington Oil didn't spend

much money in this area. In the event of a big slick they could count on rapid expertise from the Coast Guard. It was with this thought in mind that they failed to develop their own capability accordingly. The company's hierarchy felt that spending large sums of money and resources in this area was as feasible as nuclear war insurance.

"Well, Mr. Morris," Taylor spoke again, "what about it? Is your company prepared to handle this catastrophe?"

The rage building up inside of Morris was masked by his calm exterior. Rather than telling this gentleman to go to hell, Morris regrouped and began answering the question in a practiced tone that was solemn and almost sympathetic.

"We're doing all we can right now," stated Morris, "and the answer to your question can best be found on the beaches, helping to clear this mess up."

"I trust that they won't be out on the beaches cleaning this mess up this time next year!" was Taylor's sarcastic parting shot.

Whether it was his sympathetic manner or Taylor's ascerbic retort, Morris could feel the assembled group of journalists starting to turn on Taylor. One or two reporters grumbled while Taylor began his interrogation, but now fully one-third of them were talking to each other, unanimous only in their hushed tones and their fading sentiments of Taylor.

Larry Nelson of the East Bay Gazette saw this as both an opportunity to help a friend and a chance to get Morris in his debt; to "owe him one." During Taylor's questioning, Nelson had been thinking about a possible question to ask, one that was relevant to the spill, intelligent enough so that it wouldn't be thought of as a plant and easy enough far Morris to smash back into the crowd of reporters.

Taylor's question about Bennington being prepared to handle the slick provided Nelson with the opening he needed. Now that the reporters were buzzing amongst themselves, Nelson stood up and began to speak.

"Mr. Morris," he said, "it would seem to me that training for this kind of thing, both day and night, would increase a company's spill response proficiency. How extensive is your training program at Bennington?"

"Our program," began Morris, "is to train in oil spill containment and cleanup mainly for clearing up the spills that occur during our on and off loading activities. To this effect, we have been successful."

Morris was using Nelson's question to regain the initiative and was now about to accentuate the positive.

"We've concentrated our efforts on this particular area because it is the one we encounter the most. We've never lost a tanker or a cargo on the open sea. Our record was spotless until last night."

"Well then," said Nelson," have you adapted any of this training to this spill'?'

"In the areas where we could," began Morris," yes we have. But it must be understood that what works well in port may not work at all on the open seas, and by this I include out there in the middle of the bay. Booms and sea skimmers work perfectly well in port, due primarily to the absence of wave action, which would serve to agitate the oils and move them to and fro. Additionally, oil-removing detergents cannot be spread evenly on a rapidly changing surface. Inert materials, used to absorb oil, will also absorb salt water, if agitated. Basically, hard work to limit the damage caused by this slick is all that's left to us now. Anything else," Morris concluded, "is wishful thinking."

Wishful thinking is exactly what Morris was doing now. It was now past six o'clock and most of his staff had gone home, or was preparing to. Closing time had come and gone, but he was still reliving Taylor's one question.

Roth stuck his head in the door and saw Morris staring seemingly into space.

"Dave, you all right?" Roth inquired.

Morris stopped his staring now that his concentration was broken and looked over at Roth.

"I'm O.K." was his casual reply.

"Everyone on the staff told me you'd be in your office trying to figure out if you could have answered that guy's question better. They all said that you were a hopeless workaholic."

"Taylor," said Morris in both a quiet and authoritative

51

voice. "The guy's name was Taylor, and as you're on call this weekend, if he calls you--refer him to me!"

"Yes sir," said Roth. "I've got the company approved Q and A's and a tape recording of the press conference."

"Also," said Morris...

"I know," shot back Roth, "don't forget to log all media queries received. You really are a workaholic aren't you?"

"Yes I am," said Morris, "and I am going to make one out of you if you're not careful. Now go on home, it's Miller time."

Roth turned and left the office, headed for a weekend by the cell phone. The media interest in this story was such that whoever had the weekend duty was going to be swamped. As it was a great learning opportunity, or at least that was how the staff presented it to Roth, he became the PR `stuckee'. He didn't mind much, and after a few minutes guidance from Morris, he felt he was more than ready to handle the load.

"We'll know by Monday anyhow," thought Morris.

Morris stood up and again looked at the clock. It was just after six p.m. He was about to renew his thoughts of the press conference when the telephone rang.

"Hey lover," came the cheerful introduction. "What's my favorite P. R. type up to?"

"Hi, Alice," Morris answered back. "Sorry about last night."

"Don't mention it. Oh, by the way, I saw you on television about an hour ago and I got all worked up. You were looking cool, calm and collected as the ad goes. I said to myself, `I've got to take this gent home tonight'. Sooo, I say we pick up a few steaks, a nice bottle of wine, turn off the TV and hang the "do not disturb" sign on the door."

"And do what?" was Morris' playful inquiry.

"And forget about the rest of the world for a couple of days. I'll teach you everything you'll need to know until Monday."

"Are you talking carnal knowledge?'

"Most definitely not!" Alice shot back. "I'm talking carnival knowledge."

"Carnival knowledge?"

"Yes, carnival knowledge. You know whips, chains, trapeze, trampolines, clowns, wild animals, cotton candy and a crowd of thousands."

Morris could hear her starting to laugh at the other end of the phone. He just shook his head.

"I almost thought you were serious."

"I was," she cooed, "Oh, about the part where we forget about the rest of the world for a couple of days."

"Let's do it," said Morris. "I'll see you at home."

Morris hung up the phone and turned back to his desk. He started reading one of the numerous documents stacked on his desk. Half way down the first document he paused and began considering the alternative with Alice.

"What the hell," he said, "consecutive fifteen hour days are enough. Its Miller time."

With that he selected the most pressing items from his desk, put them in his briefcase, turned towards the door, hit the lights and began arranging his weekend.

He was planning on staying home in case Roth needed him. It was, after all, still a great opportunity to rest up.

"For the next two days the world will have to try and get along without me," mused Morris.

CHAPTER 5

FAMILY FIRM/FIRST STRIKE

The last few days were extremely fatiguing for Edward Montgomery Richardson. Being the chief executive officer of Montgomery Oil and Petrochemical, known simply as Monty-O, was tough enough. But add to that the events of Thursday night/Friday morning's tragedy and it became "downright hellish" as Richardson's wife of twenty-seven years so aptly put it.

Richardson had been involved in every aspect of the crash since the moment it happened. That's simply how the man operated. Knowing every little detail of what was going on and how it could affect the company was what Richardson considered to be his primary role in the company. That, and being the boss.

He personally selected company members to assist each of the families of the lost crew of the Pacific Patriarch. He kept in close contact with the spill contingency crews and had contacted the mayor or city manager of every city that was, or would be, affected by the spill. He gave them all his personal assurance that Monty-O would do all they could to contain this slick.

But all of that took place on Friday and Saturday. Last night was his first near full night's rest since the collision, and he took advantage of it

As is his custom on Sunday, Richardson arose at 7 a.m.,

put his robe over his nightclothes and took a slow stroll around the grounds of his Hillsborough mansion. It was closing on 8 a.m. when he arrived at the patio. His wife Carole was already there and was just waiting for him to arrive before she had breakfast served.

"Enjoy the walkabout," she asked.

"Nothing like the fresh air in the morning to start the gray matter," he replied.

He sat down, and after taking a moment to make himself comfortable, motioned to one of the servants to bring breakfast. Making himself comfortable was a ritual that Richardson engaged in almost every meal he ate. It consisted of arranging and rearranging the silverware and napkins till they were just right in his eyes. No one knew exactly why he did it, although Carole once suspected to a friend that he did it to make sure everything was all right before he started. As she put it, "He pretty much runs every aspect of his life the same way he runs his company."

Richardson was just about to prepare his plate when he noticed his butler, Howard, standing in the doorway of the house. Something was not right about the way he looked, and Richardson was quick to pick up on it. Howard had been with Richardson for almost twenty two years and exemplified the essential British butler. Ramrod straight, seemingly emotionless and unshakable were the very attributes that Richardson saw in him twenty two years ago, and now in his late forties he was still head and shoulders above most of his profession.

Right now, however, Howard was both tense and concerned. In fact, his appearance exhibited tenseness far in excess of his English training, and his concern was genuine.

"Howard, what's wrong?" inquired Richardson.

Howard stepped out of the doorway and approached Richardson. He was holding the Sunday edition of the San Francisco Chronicle/Examiner and his expression was dour; much like the unfortunate serfs who brought the bad news to the king, knowing that the king held no affinity for that kind of news or those who brought it.

Howard knew that Richardson would not be angry with

him; after all he was just bringing out the local paper. He half assumed that Richardson might have already seen the news online, but one thing he was certain of. He knew that Richardson was about to get angry.

"Sir," he began, "I hate to spoil your breakfast, but I felt that this should be brought to your attention immediately."

Richardson gave his butler a puzzled look.

"What are you talking about?"

Howard moved the plates and silverware aside and opened the newspaper. He turned to page nine and there, laid out before Richardson, was a full-page advertisement from Bennington Oil.

He started reading the advertisement. His wife looked at him as he became totally engaged with that one page. He was seemingly lost in the text of that one page, staring at it, reading it and looking at it as though it were being burned into his mind, never again to leave his memory.

His wife had gotten up and moved over next to him. She was unaware of the content of the article, but she wanted to be near him when he finished it in case he needed someone-a shoulder to cry on or a friend to talk to.

The Richardsons treated Montgomery Oil as if it were family, and in fact 18.6% of it was. Their lives still revolved around Monty-O. They felt its good days and they reeled with its bad ones. Whatever happened to Monty-O at 9 a.m., happened to the Richardsons by 5 p.m. Carole's life was also structured around that large corporation headquartered in San Francisco. While it separated her from her husband far too often, it also placed her in the cradle of San Francisco society. Taking both the good and the bad, they accepted the conditions that came with her husband's position. However, for the past few days they took more bad than good.

Everyone on the patio saw Richardson turn a dark shade of red as the rage built up within him. His wife's compassionate motion, to be close to him, went unnoticed; Richardson was a man of action, not affection. He pushed his chair back, stood up and turned towards his wife.

"Carole, those bastards at Bennington have gone too far this time, too damn far!"

With that, Richardson spun around and looked at Howard.

"Thanks for showing me this," Richardson said to his butler, "I'll be in the study for a few minutes. After that I'm going to the office. Call Gerard and tell him to be there in one hour. And tell him to read the Chronicle before he gets there-- he'll know what I want."

Richardson walked up to the house, opened the door to the patio and disappeared inside. Carole watched him walk up to and into the house; she knew from the gait in his stride that he was extremely upset.

She reached out and grabbed the Chronicle that her husband had left and looked at page nine. The first thing that she noticed was the heading, which read " A Message from Bennington Oil to All Californians."

She turned her attention to the body of the text and began reading.

"Last Thursday, one of our oil tankers was involved in a collision outside of the Golden Gate. Thirty-seven lives were lost and a massive oil slick was released.

The accident has not only affected the two companies involved, but the lives of countless people who live, work and enjoy the recreational aspects of the San Francisco Bay Area. The oil slick has soiled and damaged the shoreline for over one hundred miles, both inside and outside the Bay. It will be months before the true cost of this calamity can be determined, both in dollars and environmental totals.

We at Bennington Oil are saddened, not only at the high loss of life and the calamitous effects of the oil slick, but also by the fact that today, in an era of high technology and advanced communications, a catastrophe of this magnitude can still occur

We have constantly striven for the most technologically advanced equipment on board our tankers to prevent such an occurrence. Millions of dollars have been spent on our tanker fleet to ensure that they are the safest ships possible. Unfortunately, that can't be said for all oil companies. The sad part is, it is these companies whose overwhelming quest for profits and total lack of respect for environmental and safety laws that taint our industry.

You can rest assured that we are doing all that we can to clean up the effects of the spill. We have received, or ordered, tons of environmentally safe materials to help absorb the oil. We will continue to do what we can to help clear this mess off of our shoreline.

Only by conscientiously planning and preparing for the prevention of these kinds or accidents will they truly cease to occur. But this is a policy that must be adhered to by all, and not just the select few.

Until all oil companies adhere to a policy of safety first, this kind of unfortunate occurrence will happen again.

We here at Bennington Oil are doing all we can to see that it never happens again. Here, or anywhere else.

Sincerely,

Chief Executive Officer
Bennington Oil and Petrochemical Company

Carole sat in her chair with her mouth open, not believing what she had just read.

One of the servants noticed Mrs. Richardson focusing intensely in this near catatonic state and came over to offer assistance

"Mrs. Richardson, what's wrong? You look as though you've seen a ghost."

Carole regained herself and slowly looked up at the servant. With a degree of difficulty she spoke in a shocked and hurt tone.

"Bennington Oil is blaming us for the crash," she said.

Richardson didn't say a word during the entire trip in. Tight lipped, he sat looking out the windows of his limo as he decided how best to strike back at Bennington. The editorial attacked his company and his sense of propriety. He couldn't allow that.

"They won't get away with this.."

His limo drove up to the front of the building and

deposited him near the private entrance. He entered the VIP elevator and quickly rose to his penthouse office.

Charles Gerard, the chief of public relations for Monty-O was in the receptionist's lobby.

Richardson was quick and to the point.

"Did you see what those bastards printed today? They're blaming us for the crash."

"They didn't mention us by name," Gerard interjected calmly, "They just described us totally and said that the offender they were referring to has the initials Monty-O. I've seen this trick before. The public's outrage hasn't peaked yet. When it does, they'll want blood. Bennington Oil decided to give them ours."

"Where do they get off pulling some shit like this?" Richardson stormed. "Hell, the Coast Guard isn't even going to start their investigation for two more days. This madness in the paper is just so much unsubstantiated tripe. And what's worse is that most of it is not true."

"You know that, I know that and yes, Bennington Oil knows that. But the 2.5 million people who'll read those newspapers or goes online may not."

Richardson picked something up in Gerard's statement.

"What do you mean 'those newspapers?' It's not just in the Chronicle?"

"No," said Gerard. "It is also in the L.A. Times and maybe others. It's on the web as well. We're still checking."

"That's just great. You're a PR type, what are they trying to prove?"

"They are not trying to prove anything," said Gerard. "What they are trying to do is strike the first blow. The public is going to raise their banner to the side that they believe is right. And so far, Bennington Oil has made the most spectacular play.

Gerard looked at his boss. "They're getting ready for a fight. They've already flung the gauntlet at us. We can sit here and try and figure out why they did what they did, but that's counterproductive at best. The deed is done. What everyone everywhere is asking is what do we intend to do about it."

"I'll tell you what we are going to do about it," growled

Richardson. "Call in your staff and tell them to prepare a statement countering Bennington's diatribe. I want it to be hard--hitting and I want it to hurt them. It should play up our superlative safety record while illustrating their despicable one. Jesus, you're my public relations guy, you know what to say. Make it hit like Mike Tyson. I don't want some cream puff piece. Also, call the marketing and advertising folks. They'll write the checks you'll need to get this article in the same forums that those bastards at Bennington Oil used. I'll be in my office until you're ready to send that piece. You got four hours to get it ready. Questions?"

"Just one," inquired Gerard, "Actually, I've got a better idea. Do you want to hear it?"

A grin came across Richardson's face. Keeping one step ahead at the public and the media was Gerard's job. It suddenly occurred to him that Gerard had probably been working on a contingency since he saw the ad this morning.

The grin, however, was soon replaced as Richardson gave Gerard a slow, cautious look. His blood rage of this morning had not waned one iota; he still wanted to blast Bennington Oil in the same way that they had attacked Monty-O. He was interested in Gerard's proposal, but only to see if it harpooned Bennington Oil worse than his own idea did.

"Go ahead," said Richardson, but before you do, does your method have teeth?'

"You tell me," asked Gerard. " I figure that they spent around $500,000, give or take a few grand, getting those full page ads and whatnot. That's a lot of money to put one's point of view forward. But it turns out that it was a relatively transparent effort."

"Transparent, said Richardson incredulously. " They've put their point of view in the laps of millions. I consider that to be a very cost-effective transparency. But that doesn't explain your concept. Why does paying for this ad make their effort transparent'?"

"When you pay to run an ad," said Gerard," it goes without saying that you'll get your point across. The money buys you that. What it won't buy you is credibility. People think one of two things whenever they see a paid ad; 'So this is Company A's stance' or 'These bozos had to actually pay a respectable outfit to run their side of the story.'"

Gerard looked Richardson in the eye and added. "This morning, countless people were saying to themselves, 'What is it about Bennington Oil's side of the story that was so weak that they were forced to spend money to tell us about it? Why doesn't it stand on its own?' "In the midst of a crisis like this," Gerard injected, "their point of view should be a news item and not an advertisement or an editorial. Follow me so far?"

Richardson looked closely at Gerard for a sign that might tell him what was coming next. It was for naught as Gerard's face was free of emotion. Gerard was now relaying pure information upon which a very important decision would be based. The facts were all that mattered.

Gerard not only knew that his plan of action was solid, he was certain of its success. But the order to implement it was not his; it rested with the stern-faced gentleman in front of him. Gerard was facing his toughest critic and it was imperative that he win him over. If he could sway Richardson, everyone else would be a piece of cake. Richardson had come into the office with blood in his eye and wanted to extract his pound of flesh from Bennington Oil. Gerard wanted to convince his boss that responding in the same way as Bennington Oil did was a mistake; that even trying to respond in a similar manner was a fool's errand.

The plan he devised was a flanking maneuver; first to destroy the credibility of Bennington Oil's advertisement and then that of the corporation itself.

Richardson looked up and said, "I'm following you, so far. What you're saying is that Bennington purchased that ad because no respectable medium would run their point of view for free?"

"Exactly," said Gerard. "Now all we need to do to come out ahead is to get our side across," he said with a pregnant pause, "without paying for it."

"Yeah, right," was Richardson sarcastic reply. Richardson made no attempt to hide his cynicism. "You said they probably paid a hundred grand to those newspapers to get those full page ads. Just what makes you think they'll run our stuff for free?"

For the second time since their conversation began, Gerard smiled. He had been waiting for this moment ever since he started baiting the CEO on his plan.

"Boss," Gerard said, "it all depends on how we package it. Bennington's ad slimed us by insinuating that we have a poor safety and environmental record. Nothing could be further from the truth. In fact, our safety record is the industry standard, or close enough to be.

"Go on," Richardson added impatiently.

"If you were a newspaper," Gerard started, "or a television station, what kind of space would you devote to an exclusive, one that showed that Bennington Oil intentionally tried to deceive the public through the use of an advertisement that they knew was false-a lie if you will?"

Richardson's eyes lit up and his attitude changed from one at barely veiled impatience to total interest. For the first time since the tankers collided he was anticipating something that he knew he was going to like.

"We bust them," he said, "by proving that their ad was a deliberate falsehood."

Gerard nodded his head in the affirmative. 'The boss liked the goal of his intended effort and as far as he was concerned, the battle was half won.

Richardson leaned back in his chair and, for a few seconds, let his mind enjoy the possibilities that Gerard's plan invited.

"Not bad Gerard, not bad at all. It's a good idea Gerard, but how do we do it?"

Gerard turned and walked over to two stacks of papers on the secretary's desk. Richardson had never noticed them, even though they were only a few feet away from where he and Gerard were talking before they drifted into his office.

"Each of these two and a half inch stacks contains three copies of all of the spills, accidents and safety violations of both of our companies. They are all on file with all of the appropriate state, federal and local safety and environmental agencies. In short, they are part of the public record. You'll notice that the Bennington Oil list is larger than ours, much larger."

"Okay, said a thoroughly hooked Richardson. "What's next? How do we turn this pile of computer printouts into favorable public opinion? Or more importantly," Richardson added, "how do we stick this up Bennington's ass?"

"Easy. What do Americans like more than anything else? They like to see the underdog win. Bennington Oil has taken the first shot through their ad. Getting even will be simple; we give one of these stacks to a fair sized East Bay paper. They then run Bennington Oil's despicable safety and environmental record as a direct contradiction to the essence of their ad. As I envision it, a small hometown paper in one of the cities who's shoreline got lubricated takes a big bad oil company to task for either lying about or distorting their record."

"Good Lord," said Richardson, "Once that story hit the streets even the wire services might pick up on it. It could be David and Goliath again."

"'That's right," said Gerard. "The collision and spill made the front pages of every newspaper in the country. Editors will cream when they see the power of the pen cutting into a massive profit-driven oil company. It's not a front page story by any means, but we can rest assured that the San Francisco and Los Angeles papers will pick up on it. They'll worry about their objectivity if they don't. Any other newspapers will be gravy. And it won't cost us one red cent."

Richardson was beside himself with elation. "Trifle with Monty-O will they. This will teach their asses." Even in his enjoyment it didn't take long for the logical Richardson to emerge again. "What if your anticipated groundswell doesn't happen? What then?"

Gerard was more than prepared for this question. "Since the local newspaper ran it, every newspaper, radio and television station in the Bay Area would be quoting it. They'll he quoting our side of the story in the name of quality journalism. The people who are affected will see firsthand, our record. It will also reek of credibility because it's coming from someone other than us."

"We'll drive this story," Gerard continued, " and there will be no direct tie-in back to us. All of this information is in the public domain. When the ships collided, I figured I might need an ace in the hole, so I sent someone to the state, county and city records repositories. These lists represent the last four years of operations for both of our respective companies. Every little violation from the both of us is in here. I knew some intrepid reporter would want this and given time, they'd assemble it on their own. But I'm going to save them considerable time. They'll get hold of this and they'll randomly check some of the listings to ensure accuracy. Once they're certain that the information is factual, they'll run it. It's Sunday now, I expect to see this info in a story in the Tuesday morning edition of the East Bay Gazette."

"The East Bay Gazette," Richardson echoed. "What makes you so certain that they'll run it?"

"I've already spoken to them. About an hour ago. They're sending someone over for one of these lists at two o'clock."

"You sly bastard," Richardson grinned. "You knew all along that I'd go for it didn't you?"

"I'd hoped you would," Gerard replied. "With the money we lost in the crash and the money we're spending in the Louisiana Project, I figured it was an easy way to save us a couple hundred grand. And more importantly, it gets our point across."

Richardson sat down behind his desk, his happiness evident. He stretched across the large mahogany expanse and reached into a small wooden cask sitting near the far right hand corner. When he had withdrawn his hand, it held two very expensive-looking cigars.

Richardson extended one of the cigars to Gerard and placed the other one between his lips.

"Gerard, my good man," he began, "you're one in a million. Thanks."

Richardson's sincere tone surprised Gerard.

"Just doing my job, sir, just doing my job."

"Speaking of just doing their jobs," echoed Richardson,

"why do you suppose your counterpart ran that ad?"

"I've known Bill Martin for three years," said Gerard, "and nothing about him surprises me. He's unscrupulous and has no professional ethics whatsoever. I'd hate to be on his staff." Upon a moment of reflection, Gerard added, "I'm sure they had a reason for running that ad. Our stuff won't hit the streets until Tuesday. Our stock dropped on Friday due to the crash. That's understandable considering we lost a tanker and its cargo. However, this kind of negative publicity could add to that in some small way.

"You said your counterpart at Bennington was unscrupulous," Richardson queried, "but to the point of lying to the press? You don't need to be an Albert Einstein to know that if that backfired, they'll filet your ass for lunch."

"Remember, in that ad this morning where Bennington said that they were buying tons of ecologically safe and environmentally compatible materials to absorb the spill. Do you know what they were talking about?"

Richardson stopped and concentrated a minute. All of the materials that he'd known about for cleaning up oil were either toxic to marine life or at least a hindrance. None were exactly safe or compatible with the marine environment. He wracked his mind searching for an answer before turning to Gerard with his negative reply.

"I told you before that any story's success depends on how you package it," Gerard stated. "The material that Bennington was talking about is your average, ordinary, run-of-the-mill, dime a bushel.... straw."

"Straw," added a disbelieving Richardson, "the stuff they make brooms out of and feed to cattle."

"One and the same," answered Gerard.

Richardson started laughing and Gerard joined in.

Gerard looked at Richardson and inquired, "What kind of people are we dealing with?"

Richardson's reply was short and to the point. "I don't know, but I don't think that I can trust them to be anything but unpredictable"

In the time that Alice and Dave had lived together, she'd never seen him like this.

"Upset is an understatement," she thought.

Morris was now across the room, telephone in hand, furiously trying to contact Bill Martin.

"I sure don't envy Bill Martin." Alice thought.

Fifteen minutes earlier she had given Morris the Sunday San Francisco Chronicle while she kept a different paper, the East Bay Gazette. It was a slow Sunday morning. They were just getting into the day and had planned nothing more than to kick back and relax. After breakfast they were planning to go out for a walk and do a little looking around San Francisco.

The eggs were still on the stove and the croissants still in the oven when she gave Dave the paper. Sundays were always informal, with both of them eating while reading papers, stopping only to converse about a particular story that attracted their mutual interest.

Then suddenly, Morris stopped eating and began focusing on a single story. For about three minutes his gaze was fixed on one page, one story of the paper. At that moment, at least for Morris, the rest of the paper ceased to exist.

In a few short moments he finished reading the full-page ad from Bennington Oil. He was livid. His feelings ran the gamut of emotion, but rage, anger, pain, betrayal and consternation were the ones he kept coming back to.

"What the hell is this madness?" he shouted.

He jumped up so quickly that his milk and juice, poured in their respective glasses, spilled all over the dining table. Alice watched as rivulets of the liquid ran over the edge of the table and began dripping onto the hardwood floors. She turned her head in time to see Morris walk over to the phone and snatch the receiver from its cradle.

She went into the kitchen and returned with a dishcloth. As she started wiping the table she looked into the living room and saw Morris sitting on the couch, obviously lost in thought.

He's planning his words carefully, she thought. "What's he so upset about?"

She walked over to where he sat for breakfast and saw

the advertisement that set him off. She turned the paper so that she could get a better view and began reading.

As a lawyer, she easily deciphered the meaning of this letter in a heartbeat. It was meant to focus the blame of the crash from one party to another. She assumed that Morris' role as Bennington's public relations official in charge would have led him to this course of action, and as such, she didn't quite understand his reaction.

"Dave," she asked, "what is wrong with this article? It looks alright to me. I mean, it's you guys blaming the other company without a shred of hard evidence, but that's what public relations is all about." Her attempt at humor failed.

Morris stood up and walked over to Alice. He stopped right behind her and stared down past her at the article. She twisted in her seat to look at him.

Without looking at her, he simply stated, "There's nothing wrong with the article, except that it's the first time that I've seen it."

Alice took her eyes off of Morris and looked down at the article again. After a few seconds she glanced back at Morris.

"What do you mean it's the first time that you've seen it. It would have had to come from your office. There's no way you couldn't have seen it."

"Yes there was," said Morris, "if no one showed it to me. I've run the office since the crash and I didn't task any of my people to do this. But Martin has been out of the office since this incident started, doing God only knows what. He's got to be the one behind this; it reeks of his style."

Alice's concern over his next act was growing. He hadn't cooled off, and she recognized the dangers of allowing him to call on his boss in his current mindset and using less than glowing adjectives. She used the direct approach to try and get him to think about his next step.

"Can you prove it was Martin?" she inquired.

"Always the doubter, eh, counselor," was his sarcastic reply.

She noted the sting of his comment, but chose to let it ride.

"No," she answered, "but you ought to be prepared when

you call up your boss and accuse him of something that he may have played no part in."

He looked at her and then looked back down at the article.

"I know you mean well and I'm sorry if my responses were curt. But it was him alright," said Morris, "and I need to know why."

Even though it was a Sunday, Bill Martin was preparing to head for the office when the phone rang. He walked over and answered it and when he did, he knew immediately that he wasn't going to like the conversation.

"Bill, this is Dave. We need to talk."

Martin was expecting this call and had taken time to prepare for it. He knew Morris was going to be livid, he wouldn't accept the fact that the answers he was about to receive, and that he would be vocal in his complaints throughout the company's hierarchy. Martin needed to stop Morris cold.

"Dave, Martin started, "you're calling about the ads in the papers this morning, right?"

"Damned straight I am," Morris snapped. "I'm supposed to be handling the company's efforts in this spill and you come out with a bullshit piece like this and then get the boss to approve it. What are you trying to do?"

"Dave, there's a purpose to that ad."

"Good," Morris shot back. "I'd like to hear it!"

Martin had enough. Morris wasn't informed of all the things that Martin knew, and until he was, he was going to be kept in the dark, like almost everyone else. But Martin was not going to take abuse from a subordinate, regardless of what role they were playing in the company.

"Morris," Martin angrily responded, "There's something going on that you are not aware of. You may never know about it, and that's the CEO's policy. But I was the one who ran that ad. There's a purpose for that. I can't tell you anymore except this. Don't ask questions or look any further into this matter. You'll be asking for trouble if you do.

Secondly, I run Bennington's PR, not you. You'll do well to remember that before you speak to me in that tone again. I'm busy Dave and I have to go. Remember what I just told you."

Morris heard a hard click at the other end of the line. Something big was going on and Morris was being left. He didn't like that at all.

He looked into the dining room from where he was standing and saw Alice staring at him. She looked worried. He was about to walk over to her and relay Martin's conversation, but as he got up all he could do was look back down at the phone and shake his head.

"I'll find out what that bastard's up to if it's the last thing I do," Morris said. "And when I do, I'll fix his ass!"

It was nearly 9 p.m. on Sunday, yet in a small, cluttered little cubicle on the third floor of the East Bay Gazette building, Larry Nelson was pounding away at his laptop, putting the finishing touches on a paragraph he had just revised. He had spent three hours cross checking parts of the information he received from Gerard with articles in the newspaper's morgue. His quest for accuracy proved fruitful- the information provided by Gerard matched perfectly with the information contained in the paper's morgue.

Since three o'clock that afternoon, Nelson had focused on his article. It was an investigative reporter's dream-he would have the opportunity to write an exclusive report detailing the hypocrisy of Bennington Oil's advertisement.

"They are a publicly owned pollution source" thought Nelson.

"Just look at this from just this year alone," Nelson pondered aloud, "January 3rd- 5000 gallons of heavy crude spilled when a steel hose ruptures; January 23rd- corroded storage tank valve flange allows 250,000 gallons of gasoline to escape, luckily held in check by the berm built around the tank - 96% of the spill recovered; March 29th-tanker aground off of Galveston Island in Texas - 8800 barrels spilled on an outgoing tide. No oil reaches land-tanker repairs exceed $1 million."

"This is just the tip of the iceberg," thought Nelson.

Nelson had double-checked the facts in his article with those from the newspaper's records. His accuracy guaranteed, all that awaited Nelson now was an 8 a.m. call to Bennington Oil's Public Relations Office to get their point of view. This call to Bennington Oil was important, because it provided all sides of this issue an opportunity to comment. Whether they accepted it or not was irrelevant-the opportunity to comment was forwarded to Bennington Oil in earnest. How they chose to accept and exploit that opportunity was not Nelson's concern. He simply wanted to make sure that they could claim that they had not been approached on this matter before it went to press. Nelson had also taken one additional step in contacting Bennington Oil.

When Nelson contacted the on-call representative from Bennington Oil's PR staff, he was connected to Alan Roth. Nelson explained that he wanted a representative of the Bennington Oil PR staff to call him on Monday, but he took the added step of asking that the reply come from none other than Bill Martin, the chief of Bennington Oil's PR office. His motives for this were many. He didn't like Bill Martin, and he knew this story would not sit well with him. Secondly, he did like David Morris, and he didn't want Morris having to respond to questions about Bennington Oil's hypocritical advertisement. Nelson figured that Martin would delegate this request to Morris anyway, but if that happened, it would be Martin, and not Nelson, putting Morris on the spot.

Roth took Nelson's request and told him that he would make certain that Martin got his message.

After making sure that Martin would call him tomorrow, Nelson leaned back in his chair and tried to figure out if he had left out any pertinent facts or details that could affect the article. He was working a major article and he wanted no discrepancies, no nit-picky and insignificant details to exist that could rob it of its punch, its impact or its credibility.

He read the article twice before he was assured of its thoroughness. He saved the article into his office computer's hard drive, as well as making a backup copy to a flash drive. Like most computer users, he had learned the importance of backing up all of his documents the hard way-an important file flashed from existence in the speed of an inadvertent keystroke. Accordingly he made a backup copy whenever he was working on a major project. He had never worked on as major a project as this.

He took the flash drive off of the computer and put it in his shirt pocket. He had no idea of how Bill Martin would respond to his questions, but he decided to worry about that tomorrow.

CHAPTER 6

FIFTH ESTATE/ECONOMIC REALITIES

Bill Martin's Monday morning was starting out well. The commute had been trouble free, with no stalls or crashes to tie up the daily lemming-like parade of the countless souls who crossed the Bay Bridge.

Martin was in the elevator on the way to his office when he glanced down at his watch.

"Three minutes to eight," he said. "I could sure use an easy day."

He turned into the corridor and headed for his office, arriving and sitting down behind his desk two minutes later. It was the first time he'd been in it since before the crash. As his responsibility for the last four days had not been here in his office, but on a still-undisclosed endeavor, he'd delegated the entire spill effort to Morris while he, the chief of strategic planning department and a select few others worked on a different matter. While he may have wanted to, he couldn't tell the rest of his public relations staff about what he was working on, at least not yet. That would require clearance of the highest order; a clearance he didn't possess. He pondered for a second, and then dismissed the entire train of thought.

It was exactly eight o'clock when the ringing telephone interrupted him.

Ten minutes later Martin was using all of his strength to

keep from literally exploding. Larry Nelson of the East Bay Gazette was as good as his word and had called Martin for Bennington Oil's response to his article. After listening to Nelson's proposed article, Martin's reply was short and concise; as lucid as it was direct.

"Print that story and you'll regret it!"

Martin had immediately grasped the nature of the story and its worst case consequences.

At a time when truth and credibility were most important, this story could serve to destroy both for Bennington Oil. Martin could not, and would not allow that to happen.

He picked up the phone and called the CEO's secretary.

"Mary, this is Bill. Tell the boss that I've got an emergency and I'm on my way up."

"Will do."

Five minutes later, Martin walked into the CEO's office; first to brief him on the article and secondly to tell him what he planned to do about it.

In his haste to enter the CEO's office, Martin failed to close the door. As he began talking the secretary sat at her desk, pretending to be reading a document while registering every word the two men spoke. For her, this would be another juicy tidbit that she could trade upon. As the CEO's secretary, Mary Nesbitt enjoyed a position of being the first to know when every decision is made. This knowledge was power, and it made her a demigod in the eyes of the other secretaries, and even to some in the executive cadre. She had seen the scurrying about and the closed meetings and she knew something big was up, but even she took exception when the doors to the boardroom closed, and she was still outside them. She watched with disdain as "that little tart" as she called Jenkin's secretary at Strategic Planning, walked into and out of each of these meetings, each time learning more about this puzzle than she could talk about, and yet letting everyone know that she was involved. She had hoped through this ongoing conversation to learn about what was going on.

"You know" Martin said, "that there is another hand behind this article. The timing was too soon and it would have taken them much longer to compile the information, especially since all the agencies that he'd need to work with would have been closed for the weekend. And not all of this information is available online."

The CEO thought for a second. "We have two problems here. One is this article and the other is the hand behind it. As far as who put the paper up to it, we can wait until we're into the retribution phase of this operation to deal with that. What we plan to do about the article is our first and foremost concern. What's your plan?"

"Well," said Martin, "I thought we could start with..."

Martin abruptly ended his sentence when he noticed the open door. He stiffly got up and went over to it, looking out from behind it as if to see who might have been listening in. His icy stare fell upon Mary, who immediately assumed an air of innocence and asked what might be wrong.

Martin ignored her question and disappeared back into the office. The look on his face when he gazed at her was harrowing and all of a sudden, she realized that she not only had a lot of work to do, but that she had lost all interest in what was going on.

"Whatever it is," she thought, "I don't want any part of that man!"

By one o'clock that afternoon, with the CEO's blessing, Martin had contacted all of the necessary departments within Bennington Oil and had prepared a reply to the East Bay Gazette's inquiry.

It was one that no one had expected, and it came as a shock to everyone, especially to the intrepid reporter, Larry Nelson.

At five minutes to three Robert Schilling, editor of the East Bay Gazette and five of his major subordinates were headed into the newspaper's conference room. Every day, at three p.m., the key Gazette staff members held an editorial board to determine what would go on the front page and news section of the next day's paper. Three o'clock was the perfect time for this, as it allowed the high powered governmental and financial centers on the East Coast to close. Thus, no major policy or financial issue would escape their purview, or worse, occur after they went to press.

Along with Schilling were the city editor, Joyce Elliot; the editorial staff head, Sidney Howard-Morton; financial editor, E. Joseph Harper; the features editor, Jewel Ruttman; and the managing editor John Mason. The advertising editor, whose role was strictly advertising and policy adherence, was conspicuously absent.

We'll go with the oil stories on page one," said Schilling. "Our lead piece will focus on the Coast Guard investigation. Following that we'll..."

The door opened and the entrance of two men stopped the meeting. Jack Abbs, the advertising director entered, followed by Louis Pierce III, publisher and owner of the Gazette. Their arrival together came as a shock, as the publisher rarely came to these editorial meetings. Only when an important announcement was imminent did he "ever grace the meetings with his presence," as Schilling would sarcastically mumble.

Pierce's position with the paper staff was one of omnipotence. Many arguments between staff heads had been solved or calmed with just a few words from him.

His presence at the staff meeting however, brought with it an air of curiosity and apprehension. Ruttman, the features editor, leaned over to the city editor and quietly proclaimed "Something big is up, and I don't think Schilling's going to like it."

Schilling took the offense and spoke first.

"Jack, I take it you've got something for all of us." It was phrased as a statement and not a question.

Abbs tried to smile and put on his best face, but the assembled group wasn't having any of that. They felt that something big was up, and they wanted to have it outright. Abbs prepared himself to oblige them.

"Robert," Abbs began," Advertising is the lifeblood of a newspaper. Editorial policy sets the nature and the character of a newspaper if you will, and it's also what sells the paper. But no large American metro could survive on just its circulation. Whether we like it or not, our life's blood comes from advertising, from those who buy the ads. It's even more important now in this digital age."

"Jack," Schilling said bluntly," what are you getting at? What are you trying to say that we don't already know?"

Abbs continued. "It has come to my attention that we're planning to run a major piece in tomorrow's paper on Bennington Oil's poor safety and environmental records. A major negative feature like that could affect our relationship with one our top advertisers."

Schilling fired back, not trying to mask the disgust he felt over what he knew was coming next.

"You're right, we're doing a piece that harangues them for their sorry safety record. It's part of the public domain and was drawn from purely public sources. It's true that it's a negative piece but the truth is that it contradicts some of the claims they made in their Sunday article."

Abbs and Schilling were staring intently at each other. The fact that the two men disliked each other was obvious; they had quit trying to get along ages ago. Since then, their relationship had been cordial and professional-nothing more. Their dislike was based more on their differing philosophical opinions than anything personal. Both of them had been with the Gazette far too many years to remember, and in their respective jobs they were amongst the best in the business. Their one overwhelming point of contention was that at times they wondered who worked for whom. It was during these times that the publisher had to assert his authority and put one of them down.

As advertising director Abbs would either harp on Schilling for running articles that maligned his advertisers, or he'd request more advertising space which, while earning more money for the, paper, served to take away valuable editorial space.

Schilling on the other hand was the editor, and his word was the one that counted. This single fact perturbed Abbs to no end. Because his advertisers paid for the paper, Abbs felt that they needed to be treated with a heightened degree of respect if the Gazette were genuinely interested in keeping their business. Abbs used to state, only half-jokingly, that Schilling's treatment of his advertisers was about as tactful as a Nazi reunion at a B'nai B'rith meeting.

When the two of them were on a collision course, the publisher had to step in. He had to perform the arbitrator's job, stepping in between the warring factions and trying to reach a happy medium. This position was one of walking the fine line of editorial integrity and profit making. As the Gazette was not a charity project, it either made a profit or it scaled down its operations. The profit line determined a great deal of what might be included in a newspaper.

Abbs was still standing and staring at an increasingly incensed Schilling. Schilling's newspaper skills had alerted him as to what was going to happen next, and he was planning to fight it.

"So we're still planning on running that Bennington Oil piece?" questioned Abbs.

"No," said Schilling adamantly," We're not planning on running that piece. We are running that piece. If Bennington's so damned ashamed of their safety and environmental record, they should improve it!"

Abbs took a long look around the table and looked back at Schilling. "Haven't you been listening? I'll make it as clear as possible. Bennington's reply to that article was to threaten to pull their advertising away from us if we run any item with their safety record in it."

"Tough shit," Schilling shot back. He slowly rose to his feet, pointing a finger agitatedly at Abbs. In a stern voice he stated," They don't set our editorial policy, I do. And I'll run whatever I like, regardless of who they think they are!"

Schilling's reaction and reply made Abbs certain that having the publisher come down was the right thing to do. Schilling was making this issue a personal crusade and Abbs knew that he wouldn't back down unless ordered from above. He looked over to the publisher and gave Pierce a puzzled look. It told the publisher everything he needed to know; that Abbs had reached an impasse and needed his help. Pierce got up and walked to the front of the room.

"There's more to it than that," Pierce started. "Bob, before you became our editor we were in a terrible financial state. In fact, those were our worst years ever. You were here then, you know how bad it was. For three years we barely hovered near the break-even point. Unfortunately we were hovering on the loss side of that line, not the profit side. During that period we lost close to thirty seven million dollars.

"Almost two years ago we stemmed the loss. Last year we had a healthy profit and we're well on our way to total recovery."

Schilling was well aware of how Pierce did his bidding. After beginning with the bleak picture, Pierce would then talk about the problem times and swing into how a certain course of action could affect the entire picture. He glanced over to Abbs and detected a slight smile on the advertising director's lips. At that point, Schilling recognized that Abbs had won this battle, and that listening to Pierce was just a formality.

"While we're on our way to a total recovery," stated Pierce," we haven't reached a point where we can afford to lose a multi-million annual account. No other paper in the Bay Area will be running this kind of story because they all want to be in good position to gain this contract if we should lose it. I've already checked with three other papers about this and they've all been told by Bennington Oil that we could lose their contract immediately, and that those papers that show themselves to be 'objective' could be in a great position to receive it.

"Win can't lose many contracts like this one and expect to stay alive. It's as simple as that."

Pierce looked over to the editor and in a direct tone said," Bob, you know what you have to do in this case."

"Yes, sir I do."

Pierce turned to leave the room and Abbs stood to follow.

Schilling shot a glare over to Abbs, who was trying hard to suppress a smile while leaving the room.

"This round went to that bastard," said Schilling after Abbs and Pierce had left the room, "but the next one will be mine!"

"Bob," said Elliot, "Pierce said that you knew what to do in this case. What: did he mean? What are you going to do?"

"I don't have an alternative, Joyce, I'm going to pull the Bennington story out."

CHAPTER 7

TRUE FRIENDS/UNTRUE MOTIVATIONS

"What the hell do you mean you had to kill my story," screamed Larry Nelson. "It was a damn good story and it should be run!"

"I know," said Schilling, "You did a lot of research and checking for that story, and I'm sorry that it's not going to happen. God knows you have every right to behave like a totally irrational jerk but like I told you, it got OBE'd."

"OBE'd?" said Nelson, "What the hell does that mean?"

"Overcome by events" said Schilling. "Bennington Oil threatened to yank millions per annum in advertising if we ran that story. The paper's just come off of some pretty lean years and simply can't really do without that kind of income right now."

"So they strong-armed us?" Nelson blurted.

"That's exactly how I'd phrase what they did to us," said Schilling.

"So what are we going to do about it?"

"Me," said Schilling, "Nothing. You, however, are going to do some checking on Bennington. They're not to be trusted. Do you have a contact over there?"

"As a matter of fact," said Nelson, "I do. I wasn't going to use him in my story because I wanted to avoid any conflict of interest problems."

"You got a name for this person," questioned Schilling.

"Yeah, his name's David Morris. He's the number two man in their public relations department."

"Give him a call," Schilling directed, "And see if he can give you the scam on Bennington. See if they're up to something. But be careful, because if he's PR he'll know how to handle a reporter."

The first thing Morris saw on his desk Tuesday morning was a note on his phone to call Larry Nelson at the East Bay Gazette. He took the note, folded it and stuck it in his pocket.

Monday had not been a good day for Morris. He avoided Martin and spent nearly the entire day discussing PR strategy with his staff and arranging media visits at the company spill control center. His intent to find out what Martin was up to would have to wait until time permitted.

He put his briefcase down and picked up the phone, dialing Nelson's number. After a moment of Gazette editorial types searching around for him, Nelson answered the phone.

"Hello, Larry Nelson speaking."

"Man, you sure sound formal for a media slug," joked Morris.

"Dave," Nelson answered, "How goes it?"

"Not too bad. Yourself?"

"No real complaints," said Nelson. "Actually, I do have one and it's a biggie."

"You know my motto Larry," said Morris. "Just ask and ye shall be denied."

"Yeah, right. Resubmit in ninety days for final disapproval. You sound like you're still in the military."

"No way," said Morris. "But when you're in a runaway bureaucracy, it just seems like it. What seems to be your problem?"

"Well Dave," Nelson stated pensively. "There have been a few things puzzling me and I need your help in getting some answers. You know the ads that you guys ran Sunday?"

"Yes, I know them." Morris answered, deliberately leaving out the fact that they were run without his knowledge.

"Well I was going to run an article with your company's safety record and show how the truth contradicted your ad."

"I see," said Morris. "Before you do, I would ask that you give us a chance to peruse the article and..."

"You're kidding aren't you?" Nelson bluntly interjected.

"No, I'm serious. I'd like to see what our record really is in light of what you're planning to say."

The line went dead for a second as Morris waited for Nelson to reply.

Nelson stood flabbergasted.

"Dave, we're not planning to say anything. I called Martin with the story yesterday to get your company's point of view. Yesterday afternoon he called our advertising director and threatened to pull all of Bennington's advertising from our paper if we didn't yank the expose. I guess my question to you is why? We've always been on the up and up in our dealings and now... Dave, why these tactics and why now?"

Morris sat in his chair dumbfounded by this new and shocking revelation.

"You can't be serious?" inquired Morris in a solemn tone that was barely audible.

"You've got to be joking - tell me you're joking?" Nelson could tell by the sound of Morris' voice that he was serious. As much as he would have liked to tell his friend otherwise, he restated the truth.

"I'm totally serious," said Nelson. "They've got me working on a story about some old geezer who's about to have a heart-lung transplant. After that I've got to do a piece on airline safety. Seemingly, anything but stories on oil spills in the Bay Area."

Morris was so engrossed in this new turn of events that he didn't notice Nelson in his moment of self-pity. He pressed the reporter for further information to find out what was going on. "Martin called your advertising people? Are you sure it was him?" Morris questioned.

"Yeah it was Martin," came Nelson's near cynical answer. "And from what I hear he didn't pull any punches or mince any words. Just 'Pull the story or else."

"That's Martin all right," said Morris, "...a real sultan of subtlety."

"Larry," Morris began, "I didn't know about any of this,

about any of what Martin did to you guys. But I will check into this. Needless to say, this isn't the kind of relationship that we want with the press."

"Thanks Dave," Nelson replied. "By the way, what are you doing after work?"

"Not much, why?"

"Meet me at Rosey's in Jack London Square. We'll have a drink and you can tell me what you've found out."

"Jack London Square," Morris stated. "That's way on the other side of the bay. If you want to see me so badly you can come to my side of the bay - the good side."

"Tell you what," said Nelson, "I'll buy the first round."

"In that case, see you at about six."

Morris' day had been pretty much set aside. Media coverage from the spill was starting to ease, and the focus was fading from the event to its cause and eventually who was to pay for it. As the media's focus shifted, so would Bennington Oil's public relations effort. Instead of concentrating on the cleanup, the onus of their efforts would now fall upon the Coast Guard investigation, which was beginning at 10 a.m. As that was a closed door affair, only the crew members and their counsel, as well as the two corporate legal representatives, would be allowed. Morris would learn of the investigation's outcome with the rest of the world.

Unlike the interested public, Morris had to be ready to react. He needed to have plans ready for all possible outcomes, from the crash being caused by negligence to it being a genuine accident; from the collision being Bennington's fault, to it being caused by the Montgomery Oil tanker.

He was sketching out a straw man diagram of what he planned to do in each circumstance when he saw Martin enter his office.

Martin had walked in and placed his briefcase down near his desk. He had no more removed his coat when he heard a knock on his door. He saw it was Morris and invited him in.

"Morning Dave, how's business?"

"Not too badly," Dave replied. "Yourself?"

"No complaints," Martin replied. "By the way Dave, I want to apologize for snapping at you on Sunday. It shouldn't have happened."

Martin's apology caught Morris by surprise. He hadn't expected it, but he wasn't complaining.

"Funny you should mention Sunday," said Morris, "That's partly what I wanted to talk to you about."

"Just a minute," Martin cautioned. He got up from behind his desk and walked the fifteen feet to the door and closed it. As the latch clicked, Martin had already turned, walked back to his desk and sat down.

It was then, for the first time, that Morris noticed how Martin used this desk as a power implement. The broad expanse of its surface was clear, making Martin the only thing a visitor could look at. Morris remembered that every time he spoke to Martin, he retreated to the safety of this cherry wood island in a sea of carpeting. Behind Martin was the only window in the office. When the sunlight shone through, it bracketed and framed Martin, giving him the deified blessed by God appearance.

"He's really into this powerplay crap," thought Morris. "Why else would he have natural light shine on him while the rest of his office, not to mention we hoi polloi, get illuminated by the phosphorescent tubes in the ceiling?"

"Now you wanted to talk about Sunday, or some particular aspect of it?" said Martin.

"Bill, I'm going to put it to you straight. In Sunday's advertisements, we made a lot of insinuations. If any media call up, I'm going to need to know if we can back up what we said. I'm not going to risk my integrity defending a lie."

"What are you aiming at, Dave?" Martin asked.

"I need to know what proof we have to back up what we said Sunday. We all but blamed Monty-O for that crash. Give me some substantiation."

Martin eyed Morris. The image was magnified by the distance it covered over his immense desktop. Morris was eyeing Martin just as intently, neither man seemingly willing to back down or look away.

Martin looked down at his desk and then back at Morris.

His expression was stern. "I thought I told you not to look into this matter any further?"

"You did," Morris replied. " You also told me to take over the department during the spill control operations. This stuff could spill over into my efforts there. I could care less about what project the CEO's got you working on, but if it could affect mine, then I need to know."

While Martin had begun to get angry with Morris' tone, he knew Morris was right. He had his tasks to do, and the job wasn't made any easier by Martin's ad on Sunday.

"OK, Dave" Martin began. "This is for your information only. Our guys are testifying about the crash at the Coast Guard hearing today and tomorrow they are going to tell the Coast Guard what I already know: that the crash was the fault of the Pacific Patriarch. They cut in front of our ship and caused the crash. Everything I said in Sunday's ad was correct and substantiated by our crew, the only eyewitnesses to the entire accident. Our guys got cut off and sliced into their ship," Martin continued. "They told me this when I went to see them on Friday. I asked them to tell me exactly what happened and they did. From there, you've seen what I've done with that information."

"I see," said Morris. "But why did you keep me out. I could have kept that quiet."

"Until they're under oath and testifying," said Martin thoughtfully, "it's just so much of our word against theirs. Since their crew died with their ship, it would have looked as though we were taking advantage of their situation. Also," Martin continued, "the closer we kept these cards to our chest, the less chance they'll have to respond when all of this comes out into the open. I'm sorry, but we had to keep this quiet. Until this investigation is over, we still need to."

Morris nodded his head, finally understanding the need for secrecy. While he still didn't like being on the outside, at least he accepted it better.

Martin saw Morris' mood change from one of concern to contentment. He was certain that Morris had found the answers he was searching for. Rising up from behind his desk, Martin escorted Morris as far as the door. Standing there for almost another five minutes, Martin explained why he treated the East Bay Gazette to such drastic measures. Morris took the opportunity to express his views, and his desire that a step such as that not be repeated without his knowledge. Martin apologized, saying that the time factor alone was the reason he did not include him in the coordination loop. After their brief conversation, Martin dismissed his subordinate with all of the standard pleasantries.

Martin watched Morris go back into his own office before turning back to his desk. Smiling as he walked back to his cherry wood shrine, Martin sat down, happy in the knowledge that he had easily dispensed with Morris by telling him only the merest fraction of the truth.

Morris directed his staff to probe into all possible courses of action dealing with the investigation. He concentrated his own efforts on emphasizing the only possible conclusion that the Coast Guard could come to, and he planned to give it maximum publicity.

He was so lost in his planning that he didn't realize when five o'clock rolled around. Only when Roth stuck his head in the door and said "Hey Dave, Its Miller time!" did Morris realize it was time to go home and that he had a drinking appointment across the bay. He now regretted taking up Nelson's offer, because it meant crossing the Bay Bridge at zenith of rush hour.

Traffic was smoother than usual and only took forty minutes to get from downtown San Francisco to Jack London Square. He parked his car near the KTVU television center and walked the short distance back to Rosey's, arriving exactly at 6:20 p.m.

Rosey's was a major Eastbay hangout, overlooking the Alameda channel and the Oakland Marina. Members of the banking, finance and media communities converged on it after work, to be part of the 300 people legally allowed entrance by the Oakland Fire Department. The crowd at Rosey's nearly always exceeded the limits, and this Tuesday night proved no exception.

Walking towards Rosey's, Morris could make out the unmistakable spell of oil. "It made down this far as well," he thought.

After walking through the front door, Morris scanned the sea of business suits and skirts trying to find Nelson.

"This is going to take a while," thought Morris.

A smiling face broke through the crowd and approached Morris. "Damn man, it's about time you showed up!"

"Right!" Morris shot back to Nelson, "I've been here searching for you out there in the Great Yuppie Sea."

"Not to worry," said Nelson. "I've got a reserved table."

"How does a reporter rate a reserved table in one of the most popular hangouts in the Bay Area?"

"Easy," stated Nelson matter-of-factly. "One, ours is a great responsibility entrusted to only a chosen few. Two, some recognize the press as the all-seeing, powerful eye which watches us and can affect us with just the slightest glance."

Morris figured that Nelson's last statement might be an expose on a bar that allowed, on a regular basis, 20% over the fire ordinance maximums. Such an article would probably close this place down.

"Thirdly," Nelson continued, "my uncle owns the place."

"Nepotism," said Morris in mock surprise, "that's so beneath you."

"Yeah, it is," laughed Nelson, "but it gets me inside."

The drinks they'd ordered had just arrived when Nelson spoke up.

"Well Bill, what did you find out about the Sultan of Subtlety's decision to cancel my article?"

"I talked to Martin about that this morning. He told me you were doing a slime piece on us. Basically the piece you were going to run was intended to contradict Sunday's ad, to catch us in a lie, so to speak."

Morris looked Nelson straight in the eye and said," We couldn't let that happen."

Morris' "company-man" stance mildly surprised Nelson, who nonetheless pressed for the advantage.

"We," Nelson replied. "Hell you didn't even know about it until I told you this morning. And now you condone it?"

Morris let Nelson's comment go unacknowledged.

"I didn't know a lot of things this morning. Martin made

the tie-in to Sunday's ad and told me that killing it was our only course of action. In light of that, and some other information that you aren't aware of, I fully concur with his course of action."

"Not a whole lot you can do-after the fact!" thought Nelson. "What's this unknown you're referring to?" asked Nelson.

"Can't tell you yet, but you'll know soon," said Morris, referring to the Coast Guard findings he felt would be released in a few weeks.

"Anyway," he added, "if the wire services picked up a story showing us in a negative light and ran it, that, coupled with the loss of a tanker and a crew plus possible liability suits, would serve to unnerve our investors. If too many of them got frightened and tried to sell their shares, it could drive our price down. A depressed stock price doesn't do any of us any good."

"The advertisement you did on Monty-O Sunday isn't doing them any good," said Nelson. "That, the collision and the spill has dropped their stock several points. Their situation is so bad that demonstrators have appeared outside some of their stations."

"They deserve it," thought Morris, *"the collision was their fault."*

"And besides," added Nelson," the information in my story is public knowledge and came from public sources.

"I figured that," said Morris, "but it isn't exactly flattering, is it?"

"But it's true!"

"And it comes at our worst possible time," said Morris.

"Well what about the public's right to know?" interjected Nelson.

"That extends to governments, not corporations. The U.S. Constitution guarantees a free and fair press," Morris added. "Ours doesn't."

"So you guys will just keep on sending us the good news and not the bad?"

Morris realized that his point of view was not getting across to his erstwhile friend, so he tried a different tack.

"Look at it from our perspective," Morris began. "Your newspaper is owned by one man. My company has 150 million owners, each of them at today's quote would have had to pay $45 to $50 dollars a share for that privilege. For that money, they get to elect representatives to run the company. These representatives, or board members, pick someone to run the day-to-day operations of the company, the CEO. By and by everything we do is to placate the shareholders."

"If they see a story in the paper that berates us, do you think for a moment they'll sit there and smile.

Hell no!" Morris stated emphatically. "They'll either bitch to us or sell their shares. If enough of them do it, it'll drive our share prices down

"You see Nelson, you have your public to answer to and I have mine. I don't think either of us is going to put the other's views over his own."

"I understand," Nelson replied. "I've got another question for you. Why did you guys write that letter for the Sunday papers? Under the circumstances, it was uncalled for, and some would say that it was callous. Even you have to admit that it went beyond the bounds of good public relations."

Morris had thought about that same question since last Sunday. Even though he had spoken to Martin about it, he was no closer to an answer than Nelson was.

"Since you won't talk to me about it," said Nelson, "can you look around your company and see if anything funny is going on?"

Morris was taken aback by this unusual request and let Nelson know it.

"Don't you think I've said enough to you already?"

"Yes you have," Nelson said," but I'd just like to know why that ad was written?"

Morris, the number two man in the Bennington Oil Public Relations department wanted that answer too. He needed it; his ego required it.

Morris worked long and hard rising up through Bennington. He always prided himself for knowing what the company was doing. He couldn't quite say that now. And to add to that, Nelson was speaking to him in a manner that implied that Morris was not even involved in his own department's decision making process; that Morris' role was simply to react to what Martin was doing. Nelson was treating Morris as if he were an outsider to his own company. And though he tried to camouflage it, Morris knew that Nelson was right on the money, and it hurt.

"I'll look around," Morris said to Nelson, "but for my own reasons. I'll decide what you need to know, and all of it will be off the record and for your information only. In short, it's friend to friend. If you understand that none of this is for publication, I'll let you know what I find out. O.K.?"

"Sure," Nelson replied. "I just want to know why your guys had my article pulled?"

"I understand" said Morris, "but that will be it. No more."

"But no less" Nelson answered.

CHAPTER 8

FLEDGING STEPS

The early Wednesday morning saw one of the numerous express elevators in the Bennington building close its doors in preparation for yet another of its journeys.

As soon as the doors touched, the elevator and its sixteen passengers began their skyward ascent, covering the forty-five floor climb in less than sixty seconds. Most of them were heading to the same destination: the petroleum company that occupied the uppermost floors of the building named after itself.

While fifteen of the passengers were headed for another day at the office, one of them, a tall slender man with a certain air of commitment, was preparing to engage in an activity that he'd been warned not to.

Morris was going to start looking for answers. His answers. He'd been the non-participating witness to two major decisions; judgments which he should have had input. He was aware, and concerned, that he was being intentionally left out of the loop.

From what he'd ascertained, two things were happening. Something big within the company was occurring, and whatever it was, it was being kept close to heart by those individuals in the know.

But despite all of this, Morris was optimistic. The headquarters of a major corporation is a bureaucracy, and bureaucracies are made up of layers of people. Whenever the CEO gives an order, countless people are required to carry it out. Morris planned on tapping these middle and lower level executives to try and find his answers. He was banking on an instinct that some orders connected to the "veil of secrecy" had already been given, and that somewhere, Bennington executives and subordinates had been tasked to perform them.

The elevator doors opened on the forty-fifth floor and the Bennington Oil contingent spilled out to attend their respective offices. Morris had turned the corner into the public relations department when he stopped to look into Martin's office. As he anticipated, it was empty.

"Leadership by absentia," Morris uttered under his breath.

He walked the few feet to his office and found Alan Roth III waiting within.

"Hey Dave," Roth began, " I hope you don't mind me waiting in your office. You weren't here so I thought that I'd...."

Morris politely cut him off.

"No problem, Al. You know you're welcome here at any time. So what brings you here so early?"

"Well, Dave," Roth started, "there's a few things going on that I don't understand."

"Yeah, I know that feeling," Morris added sarcastically.

"Pardon?"

"Nothing, just thinking out loud."

"Anyway," Roth continued," I wanted you to take a look at this video of last night's news." Roth walked across the office to where a television and video recorder were positioned on a small wall unit.

Roth turned it on and fast forwarding it until came to the feature he wanted. He paused the video playback and turned back to look at Morris.

"Dave," he said, "the rest of the news, or at least the part before this segment, concentrated on the spill. This piece brought attention to a bizarre occurrence, a sort of sideshow to the main event. Take a look."

The segment had already begun and the reporter had

apparently already identified himself. Roth made no attempt to rewind the videocassette; it didn't matter. The issue was the news and not the person reporting it.

"Demonstrators by the hundreds have begun picketing Montgomery Oil service stations." stated the unidentified news reporter. "Starting Sunday in a few of the busier San Francisco and Oakland stations, groups of protesters have begun demonstrating at Montgomery stations as far away as Redding in the north and Monterey to the south. As of this morning, company officials have announced that 162 stations, some thirty percent of all Montgomery stations have, or have had, pickets or demonstrations. One major impact of this protest, obviously formed because of Montgomery's involvement in last week's calamitous tanker collision and oil spill, is that thousands of potential customers are going to other service stations in order to avoid the controversy. One of those benefiting from this circumstance is Bennington Oil, where a lot of these customers are taking their business. It's ironic that one company is being lambasted for its role in a maritime disaster while another one is seemingly profiting from the same thing."

At that point, Roth walked over to the video recorder and stopped it. He looked over to Morris and asked him the question that had been bothering since he'd seen this particular news segment.

"Dave, what do you make of that?"

"To be perfectly truthful" Morris calmly replied," I expected it. You see, demonstrators and people verbalizing their beliefs are as much a part of California as redwoods and earthquakes. However, I am concerned about the size and speed of the protest. To discover the locations of 162 stations, and then round up enough demonstrators to picket them all requires an organized outfit. This could be turned against us too, and we're currently no better prepared for it than Monty-O. This is your baby Alan. Look in our guidance book on demonstrations and come up with a course of action in the event that we should be blessed by this occurrence."

"And Alan," Morris continued, "Thanks for bringing this to my attention."

Even though Roth had turned and left the room five minutes ago, Morris was still wondering about the size and the speed of the Monty-O demonstrators.

"Californians are volatile," he thought, "I don't envy Gerard over at Monty-O."

Morris reached over to his phone directory and found the number to Charles Gerard, chief of public relations at Monty-O. He dialed it quickly and waited for someone to answer the ringing phone.

"Hello," a monotone voice replied, "Montgomery Oil Corporation, may I help you?"

"Yes," Morris answered, "I'd like to speak to Mr. Gerard?"

"One moment please," came the automatic reply.

"Hello, this is Jeff Randolph. What can I do for you?"

"Jeff, this is Dave Morris over at..."

"Over at Bennington," Randolph finished. Morris noticed that Randolph's tone was a lot less friendly than when he first answered the phone. "What can I do for you?"

"Actually," Morris began," I wanted to speak with Gerard."

"He's in with Richardson. He's probably receiving the grilling of his professional career. The story in the Eastbay Gazette was to be our counterstroke to your Sunday ad. It was an inspired ploy too, if you ask me. But I don't think anyone thought that you guys would pull train on the newspaper."

"Pull train?" Morris inquired.

"Yes, it means you screwed them over. A lot like what you're trying to do to us."

"Let me get this straight," said Morris, "the newspaper got their story from you?"

"Not their story," said Randolph, "just the facts behind it. The safety records of our two companies came from us. The reporter added his flair to it, but it pretty much covered everything we wanted. Don't get me wrong, however. The reporter wrote the article, we just helped him with some facts."

The line was quiet as Morris grew silent. He was thinking

how he'd phrase his expletives when he next saw Nelson. "Monty-O used him and now he's using me," thought Morris. "Go and check around your company for answers about why my story was killed," Nelson's quote was reverberating throughout Morris' head. He was not thrilled that Nelson shared such a cozy relationship with Monty-O or that Nelson wanted him to look throughout his company for some kind of tidbit.

"I'll be damned if I'm going to lay Bennington on the line for that two-faced...."

"Hello? Dave you still there?"

"Jesus," thought Morris, "I forgot all about ...."

"Sorry Jeff," said Morris, "My train of thought got derailed."

"Yeah I know how that can happen," said Randolph. "Look, Dave, with the situation between our two companies the way they are, I think that it would be best that communication between our two companies should be at the department head level. I'll tell Charles that you called, and I'll have him call you back."

"Don't bother; I just wanted to find out how he was planning to handle the demonstrators."

"I'll have him call you," said Randolph.

Morris put the phone down and entered a period of reflection. His plan for the day was to go throughout some of the major corporate divisions and try to piece together what was happening. The need to understand the events that were occupying 100% of the public relations and strategic planning department heads' time was beginning to gnaw at Morris. He needed to know before they performed another assault on his credibility and integrity. And then there was the Eastbay Gazette.

He had planned on sharing everything he uncovered with Nelson. That was before he discovered a tie between Nelson and Monty-O. This conduit could not be allowed, and until Morris was certain that it no longer operated, he couldn't trust Nelson.

But the more he thought about what was going on, or at least his lack of knowledge over what was going on, the more he wanted to learn.

"My plans for today stand," Morris thought aloud. "I'll figure out what to do with any answers after I discover them."

A quick glance at his watch revealed that it was closing on ten o'clock.

With that, Morris rose from his desk and headed towards the door. He looked over at the secretary and gave her a rough agenda as to where he planned to be. As the crash was six days ago, interest in the oil companies themselves was waning. It was being refocused on the Coast Guard inquiry, which began that morning. From his talk with Martin, Morris was pretty sure of how it would turn out. But until the inquiry was finished, he couldn't tell anyone what he knew. Needless to say, however, his workload was to plan his company's response to the inquiry. He had already shown the media the work being done at the animal aid centers, and he'd filled them in on all he knew to be true and everything that his company was doing to combat the pollution. Now that something resembling a lull in his schedule was appearing, he was going to spend it looking for answers.

His answers.

The ceiling and basements of today's modern business skyscrapers are packed with the electronics needed to ensure the massive computing and telecommunication needs of the contemporary business environment. Bennington's was no different, with one exception.

In the basement of the Bennington building was an extremely powerful telecommunications computer, one capable of thousands of functions within the blink of an eye. Amongst the myriad of capabilities possessed by this computer was the ability to monitor every phone call going into and out of the Bennington building. Its silicon brain could reveal from where a call was made, directed and received. With a little additional programming, accomplished when the system was installed, it was possible to have the computer inform select higher headquarters officials when certain phone numbers were accessed/contacted. Montgomery Oil was one of the listed numbers. The East Bay Gazette was added after Nelson's aborted story attempt of the day before.

This capability was not known throughout the company, or widely publicized throughout the Bennington building. Bennington Oil officials wanted, and got, the ability to see who was saying what to whom. With this system, on-going leaks to the media and others were non-existent, due to an almost 100% ability to track down the leakers.

Unfortunately, Morris knew none of this. While he was talking to Randolph at Monty-O, and earlier when he talked to Nelson, the computer processed his outgoing calls and determined that they were on the restricted list. It alerted an aide to the chief of security, who took the name and number of the caller and the called. The aide then logged the information and passed it onto the Chief of Strategic Planning, who set to work on it immediately.

CHAPTER 9

MARITIME PERSPECTIVE

Deciding to begin his search for answers at the department most affected by the collision, Morris went down a flight of steps to the forty-fourth floor and entered the Maritime Transport department. When all of the public uproar was over and the spill relegated to page ninety-nine of the newspaper, the Maritime Transport department would still be one tanker short.

The department was an orderly array of desks, computers and maps, each playing its part to see that Bennington's six remaining tankers picked up their loads and dropped them off at the proper destinations. Bennington's refineries processed 360,000 barrels of oil a day, and shutting one of them down because of a tanker related problems, for even the shortest periods of time, would cost the company hundreds of thousands of dollars. Needless to say, close track was kept on all tankers.

Morris had telephoned ahead and let them know he was coming. Fred Avey, the department head, welcomed Morris' visit and said that he would personally host him.

Morris liked Avey. Avey had spent umpteen years in the Navy, sailing into what he described as "every port where there was bad booze and worse women." Five foot ten and solid, easily passing 200 pounds, Avey wasn't as refined as most of the other execs. Not in demeanor, in style, and definitely not in language. But he could put a tanker into port, load it up and have it reach its destination on time and without a hitch. Most didn't think of the word 'executive' when they saw him for the first time, but everyone thought of the title 'executive' upon reviewing his track record at Bennington. He had a rough job to do, but he saw to it that it was handled professionally. The fact that the events of the previous week had made his job more difficult was not lost on Morris, and he planned to take as little of Avey's time as needed.

Morris had barely entered the Maritime Department when Avey greeted him.

"Good mornin' Dave, how's biz?"

"Not too bad Fred, yourself?"

"Man we've been busier than a one-legged man in an ass-kicking contest!"

"Typical Avey," Morris laughed. "But I can imagine you guys down here have been feeling the strain. How are you guys going to make due with one less tanker?"

Morris had told him what he was coming down for, so Avey had time to do a little preparation.

He thought about the question, furrowed his brow and frowned.

"It's not going to be easy" Avey began. *"At* any time we need about 2,000,000 barrels of oil on the roll. We've got to service three refineries— one in Texas and two in California. The Texas refinery gets its oil from our Texas oil fields via pipeline. But they get almost 10,000 barrels a day more than they use, so we either ship it here to California, or we sell it on the East Coast. We also get 75,000 barrels a day from Alaska. Every eight days, our operations in Alaska receive enough oil to fill one of our tankers. But we have a 1.3 million barrel tank farm up there where the oil just sits until a tanker comes and gets it. When that tank farm fills up, we have to start thinking about shutting wells or some other equally drastic measures.

"Anyways, a round trip from Alaska to L.A. takes about three weeks, more or less, depending on the weather. A similar trip to our Benicia refinery takes about three days less. So three of our tankers make the L.A. run and three of them make the S.F. to Alaska run.

"We keep our biggest tanker, the Walter J. Bennington, a beauty of just under 160,000 tons, on the Gulf of Mexico to East Coast run. Funny, while we have a big refinery and a lot of oil fields in Texas, we don't seem to have much of a market there. Almost all of our petroleum products are sold to East Coast petro-brokers who either sell it under their own names, or to the independents. I'm just telling you all of this so you'll know where exactly it is we stand."

Being the number two man in the public affairs office, Morris was already aware of most of Avey's conversation. He simply nodded his head in affirmation and waited for his host to continue.

He did.

"The entire output of our Texas refinery goes out on that one tanker," Avey said. "When the backlog gets to be too much, or when the Walter J. Bennington goes in for repairs, we get a charter to help handle the load. But until then, that ship is the rock that holds up the Texas refinery. Unfortunately, that ship is tar too important to move onto another route."

"That's one of our seven spoken for," Morris added wryly.

"That's right," agreed Avey. "Another one of our tankers is just outside the bay, painting the shoreline in oil."

"So that's two of our tankers accounted for," Morris added.

"This is where our problems really begin," Avey sighed while looking back at Morris.

Avey walked over to a huge electronic wall map that showed the entire West Coast, from Alaska to the northern part of Mexico. Five red dots showed the location of each of Bennington's five remaining tankers.

"Here's the rub," Avey announced. "We've experienced a rise in usage in the L.A. area. It may not be reflected throughout the industry, but it is throughout this company. I'm sure its due to those great advertisements you guys put out."

Morris just smiled and took the complement. The advertisements came out of the marketing department and not Public Affairs, but Morris saw no need to correct him.

"So," Avey continued, "the L.A. area needs more of our oil. Since we've gotten a large surplus stashed at our Benicia refinery, we were diverting some of our S.F. shipments down to help out in L.A."

"That," Avey sadly explained, "was where the Guardian was headed with 50,000 tons of crude."

"Anyway', he said, "with just two tankers now, the L.A. refinery is just going to have to sell what they've got, or close or ration. But whatever they do will be up to the folks upstairs. I've got a charter lined up, and if the boss wants to go with it we can be ready in just a few days. It'll cost us plenty, but it'll move our oil up and down the coast."

"A charter?," questioned Morris "how about a replacement tanker? Surely the transport of that much oil should take a higher priority.

"It should," Avey replied regretfully, "but it don't."

"What do you mean?"

"I've already asked about that," said Avey. "Even though the Guardian was the sorriest piece of shit ever floated, it won't be replaced; not any time soon at least."

Morris sat puzzled, not believing this latest revelation. Carefully looking at Avey's face, Morris saw no sign of mischief that would give him the impression that the maritime transportation chief was joking. Avey was very serious.

"Moving oil is like our circulatory system," Morris began. "Without it, we die. And now you tell, me that they won't allow you to get another tanker to replace the one we lost? Why, for God's sake? I know the one we lost was fully insured, so money should not be a problem and..."

"Let me fill. you in on a few things," Avey interjected. "First off, that damned boat wasn't fully insured. In fact, it was insured for no more than 50% plus cargo."

Morris shook his head from side to side, reflecting his incredulity in what he was hearing.

"Nobody, but nobody, insures a ship for half of its value. It doesn't make sense. If you lose it, you're out of one ship. And half of the loss comes out of your own pocket. How could we allow that to happen? I mean how can that be allowed to happen in a publicly traded company?

"Easily," said Avey. "Don't tell anyone what I'm about to tell you, and you didn't hear it from me. The Guardian was the worst ship afloat. It had problem upon problem and should have never gotten past her sea trials, let alone put into service with us."

Avey got up out of his chair and walked over to the door and shut it. He didn't want anyone to hear what he was telling Morris.

"That ship," he continued, "was all messed up. Before he sailed from BeniciaBenicia, Marlowe came over here and tried to talk to the CEO about the Guardian. Seems it gave him trouble their entire way down from Alaska and the radar was iffy at best. It was just about all he could do to get it to Benicia."

Avey stopped talking for a second, resting his head in his hands before he went on.

"Marlowe wanted repairs done to that ship immediately, if not sooner. I went with him to the CEO's office to help plead Marlowe's case. I thought about making that decision myself, but the possible effects, and ramifications, of taking a tanker off line were such that I felt this should go to the top for an answer."

Avey's voice trailed off as he looked away from Morris and stared into space, looking back at and then through Morris as if he weren't present. His thoughts were engaged in their own private conflict, fighting to see exactly how much, and in what detail, they would reveal themselves to Morris. The battle apparently ended when Avey continued.

"Dave," he began, "It was amazing! They reacted as though I shot the Pope. Basically, the answer was not only no, but `Hell No!'. Oil needed to be moved to a demanding market and taking a tanker off-route was out of the question. In fact Jenkins in strategic planning had the audacity to say that "if the ship made it here without so much as a mayday, how bad could it be?"

"Can you believe that shit! They take the rationale that because the ship completed one leg of its mission that it would be safe for whatever."

"The bottom line was simple—oil needed to be moved,

and if it had to go out in a troubled ship than so be it."

"Mark my words" Avey started, "they're up their now behind closed doors trying to figure out how to explain this debacle to the board and the shareholders. When they find out how bad this ship was, and that the executive suite sent it out anyway, there's going to be hell to pay."

Avey looked over at Morris and chuckled. "The board and the shareholders will never find out how bad this ship really was, will they?"

"No." Morris replied, "I don't think that those who made that decision are going to volunteer information about the ships ability to function. And Fred," Morris cautioned, "you do realize that this is a very dangerous train of thought we're discussing."

"Don't worry Dave," Avey replied, "it's not going outside of this office."

"Anyway, back to what we were talking about," Avey continued.

"After Marlowe and I finished our discussion with the powers that be, they excused Marlowe from the meeting and then they fried my butt. I won't go into the details of that meeting save this. I have never seen the kind of shortsightedness or myopia they exhibited, once faced with conclusive evidence."

"Conclusive evidence," questioned Morris, "what did you tell or show them?"

"I told them just what I'd told you," Avey said. "I told them that the Guardian was trouble from the day we got it and it has been trouble ever since. Its eleven years old now, and its been dry-docked no less than five times to work on a faulty rudder and twice for engine problems. With the exception of two of those rudder problems she had to be towed to port."

"You want to talk about another large, unscheduled expenditure," Avey joked, "try having a fully laden oil taker towed."

"Anyway," he continued, "add to all of that a radar that was suspect at best and you're starting to get the picture."

"The Guardian started her career with us on the Texas run. But on one run her rudder seized up and for four hours she circled out in the Gulf of Mexico. Then, just as sudden as it happened, she straightened out. No one, to this day, knows what happened and why. Also, there was a problem in the propulsion system that could push the ship up to two knots faster than the eighteen knots that she was supposed to go. While that may seem a small problem, it means that she was burning through fuel and could also take her an extra half-mile to stop. Who knows what kind of difference that could have made out there before the collision?"

"These problems just serve to illustrate what kind of ship the Guardian was. Believe it or not, on our most important run, we had our least reliable ship. Try as we might, we couldn't get a new ship to take over the Guardian's duties. That was where luck stepped in. The Guardian started spending more time in drydock and repairs than it was spending in the water, and that simple couldn't continue.

So to make a long story short, I had it removed from the Texas run and put it on the S. F. to Alaska run. It was a pain on that run as well, but it carried less responsibility. As you can see now, I didn't think much of that ship. As much as I shouldn't be saying this, Thank God it's gone. Now it can't hurt anyone anymore."

"Yes it can," Morris ruefully added, "It's killing Monty-O."

"Yeah," said Avey, "I know what you mean. It went down it some deep water not too far out, and subsequently spewed its load. But that's not the only thing ailing those guys. You guys got a jump on Monty-O and blamed them for the crash, and it seems the public believes you."

"And," Avey continued, "you have to know that the Coast Guard and the National Transportation and Safety Board are interviewing the crew today. Hell, from what I've heard its pretty much cut and dried."

"What have you heard?" Morris suddenly asked. His point blank manner caught Avey by surprise, but he replied nonetheless.

"I heard that they cut us off in the fog," Avey stated. "The Coast Guard's already got divers who've seen the intact bow of the Patriarch. Its laying upside down, but its in one piece. The bow that is. What that shows is that they crossed our bows and not vice-versa. With our witnesses, they could make their findings known in just a few short weeks."

"How much truth," Morris asked, "can you place in the fact that all of the eyewitnesses were from only one of the ships involved? I mean, they could just be covering themselves, or evading their responsibility."

"I thought about that," Avey responded, "but finding their bow intact gave our side a lot of credence. It showed that something got in front of us, not that something hit us."

Morris thought back to his conversation with Martin on Monday. In their meeting, Martin told him that the crash was Monty-O's fault, but that it couldn't be announced until the Coast Guard actually released it.

"For a change, that bastard could have been right," muttered Morris.

"What bastard?" asked a puzzled Avey.

"Nothing, skip it," Morris hurriedly replied, trying to cover his being caught thinking out loud.

"Not to change the subject," Morris added, "but you said the ship was only insured for half value and cargo. Why was that?"

"Easy," replied Avey. "Our insurers were aware of the Guardian's reliability record too. They knew that she was an accident waiting to happen. Ships are like people, no two have the same personality. The Guardian's two sister ships run the Alaska to L.A. route with no problems whatsoever. But the Guardian turns out to be one temperamental old bitch. As a result of all of her problems, the insurers upped the premiums. They've now upped them to a point where, based on our budget here in maritime transport, we can no longer afford to insure the whole ship. So, we've reduced the insurance coverage in an attempt to make the premiums 'livable'.

"The sad part is, we were preparing a package to the CEO to show him how badly that ship needed a refit. By showing him how much money we'd save in premiums and operating costs if we took the time and effort to fix her problems, I felt we had a real good chance of taking her off the line in six to eight weeks. I already had a dry dock lined up. A little more time, and I believe we could have turned that ship around."

"No need worrying about it now," he resignedly added.

"How much have the insurers offered us for the ship and cargo?"

"Thirty million even," was Avey's disgusted response. "Twenty-eight million for one-half value of the ship and two million for the cargo, although it wasn't quite worth that much."

He looked over to Morris and sarcastically added, "Hardly worth filing the damn claim!"

"We won't be able to get a new tanker for that will we?" Morris asked. "If they're going to be so funny with insurance premiums they probably won't let you draw from existing accounts to replace that tanker."

"You don't know how right you are," said Avey. "As far as us getting a new tanker for the insurance claim, the answer is no. That's the same answer I got when I asked about getting a new tanker, period. The boys in finance have told me that there is no money available for a new tanker."

"Are you kidding?," was Morris' shocked reply. "What do they mean telling you that no money is available for a new tanker? Don't those finance guys read our annual shareholder statement? Four months ago, a consortium of banks extended to us a line of credit totaling some five billion dollars. Last year we had a profit of over one billion. Now they tell you that they can't come up with fifty million for a new tanker?"

"I tell you Fred," Morris began, "something funny is going on."

"Maybe so, Dave," Avey replied, "but not here. You've seen what I'm up against. I've got to move the same amount of oil with one less ship. It's O.K. now, but it'll get real tight in a month. You want to see a sight, come look in here then. I'll show you a madman that'll make Capt. Ahab look like Mr. Rogers."

Morris laughed at Avey's simile and politely added his departure.

"I know you guys are busy, so I'll let you go. Thanks for everything."

"No problem," said Avey, "just keep it under your shirt."
"I will," replied Morris
"Later, Dave."

CHAPTER 10

BEAN COUNTER

Traveling from the maritime department to finance took just three minutes and two floors. Walking down the stairs, Morris entered the corridor leading to the finance department, passing on the way the geology department. Morris entertained the thought of paying them a visit, however the three departments he'd selected over the numerous areas of expertise contained within Bennington, were the ones he felt could give him the most answers.

The maritime transport department had given him plenty of information, and Morris was hoping that finance would give him more.

He still didn't know what to expect from the strategic planning people.

Coming to a set of double glass doors containing the offices of his destination, Morris entered and found himself in an empty lobby.

The secretary's desk was positioned at the other end of the lobby; its perfect vantage point of all who entered was wasted, as the secretary wasn't behind it.

Morris scanned the furthest three of the seven doors that exited into the lobby; doors that led to the offices of Bennington's key finance officials. One belonged to Robert McIntyre, Bennington's head of finance. Another went to his deputy. The number three man in Bennington's finance arena also had one. These doors were all located at the back of the lobby, behind the protective countenance of the secretary. The other four doors led to two large working areas, two on each side of the lobby₄

Morris stuck his head around the corner and took a quick look at what was going on. About 13 people were behind computer terminals, busily crunching the numbers that told the story of Bennington Oil.

"They could know the true state of this company eons before it was ever reflected in our stock prices," thought Morris. "Now there's a great position to be in," he mused before turning back to the other doors.

McIntyre's door was closed, and Morris could hear voices on the other side. It didn't sound like a discussion—both sides taking part in the exchange of information. This, thought Morris, was more like a lecture—one side talking and one side listening.

Morris didn't know who else was in on the meeting, but guessed that McIntyre's number two was involved, especially when he peered around the corner and saw his empty desk with the room lights still on.

"Finance folks don't even go to the bathroom without turning off their lights," Morris joked. "That way," he added in his best accountant's nasal whine, "we can conserve at least .000067 of a percent's worth of electricity, which when multiplied by the countless offices in the building over a year, could add up to a whopping $13.67." He chuckled at the degree of ridiculousness he felt some people had to go through in their day-to-day jobs.

He turned to leave, planning to come back later in the day, when Jacob "Jake" Lawson came into the office. Lawson, Bennington's number three man in the finance department, was just returning from a meeting when he saw Morris turn to leave.

"Dave," Lawson yelled, "you're not planning to leave without saying hello?"

"Just as I figured Jake," Morris replied, "nobody works down here. How's it going?"

"Not too badly," said Lawson, "though you caught us at a

bad time. I think everyone's in with the CEO or," he paused, looking at the chief financial officer's door and hearing the murmur of voices behind it, "they could all be in there.

"Anyway, what brings you down here where the shekels get counted?"

"Actually," Morris began, I've got some questions I need answered and I was hoping you could help me?" Morris knew that Lawson would be extremely cautious and immediately planned to set him at ease. As is everyone else who is not in Lawson's chain of command, Morris was a half second too slow.

Lawson answered Morris' request in the affirmative, while simultaneously shifting all of his faculties into a vigilance mode. On more occasions than Lawson remembered, whenever anyone wanted to talk, it was usually about something that they didn't need to know, or to help them out of a hole of their own creation. In his twenty-one years with the company, he'd just about seen it all. His favorite example was of a young executive who'd siphoned over two million dollars from corporate accounts and then asked Lawson not to do anything more than to let him have a few minutes alone with the finance computers. Lawson had spotted the leak, traced it, identified the perpetrator and confronted him. The exec offered Lawson 50% if he'd allow him to10 minutes with the computers to further alter the records to show that everything was correct.

He refused.

In fact, Lawson not only refused, but his testimony and two million ill-gotten dollars got the gentleman twelve years in prison. Before leaving court, the exec told Lawson that he would, upon his release, seek his revenge. Lawson curtly told him that if his vengeance were no better planned than his embezzlement, than he had nothing to fear. While that was eight years ago, Lawson reputation as a tough but fair man continued throughout the company. He was also known for standing firm. Some said that his lack of give and take was why he'd risen no higher than number three in his department.

"Jake," Morris began, "I just spoke to Avey over in Maritime Transport and he told me that he's not going to get a new tanker. What's up?"

"Dave," Lawson replied, "Its too soon to be talking about a new tanker. Hell, the old one is still warm. After all, its been less than five days-we're still working the slick."

"But Avey said he talked to you guys and that you said no."

"What we've done," said Lawson, "was get together and talk to the insurance company, who I might add made a piddly-ass offer for our ship and cargo. Its less than one-third the loss we sustained. What we in Finance told them in Maritime was that we could not afford to get a new tanker right now, and to an extent that's true. Until we know our exact level of liability in this matter, I don't think its prudent that we go about investing massive sums of money--as much as 160 million dollars for a new state of the art 150,000 tonner. I think you'll agree.

"Well last year we made 107 million dollars in profit," said Morris, "and more recently we took a line of credit for 1.5 billion dollars. What about all of that?"

"I," Lawson started then stopped. Replying stoically, he added, "We were told not to touch a dime of that."

"When?" Morris inquired, "and by who?"

"Not too long ago, probably within the last week," Lawson answered. "The who is the CEO."

Lawson noted Morris' quizzical expression and motioned for him to go into his office. Morris obligingly left the lobby for Lawson's more private office. Lowering himself into one of the office's plush chairs, Morris subconsciously acknowledged that his little investigation was turning from the curious to the bizarre.

"Its not just us, but finance too," he thought.

Morris turned to look back at Lawson, who was staring at him.

"Its a funny feeling Dave," Lawson stated, "when someone way above your pay grade starts doing your job for you.

Listening to Lawson continue, Morris almost missed the change in his tone; from one just shy of confidence to one of humility.

"I checked with geology," continued Lawson, "to see if we were purchasing any new fields for exploration. Even before the collision, I checked with Maritime Transport to see about undersea pipelines, tankers or new off-shore rigs. I even met with the Human Resources, or whatever the personnel people now call themselves, to see if we were going to experience any major manning changes. I even talked to our refining people about an improvement or upgrade in our refinery capability and like everyone else, they said no!"

"All of them," he added, "all of them but Jenkins in Strategic Planning. He very matter-of-factly told me that only the CEO could have those answers."

"In short," said Morris, "you've been told nothing more than to keep your hands off of that money."

"Bingo!," Lawson exclaimed. "So while we sit here cooling our jets, over two billion in operating profits sits in the bank drawing passbook interest and a five billion dollar line of credit, with its incredibly large finance charges, awaits for us to only find a use for it."

"That's puzzled me ever since I heard about it" said Morris. "No offense, but I first found out about the loan in the Wall Street Journal."

"The press release on it came from the bank. We wanted to downplay it, you know, keep it close to heart."

"Why?" questioned Morris, "what are we planning on doing with $5 billion?"

"I can only think of two alternatives," said Lawson. "One is a takeover and the other is a partnership."

Lawson thought for a moment and then began anew.

"No, it can't be a partnership; that's definitely out."

"Why is that?" asked Morris.

"Between you and me," Lawson started, "Our higher ups aren't very well liked or respected in the business world. We were absolutely shocked when our request for the line of credit was accepted. However, as we're a self-contained company we have an edge over the opinions of our contemporaries."

"How so?" asked Morris.

"Well, regardless of what they think of us, they can't

harm us. We have everything we need, oil fields, rigs, pipelines, refineries, distribution facilities, gas stations and the like. But back to my original point.

"We have decent reserves, so a partnership isn't really needed to fulfill any petroleum related need. So unless there's a target in a non-oil field, I can't imagine a takeover, unless of course, we can score a large oil reserve. But that's about the only thing we could use. Anyway, we'll know shortly."

"Shortly?" asked Morris.

"Yeah, shortly," said Lawson. "We've been told to get the line of credit ready for action, so whatever they're planning on doing with it they plan to do it soon."

"How soon do you think it could be?"

"Ask the guys in Strategic Planning," said Lawson. "But be careful of Jenkins. He's real bad news. He's a bastard for no better reason than he just likes how it feels."

"I will," said Morris. "Thanks for your help."

"Sorry I couldn't help you more," was Lawson's parting shot.

CHAPTER 11

MORE QUESTIONS-LESS ANSWERS

Of the three departments that Morris had planned to visit, the Strategic Planning division was the one that he was most uncertain and apprehensive about.

The entire corporate staff had seen or felt, at one point or another, the tirades of that ogre Stan Jenkins. He was as feared for his behavior and temperament as he was for his tactics and methods. Those who stood up against Jenkins have, on occasion, discovered that the future of Bennington Oil included neither them nor their departments. He was indeed a man to be feared throughout Bennington, and now Morris was walking into his lair. He wasn't enjoying it, but he needed some answers that only Strategic Planning possessed.

Strategic Planning, known throughout the company simply as Strat Plan, was charged with determining the long range outlook for the company. Which direction the company traveled tomorrow was decided by Strategic Planning today. Theirs was a tremendous responsibility-determining the promise of tomorrow. Assisting Jenkins in this role was a staff of sixteen experts in all areas of the company's operations. They were constantly on the lookout for opportunity, and they geared the company to pounce if one presented itself. They were working on that very subject when Morris arrived.

Jenkins wasn't in when Morris called, a fact Morris welcomed openly. He was still figuring out whom to see next when a young, blond headed and well-dressed exec, reading some sort of office correspondence, walked up to him.

"Excuse me, but do you have any business in this department?" was his curt salutation to Morris. From the young exec's first word on, Morris felt he was being addressed in a tone somewhere between indifference and arrogance, as if he were doing Morris a favor by talking to him. This attitude would pervade the rest of the conversation.

"Actually," Morris fired back, "I do. But it's with your boss, not you. No offense."

The young exec gave Morris a once-over glance, in effect, sizing him up. Without saying a word, but exhibiting what could best be described a haughty attitude, he went back to reading his message. In doing so, he positioned himself so that he could see every move that Morris made. From the man's reaction, Morris knew he'd struck a nerve. It was the intended result.

Morris had deliberately responded in that fashion to alert his young friend that his attitude was neither warranted, nor necessary. With that Morris turned and looked at the vacant office of Stan Jenkins.

It was his plan to get some answers from Strategic Planning, but as its leader was out, that little task was made harder. Morris looked over at the exec he'd just corrected, who was still standing nearby. Feeling that his little cannonade had done the trick on his disrespectful conversant, Morris relented and spoke to him.

"Maybe you can help me," offered Morris. "The guys in finance tell me that you've assumed all control and responsibility for almost five billion dollars in corporate funds? What's up?"

The exec's attitude changed immediately; he seemed to almost gloat about the possibility of talking about this topic. As young men do when they want to show their maturity, they tell their "war stories" in the hope of impressing their elders. This one was about to try and impress Morris.

As he began speaking, Morris noticed the indifference leaving his tone. The haughtiness and arrogance was still there, but more subdued than in their earlier communication attempt.

"I'm surprised that you haven't heard," was his first deliberate statement. "All of the necessary company officials have been briefed."

Morris caught the barb and tossed it off, thinking to himself *"OK, obviously an asshole of the highest degree!"*

"Actually, you don't need me to tell you," said the exec, adding "Your boss in PR has been to all of the meetings. In fact, it was his suggestion the night of the crash. You ought to get him to tell you. Aw, what the hell

"This guy is the cat that toys with the mouse before dispatching it," thought Morris. *"Just get on with it!"*

"This is going to put us into the papers. It'll be San Francisco's largest business venture of the year, and it'll be Bennington Oil pulling it off. We're about to…"

"WHAT THE HELL IS GOING ON HERE?"

The young exec never finished his statement as the booming voice of Stan Jenkins filled the air.

Realizing that he was out of place, the young exec tried to back pedal.

"Sir, I was just telling him about the…"

"Don't tell him a thing," said Jenkins. "He works for PR and God knows they only want to get into the act and hoard all of the glory. Well, the sheer size of what we're doing will generate more publicity than you clowns in PR ever could.

"If those damn tankers hadn't collided outside the bay, this matter would." have been over and done with long ago. But since it isn't, I don't know about you, but we've got a lot of work to do before today is over and we won't get it done talking to the likes of you. Good day!"

With that, Jenkins and his young exec disappeared into his office.

"So much for that kid's rites of manhood," smirked Morris.

As he turned to leave he looked into one of the Strategic Planning department work areas. For the first time since he'd entered the department he noticed something peculiar.

With very few exceptions, the computer terminals in Bennington Oil were all Compaq's, connected to the corporate mainframe. When Morris looked into the group of computer operators in Strategic Planning, he also noticed that the hardware they were using was unique; unlike almost any he'd seen in the rest of Bennington Oil. That fact stuck in the back of his mind, and he made a mental note to look in on it when he had the opportunity.

After stepping out of the Strategic Planning offices and back into the hallway, Morris looked at his watch. It was nearly 10:30 a.m.

*"Time to get back to the matter at ha*nd," he thought.

Upon returning to his office, he received a briefing from his staff on the events pertaining to the spill. As it now was 'on the beach' not much media interest was being generated at the company headquarters. Most of the media were down on the beaches trying to develop their own particular angles to this accident. As he had representatives at the three spill control centers run by Bennington, he wasn't too worried about what the media might try and do.

"In a way," Morris mused, "this company was lucky that the spill was so close to shore. Any further out and we would have had to deal with the drama of a slick 130 miles off shore coming inland at twenty to thirty miles a day. The press would've loved it."

The meeting with his staff was short, mainly discussing the press' migration to covering the shorelines and those laboring there, and the joint Coast Guard/National Transportation and Safety Board hearing that started earlier that morning. Ten minutes after the meeting started, it was over.

As the last of his briefing staff was leaving and while he was thinking about the spill, Alan Roth entered his office. Morris had noticed Roth's absence in the meeting that had just concluded, and would have found out why had he not come rushing up to his desk.

"Dave," Roth started, "have you been listening to the radio? Some group called the Coalition for Clean California Shorelines has filed a one billion dollar suit against Monty-O. I can't imagine them not filing one that size against us."

"One billion," Morris whistled. "It couldn't come at a

worse time for them. The word on the street was that they were strapped for cash before all of this happened. Add the crash and the boycotters and this has to be hitting them hard."

"But," Morris added, "That's Monty-O's problem and not ours. That group may decide to come after us. So Alan, I'd like you to alert our legal department and I want you to follow this closely. Monitor Monty-O's responses to all of this and see what they do and how they handle it. No need re-inventing the wheel unless we can do it better."

"I already called the legal beagles," Roth began, "and I wanted to talk with the Monty-O folks to see how they were planning to play this. But given our current cold war with them, what with the newspaper editorial and all, I thought I should check with you before calling."

"Smart moves," said Morris. "However, I want to keep all contact between Monty-O and Bennington on the department head level. After that editorial madness, I don't trust them. It wouldn't look good if they pulled something over on us. Give me any questions you might have and if they ever return my call I'll pass them on. Alright?"

Roth nodded in agreement, rose and left for his office.

Morris smiled as Roth left. He found Roth's advancement encouraging, and made a mental note to pass that on to him when this whole matter was over.

Turning back to his desk and viewing the piles of work waiting for him quickly drove the smile from his face.

But before he could muster the resources to tackle any of his other duties and responsibilities, Morris thought back to his run in with Jenkins, and the unusual computers he'd seen in the Strategic Planning department. There wasn't much he could do about Jenkins, but there were others he could turn to about the computers.

Picking up the phone, Morris dialed the four-digit extension to the section that ran Bennington's information systems.

"Yello," Information Services Department, Johnson here."

"Why do you always answer 'yello', the word is HELLO," Morris laughed.

"Oh no, not Public Affairs," came a pained groan, joking from the other end of the line. "What is it now? 60 Minutes, 20/20, Nightline or somebody called and you need a handsome intelligent stud to speak to the press?"

"Nothing that drastic Johnny, however I do have a few questions I'd like to ask you about, if you have some time?"

"Sure, Dave go ahead," was Johnson's jovial reply.

"OK," Morris began," I just spent some time in Strategic Planning and I noticed that they had a computer system up there that's unique to their offices. What's the deal on that?"

"You're talking about the Mortenson 31002's," said Johnson. "They're not unique to Strat Planning. There are two terminals in finance and a couple in, just a second o.k."

A strange computer-sounding version of Morris Albert's "Feelings" wafted into the line as Johnson put Morris on hold while he checked into a couple of facts.

"Sorry about that," Johnson started, "but I needed to verify something. Only Finance and Strat Planning have the Mortensons, and finance only has two of them. Seems they're great for crunching numbers, but they're very limited in word processing applications. Not really limited but sort of user belligerent for non-numerical uses. Seems we wanted them more for word processing than anything else, so we bought a small number just to see how they worked. Between you and me we should have just leased the damn things for a test period and bought them if we liked them. Buying twenty terminals and a small mainframe set us back much budget, and down here it cost us a buyer."

"How did it cost you a buyer?" Morris asked.

"When they found out it wasn't really anywhere near what we wanted for the company, someone had to pay for the small fortune we spent. That someone was the buyer. We were about to try and dump the system when Jenkins up there in Strat Planning pitched a bitch. He'd been whining for a self-contained computer capability and recognized an opportunity when he saw it."

"And that's how they got the computer system up there?" asked Morris.

"Precisely," replied Johnson. "And they would have

gotten all twenty terminals if it hadn't been for a gentleman named Lawson in Finance. Because of his concerns, one terminal went to the CEO's office and the other two went to finance."

"Yeah, I know good ole Jake," said Morris. "So he stuck his foot into the matter, eh?"

"You don't know the half of it. He told the powers that be that they couldn't give the folks in Jenkins' department a computer system with no form of checks or balances attached. He said that no agency in the building with fiduciary capability should be allowed to act without even the CEO's knowledge or supervision. Needless to say, this went over with Jenkins about as well as a piranha in a hot tub. Jenkins made no bones about it-Lawson was a marked man."

Morris waited a second to comprehend all of this conversation; he was unable or at least reluctant, to believe what he was hearing.

"How do you know all of this?" Morris inquired.

"Lawson's a good friend of mine," Johnson answered, "he's a straight shooter and a hard worker. But to make a long story short, Jenkins told him that he's peaked at this company and if he didn't watch his step he could fall off of that peak. Lawson changed a bit after that. He checks and double-checks everything that comes through his office. It has affected his family life, and I wonder if he and his wife aren't on the verge of a divorce. He put some resumes out to try and find something else, but Jenkins had already put the word out on him. Adolph Hitler has a better chance of working in San Francisco than Lawson does anywhere else but Bennington.

"Jenkins has been putting the screws to Lawson ever since this happened, about two years ago. Lawson's become so meticulous that they'll never be able to fire him for a work-related cause. But time is on Jenkins' side, and he knows it. Being a super troop in finance is costing Lawson his personal life. If his marriage breaks up or if he starts drinking or if he just plain stresses out, Jenkins will swoop in and finish him off. Personally, I don't think that time is too far off."

"Back to your original questions though, Strat Plan wanted a totally separate computing capability so that they wouldn't need to worry about any unauthorized tampering. At least, that's what they say. The feeling around here is that they wanted the system so that they could develop their own initiatives without interference from the rest of the headquarters staff. You can take that for what it's worth."

"Anyway, if any of their information from the Mortensons' is needed throughout the rest of the corporation, it is drawn up and a hard copy printed. From there they simply put it in an optical character scanner and load it up into our mainframe's memory. It's a bit tedious, but it gives Jenkins the peace of mind he's always wanted. Funny part is, we could go up there in an hour and install an interface between their system and the one we all use, but Jenkins doesn't want us anywhere near his system. He even out sources his repairs and maintenance. "

"So as it stands," began Morris, "Jenkins has access to the company computers, but the ones in his offices are pretty much off limits?"

"That's about the size of it," said Johnson. "Even if someone got into Strat Plan, it wouldn't make much difference. Those Mortensons are a bear to operate for the unenlightened. And from what I've seen of it, Jenkins' people have installed a few safeguards into the system to keep prying eyes, mainly those in finance, away from their files."

"Anyway," said Johnson, "That's the quick and dirty on that Strat Plan system. You got anything else I can help you with?"

"No," said Morris, "but thanks for your help. It has answered a lot of my questions. Take it easy."

Morris had nearly hung up the phone when he realized that he had another call to make. He wanted to contact Larry Nelson and set up a meeting at Rosey's in Jack London Square.

Initially, he was going to listen to Nelson's explanation of the Monty-O connection and, if he was satisfied, tell him about the things that he'd uncovered at the office. Morris knew something big was going on, something mysterious and unknown, and he thought that Nelson might be able to help him find out.

He dialed Nelson's number and waited for a reply. After seven rings, the call was answered.

"Hello," began the response, "Larry Nelson, East Bay Gazette."

In the basement of the Bennington Building, another call to a restricted number was logged, determined and passed on to the Director of Strategic Planning, Stan Jenkins. Unbeknownst to Morris, he'd just made one call too many.

The final four hours of the working day saw Morris working Bennington's public relations crisis control. But regardless of how hard he worked, he couldn't clear his mind of Jenkins' verbal assault. Morris had never expected that kind of hostility from someone within the company. In fact, he felt that in being part of the same team, he'd receive anything but that. He knew differently now.

The sharpness of Jenkins' words hurt, but Morris had gotten over that quickly. What was still playing on his mind was Jenkins' last statement.

"How," thought Morris, "could *a maritime accident over twenty miles outside the Golden Gate affect a transaction that could involve several billions dollars?"*

Morris also reflected on the number of experts he saw working so hard in the Strategic Planning department.

"What is it that they needed to finish so badly by the close of business today?" he asked himself.

Morris had been scanning the Internet, looking at the stories surrounding the half-billion dollar lawsuit filed against Montgomery Oil. What caught his eye was an article that stated that all trading of Monty-O shares has been suspended by the New York Stock exchange until tomorrow morning.

News of the lawsuit helped drop the stock another 3 points, in addition to the points it has already dropped since the crash and the controversy.

"Damn," thought Morris, "Exxon or Chevron stock wouldn't have even flinch at this collision and it's dropped Monty-O almost 25%.

"The suit gets thrown out, the oil on the beach evaporates

and the protestors get bored in two weeks, and Monty-O will be back where they should be at $58-60 a share."

Morris was even contemplating buying some of Monty-O's stock while they were down. He was being enticed by that old stock market credo of "Buy low, sell high!" How a high flying company's stock wound up being driven to unforeseen depths was not Morris' worry. He's heard of it happening before. When some psychopath poisoned Tylenol packages, Johnson and Johnson stock to a nosedive. But if you bought it when it hit rock bottom and held on to it for six months you would have made a small fortune. Morris saw this as his chance to make a quick profit.

He looked at his watch, and upon noticing the time realized he still wanted to talk to Fred Avey in Maritime Transport. The Coast Guard was interviewing the surviving crew members from the crash and Morris wanted Avey's take on how the day went. He called down to Avey's office but the line was busy. Rather than leave a message he hung up the phone and strolled down to Avey's office.

As he turned the corner and looked into Avey's office, he suddenly realized while Avey was busy. A local reporter wanted to ask some questions about tanker explosions and Morris had dispatched Alan Roth to work with Avey to respond.

They both looked up at Morris when he stuck his head in the door, but then went right back to business. Morris stood silently in the doorway waiting for Avey to finish with his phone call.

"Can fumes in an empty tank blow a tanker apart?" Avey repeated. "Hell yes!" Avey looked over and saw the pained look on Roth's face at the use of a cuss word. Avey smiled and continued.

"It used to happen all the time. It's not as frequently now as it used to be. For a while these things would blow up pretty regularly. You name it, lightning, static electricity, a rogue electrical spark. Any ignition source that came into contact with the leaking gas would ignite it. But I digress. Anyhow, when you offload, or drain, a tanker at a refinery or tank farm or what have you, up to one or two percent of the cargo will stick to the tanker's internal walls and stuff. A tank inside an oil tanker is not just a large pool or empty tank type deal. Each tank has framing, support beams, pipes and all sorts of stuff running through it. The cross members that actually give the ship its structural integrity run exposed throughout the ship's cargo holds. Anyhow, globs of paraffin, tar and some of the other heavier petroleum elements will stick to all of those exposed areas, be they steel walls 50 to 60 feet straight up, or all of those other beams and steelwork running through the tanks. And each of those globs of oil gives off gas."

"Why doesn't this happen when the tanks are full of cargo?" Avey leaned back in his chair and rolled his eyes at the naiveté of that question, but he replied to it nonetheless.

"Hell man, it does happen, but since there is no place for the gas to go in a tank full of oil, it just stays there in solution. But once you begin offloading cargo and the oil level starts dropping, the pressure on the oil is off and the gas will begin separating from the solution. This is one of the major reasons we do tank cleaning; to remove this gas buildup. When the gas in the tank builds up and the air in the tank reaches a certain fuel-air mixture, you have the recipe for a major explosion. Imagine how you'd feel if you were 300-400 miles out to sea and your ship blows up! That'd be a hell of a lot of dogpaddling' to get back to shore."

"Believe it or not, I had talked with a structural engineer this morning about these kinds of explosions and their effects. We were trying to make sure that we didn't get screwed by the insurance company so we want to know, or at least find out, as much as we can about what we think might have happened to our ship during the collision." Avey looked at Roth after that last statement and saw the same pained expression from a minute earlier. Roth was about to tell Avey not to impugn the insurers, but Avey continued.

"To answer your first question, the gas won't become explosive until it reaches the proper fuel and air mix. For natural gas, for example, the most explosive mixture is somewhere around 6-8% gas and 92-94% air. More gas than that and you'll have a lesser explosion, or possibly just a big fire—too much gas in the mixture will actually prevent combustion. You see, you have to have the right mix of gas, heat and oxygen. Too much gas might prevent enough oxygen from getting to the tank to help create the combustion. Also, while cargo tanks full of gas may actually prevent an explosion, they are notorious killers of crewmembers. Anyway, a lesser percentage of gas and you might not have enough to create a combustible environment; it won't so much as explode as just burn off. That's not a good thing either, but better than a shipboard explosion."

"In our case," Avey offered, "we seemed to have had the exact percentage of gas and air mixture in those tanks. That's why we had the blast."

"As far as the effects of the explosion being so bad, you have to consider just what was happening in those tanks during the explosion. An explosion is nothing more than an incredibly rapid combustion. Instead of a slow burn where all the energy can be controlled while it's being released—the total of all of the energy generated during an explosion is released at once. When an explosion occurs, it starts off in stages. That might seem a bit crazy, but every blast starts off small and grows in intensity. Mind you, it goes from small to devastating in $1/100^{th}$ the time it takes you to blink your eyes. As the explosion grows it expands outwards. If the explosion takes place in an area that is vented, or contains other orifices to allow the pressure to escape, the explosive power created by the blast will force its way through these openings. Thus, a portion of the blast will actually be expended through this venting process. In short, the explosion may not reach its full fury because a portion of the blast was expended through venting."

Don't get me wrong, the site of the blast will still be pretty fucked up, but it will be better than if the blast was contained in an area that provided no venting." Avey didn't bother to turn and look at Roth. He could feel the heat of Roth's stare burning into the back of his neck. He continued.

"An explosion in an area with no venting forces the blast to reach its full potential without any of its fury being allowed to escape. Actually, it doesn't so much as reach its full potential as it simply grows to a point where the vessel containing it can no longer withstand the pressure and is subsequently breached. That is pretty much what happens in a tanker explosion."

"Remember how I told you that a lot of the structural frames and members run exposed throughout the tanks. For normal operations these beams help gives the ship its integrity. But during an explosion they are not our best friends. All of that hardened steel welded together to make a leak proof tank also prevents a low-pressure explosion from creating a small breach or a vent. The outside water pressure against the tank walls also enhances the strength of those walls. So because the tank is so strong that no low pressure explosion can blow out some of the ship's plating, the force of the blast grows in intensity until it is forced to breach the tank. When this happens, the explosion is usually so massive that it not only breaches the tanks, but it blows the ship apart. Also remember, that the walls of the outer tanks also form the sides of the ship. Breach those walls and you have breached the ship."

"What I suspect happened on the Pacific Patriarch is that when one of the ships collided with the other, one or more of the outer wings tanks, and possibly the center cargo tanks, suffered a catastrophic rupture. Both air and water rushed into the tanks, creating an agitation of the gas and air in the tanks. Add to that the rising water levels in the breached tanks and you have the fuel air mixture being forced to the top, upper portions of the tanks. This compression of the gas and air mixture served only to concentrate the explosive effects of the blast towards the top of the tanks. Sparks from the steel grinding on steel from the collision gave it the heat source it needed and the rest is history. I doubt there is a ship afloat that could have withstood that blast. Obviously ours didn't

So the blast grows in intensity, and the structural steel framework throughout the cargo tanks gives the center tank so much strength that a low-pressure explosion can't create a breach. Since the explosion could not expend itself through a vent, it created its own vent. "

"Hey look, I know you have more questions but I have to go. No...No... Look, call the guys in PR if you need more help. They got a stellar guy up there named Roth who'll be more than happy to help you. Give him a call in five minutes. Bye!"

With that, Avey hung up on his insistent inquirer.

"Damn, I hate the press!" he added for good measure.

Roth was about to start briefing Avey on his responses to the media when Avey told him that he would be getting a call in five minutes and he should be at his office when it comes in.

Roth wasn't ready to leave yet. He was planning on letting Avey know that he considered his conduct unprofessional and that the company deserved better spokespeople. Morris stepped in and saved Roth from himself.

"Alan," Morris began, "I'll talk to Fred and you go back to your office and await that call."

Roth, figuring that Morris would straighten Avey out, grabbed his things and left.

Well Dave, you came all the way down here. What can I help you with....Again?" Avey started. "Oh and by the way, I came up to see you just before we called this reporter back. You were looking at something pretty intensely, so I just went and got Roth and came back down here. To tell the truth I thought you were sleep, being that it's after closing time and all."

"I wasn't sleep," Morris replied, I was dreaming of the good life. To be honest I was surprised to see anyone down here after four o'clock. "

"We work harder than you guys," Avey replied, "Look at you, up there reading horoscopes and all."

I'm just trying to predict my future," Morris said, "not with a horoscope but possibly with a gamble."

"Funny you talk about the future," Avey added in a manner that Morris found strangely solemn and emotional. "And about gambling; a gamble that I think is going to go real bad."

"What's up Fred," Morris said

"Dave" Avey began, "this morning I told you that all of

our crewmembers were going to testify to the Coast Guard today. "That's why I came up to your office."

"Well anyway," he continued, "they all gave their sworn testimony in writing, which is strange, but legal. All of them, in their own words, described their versions of what happened in the crash to the Coast Guard tribunal."

"All of them," he stopped, "All of them except the Capt. Marlowe. Capt. Benjamin Marlowe. He wouldn't write anything and when they spoke to him he refused to respond to the tribunal. He didn't plead the Fifth Amendment protection against self-incrimination, he didn't say a word. He just sat there. It was like a scene out of Conrad, you know, Lord Jim, where the kid wants to be tried and found guilty of abandoning a ship load of pilgrims during a storm, while everyone else said he and the crew did the right thing."

"Well anyway, for not providing his testimony they are recommending revoking his master's license. They'll announce what they plan to do to Marlowe with the rest of their findings, in about two weeks. Because of public sentiment and the fact that the cause of this crash is pretty cut and dried, they're trying to expedite their findings."

"Either way," Avey went on, "It won't help Marlowe any. I saw him the day after the crash and he was really broken up about it. You know, real sorry about what happened kind of stuff."

"But today he was different; it was almost as if he didn't care what happened to him. I know he's got a lot on his mind, with the crash and...ah Hell, he'll be alright...I guess."

By just listening Morris could tell that the end of Avey's statement lacked conviction. Morris recognized it and offered his own reaffirmation of Marlowe.

"He'll be OK Fred," Morris added, "besides you only pick the best."

"Thanks Dave," Avey replied, "I'll be glad when this whole thing is a memory. By the way, did you ever find what you were looking for?"

"Yes I did," Morris started, "and; Hold it! What time do you have?"

"About a quarter to six. Why?"

"Sorry Fred I'm late, I've got to go."
"Knock 'em dead, Dave," was Avey's parting reply.

CHAPTER 12

MEETING OF THE MINDS

"What took you so long?" Nelson asked, "You said 6 p.m. and it's almost 7."

"Sorry" Morris began, "I got held up. So what have you been up to?"

"They got me doing a piece on airline safety" Nelson said, "You know, you'd be surprised at what little insignificant shit could knock a jumbo jet out of the sky."

"Really?" said Morris.

"Yeah," said Nelson, "Couldn't care less could you?" Nelson added.

"Not one iota," said Morris.

"Me neither. And I have to write that crap."

"Is this what they've got you doing?" Morris asked sympathetically.

"Hey, it beats the hell out of the piece I had to do on an old geezer getting a heart lung transplant and his new outlook on life.

"But enough about me," Nelson said, "What did you find out?"

"Larry," said Morris, "before we go on there is something I need to know. How close are you to Monty-O?"

"What do you mean?" said Nelson.

I know they gave you the oil spill information for your article. It got pulled because it slimed us and we had recourse.

I want to know if you were part of their plan or if they just used you as a target of opportunity."

"Dave" Nelson began, "I've known you for a long time. I've also known Charles Gerard at Monty-O for a long time. I called him and asked him for information on their pollution record. He gave it to me. I had plenty on you guys at Bennington before I called Gerard, but as he had it all printed out, he gave me a copy. I checked it out to make sure it was genuine. He saved me time and effort, but giving me that information only sped up the story by a day, two at the max. If you think I'm playing one side against the other, you're wrong. This was a target of opportunity, but it was my target of opportunity. This was a story screaming to be written and I wrote it."

"Didn't get it published," he added sarcastically, "but I wrote it."

"Dave, I'm not in their pocket, if that's what you're worried about."

Morris looked at Nelson and he was satisfied. He'd hoped Nelson wasn't on Monty-O's payroll or otherwise owing in loyalty. He had a sneaking suspicion, deep down inside, that he was going to need Nelson, or someone like him, and he wanted to be able to count on him.

He dropped his defensive posture and smiled.

"I believe your question was something about what information I may have found out about my company's activities?"

"Plenty and nothing," was Morris' cryptic reply.

"Riddles and conundrums I don't need." Nelson started. "What I need are substantiated facts? Got any of those?"

"Yes" Morris started, "Listen to this. We lose a tanker and cargo in an underinsured tanker. Last year we had a record profit, over a billion. The year before, we did almost as well. Earlier this year we take a $5 billion line of credit. In essence, we have access to over $7 billion dollars, and we can't touch it."

"Why can't you touch it? asked Nelson.

"It's been put off limits for something big happening soon. It's real big, and whatever it was got held up by our tanker collision."

"That's understandable" Nelson said, "With the crash and all, your higher ups decided to pull in the reigns and slow down a bit. It's been pretty hot and heavy these last few days. Spending billions of dollars takes lost of effort.. Hell I have enough trouble writing my own checks."

"Well on top of that," Morris continued, "my department, with the exception of Bill Martin, is being kept in the dark."

"I think I know what it might be," said Nelson, "Your company is preparing a hostile takeover. Wouldn't that explain the cloak of secrecy?"

"Yes it would," Morris answered. "But of whom and of what would we be trying to takeover?"

"How should I know?," Nelson said while slowly sipping his beer. "You work for them, I don't!"

"Did you task to the guys in Finance," he added, "Maybe they could shed some light on this?"

"I did," Morris began, "they didn't! Something big is going on and the fact that PR isn't involved scares me."

"Do you think that they could be up to something criminal?" asked Nelson, "I mean, God knows if an oil company would resort to doing something crooked, yours would. No offense!"

"No Offense! How can you say something like that and think that a 'no offense' tossed in like an afterthought is going to get you out of it? You've hurt my feelings to the tune of a beer."

"Coming up." Nelson replied.

The wait staff brought the drinks and Morris and Nelson sat at their tables talking like the old friends they were. After ten minutes of light hearted bantering and reminiscing seemingly flew by, Nelson got serious again.

"Dave" he started, "sorry if I offended you, I mean with that comment about your company and all. It's just that I'm going crazy trying to figure out wht my story got cancelled. God knows the assignments they've given me since then don't mean squat to me on an intellectual, professional or personal level, and its showing up in my writing and attitude."

"Don't sweat it," said Morris, "you're not the first to

echo those sentiments and I'm pretty certain you won't be the last. But I'll tell you what. After this drink I've got to go back to the office and...

"Just like you Dave," Nelson said, "to leave the bar before your round comes round."

"Nelson," Morris began, "you are the last of the big time whiners."

"From you buddy, that's a complement," Rucker shot back. "Tell the truth. The reason you're leaving is because you can't hold your liquor. One beer and he's waxed."

"I'm leaving to go back to my building and see if I can find any answers. Yours and mine."

"Dave, can you let me know if you find anything?"

"Geez Nelson, I don't know if I'm looking up this stuff for me or for you."

Nelson smiled.

"Look," Morris began, "I'll tell you whatever I find out. But it's for your information only. Not for print."

"OK" said Morris

"OK" Nelson replied.

CHAPTER 13

THE PERFECT IMPLEMENT

Morris' drive back to the Bennington Building was about as eventful as watching the spilled oil congeal on the shoreline.

Clearing the throng at Jack London Square, he turned onto the freeway and headed for the Bay Bridge.

The normal jostling of cars on the I-580, all of them seemingly trying to get into the two Eastbay lanes, was of no consequence to Morris this evening. He was further away, focusing on what he needed to do once he got back into his office and what he was hoping to uncover.

Motoring across the Bay Bridge, he casually glanced over to the City's business district. In the fading evening light he saw the numerous gargantuans towering over the city, each looming as would a silent be-medalled sentry standing watch over a sleeping metropolis. These sentries were the skyscrapers and their decorated chests nothing more than the countless windows of offices that, for whatever reason, remained lighted long after their last occupants had departed.

Morris was always intrigued at those lighted buildings, and the many different designs the burning lights made. He didn't drive across the bridge everyday, but when he did he always made a point of acknowledging that he would probably never encounter that same pattern of lights again; that each of these lighted visions, night after night, was unique unto itself.

The "courtesy" of another California driver, swerving from lane to lane without so much as the thought of using his signals, brought Morris back to reality.

"Lost in the wonders of the universe again, eh Dave," Morris chuckled to himself.

Fifteen minutes later he pulled into the underground driveway of the Bennington Building and parked. Getting out of his car, he noticed another one parked just a few feet away in the position reserved for the top finance officer. Except for the cars parked in the spots reserved for security, these were the only other cars in the lot.

Knowing that after prescribed business hours anyone was liable to park anywhere they wanted, Morris didn't quite recognize the offending auto. Walking over and taking a quick look, he saw that the car was about eight years old and in a pretty sorry state of repair. Flaking blue paint gave way to an earlier light-blue coat, neither of which was the original or could be mistaken for quality paint.

Peering inside the window, he noticed the front seat covered by an imitation sheepskin, which was nearly threadbare on the driver's side. It was the only thing that Morris could make out inside the car. Parked directly under a parking lamp, the little light that wasn't blocked by the car's roof was being reflected back by its slightly angled windows.

After taking the license plate number and a general description of the car, Morris strolled over to the elevator that would whisk him up to the lobby.

As a security precaution, all parties entering the building after working hours had to stop by and register at the security desk in the lobby of the building's first floor. The elevator that Morris was on, controlled and programmed by computer, only went as high as the first floor. From there, he'd have to check in with the guard on duty and take one of the other elevators to the top.

The doors to the elevator opened and Morris stepped out, turning to walk the thirty feet to the security desk while reaching into his pocket to retract the security ID needed for entry.

It wasn't until he'd almost approached the security desk that he first noticed the guard. If he hadn't been in such plain view of the man he would have succumbed to the fit of laughter that was rapidly building up inside him.

There in front of him, sitting in his station with his head buried in a webmaster design manual, was the security guard, Phil Jeffries. Five foot six and topping the scales at an impressive 127lbs, Phil was totally oblivious to his arrival.

Morris was certain that Phil noticed when the elevator arrived in the lobby and opened its doors. But as he stood there, about ten feet away from the guard, Phil read on as if he were in the San Francisco public library. He simply did not see Morris.

While Morris marveled at the physical specimen in front of him, he took the time to give him a sizing up. It wasn't until he started wondering about the vigilance of this guard when he noticed the extremely thick lenses of Phil's glasses. Morris had talked to Phil on several other occasions, but it had always been up in the building, never as security's point man. And on each of those meetings Morris had never noticed the huge lenses of Phil's glasses. Now, however, Morris suddenly began to feel small for laughing at Phil. He never realized, till just now, that the man's eyes might not be what they could. In his talks with Phil, he'd always thought that the man was all right.

A tad puny, but all right.

Deciding at that moment not to embarrass Phil, Morris slowly walked backwards toward the elevator. Making hardly a sound, Morris wanted to be closer to his point of entry when he made his presence known.

He silently edged his way back to the elevator doors and with pushed the button for the first floor, summoning the elevator back up from the garage. As it had never been signaled to descend, the elevator stayed at the first floor. When Morris called for it, it was already there, and the doors opened instantly.

Morris stepped back into it, and clearing his throat as loudly as he could, stepped out.

Hoping that the sound he'd just made would alert the

guard to his presence, Morris was surprised to see Phil still looking down into his books.

"*Damn,*" Morris thought, "*is this guy deaf too?*"

Morris took his briefcase and held above his head, using both hands so that it would be perfectly flat. He waited a second, and then let it fall.

With a loud report resounding like a gunshot, Phil immediately jumped out of his chair, lost his balance and fell to the floor.

By the time he had regained his composure, Morris had reached the desk.

"I'm sorry," began Morris, "but my briefcase slipped. Hope it didn't frighten you.

"Nah" said Phil in a high nasally tone, "I was just reaching down to the floor to pick up something I dropped."

"*Yeah,*" thought Morris, "*like lunch.*"

Morris left the elevator and entered his office. Knowing that Lawson was in the office changed a few things. For one, his skulking about might now be witnessed, and not being seen was the exact reason that Morris came back after everyone else had gone home.

Morris sat down, pondered for a second and then phoned the security guard he had just left in the lobby. He was hoping that the guard might have some insight into why Lawson was still in the building at this late hour.

"Yeah, Mr. Morris, he's been up there awhile," came Phil's nasal reply. "He's been wracking his brains out all evening. He left at closing time and came back about an hour later. I think he just left to eat."

"Thanks Phil," said Morris, " and by the way, you don't happen to know when he's leaving do you?"

"No, sorry I can't help you on that one. Anything else, Mr. Morris?"

"No Phil that'll be all. Thanks."

Morris heard the receiver at the other end go dead before putting his phone down.

"*What's he doing down there?*" thought Morris. He couldn't

think of a legitimate reason for Lawson to be in the building. The fact that he also had no legitimate reason for being in the building at that hour was not lost on him.

"What the hell, why not just pop on down there and pay him a visit?"

With that, Morris got up and walked over to the Finance Department.

Trying as he might, Morris couldn't think of the proper salutation for asking someone why they're in their office four hours after closing. As in any other time in which words failed him, Morris just relied on subtlety.

"Hey bean counter, what're doing here so late?"

"I could say the same to you," Lawson replied. Morris noticed that while Lawson was startled at first, his voice had a friendly tone to it. He was obviously happy to see someone this late; someone, that is, that he didn't work with.

"What's shakin?" asked Morris.

"Nothing much Dave, just my house, my job..." He faltered a moment before continuing. ."..and my livelihood."

"What's the problem?"

"Its this damn office" said Lawson. "I got called in at three o'clock this afternoon and told that the head lizard himself wants Wahtash here.." he said while pointing to his own chest, ."..to brief the board on our financial condition, first thing in the morning."

"Whoa, hold on a moment," said Morris. "What the hell is a Wahtash?"

"I think it's an Indian word," Lawson began. "It means something along the lines of `the last brave in the teepee', you know--the fourth person in a three person line."

"I think," said Morris, "that it probably translates over in to something like `stuckee'."

"Precisely," added Lawson. "Anyway, to make a long story short--I got tagged with this monster. So I decided to get a jump on everyone by having a computer print-out for each and every one of our board members. But before I ran off thirteen copies, I decided to look one over for any blemishes or discrepancies."

"And you found one?" inquired Morris.

"Did I ever. Either this machine is broken or someone within our company has spent megabucks in the last few months," said Lawson.

"How much is missing?" asked Morris, "...what, a couple hundred thousand, half a million to a million dollars?"

"Try eight hundred eighty two million dollars."

"Eight hundred eighty two million dollars." Morris exclaimed, "That's serious money. Why you'd need the approval of the Chairman of the Board to lay out that kind of money. What did you guys spend it on?"

"That's the kicker," said Lawson. "We didn't spend it. And neither did Research & Development, or Production or Exploration or Shipping or Refining."

"I'll also bet," Lawson groused, "that was the reason they waited until so late in the day to have me prepare this stuff -- so that nobody who knows about any of this will be available why I'm trying to make sense out of it."

"There is," Lawson continued, " one agency I haven't checked with, but I don' t have access to their records or databases. But the most they've ever spent at one time was twenty-two million dollars, and that was for a three year study on the effects of gas recharging our offshore reservoirs back in..."

"Who are you talking about?" Morris interrupted.

"Strategic Planning," said Lawson.

"But they couldn't just up and spend that kind of money, could they?"

"No," Lawson stated. "Even they would have to get approval from on high to spend that kind of money. They do however have a direct track to the CEO. But until tomorrow, when I can ask Jenkins personally, I can only guess. But the more you consider it, its got to he them because...."

Lawson suddenly stopped in mid-sentence and appeared to Morris to be reflecting. It only lasted a few seconds.

"You know," Lawson began, "Jenkins was down here a little bit earlier and he brought a bunch of stuff with him. He was in there with my boss for quite some time. You know my boss Bob McIntyre don't you?"

Morris nodded in the affirmative

"In fact," he continued, "it wasn't until Jenkins left that McIntyre tagged me with this bull. You know, now that I think of it, maybe there's something on McIntyre's desk that can clear this up. Let me just go over there and take a look."

"Maybe McIntyre's desk holds the key," offered Morris cautiously, "but even if you could, is it advisable to go snooping around your boss' office when he's not around?"

"Don't worry about me" Lawson smiled. "If it weren't for my nocturnal raids on his office I wouldn't know what's going on around here. Just keep it under your hat, all-right."

"Somehow," chucked Morris, "I don't think anyone would believe me if I told them."

Lawson was gone less than five minutes when he returned from his boss' office. A slight glance was all it took Morris to see that something had gone amiss in those few minutes.

Lawson came back to his office and gave Morris a straight glare.

"Dave" he began, "I took a little look around my boss' office and to tell you the truth I stopped after a few minutes. I now know why they waited until so late in the day to give this to me.

"What is it, Jake?" Morris asked.

"Dave, on the desk in that office are answers and questions that we're not even supposed to know about. I work in finance and I can only fathom a guess as to what's going on here."

"Jake," Morris asked again, "What did you find out? What did you see?"

"I saw nothing that I'm supposed to know about. There's info up there that tells what Strat Plan did with the $800 million. There's info in there that talks about our $5 billion line of credit. There's info in there on something called the 'Louisiana Project.' I didn't read any of that stuff I just glanced at the titles and the captions to try and see what they were."

"But while there is a lot of info up there, almost, if not all of it, is for an activity of which I know nothing about. It's also information that no one in an official capacity has shared with me."

"Which means, Dave" Lawson continued, "that while this may be the info you're looking for; I can't get it for you."

"Why not, Jake?"

"If I give that info to you, or use any of it in my presentation tomorrow, I'll tip my hand and they'll know exactly what I've been doing. I don't know what my boss will do, but Jenkins will bury me."

"Or" Lawson smirked, "at least try to again."

"I'm going to deal as best I can without this information at the Board of Director's meeting tomorrow.

"I'm going to keep working here for about 20 minutes and then I'm going home."

"Dave" he added, "Since Jenkins brought all of this information down this afternoon it's probably all in the Strat Plan computers. If you look there I'm almost certain that you'll find some answers. But you'll have to do it without my assistance.

"We both know that there is something strange going on here at Bennington. But unlike you, I can't go any further to find answers. I've told you where I think your answers may be found. The question now is what are you going to do?"

"Jake, can I access the Strat Plan computers through your system here?"

"Yes," Lawson replied, "if you had someone who could get you in. It won't be me."

Morris nodded in silent acceptance.

"But," Lawson continued, "I know someone who can. You have to wait until I'm gone, but getting into these systems shouldn't be a problem for a computer genius like him."

"So where do I find this person?" Morris asked.

"Are you kidding," said Lawson, "He's right under our noses. Did you see that dorky looking security guard in the lobby, the thick glasses, about 90-95 pounds and absolutely no threat whatsoever to a relatively healthy intruder?"

"Phil?" Morris replied incredulously.
"Phil!" said Lawson.

CHAPTER 14

CAUGHT

"Mr. Morris, if anyone sees me they'll fire me on the spot." said Phil. "If I lose this job I'll have to drop out of college." He was shaking all over, like a scared rabbit.

"Look Phil," Morris began, "There's $25 bucks in this for you and I guarantee you a job. Now start hacking."

Thirty minutes later, Phil walked into Morris' office. "I think I got something for you."

"Let's have it," said Morris

"Don't you want to know how I got into the system?" Phil asked. He loved being acknowledged for his computer skills.

"Shoot" said Morris. Knowing that he would soon have answers to questions he spent two solid days looking for put him in a jovial spirit.

"As I looked at the monitor," Phil began, "I knew that there would be some kind of safeguard a code that needed to be discovered. I found it too.

He continued. "After requesting access to the Strategic Planning files, I was confronted with a nine-digit access code. That meant that there were 999,999,999 different combinations. That's why no one would even try to get into this system. At ten combinations a second, it would take years if the combination was high enough."

"But I said to myself, "Which nine digits could it be?

What's the magic number? Then it hit me."

"When I was studying computer security we were told how people almost always used some number or sequence that was familiar to them, even though they were almost always told not to. The general rule of thumb was that if a password or code was too familiar to you it would be too easy for some malevolent type to get it. Hell I once had a programming class where we were told to secure access to our work. We used credit cards numbers, telephone numbers, driver's license numbers and the ever popular social security numbers. That night the professor cracked all of our security protocols with ease and erased our programs as punishment for lax security. I learned security that night.

"Anyway, while we computer geeks go with random, hard to decipher security access codes, those like yours friends here in Finance still want the comfort of some familiar code or sequence, like a Social Security Number, that we can access if mere minutes.

"Morris was noticing that Phil was almost reveling in his accomplishment. *"It seems,"* thought Morris, *"that there is an arena where this mouse can roar!"*

"People create these codes to try and devise a number that is familiar to the user but still too random for an intruder. Your phone number has seven digits. Your house number has four. Your birth date has five or six. But it doesn't matter. I could access of this information and more from their personnel files. I tapped those files and got the top ten Finance officials' SSNs and ran them through. I took Lawson's SSN out because I didn't want them to think he was the one seeking access. But on the fourth number I ran the system opened up and let me in.

"Phil," Morris began, "You're a genius."

"Well," Phil began, "you'll have to come over to the monitor and see if you can find what you're looking for.

"Sure, but why not just run up a print out?"

"I just got you into the system," Phil answered, "I have no idea of what you're looking for."

"Just in the event we were successful I brought a flash drive with me. Do you think we'll be able to download anything to it?'

"We can give it a shot," said Phil.

After walking back to the Finance offices, Morris looked to Phil and said, "Let's see what you got."

"Here it is," said Phil, "Look at this list. This is a list of everything your Strat Plan boys are up to.

Morris sat down behind the monitor and began looking at, what he hoped, would be the answers he was seeking. He knew. However, at that time, that the documents he was viewing were another conundrum altogether, and that he would still need time to sort things out. All he knew for certain about his company and the officials who ran it, was that nothing he knew about any of this was certain.

He was going to need some time to fully interpret the documents now available to him, and that was why he brought the flash drive. "*Its six gigabytes of storage should hopefully be enough*" thought Morris.

Morris again scanned the list to see what the Strategic Planning staffers were working on. He noticed a letter that was faxed and mailed to New York and Washington D.C. He noted another letter that was sent to London, and referred to the other two letters. Another file contained a letter that was to be sent to the Security and Exchange Commission offices in San Francisco in two days. Letters to four of the country's largest brokerage houses were also included. Lastly, the was a file simply titled "Louisiana Project"

"Phil," Morris asked, "Can you save all of this on the flash drive for me?"

"Sure Mr. Morris," Phil replied

Phil stuck the drive in one of the available ports and began the process of downloading the information.

"Mr. Morris, if you don't know what this stuff is how do you know it'll be useful?"

"I'm hoping it'll hold some answers for me" Morris replied. "Besides if this doesn't work we can always come back and look at another...

"Damn!" Phil blurted.

"What's wrong Phil?" Morris asked

"We just stumbled over a trip wire." Phil replied.

"Just a second ago a blank seven digit line appeared across the bottom of the monitor and wants to know my Strategic Planning access number."

"I was afraid of this" said Phil

"Afraid of what?" asked Morris.

"There's a code I have to break and there are several crazy things going on" Phil started, "In the bottom left of the screen there's a static numbers 16 and on the right bottom there's a running number. It's at 26 now, but it started at 45 at the same time I started downloading your...."

"Aw Hell" Phil stated. "I know what this damn thing is. It's a defense mechanism built into the catalog. When we tried to download any of the files we set it off."

"Is it allowing us to download?" asked Morris.

"I think so," added Phil.

What does this defense mechanism mean, and what can it do to us?

"I don't know," said Phil, "but we'll know in 14 seconds, when that number on the right hits zero."

They were both looking at the screen as the numbers turned to three, then two and then one. When the number turned to zero the number 16 on the left bottom of the monitor turned to 17.

"Did you see that? asked Phil.

Morris slightly nodded his head in the affirmative.

"Correct me if I'm wrong Phil," Morris began, "But someone in Strategic Planning checks this system every morning and night and logs off all pertinent info. Right?"

"Right" said Phil

"And that number on the left side of the monitor, the sixteen that became seventeen, was probably logged in somewhere as a sixteen earlier tonight?. Right?"

"Right," Phil repeated.

"And chances are that when they see the seventeen, they'll know that someone has been in their system. Right?"

"Right" said Phil.

"What will they do then, Phil?

"Chances are that they'll make several copies on a transferable medium, a disk or a flash drive or two, then they'll purge their entire system of this information anywhere, except the ones that they have.

"And what about us," Phil continued. "What will they do when they find out that we tapped their files?

Morris thought about that for a moment. Getting information was his goal. He didn't contemplate getting caught and having to deal with higher ranking corporate officials.

"What else can they do," Morris answered sarcastically. "We'll either be free-lance or work as consultants because they'll see to it that we never work steady here again."

"Great" said Phil. "A free-lance security guard." Phil began shutting down the computer and suggested that both of them leave immediately.

They did.

CHAPTER 15

REFLECTION

Morris and Phil sat in his office trying to figure out what they should do next. Morris' desires to find out what was going on was not yet bordering on obsession, but it was a constant gnawing at him that was driving him to do things he ordinarily wouldn't. As he sat behind his desk, he was only now beginning to understand the complexity, and the consequences, of his actions.

Even he realized that he should have considered all of this before his incursion into the Strat Planning computers. But it was too late for this. They had been caught, and now they were left with their thoughts to determine just how bad this could get.

"They'll know someone was in their system by noon tomorrow won't they Phil?"

"More like 9 a.m." was Phil's laconic reply.

"Is there anything you can do to purge our efforts?" asked Morris.

"If it was the Bennington mainframe I could erase all knowledge of our hacking in a New York second. But these are those damn Mortensons. I just now walked us into a booby-trap, and I don't think I'll have better luck trying to purge our incursion from those databases. When Jenkins finds out what we've been up to he's gonna be pissed."

"You have any idea what happens in this type of

situation, Phil?"

"To an executive or a security guard?"

The phrasing of Phil's answer told Morris more about Phil's concerns than any other words he uttered. Phil was afraid for his job.

"I better go back to my post Mr. Morris. I'll be there if you can think of something that could help us."

With that, Phil stood up and left Morris' office.

Morris looked over at the pile of documents that he and Phil had downloaded. They had taken the flash drive back to his office and printed hard copies of the files. Phil suggested that course in the event the files had some timed self-deletion tool.

The files were by no means complete, and Morris didn't even know if they made sense to him. But he was also aware that the very people whose actions he wanted to know about were going to know that he was in their computer databases. Morris was also aware that those people had a reputation for being excessive in showing their displeasure.

Morris was not looking forward to tomorrow. He knew it was going to be a very bad day. He was unprepared for just how bad it would actually be.

CHAPTER 16

HARSH REALITY

Jenkins waited impatiently in his office for his 9 a.m. appointment. The news he held in his hands was disturbing and, as was his way, requiring of immediate and decisive action.

Jenkins' role as the chief of strategic planning was to plot the course that the corporation was to follow. He looked upon any eventuality as having a positive or negative effect on his company and he made sure that -- either way -- every possible outcome was considered and covered. From details as large as determining a third world country's political leanings to issues as small as the color of his office, Jenkins considered every aspect of any occurrence that might affect the company, and he put them into his equation to measure how their impact might affect Bennington. He had done this with every conceivable aspect of the collision and was certain that he had a grip on the spill's effects on the company.

But Jenkins was not just focusing on the spill. He was beyond that now. He had already considered the effects of the loss of a tanker to the company's operations and bottom line. The cost of clearing the spill had already been calculated and analyzed as to its effects on future earnings and operations. He even had his staff work on how the public's perception of fault in an oil spill could affect the company's current and future operations, as well as their share value. Jenkins had made it a point to cover every aspect involved in determining Bennington's future -- even to the point of providing an in-house surveillance of the computers in his offices and a computerized logging system that tracked every phone call out of --and into-- Bennington. He smiled grimly knowing that his foresight had borne results and that someone was about to pay for, as he saw it, their treasonous transgressions into his computer system.

Running the page he held between his fingers, Jenkins thought aloud.

"It seems I've caught a rat," he snickered, stopping to correct himself, ."..or a mole."

Jenkins was a very smart man. An Ivy-league MBA provided him with the foundation to work, thrive and, as far as he was concerned, lead a Fortune 500 company. He was well on his way to that goal when his world was turned upside down by the go-go eighties. His company, Jupiter Oil, wound up on the losing side of a hostile takeover. When it was all said and done, Jenkins neither had a job or his dream. They both disappeared as some multi-billionaire he never heard of tore the company apart in the belief that it was worth more dismembered than whole.

Jenkins quickly recognized what was about to happen. Since oil companies being rendered apart had no need for strategic planning specialists to plot their futures, he was being made worse than expendable. He was becoming useless.

The years he spent making the right contacts, doing the best he could and creating innovative paths for the Jupiter Oil to follow to prosperity were now nothing more than wasted forethought. The new owners were only interested in Jupiter's petroleum reserves. It didn't make economic sense to drill for oil at $10 a barrel in the ground when you could plunder an oil company for $6 a barrel on the stock market. The hard resources would be sold, shut down or dismantled. The soft resources, all four thousands of them, would simply lose their jobs.

Jenkins was but one.

But it wasn't losing his job that bothered Jenkins as much as it was how. It was a discovery he made toward the end of the takeover that changed his attitude towards business for good.

During the latter stages of the takeover Jenkins discovered how Jupiter's takeover defenses were consistently being trumped. Their opponent was not better organized, better financed or better prepared. They were simply better informed. Two staff members at Jupiter were providing their attackers with information about every move that Jupiter was planning to take--allowing them time to trump Jupiter's every move, at every turn.

Attempts to woo white knights failed not because the intended saviors were afraid of Jupiter's aggressors, but because Jupiter's aggressors were so informed as to Jupiter's efforts that grave concerns arose as to the protection of the white knights interests. The level of infiltration was so encompassing that it became a cancer to Jupiter, and a perceived cancer to all that were interested in assisting Jupiter. A white knight out to make a bid for Jupiter might find itself fighting for its own life against a wretched financier who had an information stranglehold on Jupiter. Potential white knights backed out, fearful not of the large company they might gain, but of the unknown infiltration killing Jupiter.

The "moles" were not high placed executives with access to corporate secrets, but the director of the document-processing center and the director of information services--the computers. Disks and flash drives were simply filled from downloaded information and passed onto willing recipients. E-mails and other electronic transfers were sent and deleted before they could be acknowledged, let alone traced.

Every letter, telephone call, memo or agreement from Jupiter went through the departments one of these two executives controlled. So trusted were they that they were tasked with preparing the security to prevent the kind of infiltration that they were committing. With the exception of their own activities, they safeguarded the firm's confidential materials with the utmost in diligence. When the corporation began discerning a pattern from their opponent's superior knowledge, it was these very two people who were asked to bring in outsiders to protect the company's confidential materials. They even served up a young executive as a potential mole and prepared enough incriminating evidence to have him fired for leaking classified materials. It was here that Jenkins first suspected a problem.

The young exec that had been sacrificed worked for Jenkins and Jenkins knew the exec didn't have access to the information he was accused of stealing. Jenkins quietly backtracked the whole chain of events and realized that the two department directors were leaking the information and selling out their own company. But he found out too late.

A week later Jupiter was sold and the dismantling began. Before he could prove his findings, Jupiter's computers were erased and replaced, and when that occurred, for all intents and purposes, only Jenkins knew of the department directors' treachery. He lost his job before he could even confront them.

Jenkins was bitter. He could care less about the company or the thousands of unemployed workers. He was angry because his dreams and plans had been skewered for a promise of future employment and a few shares of stock. Valuable information hemorrhaged from the company from a spot not even contemplated and the net results, in his eyes, were his shattered plans and dreams. While Jenkins knew that any form of revenge was useless, he thought that the CEO should know.

"It can't be easy to have a profitable company yanked out from under your feet," thought Jenkins, *"especially if you had no chance from the start."*

If only a symbolic gesture, Jenkins told the CEO what he had learned. Even Jenkins did not suspect what was to happen.

Three weeks to the day after Jenkins told the CEO what had happened, a savage retribution took place. As Jupiter's former word processing director entered her car after work, a van pulled up and two men leapt from the vehicle, abducting her. She was located the next morning, barely alive. The ferocity in the manner in which she had been assaulted stunned even the police. Across town, just moments after leaving his apartment, the former director of Jupiter's information services, was found beaten to a pulp, with knees so badly broken that they would eventually have to be fused together.

The newspapers covered the attacks in separate insignificant stories, chalking them up to the random violence that plagues modern society. Jenkins recognized the names of the victims in the news reports he saw and he began to fear for himself. He knew this was no random act but a signal; not just to the victims, but to those corporate decision-makers who had enlisted their aid. Jenkins had thought about going to the police and revealing what he knew about the attacks but he had two problems with that course. One was that he had no hard evidence about who actually performed the attack. And the second was his own complicity in this matter. If the authorities misconstrued his reasons for telling the former CEO about the traitors in their midst, he might be held as an accomplice to a pair of vicious assaults. He was still evaluating his options when the decision was made for him.

Jenkins was still shocked by what he had read when the phone rang. An emissary of the CEO called and told Jenkins that he would be coming by later and would ease his mind as to the current events still unfolding. The words "still unfolding" were echoing in his mind when the emissary told Jenkins that his fears would soon be laid to rest.

That night at his house, the CEO's representative told him not to worry, that the CEO was grateful for his efforts. The former CEO was engaged in working out the details of his severance package when Jenkins had come to him with the information about the two turncoats. The CEO immediately suspended discussions about his compensation and told the new owners of Jupiter that they would receive a sign that would lead them to do what was right by the departing chief executive. That sign was last night's attack upon the two former Jupiter executives.

The emissary told Jenkins that the attack had served the intended purpose. Earlier today, Jupiter's new owners gave the CEO a compensation package far in excess of the one they had haggled over. The reason was plain.

In one fell swoop, the former CEO had shown his adversaries what he knew, and what he was capable of. He knew that they had engaged in insider trading and other securities violations to win Jupiter, and that the slightest disclosure of this could mean jail time and/or a disgorgement of millions of dollars for Jupiter's new owner. As far as what he might truly be capable of, that spoke for itself. He now had both the ability to disrupt this takeover and, as he had shown, the audacity to use whatever method necessary to achieve his objective. And he had shown all of this to his adversaries without so much as a hostile word or gesture directed to them.

What had started as nothing more than an asset grab of Jupiter's reserves had now turned into something more insidious. Jupiter's new owners had neither the stomach nor the inclination to escalate this matter; they simply wanted it over. For twenty-four million dollars more than the total they haggled over just two weeks earlier, it was.

The emissary told Jenkins that the CEO was going to retire. He added that the CEO had a friend looking for a new chief of strategic Planning and that he had given them Jenkins' name with the recommendation that he could be trusted. When Jenkins asked why the CEO thought he could be trusted, the emissary simply replied, "With what you knew, you could have cut yourself a better deal. And you didn't have to tell the boss. The Boss appreciated your loyalty, even when there was nothing to be gained by it."

Jenkins had never considered that what he had uncovered about the two turncoats could have been used to his advantage. This revelation enlightened him. He began seeing things in a different light, one that shone on his future instead of everyone else's. Shortly after that, Jenkins became the new Chief of Strategic planning at Bennington.

Before the CEO's representative left, Jenkins asked him one final question. He wasn't sure the emissary would answer it, because it would mean complicity in something far more heinous than anything he'd ever done.

"Were you involved in what happened to our two former friends from Jupiter?" The emissary looked sternly at Jenkins and replied. "Yes. There are times when things must be done to keep the world in its proper balance. Two people above all cost four thousand people their jobs. They also cost ours," he spoke collectively now, for himself and the former CEO that he continued to serve. "The boss will never find work again. But he's not ready to retire. I guess he'll just find some way to...exist. All that was done to our two friends was to place them in the same position that many of Jupiter's older employees now find themselves in. Plain and simple, many former employees will never work again. And neither will, shall we say, Judas I and Judas II. So far, they have been nothing more than a signal to Jupiter's new owners to pay up. But in a few months, they will find that thirty pieces of silver doesn't go as far as it used to. Only then will they feel the retribution for what they've done."

The emissary slid Jenkins a business card with a phone number written on the back. That is the number of the priest that I talk to when a certain kind of job has to be done and I need help in getting it done.

"Like the job done on those two folks who betrayed Jupiter?"

"Exactly"

"How the hell can a priest help you with something like that?"

"This priest has nothing to do with God!" While that statement hung in the air, the emissary rose and started for the door.

"Take care of yourself!" Those were the last words Jenkins would ever hear from any of Jupiter's four thousand employees. As the vanquished, they could teach him nothing.

Jenkins had learned some very valuable lessons from working at Jupiter and in watching its demise. The first was to trust no one. The second was that it paid to have someone in your pocket to do the kinds of things that no one else wanted to or could do -- but things that nonetheless needed to be done. But the lesson that affected him the most, to the point of changing him, was that knowledge, no - information, was power and that you empower everyone, from families to friends to enemies, with what you tell them.

Jenkins had come to know that true power lay not in position but in information. The smartest CEOs have been removed by lesser execs armed with salient information.

Countless incompetent CEOs who have literally driven their companies into bankruptcy have at least had the foresight to cloak themselves with some sort of talisman that allowed them to maintain their positions. As far as Jenkins was concerned, that talisman was information. The information may have been an innovative plan of recovery, a way to exploit the weakness of a competitor or just some good old-fashioned incriminating piece of evidence directed at a potential successor. Either way, Jenkins realized that information and access to it was where the real power existed.

Jenkins also realized the corollary to that philosophy; that information in the wrong hands was dangerous. As he learned to his dismay at Jupiter Oil, information illegally transferred loses none of its impact or value; it simply gains in its applicability. Information in the right hands is a powerful tool. In the wrong hands, the information was no less powerful. The extraordinary lengths taken by tobacco companies to maintain the secrecy of their research or the efforts put up by defense contractors to silence whistle-blowers only reinforced this philosophy to Jenkins.

How many business deals have fallen apart because of wrongful or carelessly transferred information? God only knows. But Jenkins wasn't planning to add another company to that tally.

As Jupiter Oil was joining the hallowed realm of oblivion, Jenkins vowed to never tell anyone more than he wanted them to know. Not what they needed or wanted to know, but what he felt they should know. He vowed to become the gatekeeper of all information under his control and to tell people just enough so that they would become dependent upon him.

He followed through on that vow when he started working at Bennington. His creed was simple enough. Since only he had an idea of what he knew, the ignorance of his knowledge by his staff would be his strongest and most important bargaining chip. In just a few months at Bennington he had made himself indispensable. He had also taken steps to stay that way. One of those steps was an in-house surveillance of the computers in his offices and another was a computerized monitoring system that logged every phone call out of --and into-- Bennington.

He waited for Martin to arrive in his office. His grim smile was gone. His face was now a mask of resolve. Jenkins was about to tell Martin of the intrusion of his computers last night, and who he suspected that intruder to be. Jenkins also suspected that Martin would be upset with the plans that he had already initiated to prevent another intrusion. He also knew that he didn't give a damn about what Martin thought. As far as he was concerned, if Martin had done his job right, this particular meeting would not be occurring.

Jenkins held a piece of paper in his hands. The paper was a confirmation from the department's computer expert that informed them that someone had gotten into their system last night. Additional investigation had shown that the security logs placed a small number of people in the building at the time of the intrusion, and only a few in the HQ section. It also showed that whoever came in had a badge for electronic entry/access. This told Jenkins all he needed to know.

When Jenkins had the security logs checked, he was only looking for one name. David Morris. When the guards found that name, Jenkins told them not to look any further. The security logs also revealed that a security guard named Phil Johnson had also left his post for almost an hour last night. Jenkins' cursory check of Johnson's background showed that if Morris needed any help in getting into the strategic planning computers, this security guard was that help.

Martin arrived at a few minutes past nine.

"You called me up here, Stan," said Martin, "What's the problem?"

Martin worked well with Jenkins, as they were two birds of a feather. Both practiced the Machiavellian "ends justifying the means" management style. It endeared them to only a few people at Bennington, but as they would both hurriedly admit, it was the few people who mattered most. While their targets were often different, they went after them with equal vigor. Bennington Oil was all that meant anything to both of these men, and now they were about to discuss a major problem brewing within it.

"Earlier this week," Jenkins began, "I asked you to cure Morris of his snooping ways. Either you didn't, which doesn't sound like you, or you did a bad job of it, which also doesn't sound like you. Either way, he's still at it."

"I talked to him already," Martin countered, "and I told him to lay off. But if he hasn't I'll talk to him again."

"If you've talked to him once you don't need to talk to him again" Jenkins replied. "I'll take care of him. He needs to know that we're serious and we don't want his, shall we say, involvement."

"Wait a minute Stan," Martin started, "Morris works for me. I'll talk to him. You deal with your people and I'll deal with mine. I'll bring him back in line."

"You'll bring him back in line, huh?" Jenkins reiterated. "Last night there was an intrusion into my computers. What was taken or viewed is still being assessed. I don't know what he has, or what he saw. I just know that, from my databases, he wasn't supposed to see or take anything."

"Anything!" Jenkins emphasized with a hostile reiteration.

"Stan" said Martin, "Don't worry. I'll stop his snooping once and for all."

"Just the same," he continued, "I've got some people looking up his personnel folder to see what we could find. If he saw what I suspect he may have, than he has become a far bigger problem that planned on. As such, I need to do something subtle to jog his memory."

"Like what?" questioned Martin.

"I've made an appointment for him to see a priest?"

"A priest?" said Martin. "If you're checking into his background, it shouldn't take you long to find that he's not Catholic?"

Jenkins looked Martin straight in the eyes and coldly stated, "As you will see, this priest has nothing to do with God."

Morris had finished working at almost 7:15 p.m. and was getting ready to leave when he remembered that Martin had asked him to drop in before he left. Morris had absolutely no idea of what Martin wanted because, for the most part, since the collision, he had independently been heading the company's public relations efforts and had neither asked nor needed Martin's counsel.

"However, Martin is my boss," thought Morris as he neared his supervisor's office," and you don't just blow off meetings with your..."

Morris had turned the corner and stared, yet again, into the empty office of Bill Martin. While his briefcase and other personals left the impression that Martin was still in the building, he was not, at that moment, in his office.

"Apparently" he murmured, "It's O.K. to blow off meetings with your subordinates."

As he turned to go back to his office and prepare to leave, he thought about where Martin could be. It didn't take him long to arrive at his first location.

He leaned over Martin's secretary's desk, which had long since been unoccupied, and began dialing the phone. After one ring, the person on the other end picked up the phone and voiced the salutation, "Hello, Mr. Jenkins office."

"Yes," Morris began, "I was calling to see if Bill Martin was there. He wanted to talk to me about something before I left. Can you see if he's available to come to the phone."

"One moment" came the reply.

Almost thirty seconds passed before a voice came back across the receiver.

"Dave, this is Bill. What I had to talk to you about can wait. Why don't you head out and I'll talk to you in the morning."

"Alright" said Morris, "So you will be back down here in the morning?" The phrasing seemed more sarcastic than interrogative. While the inflection was lost on Morris, it was not lost on Martin.

"I'll talk to you in the morning" was Martin's curt reply. Morris heard a hard click from the other end of the phone before his line went dead. Martin had angrily, and abruptly, hung up.

It wasn't Morris's intent to needlessly aggravate Martin by pointing out his absence from his own corporate post; the angered response, however, showed that that was the result.

Morris simply wanted to pin him down and discuss the ongoing public relations efforts.

"That went well," Morris stated.

He hung up the phone and in doing so, decided that this issue was, in fact, one that could wait until tomorrow.

"Well then," exclaimed Morris, "I guess its Miller time!" He walked back to his office and began assembling the materials and works that he would be taking home with him. It took him almost ten minutes before he was finally prepared to leave. Unbeknownst to Morris, a lot had happened in that ten minutes.

Martin walked back into Jenkins office after he'd gotten off of the line with Morris.

"He's leaving," said Martin. "Are you sure we need to go through with this?"

"Don't lose your nerve on me now, Martin" Jenkins snipped. "Morris went way over the line when he entered my computers. This afternoon we finally assessed what he had an opportunity to look at and guess what? He now has all the pieces he needs to put this puzzle together and scuttle our plans. We've worked too hard towards making Bennington one of the petroleum giants of this country to turn around and let to let some intrepid executive, blind as he may be to the final objective, come traipsing around and ruin everything. I will not stand for it. I would hope you would be in agreement."

"I am in agreement," Martin retorted, "and you know it. When we started this operation it was only a pecuniary event-- a money and resource grab. No body was supposed to get hurt."

"He'll be jostled a little bit and nothing more" Jenkins added. "What is about to happen to him should make him think twice about the information he has and the plans he may have for using that information."

Martin sat down in one of the office chairs and tried to take decide how he felt about what he was hearing. He still felt uncertain about the events that were rapidly unfolding. To him, Jenkins' statement lacked a degree of sincerity and if what he proposed was allowed to occur, it would drag Martin into complicity of a much larger and more sinister nature. Martin wasn't certain that he was ready for that.

He had convinced himself that Morris needed to be taught a lesson; something significant enough to cure him of his meddling. Sitting him down and informing him as to what was going on would have solved everything, but there were greater powers at work here than Martin and he didn't want to risk their wrath with a disclosure to an uncontrollable party. But just as he was certain that the full disclosure of this matter to Morris would have stopped his inquiring; so too was he convinced that what Jenkins had planned was just as extreme, and far more dangerous.

He was still engaged in his mental deliberations when Jenkins' voice broke through his menagerie.

"He's leaving," Jenkins started. "In two minutes the garage will go blind and you'll have five minutes to act. What's that? I don't think you'll need the entire five minutes either. However, the clock is running. Go to it."

Jenkins put the phone back into its cradle and shot a quick glance at Martin. He then turned to his computer and typed a short command.

Martin had met Jenkins stare and held it until Jenkins turned to one of his computers. It wasn't until Jenkins was nearly halfway through his keyboarding that Martin realized that Jenkins was using the Bennington, and not the Strategic Planning department computers.

Jenkins began speaking before Martin could react.

"It's done," Jenkins stated to Martin. "Hopefully, our problems will no longer include Morris."

By making the phone call, Jenkins had set a course of action in motion that would envelop both Martin and Morris. By making that call and uttering those few words, Jenkins had cast Martin's vote to go along with his plan without Martin's consent. Both Jenkins and Martin now knew that there was no backing down. Jenkins also knew that there was nothing Martin could do about it now

Martin leaned back in his chair and smiled. "So much for conscience," he half-laughingly admitted. Then he looked over to Jenkins.

In just seconds the smile left his face. He stood up from his chair, and looking squarely at Jenkins, spoke in a manner both firm and deliberate.

"I just hope you fully understand what you've gotten us into." "Gotten us into?" Jenkins returned. "You knowingly walked into this matter. Your eyes were then, and have remained, open as to what is going on. Any remorse about how you perceive yourself, or about what you feel I've gotten you into, you need only drift back as far as the night of the collision. You seemed pretty enthusiastic about our little plan then, to the point of talking to the crew of the Guardian and...."

"You've made your point," Martin started. Jenkins' comments had stung him and both he and Jenkins knew it. They both also knew that the deliberate nature of the retort had stung more than the context of the statement.

Jenkins was trying to handle Martin like an underling, a subordinate to be commanded into whatever state of compliance Jenkins wanted. Jenkins assumed that he was winning that fight. Martin needed to show him that the battle still remained to be fought; that throughout the coming events, he was Jenkins' equal.

"Know this Stan," Martin began, "this collateral issue with Morris is a distraction no one needs. Your hurt pride over Morris' high tech invasion of your domain is resulting in an action that has no place in this matter. I also question how well you've thought this out. What you've set in motion may bring more light to our plans than we either wanted or needed. When I said I hoped that you had fully understood what you've done, it was no reflection on my commitment to Bennington, it was an query as to whether you were trying to hold this baby so close that you wind up strangling it in your protective arms. Insider trading and other stock manipulations happen all the time. I doubt many of them ever get discovered. But your little vendetta here may bring the police to our basement. Stop and consider if that's in the best interest of what we're trying to do."

With that, Martin turned and left Strategic Planning for his own office.

He figured, at worst, his talk with Jenkins was a draw. The few seemingly insignificant keystrokes that Jenkins had performed could not possibly belie their importance. His call set a turn of events in motion that would "send a message" to a Bennington executive not to meddle in affairs beyond his station. The keystrokes would insure that Jenkins' "messenger" would not be seen or possibly identified later.

Jenkins had just sent a command that would, in 90 seconds, take the security cameras in the garage from an operational to a stand-by mode. To a casual observer in the garage itself, the only way to tell if the cameras were filming would be to look at a small red light located right under the lens. A steady red light meant that the camera was operational. A flashing red light meant that the camera was on stand-by and that no surveillance was occurring.

In stand-by, the cameras would simply freeze upon the last image they were focusing upon. If no person were caught in the frozen frame, or no other moving object caught in an awkward mid-motion pose by the frozen lens, the monitors being viewed by the security personnel downstairs would resemble large still photographs of the garage. The security guards would believe they were viewing a normal scene, for the images being sent to their monitors would be as still as a garage full of parked cars.

More important to Jenkins than the security guards being lulled into inactivity was the fact that only the two men in the garage and the two in his office were a party to the events about to happen. Three of them would keep the knowledge of their actions secure. The fourth, one David Morris, was about to become painfully aware that he was involved in something larger than he could possibly grasp, and that his involvement was not welcome.

The elevator doors to the E-level of the parking garage opened smoothly, allowing Morris to step out and head for his car.

His plans for the evening were set; he would review the materials he'd gotten from Jenkins' computers last night and try to make some sense out of what was going on. He had already read a dossier of Jenkins--which simply lowered his opinion of the man from loathing to contempt. Tonight, he wanted to see what else he had uncovered; especially a file titled "The Louisiana Project."

Morris had left the elevator and was walking past the first of the twelve stalls between he and his car, when he heard a noise.

He looked around to see who it was, but there was no one else of this level of the garage. No one, at least, that Morris could see. The noise resembled a foot stepping on a dry leaf, and seemed out-of-place in a parking garage, which simply added to the startling nature of the sound.

After doing a quick look around and seeing no one, Morris continued to his car. He had barely reached it and had just started inserting the key into the trunk when he heard a louder noise, similar to the first but sounding much closer.

He quickly turned his head to the right, to the side where the sound had emanated, to see what it might be. Before he could, a large hand grabbed his left shoulder and pulled it backwards, spinning him around.

For the briefest of moments, a fraction of a second, Morris looked into the face of pain.

As one hand of Morris' unknown attacker was spinning him around to create their momentary face to face encounter, the other hand was drawing backward and closing into a fist.

Morris had barely glimpsed at his attacker's face when he noticed the attacker's other hand, closed into a hardened, glove-covered projectile was drawing back like a viper poised to strike.

Morris tried to react and move out of the way, but could not because the attacker's other hand held him in an off-balanced and awkward position.

Before he could sound an alarm, to make some attempt to draw security or some other assistance, the attacker smashed his fist into the side of Morris' head, at the spot where the jaw joins the skull.

Morris' head snapped violently, driven by the force and the follow-through of the blow.

Instinctively, his hands drew towards his face to ward off any other blows. He tried to spot his attacker, but his vision was blurred and his motor skills dulled by the vicious blow. Had he not been so groggy from the impact of the first punch, he might have been able to avoid the next one. The attacker had rocked Morris, who had dropped to one knee to try and maintain his equilibrium. It was a simple survival technique, but it played perfectly into the hands of his assailant.

Morris was nearly incapacitated from the first blow and was quite unable to offer resistance. Swiftly moving behind him, the attacker pulled out a small metal baton, raised his arm and brought it crashing down on the back on Morris' head.

Morris toppled onto the trunk of his car, flailing wildly trying to grab onto something and avoid falling to the pavement. He slid off the trunk and half lowered himself and half fell onto the pavement. Morris turned and, through his blurred and distorted view, saw his attacker walking away, getting smaller and smaller before finally disappearing. Seconds later, the on-rushing stillness of unconsciousness overwhelmed him.

Had he but looked up a moment or two later, he would have seen a flashing red light on a security camera, not thirty feet from where he lay, switch to a steady glow. As it stood, less than two minutes after the cameras had come back on line, security personnel were rushing to aid Morris. He was still unconscious when they arrived.

Morris regained consciousness amid the frantic first aid efforts of the recently arrived security guards. Just a scant few moments earlier, one of them had looked at the security camera monitors and had noticed a figure lying prone behind a car.

As Morris struggled to regain coherence and comprehension, he ran his hand over the back of his head, only to discover a lump half the size of a hard-boiled egg. Upon withdrawing his hand, he also noticed that the lump was bleeding. He looked up at the assembled security guards, uncertain as to what he should do or say.

One security guard motioned to him that he was not to move until medical help arrived. Morris was in a daze, a stupor that was only allowing him to look at those around him in a near catatonic state. He could hear the guards asking him questions, but he hadn't yet regained the full control of his faculties needed to fashion responses.

A few moments later Morris could feel the cloud of numbness that had enveloped him beginning to abate, and with this abatement came a small dose of understanding. He could feel that he was hurt. He could also sense that he needed medical treatment. He had not yet attempted to determine what had happened and why.

The guards propped Morris up against his car. He wanted to lay down and close his eyes again, but the security guards would not let him. One of the security guards knew that head trauma victims should not be allowed to go to assume a sleep-like posture unless the doctor treating such person approves. As sleeping can sometimes mask the symptoms of a concussion, the guards had no intention of letting Morris lay down and possibly go into an irreversible sleep. In propping him up in the most uncomfortable position they could get him in, they were insuring that Morris stayed awake.

As the security guards were positioning Morris against a car, he heard one of the guards utter something like "...one minute there is nothing on the monitors and next there's this guy lying here on the ground."

The guards had brought Morris back from unconsciousness, but they lacked the training and intention to go any further than that. The ambulance that they had summoned arrived five minutes later, and Morris was on his way to the hospital.

After two hours of being checked, scanned, probed and x-rayed, Morris was happy to hear the emergency room staff tell him that he was being released. They diagnosed Morris as having a mild concussion; one that would take care of itself in the next few days. With no sign of permanent injury, the hospital staff told Morris that all they could do for him was charge him $400 a day for a hospital bed. He was discharged with the instruction to rest, take it easy and to stay home for the next two days.

Outside the emergency room Alice had been trying to get in to see Morris. Hospital security had a different idea and refused to allow her into the emergency room.

She was waiting when Morris left the emergency room, talking with a doctor. She heard the doctor tell Morris he needed plenty of rest.

"Don't worry," said Alice, "I'll see that he does."

Morris managed a weak smile at Alice. His head ached considerably, but even that couldn't stop his spirits from rising when he heard and saw her.

"Dave," Alice blurted, "what the hell happened to you? Your security people tell me you got assaulted in your own parking garage. How can that happen—the garage is guarded and secured!"

"Obviously," said Morris, "its not as secure as we thought."

"But why you-was it a robbery? Did they get anything from you?"

"No, they took nothing. No credit cards, no cash, no keys, no wallet—nothing. I almost get the impression he was just there to beat someone up and then I came along."

"No," Morris continued, "he didn't take anything, but he left a few bumps and bruises."

They started walking towards the hospital exit. As her car was parked a good way from the hospital entrance, Morris waited while she went to retrieve it.

She drove around to the front of the hospital and parked where Morris was standing. She attempted to get out of the car to help Morris, but he simply told her that he wasn't so badly injured that he couldn't open a car door and sit down.

As she steered to leave the hospital, she opened her mouth to continue the conversation they had before she left to get the car. But before she could utter a word, Morris spoke first.

"You know," he began, "I can honestly tell you that I don't know why that guy attacked me. Hell I hardly got a glimpse of him when the lights started going out."

"The lights in the garage?" questioned Alice.

"My lights," Morris replied, "I was speaking metaphorically."

"Well that's a good sign—you using polysyllabic words

in a coherent sentence."

Morris looked over at her as she drove and shook his head.

"Jeez," he said, "you lawyers and your vernacular!"

They got home just before one o'clock in the morning. The long day and even longer evening fatigued Alice. Morris was not much better, having been both mentally and physically traumatized by the events of the day. They were both looking forward for this day to end, and as soon as possible.

Morris walked up the short walkway to the front door of their house and fumbled with his keys before finally unlocking the door. He put his jacket over a chair and laid down on the couch. His eyes were almost closed when Alice came into the house. He was ready to fall asleep right then and there, and probably would have, if he hadn't noticed....

"Alice," he said with no attempt to mask his concern, "what's wrong?"

Alice face was drawn into a dour mask, a cross between a frown and a half-hearted smile concealing worry. In her hand was a single white five by seven card, and she was holding the printed side close to her blouse.

Morris struggled to his feet and walked over to where she was.

"Alice, hon...what's wrong?"

She turned the card over with just the merest of glances he realized the source of her fear and concern.

The card contained just five written words printed in bold 36-point type. The simplicity of the note betrayed the awful impact of its message. Morris looked at the message again and let its few words burn themselves into his mind.

TODAY WAS JUST A WARNING was all the entire note contained. But its definition was far graver.

Morris noticed that the card held no postmark and more importantly, that the note was hand-delivered and not mailed. It also meant that the sender knew exactly where, and with whom, Morris lived.

As Morris took the note from Alice's hands he heard her speak to him.

"Dave, what does this mean? What's going on here?"

He looked her in the eyes and knew that she didn't know a thing about the Louisiana Project or the goings-on at the company. She was as in the dark about Monty-O as everyone else except a chosen few. Morris also knew that he was fully aware of these things, and that he definitely was not one of the chosen few. He had just learned, to his detriment that someone at Bennington was aware of his snooping and would, most likely, know in a very short period of time exactly how much Morris knew.

He wrapped his arms around her in a lame attempt to comfort her fears. He knew her too well to think that this would actually work, but he felt he had to immediately steer her mind away from asking too many questions about the mess he now knew he was in. He knew way more than he could tell her, and after today, he damn sure didn't want her to know what was going on.

He didn't want whoever attacked him to go after Alice.

"*My God,*" he thought, "*Please don't let my actions bring her into this mess.*"

He put his arm over her shoulder and without saying a word led her to their bedroom.

Alice knew him well enough to know that when he wasn't ready to talk about something, he didn't. His actions showed her that he wasn't ready to talk. She began taking her suit off and headed towards the bathroom to get ready for bed.

Morris walked back into the living room. He sat down on a chair and placed his elbows on his knees and dropped his face into his upturned palms.

"*What the hell have I gotten into?*" was his only thought.

CHAPTER 17

ULTERIOR MOTIVES

Planning is an exact science where, if the variables are manipulated precisely, an event's outcome cannot only be foretold, but created. Those with this gift for subtle manipulation can, given time, lead intelligent people to conclusions that those same people would not have chosen for themselves. The manipulation will be so strong, so overpowering or so compelling that those being used might even disagree that they are being led by another party. It can be that real. But it also has to be perfect. And no one was better than Stan Jenkins.

Jenkins had made his plans carefully, and despite the irritant that a certain member of Bennington Oil's PR staff was becoming, Jenkins was moving ahead. He had taken steps to insure that the "irritant" he was speaking of was now in receipt of a message that Jenkins personally had hand-delivered last night in the Bennington Oil building parking garage.

He had laid out his plans for the takeover of Monty-O and bared them for all of the key corporate officials to see. It was undeniable now, that the takeover process was underway.

Most of those in the company with knowledge of the takeover had assumed that it would occur once the CEO gave the order. A small cadre within the company knew better. They knew that the takeover began four months earlier, when

Bennington Oil began slowly buying shares of Monty-O on the open market. Bennington Oil was hedging its bets. Their management wanted to control as much stock as possible before announcing the takeover.

It had begun four months ago when Jenkins solicited some "partners" to help in the takeover of Monty-O.

Jenkins was a cautious man. When the thought of a takeover was first raised, Jenkins agreed with it wholeheartedly. But he was not without his reservations. He was concerned that in trying to take over a company almost the same size as Bennington Oil that they might use up, or at least tie up, huge amount of both companies' capital assets. He was worried that after taking over Monty-O, the combined companies would have a cash flow issue of their own, possibly becoming targets of a takeover themselves. This was unacceptable to Jenkins. He had no intention of gaining control over Bennington Oil's most dangerous rival, only to have to loosen his grip on it because of a potential capital problem. Accordingly, in Jenkins' eyes, an option needed to be developed and implemented.

Jenkins thought long and hard about every aspect of this problem. Coming up with a workable strategy didn't take him long. Thinking and planning were, after all, his forte. But implementing his strategy would take more than thinking. Jenkins knew that the hard part would be in finding a party large enough to help them without wanting an equity stake in the combined companies; in essence, more than just profit. He would be asking for significant financial help from a third party while requiring total fealty from them. He also knew that wasn't realistic.

"It'll be a cold day if and when that happens," he thought.

He developed of a solution to this problem. He would find an intermediary to provide financial assistance, with the potential of a quick and sizable profit serving as their sole incentive. Jenkins wanted a financial partner interested only in profit. Control, or even a voice in the future direction of the target company, was not an option. In short, he was looking for a stooge, or stooges, with deep pockets. Jenkins didn't care if the company providing the financial assistance was aware that they would be playing such a role. He wanted their capital and their capacity to absorb any possible financial commitment that Jenkins would steer their way. As far as Jenkins was concerned, the other company's approval or understanding of Bennington Oil's plan were neither sought nor required.

Jenkins envisioned his third party saviors. They would be men who deal in the securities markets on a regular basis and who had the wherewithal to operate discreetly.

He found such men, three to be precise, and he had them summoned to his office. The dealt in large sums of money and other people's greed or fears—whichever brought them the most money.

The men were New York risk arbitrageurs, and they were the best at what they did. Stanley Hollingsworth, Emmett LaFluer, and Martin Hubbell had made billions for themselves and others, and they seemingly had an endless supply of capital to fund their stock purchases/forays. Jenkins intentionally did not tell them everything he wanted them to do for him when he invited them to San Francisco. He wanted access to their cash, and not their competition.

The three men accepted Jenkins' invitation and flew out to California. All three of them had directed their staffs to scour Bennington Oil and to let them know why their presence was being requested clear across the continent. By the time their planes touched down at San Francisco International, they knew everything pertinent about Bennington Oil that there was to know, even its tenuous relationship with Monty-O. They still had no idea about why they were being summoned to Bennington Oil. Each, however, suspected that the Bennington Oil/Monty-O rivalry was at the heart of the matter.

The three billionaires were interested in Bennington Oil's gambit. They knew that they were being sought out because of their capacity to raise cash. If there was enough profit in it for them they would willingly become part of this. If not, they would still get active and just try to strike a profit. Like Jenkins, they didn't much care for the goals and plans of their potential partner. They were in it to make money. If that helped Bennington Oil, that would be a benefit. If not, they would look for the most profitable position to take and participate from there.

If they joined Jenkins in his plans, they would become a part of one of the most ironic teams ever assembled. They shared neither a common goal nor a trust of each other. They were joined only by their quest for more wealth and want for more power. Strangely enough, that glue was sufficient to the parties attempting this partnership.

Neither side knew what the other side assumed the whole picture to be. The arbs thought that this was a takeover and that they were being asked in. Jenkins thought he had some deep pocketed businessmen looking to make a quick buck.

Jenkins had read the arbs like a book and realized their true position. The arbs thought that they had Jenkins read well too. They saw him as nothing more that a senior corporate type trying to make a name on Wall Street by buying up a competitor. They saw Jenkins as just another little man with a Napoleonic complex.

They had no idea how wrong they would be.

Jenkins leaned forward and motioned the mouse on his computer to the file he was looking for. For Jenkins, the time had come to brush up on some of his not too distant past.

When the arbs sat across from Jenkins four months ago, they felt that they could speak freely. It didn't matter to them if they were being recorded because the nature of the conversation was such that it could only be used for review. This was exactly what Jenkins was doing.

His office was wired for digital recording and there wasn't a spot in it where a microphone couldn't pick up the merest whispers of a conversation. Jenkins had recorded the entire conversation and was now planning on reviewing it to make sure he was certain as to what he promised them, and what their roles were.

He tapped two keys on his computer and the saved digital copy of the recording began playing back. The first voice he heard talking was his.

"We're planning a takeover of Montgomery Oil. When our bids get out everyone will try and get in on it. That'll just run up the price. I'm not interested in paying an additional 10-30% of stock price because of a rush. It's selling for $48 a share now. Buy as much as you can-quietly-a little at a time-and when we take it over I'll give you $55 a share for your holdings."

"But if you run up the price -- or get careless and run up the price--we won't move and you'll get stuck with the stock. As each of you know, you can buy up to 4.999% of the stock without having to file a 13(d) with the SEC, like you have to when you hit that magic 5% level. If you buy 5% or more, you'll have to file with the SEC. Then they'll put it on EDGAR and tell the world. Jenkins didn't much like EDGAR, the Electronic Data Gathering, Analysis, and Retrieval system used by the SEC to perform automated collection of important securities filings. It spread valuable financial information too fast for his liking.

"Wall Street will look at that and say a.) Does he have the kind of backing to pull off this deal--the answer, gentlemen, is yes. b.) The publicizing of your move will attract everyone and the price will skyrocket. We're not going past our line of credit. While we want all of Monty-O, we only need 51%, a simple majority, to accomplish our goals.

"Don't buy any more than that or you'll run the risk of giving the impression that the stock is in play. As it stands, with their computerized trading and electronic stock transaction scrutiny, enough brokerage houses are going to note that someone is buying up this stock. But if the purchases are small enough, they may decide not to get involved. However, if they do decide to get involved, and if they move before we're ready to strike, we won't buy the stock back from you. Play ball and we tie up almost 15% of the company and you're guaranteed a profit.

"Who else is in on this?," asked Hollingsworth.

"No one," Jenkins replied. *"A $5 billion line of credit from a syndicate of banks will back up our end."*

"So why do you want it?" said LaFluer.

"Simple" said Jenkins, *"they have significant petroleum*

reserves and over three quarters of a trillion cubic feet in gas reserves. We would become even larger than we are now."

While Jenkins deliberately left out confidential information he knew about Monty-O; information that he knew they couldn't get. He added, "Also, even though they don't know that we know this, they've spent a fortune on a group of wells off of Louisiana with not much to show for it. That new debt, coupled with their old, is making them an attractive target."

Jenkins wasn't lying. While the core samples looked great, at this time they had made no discovery yet.

"Why isn't anyone else interested?" LaFluer added.

"You buy an oil company and then what?" said Jenkins. *"This deal only makes sense to someone in the business. Their refineries are on the old side, but still in good shape. The oil boom and busts have played havoc in determining their value. But as long as the world's oil producers can't get their act together on oil prices and keep bickering about daily production rates/quotas, that company won't be worth nearly as much as it should be. However, bottom line--I want their reserves. We'll sell or take a charge to our earnings on the rest. We'd also keep some of their service stations in the Northwest. We also want to be the supplier for their network of privately owned operators."*

"I'm telling this to each of you in the strictest confidence. I know that each of you here could complete this deal on your own. I'm including you because this is a chance for you to make a guaranteed killing. I need you to help keep the prices down and to tie up a large block of the stock. Your profits will be my way of saying thanks."

"There won't be any anti-trust or Justice Dept. problems? asked Hubbell.

"There weren't many when Chevron and Texaco merged, and either of them was twice as large as the both of our companies combined. No we aren't that large -- yet."

"Are you three in with us?"

Jenkins leaned forward and put the recorder in its fast-forward mode, but only for a second or two.

Jenkins remembered this part of the conversation as if it had just happened. The three arbs turned and looked at each other and then two of them said yes. Hubbell said that he would join in, but he needed a little time to straighten out a railroad he just bought. He was apparently threatening a takeover when the target company suddenly acquiesced. The upper management took their golden parachutes and jumped. He hadn't planned on actually taking it over, but it was his now.

He restored the recorder to its normal playback speed.

"Give me a few weeks to loosen up some of my resources and I'll buy in" said Hubbell.

"O.K." said Jenkins, *"I picked you three because I know that you can handle your ends. I know that if you went and used every bit of your ability, any one of you could pull this deal off. Hubbell, with your railroad ploy you couldn't take this company now. But in four months you could. I talked with others in this industry and other fields and they told me that you three were good, and that you could be trusted. Trust is a big aspect in this sort of operation. Once our two companies are merged, we'll have hundreds of millions of dollars to invest. If this works out as planned, I'll remember the three of you later. Don't consider this as a one of a kind deal. Think of it as a new and profitable relationship"*

He turned the computer off and leaned back in his chair. The recorded meeting went a few minutes longer but Jenkins had heard all he needed. He remembered giving each of the three men a document that spelled out their roles and the limits of their involvement in the upcoming hostile takeover. He wanted them to take it and read it, which they did. He was not so naïve to believe that they would sign any document chronicling this meeting. That would be tantamount to a confession to insider trading. As far as all the parties were concerned, this meeting never happened.

In a little under four months, the arbs were wishing it hadn't.

Jenkins had a meeting with those same three men in fifteen minutes. He had told them that them that the collision might have changed things and that they needed to come to

S.F. to discuss the change.

Jenkins was well aware that a lot had happened since the first meeting. To start, the first six wells drilled in the Louisiana Project had shown little promise. The next ten however, showed astronomical potential. Monty-O was going full bore to bring this project on-line. Bennington Oil had to either strike soon or lose their chance of taking over Monty-O. Monty-O was still developing the Louisiana Project in secret, fearful that too many questions about the project might lead to even more questions about how they managed to gain the oil leases they were currently working. While they were still leery that their manipulations could cause the project to unravel, Monty-O held to the belief that the courts would be less inclined to overturn a Department of the Interior Minerals Management Service sale if a company had already made a sizable investment and was already producing on it, especially in a critical energy environment.

What Monty-O was not aware of was that Jenkins knew exactly what Monty-O was trying to do, and as long as it fit within his plans, he saw no need to try and disrupt their activities. That time, however, was coming; in fact it was nearly here. Jenkins had but a few more key pieces to position before beginning his gambit. He would be dealing with three of them in the next ten minutes.

Jenkins was aware that the arbs had been busy too. For a guaranteed $7 a share, all they had to do was to legally buy as much of Monty-O as possible without drawing too much attention or setting off takeovers alarms by surpassing the magic 5% limit of the SEC. The SEC's Rule's 13-d required investing parties to file within 10 days their acquisition of 5% or more of any security in a publicly held corporation.

This was a cake walk for financiers used to masking or even hiding their transactions and true intentions. While each of these arbs represented their own privately owned entity, they had each taken great strides to keep their actions quiet. Jenkins was well aware with the manner in which these companies worked and he had been keeping an eye out to see if he could detect their actions. He knew what they would do, or at least what they had planned to do.

They had, in the past, used wholly owned subsidiaries, incorporated in other states and financed by other wholly owned subsidiaries to give the appearance of several independent companies buying the target company's stock, and not just one commanding company providing guidance and opportunity in a synaptic pattern.

Stock trades between individual investors-those who actually hold the stock certificates-need no stock market or brokers to sell. This was one of the arbs favorite ploys. All that they would need is today's Wall Street Journal, a bank account for the funds transfer, the bank account number of the account that the money will be transferred from and a scientific calculator, with a ten digit capacity, to do the math and a short receipt documenting the stock transfer.

Another popular tool, while considered illegal, was stock parking and manipulation by having a separate entity buy it for them and then and sit on it until further notice.

The ability to buy options for stocks was yet another available tool. Options to buy shares simple mean that an investor could structure an automatic share purchase when the stock price hits a certain price point. Options are counted against the 5% limit under the SEC rules, because it does tie up substantial blocks of stock. But you have up to 10 days after you acquire the 5% to file the Form 13-d with the SEC. Options agreements, which can be made very hard to find if the parties so desire, can also change hands every 9 days and not be in violation. If the hands that own the options happen to change to some of those wholly owned subsidiaries, whose ownership is also difficult to ascertain, long periods of time may pass before someone uncovers those options' real owner.

The arbs knew something was up. While they had each stopped their companies from buying more than 5%, through other methods of stock transfer they now controlled over 22% of Monty-O.

The silent gloating of their 22% holdings of Monty-O meant nothing to Jenkins. The arbs were staking a vast amount of their resources and reputations on this deal. They were looking to make a major profit. They knew that the size of their profit depended on the size of their holdings. Even though Jenkins had to them not to individually go beyond the 5% threshold -- they did so emphatically.

Jenkins not only knew that they would do something like this. He was counting on it.

The arbs were simply hoping that the time had come to unload their Monty-O stock, as its price was still in freefall. Their shares of Monty-O stock had lost hundreds of millions in value, and only a pledge by Jenkins to buy it back at a certain level was buoying their feelings.

Jenkins knew they were going to try and force him to buy their stock. Buying it back would, in fact, be the smart thing for him to do, as the arbs had 22% of the target already under their control.

There was just one slight problem, and Jenkins was steeling himself for the angry outburst he knew would come, once he stated it.

In the days that had passed after the collision, the three arbs weren't nervous, but they were the slightest bit apprehensive. They had waited for the announcement from Bennington Oil about the takeover and it had never come. They had spent almost $2 billion of money they controlled and it wasn't looking too well for them. Monty-O stock continued to freefall. It dropped $4 a share the day of the collision and slick. Only the markets suspension of trading Monty-O shares stopped it from dropping further. With the inquiry testimony and the slick on shore, and with the responsibility seemingly resting on Monty-O, their stock dropped $10 more a share. Three days later came the lawsuits; and the stock dropped an additional $5.25 a share. The arbs nearly $2 billion investment had dropped, in just over the last week, more than $800 million. This is not what they had planned at all. In less than two weeks their stock had lost somewhere near 40% in value and the end was not in sight. Accordingly, they were meeting with Jenkins. They wanted a reaffirmation of Bennington Oil's offer to buy their shares at $55 apiece.

"Our shares in Monty-O have dropped tremendously," Hubbell started, "when is your takeover going to begin?"

"It has begun already," Jenkins stated.

Hollingsworth, LaFluer and Hubbell smiled. They knew that once the takeover began they could unload their holdings onto Bennington Oil. The stock had dropped from $48 to the mid-twenties in a few short days and the arbs knew that if this deal fell through that they not only wouldn't recover their purchase price for the stock, but that they would lose hundreds of millions of their, and their investors', money. Even though they had a guaranteed price for the shares they were holding, they would just as soon part with it and collect their profits.

They were, however, in for a shock.

"With the rapid drop in their stock prices," Jenkins began, "we've started making major stock purchases. The formal tender offer will go over in the morning. However, in light of their massive stock slide, I can't give you what I promised."

At first the room went silent. The arbs were used to being the ones making the demands, and Jenkins matter-of-fact tone caught them by surprise. But not for long.

"Bullshit" said Hollingsworth.

"We came in on this to help you out" said LaFluer. "Don't even think of sitting there fat, dumb and happy and even entertain the thought of screwing us."

"Look," Jenkins replied sternly, "their stock is now in the mid-twenties and could hit the high teens before too long. My tender offer will stop their slide. But I can only offer you $30 a share for them. And even that offer is contingent on the effects of further stock price degradation."

"You gotta be kidding us," said Hubbell. "Hell man, we paid up to $48 a share for some of that stock, and we definitely paid more than $30 a share for all of it. Re-member, we were your hedge against the price going up. We came into this to help you out and now you're telling us that you won't even cover the difference."

That's exactly what I'm telling you," Jenkins replied. "I can't pay you $55 a share and give everyone else $30."

"You can't," said Hollingsworth, "or you won't."

"What the hell is that supposed to mean?" snapped Jenkins.

"You assured us that we would be rewarded" LaFluer

started. "Now you try to screw us? What I mean is that I'm beginning to question your motives towards our involvement. It means I think you've used us all along."

"We get a huge chunk of your takeover target together for you and you try to nail us," said Hubbell.

"If the stock went up into the heavens you'd only have given us $7 a share profit," Hollingsworth added. "But if it went to hell, in the event that the Louisiana wells were dry or the price dipped, you'd hold out on us. You couldn't lose any way could you?"

"And," added Hubbell, "With the combined companies in your pocket, you'd have a multi-billion debt load to keep anyone from thinking of taking you over. You're a shrewd bastard, but you're trying to cheat the wrong men."

"Is that so," said Jenkins, sounding more confident of his position, more authoritative. I've thought this out. And I'm going ahead with the plan."

"Do you think so little of us that you could just walk over us?" answered LaFluer. "When we leave this room together we'll talk about combining our resources and you'll see us from a different end of the bargaining table. We have the potential to take over either of these companies without so much as breaking a sweat."

That last comment hung in the air for a moment. The four men stared at each other. Two of the arbs made no attempt at maintaining their composure. The third arb just sat and observed, which was his style. But he was planning and deciding his course of action. The other man was in charge and not only knew it, but reveled in it.

"When the three of you leave this room, you'll do nothing," said Jenkins.

"What makes you so damn confident of that, Jenkins?" asked Hollingsworth. "My first call is going to be to my bankers and..."

"And what?" demanded Jenkins. "Tell your bankers that you're going to take over a company with several billion in debt and I'm almost certain they'll balk."

"I'm taking over Montgomery Oil and that's it. The price has dropped too low for me to give you $55 a share. Everyone will back that up, including the Securities and Exchange Commission. Especially the SEC."

Jenkins let that hang for a minute, especially the part about the SEC.

"You know what else the SEC will back up? Insider trading!"

The three arbs went silent at that point.

"What could you possibly tell them" asked Hubbell, "without implicating yourself?"

"I'll simply tell the truth. If you come after my company or my target company, I'll go right to the SEC and tell them everything. The meetings, the plans--everything."

"Insider trading," began LaFluer, "is only against the law when there is a profit involved. There doesn't seem to be one here. It wouldn't stick."

"It won't?" said Jenkins. "The SEC keeps a very close eye on you arbs. Your entire field is based on insider trading."

"Our field of expertise," shot Hollingsworth, "is based on research, timing, luck and still more research."

"Your field may be," said Jenkins, "but your companies are not. The SEC has been after you gents for a while. They have been paying a close eye on you. If I told them what I know I would get fired and put to pasture. My stock options alone would keep me happy for the rest of my life. But the feds would make me states evidence against you. And remember; when we hatched this plot each of you was expecting to make $7 a share, so there was a definite profit motive involved. I'd be banned from any connection with the stock market. And when they finished with your companies, so would you. This is only my first attempt at insider trading. And I hold no stock in the target company in my name. But you three cannot say that. An SEC investigation, even if it were inconclusive, would dry up your sources for both cash and information. Your friends would find you a little too hot to touch."

"At best, it'll take you years to get back to where you are now. And there's no guarantee what the SEC will find once they get a hold of your records. You'll only lose $15 – 18 a share maximum at the buyback. If you don't take it you could lose considerably more. Once I have controlling interest in the stock, I'll buy back the rest of the company at the prevailing market value. On that day the stock may be higher than it is now, but it won't be higher that what I'm offering you. I suggest that you accept my offer before it's too late. I'm not playing games over this. I'll ruin all of you before I let you ruin my plans."

"Time is short, gentlemen. What's it going to be?"

Jenkins expected to hear the sighs and utterances of dejected men accepting their fates. He had these three men dead to rights, and their choices were to sell out at a big loss or to hold onto their stock and hope for a sudden rise in prices. He felt that they'd take his offer before they lost anymore. Their response shocked him.

The arbs looked at each other, after which LaFluer rose to speak. "I believe I speak for all of us on this..."

Jenkins smiled in anticipation.

"Jenkins, you can go to hell!"

With that the three men rose and walked out.

"The fools," thought Jenkins. Now they're going to lose hundreds of millions of dollars over this when they didn't have to. I won't feel sorry for those bastards, they had their chances and now..."

The phone rang.

The CEO was on the line and wanted to know if the arbs were on board.

"Oh yes," said Jenkins, "the arbs are committing according to my plan. They'll uphold their end of the deal."

The CEO hung up, never once noting that Jenkins had stated that the arbs were committing to his plan and not the "company's" plan. It would be more than a minor distinction.

Jenkins then made another call. This one was to an offshore brokerage company in London. His message was plain and simple.

"Everything has gone according to plan. Execute the Monty-O stock purchase order."

The real battle for Monty-O had begun.

CHAPTER 18

PAINFUL REMINDER

Morris was quiet, sullen and sore. Especially sore.

His head throbbed and he was in a lot of pain. The nature, suddenness and result of the attack were remarkable. Morris never knew what hit him, or just how badly he'd been hit. He just knew that now, he was hurting.

But even in his discomfort, he had other issues to think about. What just happened in the garage was only one of those things. Attacks don't just happen in secured garages with guards and cameras about. Another question bothering him now was, what might happen in the future? He didn't think that what happened to him was a random act of violence. The note clearly showed that he was targeted. But what it was, he was at a loss to explain.

Morris deliberately didn't tell Alice about the call to Martin shortly before the attack. She would have suspected Martin and would have "been on his ass like a cannibal on a missionary." Morris wasn't sure he wanted that. If the attack was related to his asking questions, he wanted to make sure that it didn't involve anyone else. If Alice had gone off accusing Martin, she might unwittingly be brought into danger; a danger he wasn't quite sure how to handle himself.

But there was one thing Morris was sure of. That was that he didn't want any more trouble. Someone had gone through the effort of showing Morris that his questions were not warranted and Morris had every intention of showing them that the message was received. Loud and clear.

His first call was going to Larry Nelson. Morris dialed and waited for the response.

"Nelson, here, how can I help you?"

"Larry," Morris began, "my search for information for you and me throughout Bennington Oil is over. I can't get any more information for you."

"Dave you don't sound so hot." Nelson replied. "Are you O.K.?"

"I'm alright," Morris said, deliberately leaving out the attack and the note, "but I've been told to stop snooping around or do anything outside the purview of my job. I intend to comply with that request."

"I heard you," said Nelson, "but you have to understand that I need your help to find out about my story. Finding out how and why my story got axed is within the purview of your job."

Nelson was getting defensive. Having his story ripped from print was, to him, the professional equivalent of assault and battery. He had no plans to stand idly by and let it happen, or let someone get away with it. But he also had a penchant for speaking his mind, and that didn't always help him.

"I came to you as a friend for help, you can't just walk off now. " He regretted his choice of words as soon as he uttered them.

"What the hell do you mean walk off? I put my ass on the line for you and I've paid for it. I did more for you than I have done for anyone else. And now you feel I'm walking off. You sure have a pathetic way of treating your friends."

"I didn't mean it like that Dave," Nelson stated. "It was a truthful story, one that should be told. Added to what you have told me, we have the makings of a great exclusive. Dave, we're on to something. We can't just let that go. The people of the Bay Area have a need and frankly the right to know."

"We're onto nothing. Everything I've told you was FYI-for your information. It was not for print. You knew that when I started getting answers for you. This company's onto something big, but that's not for me to say and definitely not for you. Everything I told you is moot, Larry. If any of this shows up in print you will have betrayed a trust and, he paused, you will have lost a friend. I wonder sometimes if your concern is to inform the people or just to get a byline."

The hard 'click' at the end of the line told Nelson that this argument and phone call was over.

Nelson set his receiver down. Confusion was an understatement. For the second time in a week he'd had a story killed from under him. He was beginning to hate this feeling. He thought of Morris.

"That bureaucratic chicken," he thought, *"That bastard acts like he's hot stuff but when it's time to put up he punks out. Fine I'll develop another angle and do this story."*

Yet, Nelson only half believed this. He was lashing out at Morris because he simply didn't know what to do next. Deep inside, he knew Morris was OK, and that if he was told to cool it then the pressure must really be on.

"I'll talk to him in a few days" said Nelson"

With that, Nelson went back to his research. On his desk was a portfolio of information on the American Airlines Flight 191, from Chicago to Los Angeles. In 1979, 273 people were killed in the country's worst single plane disaster when an engine detached from the wing on takeoff, leading the aircraft to stall and crash after less than a mile in flight.

The Gazette was doing a major story on airline safety and Nelson was selected to write it. While full of enthusiasm when this story was first assigned two days ago, he was now dwelling and obsessing about why his last story got the axe, and the situation his friend now found himself in.

CHAPTER 19

REMINISCING

Alice called the court and asked to have her trial extended due to Morris' attack. Dave's grogginess was gone and now replaced by a surly moodiness.

Nine hours after getting home from the hospital Morris was still moody. He stayed in bed more from Alice's angered insistence than actually wanting to.

Alice was going about straightening up the house. She put a lot of effort in the breakfast Morris didn't eat and she was getting irritated. She made no real attempt to hide it either.

By eleven a.m., Morris had spent the last four hours soul searching. He received a warning last night in the form of a knot on his head the size of a small egg and fifteen stitches. He knew what the warning was for and why it was so severe.

"They know about my computer forays with Phil and they didn't appreciate it," he thought

"Phil," Morris uttered. "Oh no!"

He called Bennington Oil security and asked to speak with Phil.

"You can't," came the reply, "he's been fired."

"Why?" Morris asked.

"Don't know why," was the retort, "I do know this. It was sudden and complete. He had a company scholarship to pay for his computer degree. He was only two quarters away from either being a senior or graduating. All that's gone now because he doesn't have any money. Hell he owes half of us money, but I don't think he planned to get fired to get out of paying us back."

Morris thanked the guard at the other end and before hanging up, asked the guard for Phil's home number, which he wrote on a scrap of paper he pulled out of his pocket.

His concern and interest into what the company was doing had turned into an obsession. It now turned into remorse for what his single mindedness had brought onto a total innocent.

"I was so concerned about what I was doing that I sacrificed Phil's future as if it was nothing. I didn't have that right."

He thought about telling Alice but stopped. She's got nothing to do with this and I've involved enough innocents. He again retreated into his thoughts.

Alice was lying on her side, totally upset. It was half past midnight, just thirty hours after Dave's attack, and things could not be worse.

First, Dave gets attacked, then the note and then came the negative attitude he had taken with not just her, but everything, for most of the evening.

She had tried to close the gap with affection. In her most sensual ways she enticed Morris into making love.

She knew there was a problem right from the start. She spent more time than ever before trying just to entice him. She recalled that he never needed much before. A quick wink and a nod towards the bedroom and he was always in the right mood.

But not tonight. It was as though he were fulfilling a half-hearted contractual obligation. The lovemaking equivalent to "Yeah, whatever."

The lovemaking was a letdown.

There was no hug, no basking in each other's arms, no afterglow. Just...nothing.

She turned on her side and fought back tears. This wasn't the first real crisis in their relationship. Like most couples they had their ups and downs. But she had always been able to handle those bad times; she didn't know how to handle this one. She had never encountered a total lack of affection during lovemaking from him before. It was as though a stranger had taken over Morris and had him trapped deep down inside. She didn't know how to reach him.

She thought about the tough times they had just getting together and having to deal with life's tragedies and the views and perspectives of family members that thought their union wasn't the best she could do.

She had first noticed him in college. He attended the California State University at Sacramento, while she attended UC Davis. As her parents were Howard and Cynthia Bradford, the successful and highly regarded lawyers from Sacramento, attending UC Davis presented no real financial problems for her. Alice's family had cash to spare, and when they felt it necessary, they used it to exert their influence. Morris was a different story.

He went to Cal State Sacramento purely because it was a bargain. He attended their U.S. Air Force Reserve Officer Training Corps program and that scholarship, added to what other meager funds he could pull together, was enough for him to attend school.

She noticed him one morning while she was running with some friends. He was leading the detachment in their drills and she was impressed with the way and the manner he was holding himself. To her, he looked as though he should be leading people.

Inquiring through a friend who was dating a member of the detachment, she found out his name and phone number. By the time that the ten days passed that she needed before she gathered the courage to call him, her friend had told her boyfriend about her interest and he relayed it to Morris.

When they first spoke she was impressed with his calm and pleasing demeanor. She thought she had hooked a live one. It would be many months before she found out that he had spent several days practicing his first conversation with her.

They spent a lot of their college days in love and making love. In their last year of college they were so inseparable that many thought that they would be married right after graduation. But the cold hand of reality, in the form of an unimpressed mother and a four to six year commitment to the U.S. Air Force, soon placed itself upon their shoulders.

Cynthia Bradford had a different life planned for her daughter, and it wasn't being a military wife following her spouse to all god-forsaken parts of the world. Alice loved Morris and wanted to marry him. He felt the same way towards her. But Alice's mother was throwing up a wall of resistance that the two were finding hard to tear down. Cynthia assumed that once he went on active duty and assigned far away, that through the stark reality of a long term separation from each other, that their daughter would see the correctness in her plans.

Alice and Morris were about to embark on their own plan of action when their situation got more convoluted. Alice received numerous admissions to law schools and had selected Harvard's. She and Morris knew that this would complicate their lives but they had planned to work through it.

In helping her with her preparations to leave for law school he barely left himself enough time to drive to Randolph AFB in Texas for pilot training.

As he was just getting ready to drive to Texas he thought *"If absence made the heart grow fonder, here was a test for the ages."*

But it was not to be.

Morris began his drive and spent his first night in Los Angeles. He called her as soon as he settled in for the night and told her of his day. She listened intently and then shared her day. The conversation ended with them telling each other that they loved the other. And that they were finding the challenges of their new lives to be exciting. He ended their conversation by telling her that he was planning to travel almost 500 miles to Tucson tomorrow and that he would call her once he got there. He would never make that call.

Morris hit the road early and after a long drive made it to Phoenix. After stretching his legs a bit and having dinner in Phoenix, Morris left for the last 110 miles of the day. Night had fallen by now, but Morris felt he had enough left in him to make it to Tucson. He had driven almost an hour and a half, and was getting close to his night's destination. It was barely 10 p.m. and Morris was just cruising along. He had made reservations to stay at nice hotel and only had to cover another twenty miles before 11 p.m. to hold the reservation.

It was here that his destiny would be forever changed by a man he would never meet and who was driving his car at over twice the legal drinking limit. Harry Wolters figured that he was so drunk that he needed to drive home fast so that the cops didn't catch him. He had no idea how impaired he was when he came down the off ramp and sped past ninety miles an hour going the wrong way. As there are few cars on the Interstate after 10 p.m., he saw no warning signs that he was on the wrong lane. He began to notice that the opposing lanes of the freeway were on the right side of his car instead of the left and began to get the feeling that something was wrong.

He looked down the interstate and saw the headlights of an oncoming car reflecting off of the supporting legs of the upcoming overpass. Wolters panicked and hit the brakes. He immediately lost control of the car, and it swerved, hard and fast, smashing into the bridge supports and, literally, exploded on impact.

The engine and most of the powertrain tore away during the crash and hurtled down the freeway into the path of the oncoming car.

Morris barely saw the accident play out in front of him and before he could even think, the engine of Wolters' car smashed through the front quarter panel, right before the driver's door and tore through the passenger compartment before exiting through the side of the car just behind the passenger's seat. Morris was still in the car as it rolled to a stop on fire. He tried to open his seat belt but his body position was all wrong. His head was nearly touching the driver side door armrest and his legs were...he couldn't really tell which direction they were pointing. He gave two hard pulls on the seat belt before he lowered his head and closed his eyes. He could smell the smoke but he didn't have the strength to get out. He pounded on the door three times before darkness overwhelmed him.

As in so many drunken driving accidents, Wolters was so inebriated that his reflexes operated too slowly for him to tense up before the impact. This looseness allowed him to emerge from the accident almost unscathed. He stood up and briefly stared at his totally destroyed car when he saw another car rolling to a stop on fire. He stumbled over to it and even in his drunken state he went to it and opened the door and dragged its unconscious occupant out before the flames engulfed the rest of the car. Wolters stayed until the authorities arrived. He had a few cuts and bruises but nothing serious.

Morris wasn't so lucky.

He was in the hospital almost a week before he regained full consciousness. When he did he never realized how badly a person could hurt and still be alive. The prognosis was bad. His left leg had nearly been severed and his right one only broken in four places, one a compound fracture. The swelling in his brain had subsided enough so that the induced coma could be curtailed. The wire holding his jaw shut prevented an airway from being inserted, but after he started breathing on his own a simple oxygen hose to his nose was sufficient. The first and second degree burns that covered a third of his body weren't that bad considering the amount of fire, and it was felt that they wouldn't leave much, if any, scarring. No additional surgery was planned for the damaged internal organs and fractured ribs, since the two he had already received were expected to do the trick.

As he was on orders and was traveling to his first assignment, the Air Force took over his care. His parents were brought to him and stood vigil over him. He was not safe yet, and any problems with his legs could mean amputation at best and death at its worst. His recovery was slated to take months, possibly years.

Alice wondered why she hadn't heard from him for three days after he left Los Angeles. Her calls to his parents' house remained unanswered as well. She had no doubts about his feelings for her, but she was concerned for the worst. Her fears were confirmed when she read an internet news article about a near fatal late night crash outside of Tucson.

She caught the first flight out and didn't even bother to pack.

The staff at the hospital wouldn't allow her into his room, but the involvement of Morris's parents made it happen. She started crying at her first sight of him. The man she idolized was now lying in a hospital bed smashed beyond belief. Her first instinct was to try and help him, but the nurses stepped in and cautioned her against that.

"He's way too hurt for you to help," was the comment she took from that day.

When they finally let her in, she didn't leave his side for the next eighteen hours. At that point he was unable to acknowledge that she was there. That didn't matter. She was there for him and that was that! She called her parents and told them of what happened and she told them that if they said one word about them breaking up that she would never talk to either of them again. Her mother realized that her daughter was in more pain that she would ever let on and she caught the first flight to Tucson. She didn't pack either, but she had her Nordstrom personal shopper call ahead and pick out wardrobes for her and her daughter.

Morris would spend the next four weeks in the Tucson hospital until he was well enough to be transferred to Lackland AFB's Wilford Hall Medical Center for continuing convalescence. They told him not to make any plans for the immediate future.

Morris kept asking questions about his time in the hospital and he couldn't get straight answers. The doctors had no answers to give him. They told him that despite the therapy and continued work by some of the best orthopedic doctors in the southwest, he was still months away from trying to stand on his own legs and that no one knew what would happen then.

Morris was facing an uncertain future. His knew his career plans were gone. So was his health. All that was left to him was his mind. And someone so dear to him that he needed to make a fateful decision for her that she would never made for herself.

He called Alice into his room and told her that she

needed to get herself to law school. She disagreed stating that her place was with him. He felt warmly about that and then started the hardest thing he ever had to do. He told her that he might never leave a wheelchair. He pointed to the wheelchair that was positioned in the corner of his room; awaiting the day he was healthy enough to try it. He told her that she needed to begin planning a life without him.

"Do you think I'd leave you because of that? You know me way better than that to think, or to say, something like that. I'm here until..."

He then turned to hard cold fact.

"The average life span a someone like me is less than fifteen years. Even if I could provide for you, take care of you or make love to you, I won't be in fifteen years. You need to start your life without me now, before you've committed too much of your life to..." His voice trailed off.

She left the room in tears.

His mom came in the room sat down next to him. She reached out and held his hand. Nothing more needed to be said.

Alice left for the airport the next morning. Her mom Cynthia was aware of everything and tried to offer some solace, although she was not unhappy that Alice and Morris were no longer going to be together. She wasn't aware that her daughter knew exactly how she felt.

As they parted for their respective airlines Alice looked back to her mother and said, "Looks like your wish came true."

Morris spent the next year and a half getting better and re-learning how to walk again. Then, to run. His whole family had spent time with him in San Antonio during the early months, but they were now all back in San Francisco. His recovery had gone so well that when he left the hospital and therapy he moved in with his parents back in SF. He got a job with a small PR firm that worked mainly for small internet startup firms. His work was exemplary and promotions came fast.

Then came the double whammy. The dot.com crash hit at the same time he found out that his beloved older sister had breast cancer. The head of his firm told a friend at Bennington Oil about Morris and they sought him out and hired him. His salary doubled and he helped his parent in their efforts to fight his sister's cancer. The whole family spent all of their waking hours either working or trying to help their ailing member. Unfortunately it was a battle against an tenacious enemy that they would not win. She fought hard for eight long years, but in the end the results were preordained. She died in the hospital surrounded by the family that loved her. The parents were devastated, emotionally and financially. It took Morris' help for them not to lose their home. It was a price he gladly paid.

Now nearly ten years after his accident, he now had to go out and get his life together. He didn't realize how fast those years had gone by.

On a business trip to Sacramento to discuss oil and taxation policy with their lobbyists, Morris stopped to have lunch in a little bistro. He and the Bennington Oil staff he traveled with always stopped here during their monthly sojourns. He enjoyed the food and the fact that he and his fellow PR staffers could have an uneventful lunch in the state's capital. On this one trip, he would be wrong.

Unbeknownst to him, Cynthia Bradford, Alice's mother, was also there. She couldn't believe what, or more directly, who, she was seeing. She stayed in the rear of her booth so that she could see him without him noticing her. The friends she was lunching with didn't seem to notice her change.

The last time she saw him he wasn't physically able to use a wheelchair. But now, save for a barely noticeable limp that she registered when he walked past, she couldn't believe that this was the same man. At six foot even, height-weight proportionate and of handsome demeanor, she marveled at his recovery. She couldn't believe it had been almost ten years. She thought that he had grown so well into himself. She saw him laughing and having fun with the other people he was with and she began to think of her own daughter and how different she had become.

Alice blamed her breakup on her parents and she let them know it. She went to law school and literally threw herself into it. 100% of her time and efforts went into her studies and upkeep. The result was graduating third in her class.

While she was arguably the best looking, most attractive woman in her class, she didn't date or even seek male accompaniment during her whole law school experience. She remained somewhat aloof in the years since as well.

Her mother privately mourned the loss of her baby daughter's happiness and had come to regret her interference. The thought that she and her husband should have stayed out of their daughter's love life and simply support the choices that they spent so much time preparing her to make, was never far from her.

Alice was highly regarded in the Bay Area legal circles for her thoughtful legal work. While her professional life was in top gear, she had no personal life to speak of. She seemed OK with this. Or so she let people believe that was the case. She knew better. So did her mother.

Her parents tried hooking her up with numerous suitors, but the result was always the same. She was not at a loss for interested partners; she just didn't care to get serious.

Her mother had tried once to ask why she didn't seem to be interested in dating and the response she received cut her to the core. Alice told her that she was looking for someone that she could love and that would meet her parent's standards. Her mom told her that they had no say in who or what type of man would make her happy. Alice told her that their objections made the one man she cared for push her away at the moment he needed her the most. He wanted her to be happy to the point that he overlooked his own very pressing needs to try and make her and her family happy. Alice told her mom that she realized that she didn't know how to love someone and make that person, her and her parents happy. So she stopped trying and just concentrated on her career.

And then she told her mom something that her body language already had. She was lonely and miserable. She told her mom that she had given thought to quitting law and moving away, as San Francisco was where everything had happened.

Her mom told her to stop crying and to take tomorrow off

and come spend the day with her. Alice agreed, but she didn't know why. She liked Sacramento enough, but it wasn't San Francisco. But then, nothing and nowhere is like San Francisco.

They spent the morning shopping and just hanging out together. The mom was realizing firsthand how unhappy her daughter was and the daughter realizing that her mother only had her best interest at heart.

At 11:30 mom said she was hungry and knew a nice little place to get a bite. Alice wasn't that hungry, but she was enjoying her time with her Mom

After they sat down and their food was served Cynthia asked Alice a pointed question.

"Alice, you do know that we were just thinking of what might be best for you, don't you?

"Yes, Mom I realize that. I didn't want to at first, but I knew that you were just thinking about my future."

"Alice, you do realize that we were wrong and we are so sorry for the pain it's caused you?"

"I know Mom," Alice replied. "And I'll try harder to make things better for myself."

"OK," said Mom. "You know that with everything I've ever done for you, your happiness was my goal right?"

"Yes, Mom." Alice continued, "Mom, is there something I should know? What are you trying to ask me?"

"No," Cynthia began, "There is nothing you should know. But if you turn around there's something you should see."

She turned around and couldn't believe her eyes. While she was facing her mom she didn't see Morris and his company lobbyists enter the restaurant and sit down.

He had just sat down and told the hostess how wonderful she looked when he glanced over and saw Alice. His double take was so noticeable that the other members of his party turned around and tried to see what he was looking at.

They saw each other across the restaurant for the first time in a decade. She couldn't believe he was walking on his own. His fear of being disabled for the rest of his life had not come to pass. She couldn't believe he was walking on his own. He couldn't believe how incredibly beautiful she had become, even more so since he had seen her.

Cynthia couldn't believe that she was trying to put them back together.

Alice looked back at her mom in near stunned disbelief.

"I saw him here last month when members of his office come up here to meet with certain governmental subcommittees and whatnot" she said almost casually. "The hostess told me that they always come here, they being the SF oil contingent, I made a few calls to friends in the legislature and found out that he'd be coming back.

"Alice, "Cynthia began, "I am so sorry that we caused you to doubt your ability to love. We only wanted the best for you, but we forgot to ask you what that could be. I don't know what's going to happen here in the next few moments, but I hope it'll help you to forgive us."

"Mom," Alice smiled, "All was forgiven long ago."

"Look at him Mom; he seems so, so…"

"Handsome" Mom started, "marvelous, cool, and good."

"All of the above" Alice added.

"Mom, it's been ten years," Alice enquired. "Do you think he could be married or have someone else in his life?

"No he doesn't" Cynthia began. "I had him checked out by some of my Bay Area friends. But you remember his sister."

"Yes, she and I got along really well."

"She passed away from cancer just over a year ago, I guess his family's struggles to help her has kept him focused on that."

Alice's eyes lost a bit of their luster on that news.

Her mom noticed it immediately and spoke again.

"Honey, you can't do anything about his loss. You can use it to try and bring back some of the good things you guys shared, you know, the times you spent with him and her. She would love to be up there looking down and seeing shared memories of her helping to make her brother happy again. I know I would."

Cynthia looked at her watch

"Damn. Where has the time gone?"

She took a credit card and a note and gave them to the hostess.

"I have to leave now. Could you please see that my daughter gets lunch and could you please hand this note to that dashing man over there. Thanks"

The note simply invited Morris to come and rest his feet under Alice's table.

They've been resting there now for four years.

Since that lunch four years ago a day hasn't passed where a happy daughter doesn't take the time to thank her mother. Or where a happy mother doesn't thank the heavens for giving her the chance to make her daughter smile again. Or where a young exec doesn't rejoice in being able to correct the worst decision he ever made, albeit with the best decision he ever made.

Alice stopped her reverie and forced herself to revisit the present. The reality of what was now facing Morris was as unknown as it was daunting. She was literally trying to resolve a problem without knowing any facts, clues or other substantive evidence.

Alice had gone back to these past memories, these happy moments, for a reason. She needed to draw on the strength of a past success, of overcoming a giant problem, to help her navigate the one before her now.

"We got through that," she thought, *"we'll get through this. I just need to figure out how?"*

While he slept she got up and went into the living room.

"Everything's gone wrong" she thought. *"He's never been this distant. He won't tell me about the note. He won't tell me about the attack. And now this."*

"What's he afraid of?"

She looked over at his neatly folded clothes in the living room. She had folded them and placed them there after they got home from the hospital and meant to move them earlier.

"It doesn't matter," she said, *"the guy who wore them last night isn't the guy here now."*

"If he'd just tell me maybe I could help....."

She looked back over at his clothes. She turned to look and see if he was still sleeping and when she saw that he was she got up and walked over to the pants.

She checked to see if the wallet was still there. After turning back to see if Morris was still sleep she gently pulled the wallet out.

She had only begun to rifle through it when she found a note. Holding it up, the note stated, 'Call Nelson about article" followed by what she suspected to be Nelson's phone number. There was another phone number on the scrap of paper as well. It was a seven digit number, followed by the name "Phil." She didn't know anyone named Phil. However, she did know Nelson.

She looked around again and got a pen and wrote down the number. She returned the wallet and neatly folded the pants again. She didn't want him to notice that she had been snooping, or that his clothes might be able to tell her what he wouldn't; or at least reveal to her a source that could help her fill in the blanks.

She had known Larry Nelson for a while, having met him through Dave. They've even entertained each other on occasion and while they have always enjoyed each other's' company, she always questioned his lack of feminine companionship. He was a little overweight and decent height and looks. She had wondered before whether he was just gay or extremely particular about the company he kept.

However none of that mattered now. She just wanted help and he seemed like the person who could best provide it.

She took her cell phone out onto the balcony and called Nelson. She had forgotten the time until she heard Nelson's groggy voice on the other end of the phone.

"Larry," she began, "this is Alice, Dave Morris's friend."

"I know you," Nelson replied, "is everything OK? Is Dave OK?"

"I don't know," she continued, "I think he's in some kind of trouble, but he won't tell me. I was wondering if you might have an idea of what might be going on."

"Alice," Nelson began, "I don't know what might be going on. He and I are working on finding some answers about a stunt that Bennington Oil pulled on my paper this week."

"Funny," Alice started, "it was in the garage of the Bennington Oil Building that he got beat up and..."

"Beat Up!" Nelson said. "He got beat up?"

"Not only that," Alice added, "but they have cameras all over that garage but none of them seem to have captured any images of the attacker. Larry I..."

"Alice," Nelson interrupted, "I'm going to tell you everything I know about what he's doing and then you can tell me everything you know. Leave nothing out."

For the next forty five minutes they told each other all they knew about Morris' travails.

They ended their conversation by agreeing that forewarned is forearmed, and that they would both have to work towards protecting Morris from what might happen next.

She hung up with Nelson with the first smile she'd had since the attack. She was so encouraged that she didn't even notice the chill of being on her balcony in her nightclothes in the wee hours of the morning.

She went back inside and got back in bed with the feeling that tomorrow would be a different day.

CHAPTER 20

ENLIGHTENMENT

Morris sat in the corner of his living room, sipping his coffee and staring out of the window. Alice told him that she has had it with his attitude and decided to go to work.

"At least there I'll get paid for dealing with rudeness," was her parting quote. It stung.

Morris knew he hadn't been on his best behavior and hurting her feelings was not what he wanted. But he did nonetheless and he realized that he would have to make it up to her. Not just the rudeness and the surliness, but the shutting her out and not telling her what he had involved himself in. She knew something was going on and she resented being kept in the dark. She wasn't used to not being able to help someone, let alone someone she loved.

Morris walked over to his computer desk and opened a small drawer. He withdrew a small flash drive and held it in his outstretched hand and looked at it. He and Phil had downloaded this information two days ago and he hadn't even reviewed it. He had simply been overwhelmed by the other aspects of his life.

As he looked at the flash drive he wondered how such a little device could contain information so important that he would be attacked based on what people thought was on the drive, and not what might actually be on it.

He shuddered at the thought of the punishment he had

taken being for naught because the drive didn't work.

"Now," he thought, "Is the time to see what all of this nightmare might be about."

He sat down and turned his computer on. In no time he was accessing the files that he and Phil had purloined.

"*So far so good*," thought Morris

They had managed to get three files before the security system closed them out, and Morris was wondering what might be in them. He scanned their titles thinking he might find a clue. One was a memo with three investors summarizing a meeting that had taken place two days ago. One was a company operating statement. The last one was a three page memo called the "Louisiana Project."

Morris printed each of the documents and turned off his computer. He pulled the documents from the printer tray and walked back over to the chair he had been in. He had refreshed his coffee and now sat down to see just what kind of Pandora 's Box he had opened.

He looked up at the clock and noticed the time.

"Looks like a good time for reading." he joked

Less than three hours later he would have most of the answers he sought. He would also have the frightening realization that he was way over his head in this matter, and had been ever since he got involved in it.

CHAPTER 21

LOUISIANA PROJECT

Hundreds of millions of years ago the earth was occupied, and dominated, by a different form of life. Among them were the largest species of animals ever to roam the earth, and the largest to ever swim the seas. They were the dinosaurs. Some were as small as house pets while others had wingspans that rivaled those of aircraft. Some were as large as a three-story house and fed on other dinosaurs, while others, even larger, fed on vegetation.

Though their numbers were countless, they all had a common trait; something that may have led them all to share the same fate. All dinosaurs shared a nearly nonexistent intelligence level.

They literally lived their long dull lives and died, accomplishing nothing more than mere existence. It almost seemed that in the overall scheme of things, they were damned to do no more than to breed others of their kind to share the same fate that befell them. How many millions of years this went on may never be known. What is known is that the valueless existence they endured in life would be directly contradicted by the valuable substance they would become in death. It seems that the works of fate are not always ended by death. The ultimate fate of the dinosaurs' remains may be history's best example of that.

The dinosaurs roamed the earth aimlessly, as their

miniature brains did not possess the power to provide them with meaning or direction. They simply lived and died. Over countless millennia, billions upon billions of these dinosaurs died, each depositing their carcasses over the generations that preceded them.

As soon as they laid down and took their last breaths, they began the transformation that still escapes total definition. Dust kicked up by volcanic activity or carried in the wind would begin settling on the remains. For the fishes and mammals that died in the seas, particulate matter carried in the currents accomplished the same tasks. The dinosaur remains would eventually become buried, and throughout millions of years the sediments over them would grow deeper and deeper, causing the remains to become compressed under tremendous pressure. This pressure, combined with time, heat from the inner cores of the earth, and the processes of nature would transform the former dinosaurs into a primordial soup that, with more time, would become petroleum. It is not known how much petroleum was contained, or better yet, derived from each dinosaur. No equation could be constructed to determine how many barrels of crude one could extract from a tyrannosaurus rex. But it must be remembered that dinosaurs were plentiful, and their time on earth is not measured in years, but eras.

The dinosaurs, in all of their varieties and species, lived all over the world and, as such, died all over the world. Each time the transformation would begin anew. And again, fate would intervene.

When millions dinosaurs around the world died, their carcasses would be scattered in millions of places, in the very spots were they fell. Thus, when the transformation that turned their remains into petroleum began, it wouldn't be in just one location, but in millions of them.

Because of seismic activity, changes in gravity or the tremendous pressures that exist at depths below two, three, four or however many thousands of feet, the individual pockets of petroleum were literally squeezed into others, forming large and sometimes immense deposits of petroleum. When geologic forces are exerted, they compressed the soil in the surrounding areas, which serves to drive out the less dense materials. These materials generally include water, minerals of lighter density, petroleum and other liquids. Stepping on a sponge full of water would represent a correct analogy. When the pressure hits a certain point, the liquid is forced out and must go elsewhere. This is exactly how major petroleum deposits are formed. Forces of such tremendous magnitude have occurred that the petroleum underground was forced out of its pockets (the pockets where it may have been formed millions of years ago) to travel through the soil in the direction where the pressure is least. Through random chance, the petroleum may be squeezed into other pockets, which would lead to the formation of large deposits. These deposits would move to the beck and call of any larger geologic forces, becoming stationary only when they have either reached a large enough size to contend with those forces, when they have come up against soil of higher density than that from which they were excluded (in which case they would have been forced back into the area of lesser density) or when they've have come up against a fault, an anticline or a salt dome.

A salt dome is a large area of salt, thousands of feet below the surface which, through earthquakes or other disturbances, pokes upward like an underground mountain. Salt provides an impenetrable barrier to petroleum, so whenever the two meet, the petroleum is always trapped against the side of the salt dome.

When a company engages in an offshore exploratory drilling, one thing that the petroleum engineers always look for is the presence of salt in their core samples. They know that there is a better chance of discovering oil off of or near a salt dome. It was exactly this that the geologist of Montgomery Oil were looking for just nineteen months ago. And they found it, too.

One hundred thirty eight miles off the Louisiana coastline, the drill ship 'Crustacean' had taken a navigational reading to verify their position. They had been at this spot for three weeks and had taken some very positive samples. Because of the glowing outlook, the morale on board was at an all-time high. The majority of drilling done by an exploratory ship generally turns out to be dry holes. But this time they knew that they were going to hit pay dirt. It was a feeling that was caused by the brownish residue that clung to the gray aggregate that they had been extracting from their test drills. The brown substance was petroleum. The grayish rocky matter, smudged with brown and black, was an extraction from a salt dome. All evidence pointed to the discovery of a good sized deposit.

The crew was ecstatic. They were all on the high that comes from success. That was, until they took the latest navigational reading. For three weeks, they had remained stationary while running test drills down to 6700 feet. Before they dropped the drill string they had made certain that they were on the exact coordinates given to them by the United States Department of the Interior.

And for three weeks, they thought they were. Then during an equipment check, one that should have been done routinely but apparently wasn't, an electrician had found a loose wire in the satellite navigational positioning system. The machine was not getting full power and at best, could not be considered accurate. Correcting the problem in the machinery was child's play for the electrician. Correcting the problem it had caused would not be.

A review of the discrepancy revealed that their true position was 23 miles southwest from where it should have been. Totally unknown to the crew, up to that point, was the fact that they had been drilling in the wrong spot.

Realizing that the company headquarters in San Francisco would not be overjoyed that the drill ship 'Crustacean' had, for $500,000 a week, been drilling in the wrong spot for three weeks, the captain and the chief engineer called for the retrieval of the drill string and set a course for the correct site. The core samples, and the test results on them, were locked away.

The crew, noticing the activity, was told of the error caused by the malfunction. The incident would have ended there if it weren't for a bizarre bit of organizational pettiness.

Johansen & Oliver Petroleum Exploration had set up a

drilling rig in an attempt to tap the riches they believed their tract held. Their 12,300 acre tract was near that of Montgomery Oil's, and they were watching Monty-O closely. It was a classic case of "if fortune finds them, then it should find us." Johansen & Oliver was banking on Monty-O finding a large deposit, and then riding on the coattails of their rival's success.

They had watched with interest as the 'Crustacean' passed near their rig and headed for its own tract. However, none of them were ready for the surprise of seeing the 'Crustacean' sail out of sight. The ship they thought would be working a few miles away from them had sailed on for another twenty-six miles before dropping anchor.

While they were surprised at this development, they shrugged it off and went to work on their own project. Three weeks later, the ship again cruised into sight, this time stopping four miles away and started what appeared to be preparations for an extended stay. The chief engineer on Morgan Petroleum's drilling rig thought that to be peculiar. He couldn't believe that they could have given up on a tract in such a short period of time. He relayed this information to the Houston offices of Johansen & Oliver. The executives there simply assumed that Monty-O had purchased more than one tract, and after hitting a few dry holes had decided to explore another tract. Just to be sure, they had placed a call to the headquarters of Montgomery Oil and asked for verification.

The chief of Monty-O's geologic section was informed of this and called the offshore supply company that had the contract to service the 'Crustacean'. They had a chopper fly out to where their ship had been and, it wasn't there.

A teleconference between Edward Richardson, Monty-O's CEO, company geologic and shipping specialists, and key crewmembers of the 'Crustacean' then ensued.

Richardson was livid, stating that "stockholders don't like to see millions of dollars being spent meaninglessly by incompetent seamen."

The captain didn't like this assault on his abilities, but he wasn't exactly in a position to talk back. Then he remembered the samples locked away below. It was his trump card and now was the time to play it.

Undoubtedly jobs would have been lost if it weren't for the fast thinking ship captain, whose next statement stopped all of them in their tracks.

While the higher-ups in San Francisco were clamoring for blood, the captain politely inquired.

"We were out there for three weeks. Don't you want to know what kind of core samples we got, and how they tested?"

Richardson immediately stopped his lambasting of the ship's captain and stared at the assembled staff. His scowl turned into a muted grin as he looked back to the intercom. Two thousand miles away, in the middle of the Gulf of Mexico, a ship's captain smiled.

"Sir, according to your geologist here on board, we may have discovered a giant deposit."

The core samples were placed on a helicopter and flown back to shore, where a chartered cargo plane waited to take them to Houston. There, an independent lab confirmed what the sea captain had said. There's oil under this tract, and lots of it. This made for a lot of happy men at the headquarters of Monty-O. But in their revelry they had forgotten one important fact. The tract in question did not belong to them. In fact it was still part of the U.S. government, as it had never been offered for auction.

But Richardson didn't get to be CEO of Montgomery Oil by taking 'no' for an answer. His philosophy was simple. "Anyone can attempt the impossible, but you've got to be one smart son-of-a-bitch to do the impossible." They didn't come smarter than Richardson.

The first thing he did was to send the 'Crustacean' and her crew back to work on their proper tract, and told them not to tell anyone of their errant discovery. With them out of the way for a while, he started the groundwork for what he would code name 'the Louisiana Project'.

But then, almost as if by design, events began to occur that benefited Montgomery Oil.

The Department of the Interior was about to allow exploratory drilling off of northern California and environmentalists went crazy. The federal government was using the highest oil prices in recent memory to try and force drilling off of California. It didn't work.

Articles in newspapers about the effects of pollution, exposes on the safety record of offshore rigs in California, and a massive media blitz against opening up the areas for exploration met the Department of the Interior's decision.

Against this media storm the department pressed on. As it wasn't an election year, the complaints weren't given much credence at the department. An injunction, however, carries much more weight. And it was just this tactic that the environmentalist used. The 9th District Court signed an injunction that told all concerned that there would be no offshore drilling off of northern California, test or otherwise, until key safety issues had been discussed. The oil industry was outraged at being handcuffed like this and they weren't about to take it sitting down.

Oil companies need to explore for oil if they are to provide energy for the nation. They go out of business if they don't. Almost all of them, however, have prepared for any contingencies, this notwithstanding. As their primary efforts had failed, the companies readied themselves for round two.

The dictionary defines the word lobby as "a group of persons who conduct a campaign to influence the voting of legislators." The petroleum industry has one of the best.

The lobbyists were now being called upon to pick up the banner of their respective companies and take the fight to the highest law of the land - Congress. The lobbyists went into the offices of hundreds of Congressmen, a lot who wouldn't have been elected if it weren't for the generosity of the oil companies and those in the petroleum industry.

They told the elected representatives that they were trying to find new oil to keep America strong and that they were being thwarted by a few active, but misguided citizens. When the Congressmen realized that offshore drilling was a sensitive subject in northern California, and more importantly out of their Congressional districts, many of them saw no need to get personally involved. While being somewhat upset at their initial lack of success, the lobbyist recognized the tenuous positions that they were asking these elected officials to make, especially since a lot of them had no stake in the matter, either legislatively or personally.

The lobbyists, realizing that traditional methods might not work, tried a different tack. They went back to the same Congressmen and asked them if they would ask the Department of the Interior to open up a different area for petroleum exploration. Thus while the issues in California were being worked out, the money and plans that had been laid out for the California tests/exploration could be diverted elsewhere, instead of sitting idle. Many of the Congressmen liked this approach and called on the Secretary of Interior with it.

Had only one or two Congressional offices called about this, chances are the Secretary would have let it ride. But when the 19th called, he knew he needed to act. The Secretary assigned a department staffer by the name of John Ralston to handle the problem.

Looking at the map of all offshore activities in the country, there were not many areas that were not already being drilled. Ralston offered the congressional representatives an area off of Alaska and the Congressmen agreed.

Two days later, those same Congressmen balked at the idea, saying it would not be economically feasible at this time for the oil companies to begin another major foray in Alaska. Ralston wondered how these Congressmen knew that fact, but he didn't ask them. They also informed Ralston that a Congressman Richard Johns would be handling this subject for the rest of them and that, as their chosen spokesman, he had their full support to do whatever necessary to close this matter. Johns was the Congressman from the California whose district which included San Francisco, the headquarters of Montgomery Oil.

Four other areas came up and were shot down. Then Ralston suggested twenty six tracts one hundred twenty six miles off the coast of Louisiana, twenty five miles west of an area currently being explored by seven companies. The Congressman called his contemporaries and relayed that information, making one more call to Monty-O's CEO and asking if that area would be satisfactory.

"No," Richardson replied, "'it's got to include the area about two to four miles west of there, or it's no good to us."

"How am I going to tell the Secretary of the Interior him to increase the area because it doesn't have your lot in it. He doesn't have to give us anything," argued Johns.

"You'll think of something, your honor, after all, that is why we contributed to your campaign," said Richardson.

Johns passed on the request to the Department of the Interior that the area be made larger so that more companies can partake of it.

"After all," said Johns,"it's still only one-third the size of the California exploratory areas. And it is within the area covered by your department's five year plan for oil leasing." Ralston had been concerned that this tract might be outside the area that the department had testified to Congress as its five year leasing plan. If it were outside the area in the plan there would be nothing more Ralston could do. But the tract was within the boundary so no problem arose. Ralston agreed with Johns and three days later announced that 129,000 additional acres off of Louisiana would be up for auction, and that sealed bids would be accepted for ninety days. At that time the tracts would be assigned.

In the headquarters building of Montgomery Oil, Richardson smiled. Before lighting a cigar and laying back in his chair to congratulate himself, he said aloud, "Mr. Johns, you were one of the best investments I've ever made."

Three months later at the auction, everyone was amazed at the size of the bids that Montgomery Oil had submitted. For three tracts totaling 26,600 acres, they had paid over ninety-five million dollars. No other company topped the sixty million dollar mark. While the other companies pondered Montgomery Oil's bid, Richardson was pressing on.

Montgomery Oil had made sure that, when the sealed bids were opened, theirs would be victorious. Now, less than sixty days later, two exploratory rigs were being towed out to the spots to begin preliminary test drilling. The costs being incurred by the operation were staggering. They were renting the offshore rigs at $150,000 a day and other operating costs had driven the expenses to almost $250,000 daily, each.

Six months after the first rig had started drilling, the decision was made. Based on the positive samples, Test wells that were bringing up 2000 barrels a day and that total expenditures on the field had passed the two hundred million mark, it was decided to bring the field into production. That decision alone would mean another billion dollars in expenditures.

In the Montgomery Oil headquarters building in San Francisco, the high—ranking executives were finishing up their daily staff meeting. It was the daily ritual they had been going through since Richardson decided to go after the Louisiana Project. Only this time, there was something different.

There was a peculiar air about Richardson. He knew a secret and was deciding whether or not to let them in on it. Smiling, Richardson stood up and looked at the assembled host. All of his life, from the days he went into the West Texas oil fields with his legendary wildcatter father, Randall Montgomery, till they moved into the Montgomery building, he'd looked forward to the day when he was the king of the heap and no one could tell him no. That day would come when thirty to forty diamond-tipped drill bits would break into an offshore petroleum reservoir one hundred twenty plus miles off the Louisiana coast.

Montgomery Oil would finally become what Richardson wanted. Looking about the room, he took a deep breath and spoke. It would be indeed a monumental proclamation.

"Ladies and Gentlemen," he began, "Steps have begun that, upon their successful conclusion, will place us amongst the major oil companies. Not just here in America, but the world."

He said this slowly and deliberately, making sure that all of them heard and digested it. All of the men assembled in the room had a rough idea of what was going on. Richardson told as few people as possible, and those he hadn't told were able to piece together their versions from the gossip and eavesdropping that goes on in a large working environment.

They were all pretty much aware of the decision to go into production, which is what they felt the next announcement had be. They knew their boss, and now they were about to find out how large the fruits of his labor were, as well as how it would affect the company from this point on.

"As you know, a tract off of the Louisiana coast has been turning up some good samples." Around the room a few men nodded their heads in silent agreement.

"Based on those samples and the recommendations of the geology department, I've decided to authorize oil and gas production of the tract." This brought a murmur from the assembled group. In hushed tones, the executives started giving each other their opinions as to what they felt was the proper course of action should be. A few even asked questions, which Richardson easily handled.

Richardson smiled and continued.

"The drilling of thirty five to forty wells would bring an additional 250,000 barrels a day to our refineries and markets. This will double our current output. But it will have more significance than just increased production. We will become one of the majors. With our increased output we'll shake the image of a small time operation."

That Richardson hated being considered a small operator was well known.

"Rough estimates have placed the size of the field at over 4 to 600 million barrels. That's more than enough to take us well into the middle of the century. Nothing can stop us now gentlemen, nothing!"

A voice from the back of the room shot back.

"What about Bennington Oil? They have a good sized war chest, and with all this extra stuff going on we now have over eight hundred million dollars in debt. A sizable part of it coming from the Louisiana Project. We're also looking at a huge expense to bring it into production. Like it or not, our current financial standing, plus the possibility of doubling or even tripling our corporate value if that field comes into production as estimated, makes us an attractive takeover candidate."

"I wouldn't worry about that if I were you," said

Richardson confidently. "First, we all know that Bennington Oil is our major and most dangerous rival, but they don't know the foggiest about the Louisiana Project. And once we're into production, in about two months max I'd say, it won't matter if they do know. They'll just sit back and watch us until I feel it's time to strike.

And then I'll destroy them!"

He sat back down in his chair and for a moment thought about that last question. He shot a concerned look over to the executive who had asked it.

"Why did you have to ask that one? That may be the single most dangerous part of this whole adventure, dealing with Bennington Oil."

Richardson had known all along that Bennington Oil would be a problem, and he'd taken some steps to keep them at bay long enough for the Louisiana Project to reach fruition. One step that he had thought might solve this problem was to go public with the information about the Louisiana Project. Once the stock markets got wind of that, the speculators, jumping onto the bandwagon to buy Montgomery Oil stock, would cause the price to swell immediately. This increase in stock prices would run any aggressors off, as they would be paying as much for the speculation as they would for the actual assets. But one thing stood in the way. Richardson was intentionally low-keying this find until it was safely into production. He was, in essence, walking a fine line. Recognizing that too much publicity about his monster deposit could let the Department of the Interior and several Congressmen know that they'd been had, Richardson was waiting for the right moment to tell the world. That moment would be as soon after another company made a gas, hydrogen or petroleum discovery of any size in the Gulf of Mexico. Unfortunately, that moment had not yet arrived. He got pensive again and then addressed the entire staff.

"Just to be on the safe side, all information on the Louisiana Project, as of this moment on, is now deemed confidential. I am the only person with release authority on information about it."

"And gentlemen," he added in a threatening tone, "I'll

have the ass of any man that violates that directive. It's imperative that we be allowed to work on this project without the meddlesome and expensive interruptions that those bastards at Bennington Oil can throw on us. The longer they stay in the dark, the better."

But even as he was speaking, plans were being made to undermine his dream.

CHAPTER 22

FERRYMAN'S RULE

Just over six months ago, on an offshore oil platform over 130 miles into the Gulf of Mexico, Richard Ferryman was mad. For two and a half years he had been a drill foreman for Montgomery Oil; a damn good one too. Over that period, working on Montgomery Oil's most demanding fields, he'd brought in over one hundred million barrels of oil and was considered one of their best. So he couldn't understand why he'd gotten the treatment they'd given him.

He was directing the drilling operation on the 'Elizabeth', Monty-O's lead exploration/production platform in the Louisiana Project. The work had gone smoothly until the drill on well no.5 started to lose revolutions. In his haste to bring the well in, he told the roughnecks to continue drilling. One suggested that they should bring the drill string up and check the bit to see if it had been fouled or damaged. Ferryman told him that if he didn't continue drilling, he'd have his ass. The roughneck did as he was told. Twenty minutes later the drill was still in operation, only now at full power, it was barely rotating.

Suddenly, the drill string shuddered and gave a long drawn-out groan. For the last half-hour the engines powering the rotary table had been straining to make the drill spin. Then suddenly they roared, releasing a big black puff of smoke, and started accelerating. The growling, roaring noises they had been making while straining to turn the drill was now replaced by the smooth hum of engines operating at the peak of efficiency. The crew looked at the pipe and then stared at each other.

"That asshole's done it now," one of them muttered.

Indeed, Ferryman had. For now the drill was turning as fast as it could, and the crewmen near the rig were racing to the controls to shut it down. To the roughnecks on the platform, the reason for what was happening was obvious. Somewhere down this sixty-five hundred foot borehole, this mile deep gamble for oil, the drill had snapped. Whatever had caused the resistance had won, and claimed the drill string as its prize.

As this was not a totally unpredictable occurrence in petroleum mining, the men of the 'Elizabeth' were prepared. They readied a "fish" to be dropped into the hole. A cylindrical clamp attached by a cable to the derrick crane, the fish's sole mission is to retrieve broken pipe stems. Its existence came about when it was discovered that it was impossible to drill in a well that has a long stretch of reinforced steel piping in it.

Initially they pulled the drill string up to see how much pipe they were going to have to contend with. Forty-seven hundred feet of it came up with no trouble, although the end of the drill string was splintered. The other eighteen hundred feet would need to be "fished" out.

Attaching the fish to the derrick cable, the crew ran it deep into the well. Deep below the floor of the Gulf of Mexico, it hit the remaining drill string. Clamping on to the bent and twisted lip where the pipe had snapped, the fish was made secure. With that, all that should have been left to do would be to raise the fish and the remaining drill string should come up with it.

Ferryman was standing there looking at the crew, waiting for the order to be given. The platform superintendent had relieved him until the damage to the well could be assessed. While snapping a drill string doesn't necessarily kill a well, it has killed the career of many of the foreman responsible. He was waiting for the drill string to be brought up to see where he stood.

Members of the crew had looked over and noticed him standing by himself, but to a man, seemingly ignored his existence.

Roughnecks are a strange breed who can appreciate and even respect a man's drilling ability while despising every other aspect of that same individual. This was exactly the case with Ferryman. More than once they said amongst themselves that they were certain that they would either find oil or murder their foreman, and that it was only a matter of time before one or the other came true.

Ferryman was good and he knew it. But while he was good, he was also abrasive. Fifteen years ago, when he was in the Navy, he got into a lot of fights because he couldn't stand being around people he thought were his "inferiors."

Ferryman's rule was simple enough to understand. Treat "inferiors" like trash and you'll know what to expect from them at all times. He applied that rule to the people who worked for him here. He maintained no loyalty to them and didn't expect any in return. This worked out perfectly because the crew didn't give a damn about any part of him, save his drilling ability. But now, even his drilling ability was being questioned. Until the crew had their answers, they'd just as soon not acknowledge his presence.

Ferryman didn't have many friends on the platform. After the drill string had snapped it seemed as though he didn't have any. He figured things couldn't get any worse when the order to begin raising the string was given.

The retrieval winches of the derrick went to work and took all of the slack out of the thick cable that stretched downward into the well. The big crane at the top of the derrick that inserts and withdraws the drilling pipe was activated. The cable grew taut and then started vibrating as it was being stretched by the pull of the crane on the unyielding pipe. For five minutes the crane struggled to pull the drill string up from the well. But all this effort proved to be for naught.

The drill string wasn't coming up.

A hard-hatted figure near the edge of the drilling deck

waved his arm up and down, signifying to the crane operator to stop. The pressure on the cable was relieved and it loosened up a bit.

The drilling foreman leading this operation went over to talk to the platform superintendent. After a brief discussion the foreman went back to the well. He waved his arm again and the crane operator began attempting to withdraw the string again.

Again, nothing.

This time however there would be no more arm waving to signal to the crane operator that this method was not working. The platform superintendent had decided, after the first attempt, to either muscle the string back up or to snap the cable while trying. If they snapped the cable, then there was no method left available to them to retrieve the drill string. The sixty five hundred foot hole, and the money it took to drill it, would be lost. They could send a second fish down the hole to get the first one, but that's all they'd be able to salvage.

The cable was vibrating wildly, as it was nearing its point of maximum stress. All of the men of the drilling deck started walking back 20 to 30 feet, looking for heavy objects to stand behind. In seconds this cable would either start bringing up the drill string and fish or it would snap. If it snapped, it would fly around the drill deck like a metal bullwhip, with enough force to cut a man in half.

Less than two minutes after everyone had found safety, the cable began to start fraying. This was the first sign that it was going to let loose. Two crewmen, behind heavy cover but closer to the quickly deteriorating cable than the rest, left the protection of the fifty-five gallon drums they were cowering behind and ran for the safety of the nearest portal. They scurried down and waited there until told it was safe again to come out.

The fraying was rapidly increasing and then suddenly, with a loud crack, the cable snapped. The men on the deck held their heads down as the cable, now a flailing scythe with the power to kill, swung no more than a foot over their crouching forms. The blunt end of the cable struck and penetrated the corrugated tin walls of a supply shed and impaled itself into a carbon steel I-beam.

Most of the crewmembers got up, followed the length of the cable and saw where it wound up. Initially, they were awestruck at the force that the cable had exerted. Their awe gave way to speculation as to what would have happened to any poor fool who found himself in front of this cable.

Then they thought to themselves, *"My God, I could have been that poor fool!"* The realization that they could be injured or worse dawned on all of them, and they unanimously realized that none of this would have been necessary if the drill string hadn't been snapped. The esteem in which Ferryman's drilling skills were held in now disappeared. The crew no longer wanted to work with Ferryman, and it wasn't long before everyone on the platform knew that.

The platform superintendent agreed with the crew's opinion on this matter and called Ferryman into his office to discuss his rapidly diminishing future.

Ferryman had gone down to his room after watching the retrieval attempt. He was there when word reached him that he was wanted by the super, as most of the crew called the platform superintendent. This was a meeting that he'd known was coming for some time, and yet he still wasn't quite ready for it. But he also knew that it didn't matter how he felt.

Walking out of his room into the narrow corridors that passed for hallways, he started for the super's office. He turned past the rooms of other crewmen, some asleep in their bunks, totally oblivious to the day's activity. He stopped and looked into the bunking area of one roughneck who was still totally asleep. *"How could he have slept through all the commotion?"* thought Ferryman, not realizing that his problems didn't quite affect everyone on the 'Elizabeth'.

He turned back into the passageway and kept walking until he came to a small collection of offices. Finding the one marked 'Superintendent', Ferryman turned the doorknob, stepped into the office and sat down. He'd never been in the super's office and he was surprised by what he saw.

A small, neat, yet dimly lit room served as the base for the most powerful man on the platform. A portal allowed a small amount of light in. A laptop computer sat on a small corner of the desk One word from him and when the next helicopter came, it took you to shore, unemployed.

The office was cluttered with drilling reports, expenditure sheets, oil projections and all sorts of official looking papers. The look of the office betrayed the power it held. A few certificates from training schools and a couple letters of appreciation from the company were the only personal effects in the office. None of them particularly appealed to Ferryman, but they were the only thing for him to read until the super came in. Ferryman had turned his head to look at a certificate on the wall when the super came in.

"There's nothing there for you!

Ferryman immediately turned and looked at his boss. At almost the same time he dropped his eyes so that he looked down at the desk and then turned his head to look out of the portal. He was doing his best to avoid direct eye contact with his superior. Particularly, this superior. He'd never been afraid of a man, but he nervous around this one. The chief stood at 6 feet two inches, and weighed an even 200 pounds. Most platform supers he'd dealt with were the accountant type; small eyeglass wearing milquetoasts who felt more camaraderie with a calculator than with other people. Not this one, though. He'd worked in the oil fields all of his life, and knew drilling. His demeanor was gruff, but he'd found out throughout the years that it helped if your men were as afraid of you as they were respectful. A scar over his right eye, caused by a rig explosion twenty two years ago, gave him an even more sinister look. Ferryman thought about the stories he'd heard of roughnecks trying to jump the super, only to regret it when they regained consciousness.

"*Those stories,*" he thought, "*must be true*"

Trying to achieve the advantage, Ferryman spoke first. "Sir, I know what we're going to discuss and I'd..."

The chief curtly and abruptly cut him off.

"First thing Ferryman, my name is Dixon. Put mister in front of that and address me that way for the remaining few minutes of our acquaintance."

The chief let Ferryman know right off the bat how this meeting would proceed, and how it would end.

While Ferryman watched him, Dixon walked over to the desk in the center of the room, pulled out the chair and sat down. A towel was draped over the top of his desk. Dixon drew back the towel and under it was five strands of dry, uncooked spaghetti, each about ten inches long.

"You know what this is, Ferryman" said Dixon. Ferryman looked at him and said sarcastically, "Lunch!"

The super shot a long, mean glance at Ferryman. "No it isn't lunch. It's a little demonstration of what happens when someone doesn't listen to common sense so he can grab a little glory. Sound familiar?" The barb at the end of that statement was not lost on Ferryman. But he knew better to do anything more than to take the abuse that the chief was about to dish out.

The chief continued. "This strand of spaghetti is a drill, turning at its proper rate and speed. All of a sudden, the drill bit at the very bottom gets stuck on something, and won't allow the rest of the drill string to turn."

Ferryman was still looking at Dixon, who pinched the bottom of the spaghetti strand to keep it from rotating.

Dixon started up again. "Now this drill won't turn at the bottom, but for some reason they keep turning it at the top. Dixon twisted the spaghetti strand until it snapped about two-thirds of the way down.

"And that, my friend is what happened. By continuing to rotate the drill, you built up so much torque that the drill string couldn't handle it and snapped. Your crewmembers tried to get you to stop and you didn't. As a result, you screwed the end of the string into something down there and we can't get it out."

The super looked at Ferryman and then suddenly, with all the rage he could muster, yelled.

"Because of your actions we've drilled a sixty five hundred foot deep hole in the ground, all for nothing. You're not only fired, but I fully intend to see that you never work in this business again!"

The super turned away from Ferryman in an effort to regain his composure, stiffly walking over to the portal and looking out into the Gulf of Mexico. Dixon stood there staring for almost three minutes, not knowing that the bulging blood vessels on the side of his face betrayed the calmness he was trying to portray. He had never been angrier, more upset at anyone or anything. He'd worked on wells that had snapped before, and they were no big deals. What aggravated him most was that this was an occurrence that didn't have to happen. Greed, stupidity and personal glory had all gotten together and caused this man to his left to accomplish an idiotic feat.

Dixon thought to himself, *"the fact that the crew tried to warn him and he didn't listen..,"* he' stopped thinking about it. It only upset him more. He looked back over at Ferryman.

The entire time Ferryman stood in front of Dixon, saying nothing and trying to figure out what to say in his defense. Dixon's outburst had caught him by surprise and left him confused, disoriented, and uncertain as to what his next step should be. He was totally lost when he noticed Dixon starting to move away from the portal.

When Dixon turned back around, his face was free of the redness that was brought on by his sudden emotional outburst. But while his face was free, his mind wasn't.

"Don't say a word," said Dixon, "it won't help you. I've called and had a chopper dispatched to take you back to shore. They're a bit tied up, so it won't be here for about eight hours. That should give you plenty of time to pack. Whatever you do, don't miss it. When it leaves, if you're not on it, I'll make you wish you were.

"Goodbye, Mr. Ferryman."

For the better part of two hours, Ferryman had, supposedly, been packing and arranging his belongings. His dimly lit cubicle, roughly the size of a small dormitory room, seemed more like a prison cell. Ferryman had turned down the lights in his room so that the mood of the room would match his; dark and surly. He didn't realize how lucky he was that his roommate was on duty, or he would have been underfoot; an unfortunate consequence in trying to maneuver two people simultaneously in these small rooms.

The meeting with Dixon was a disaster, and the word of his professional demise had spread throughout the rig like wildfire. While it wasn't exactly a party atmosphere on the drilling deck, it seemed like one to Ferryman. Most of the crew wasn't too sad he was leaving.

It was obvious to Ferryman that no one cared for him. He'd been in his room packing for over two hours and no one had come to see him.

"Just as well," he thought, *"I don't need them. Fuck all of them."*

With that statement Ferryman stopped packing and pondered a thought. *"Actually,"* thought Ferryman, *"That wouldn't be such a bad idea. Dixon has every intention of blackballing me. No one on this platform has done me any favors. Why should I do them any? My life is about to go through a wringer because of the people on this platform..."*

Ferryman knew the mechanics as well as the layout of the production platform like the back of his hand. He knew that it was a tension leg platform, essentially a floating island depending on semi rigid tendons stretching from the bottom of the rig to the ocean floor thirty two hundred feet below to hold it in place.

"These damn platforms are technological marvels," thought Ferryman. *"And their technological advancement is only matched by their cost."* He was thinking to the news article he read about an offshore production platform owned by Petrobras, the Brazilian state oil company. An explosion, of undetermined origin, ripped through the rig killing ten men and ultimately sinking the entire platform. The loss of the platform alone was valued at $350-500 million.

The cost of the platform Ferryman was preparing to depart was not much less than that. The costs of these platforms were massive figures. Massive, but not beyond the parameters of Ferryman's intended vengeance.

What Ferryman was thinking now was sheer lunacy, the kind of lunacy developed by desperate angry men.

He momentarily gave thought to possible ways of damaging the capability of the entire platform.

"All it would require," he thought, *" is an effort to affect the delicate balance between the rig and the ballast we took on to stay stable. Just the slightest screw up with our ballast would throw off our balance, and at a bare minimum all the*

wells that have been drilled so far would be damaged. They'd remember me then. The potential havoc I could create here would be..."

"I must be out of my damned mind," Ferryman thought aloud. "I want my revenge but if something goes wrong I'll be looking at 180 counts of murder or manslaughter. The way my luck is now, everything will go to hell and this rig will sink with everyone but me."

He chuckled at that thought, and the fact that, for the merest of moments, he gave consideration to toppling the half-billion dollar platform that he was being exiled from.

His anger was subsiding, and with this subsidence came clearer and coherent thought.

Drilling for oil offshore involves technology at the cutting edge of science. Floating platforms weighing thousands of tons engage in hourly battles against waves, currents and tides to remain in the same exact location to allow drilling and production activities to continue. Pipelines are laid by computer guided submersibles in water half a mile deep -- too deep for continuous human endeavor.

But the biggest leap in off shore technology is not in the construction of the offshore rigs and platforms themselves, it lies within the technology for searching and drilling for oil. Where once divining rods and intuition was all that was used to find oil, technology has since become the underground eyes and ears of the oil company.

Ninety-nine dry holes out of every one hundred drilled led to the retirement of divining rods and to the introduction of science. Now, almost one out of every four wells drilled either hits a gas or petroleum bearing deposit, or leads to the discovery of one. But while discovering oil has become more technical, drilling for oil has also technologically kept pace. Oil is now being found in venues so harsh that few, if any, living creatures dwell; in arctic landscapes so cold that a roughneck's perspiration would freeze in seconds; in desert locales so hot and barren that no natural vegetation exists. Undersea drilling efforts now took place in water so deep that the first four thousand feet of drill string and casing penetrate only saltwater.

It took a special kind of person to work and thrive in that environment. It was why Ferryman was more than 126 miles out into the Gulf of Mexico. His ability and determination made him a roughneck. But it was his arrogance that led to his dismissal.

Of the 180 Monty-O employees on the platform, only one thought that the platform superintendent had made a mistake. He was also the only one on the platform that did not consider this matter closed.

Ferryman wanted to get back at Monty-O, he just didn't know how at the moment. But he was becoming aware. He knew that his answers were here on the platform. Everything that he could have wanted to know about the production platform and more importantly, the Louisiana Project, existed in the databases of the computers in the control room. Every iota about this project, from the exact latitude and longitude of the offshore oil field to the exact acreage of the parcel they leased from the Minerals Management Service, to the depth of the test wells, the density of the petroleum or hydrocarbon equivalents discovered in the deposit to the exact size of the deposit. Everything about this project was there in the computer for the taking.

Ferryman had just two problems with this.

While numerous workers on the platform possessed laptops, including Ferryman, to Ferryman's knowledge few possessed spare CD-ROM storage disks. This was important because Ferryman was out of them altogether. He knew that if he had requisitioned one yesterday he'd probably have it by now. Ferryman also knew that if he asked for one now he would probably be denied. He also knew that his asking was bound to invoke questions, questions he couldn't answer without incriminating himself. This platform was a privately owned property and not a governmental entity. His rights to a Fifth Amendment protection didn't exist. By even trying to invoke the Fifth, the rest of the platform would know that he was up to no good. He couldn't have that, at least not yet.

He knew he could probably swipe a flash drive from someone easily enough and use it to store the information he was planning to acquire. But if that someone made any noise about some sort of storage media missing, someone else might listen. If that someone listening was Superintendent Dixon, he wouldn't need long to piece together that someone who was being banished from the platform might be the one who would try to download valuable information.

"For the want of a damn nail ...." was Ferryman's laconic pronouncement of his plight.

His other problem was that the only access to the computers was through the control room, an area that he had little clearance to enter before his dismissal. Now, he had even less reason or clearance to be in the control room.

Ferryman's plans required information, information he not only did not have, but that he did not have access to. It also required a degree of stealth.

It only took a moment's reflection before Ferryman realized that he could not retrieve the information he needed from the control room without getting caught.

"Too bad" he commiserated, "I could have made a bundle off of it."

He sat on the corner of his bed and tried to force himself to think of a new plan to get back at Monty-O, but each plan required hard evidence, the substantiation of what he would tell others lay beneath Monty-O's newest offshore discovery.

"*The computers are out*" thought Ferryman. "*And so am I.*"

Sitting on his bunk, alone in his room, Ferryman almost allowed himself to wallow in his self-pity. Almost.

He was a beaten man and he couldn't counter. It almost made him despair.

Then it just made him mad.

He had not stopped to think about his newly-imposed employment situation. When that helicopter took him back to shore and set him upon dry land, he was unemployed. He had enough money saved and invested to live comfortably for a short period of time. After that, he didn't know.

What he was thinking about in his room wouldn't help this predicament. He wasn't thinking work. He figured that he had a slim chance of getting another oil field job after what had happened earlier. He was planning on nothing less than corporate espionage.

Ferryman knew, before anyone else on the platform even suspected, that he was now playing his all or nothing gambit with Monty-O. The incident with the snapped drill string and the botched drill head recovery were accidents of judgment and not intent. In what Ferryman was planning against Monty-O now there was motive, there was intent, and there was a definite willingness to harm the company. No future employer could afford to overlook criminal activity in an employee. If Ferryman got caught trying to carry out his plan, he would never be hired again.

He hadn't stopped to consider this. As it stood, it probably didn't matter. Ferryman wanted his pound of Monty-O flesh, and he was spending his remaining time on the platform trying to figure out how to strike back at his soon to be former employer.

A philosopher once said that "It takes all kinds of people to make a world." A more true statement has never been spoken. There are those who face disaster and fold. There are those who face disaster and rise. There are even those who face disaster and strive to maintain the status quo. Then there is one other group; that .002% who face disaster with a curse on their lips and the intent of countering their disaster with a greater one of their own.

They don't seek martyrdom or victory. They seek to inflict a greater pain against those who sought to injure them. Revenge requires that one party prevails against a previously antagonistic party. Revenge dictates that in the end, the former prey stands above. Defeating a former superior foe doesn't satisfy this group. They want that foe punished for the indignity of even thinking about holding them down.

Members of this group do not want revenge--they espouse a scorched earth policy. In short, if they cannot win, then they do not want anyone else to win either. There is no end to the measures that people like this will employ to lash back at their antagonists. When angered, there is nothing that they will not try, and their ability to rage will overcome their conscious and coherent self. The goal is all that matters. The goal is to annihilate their would-be superiors.

Richard Ferryman was one of these people, and his only remaining goal was to hurt Monty-O as much as he could in retaliation for the treatment he received on the drilling platform.

In business, people like Ferryman are not just dangerous, they are lethal. They are the professional equivalent of the ebola virus, and if left alone they would insure that the business entities offending them suffered mightily before dying outright.

During the dot.com business collapse of the late 1990's and early part of the new century, thousands of employees were laid off without so much an opportunity to go back to the office and collect their personal effects. Many accepted the loss of their jobs and moved on. Many did not. There were numerous examples of employees hacking their way into their former employer's computers and scrambling personnel, inventory or financial records, often with devastating results.

In almost all cases, the companies involved did not even suspect that their employees could be capable of such an act. The destructive trait that these employees eventually exhibited was buried deep within and was only brought forth with a significant emotional event affecting the employee. In short, many companies did not know that they employed such a powder keg until they had performed some traumatic event. After that, the fuse would be lit and would slow burn until such time that the employee chose to explode.
Richard Ferryman's fuse was lit.

Ferryman stood up and walked over to the door, standing there momentarily lost in thought. Almost since he was sent to his cubicle to pack, he had been mentally sketching a plan that would not only exact his revenge on Monty-O, but one that would insure that they never forgot one Richard Ferryman.

His face began reflecting the strain of his malevolent cognitive efforts; his brow furrowing from his concentration and his mouth starting to curl into a smile. He knew what he wanted to do to this company and those who worked for it. He was just at a loss as to precisely how to do it.

Looking back over to his half-packed cases Ferryman said under his breath, *"How, in six hours, can I make these assholes pay?"*

In his mind he was only planning to do to them what they had done to him.

Thinking out loud, Ferryman claimed, *"Other foremen had snapped drill strings before and nothing happened to them. That the company was worth billions was a documented fact, so how much could one fuckin' drill string be worth to them? Hell, I've seen men lose fingers, hands and in one case both legs and the company didn't give a damn."*

In the course of just the last few moments Ferryman had become even more obsessed with the notion of revenge. But while the intention was there, he was still looking for the right method. His train of thought was focused on revenge, and only the growling of his stomach took him away from that path.

He had thought about going and getting something to eat, but he didn't dare go to the cafeteria. There was bound to be somebody there, someone who would stare at him the way a vulture stares at a carcass, someone who would look at him and say to themselves, *"How could that clown be so stupid?"*

Ferryman didn't feel up to that right now.

He walked over to the dresser in the room and started to change clothes. The oily, sweat-saturated coveralls he was in were company property, and he was damned if he was going to get billed for taking a useless pair of coveralls.

He emptied his pockets of coins, bills, a key ring and a small pocketknife and was about to pull the zipper of his coveralls when his revelation came to him. He wanted nothing more than to get even with the company, the drilling crew, and most of all Dixon, the platform super. And all of the time the instrument of his revenge was with him. It was a little brass key on his key ring that had the number twenty seven on it. Twenty seven was the number of the chartroom. And in the chartroom were the maps, charts, and geologic readings that were the driving motivations behind the Louisiana Project.

Ferryman smiled.

He held up the key ring and looked at it. There were seven keys on it. Only three applied to the platform, but he was only interested in one of them. It was more than just the key to the chartroom, it was the key to his plan, his future and his revenge.

The more he thought about his plans for revenge, the more he let his mind run. His curiosity was getting to him. Ferryman never understood why Monty-O was paying so much for this ocean acreage. He remembered right after the company bought this property that other oil companies reacted with cynicism. The industry newspapers were filled with the stories of other oil company chiefs who couldn't believe the total amount that had been spent on this tract. But Montgomery Oil never explained they just went about their business.

Monty-O was the proverbial "cat who ate the canary." They were the kids who were walking around with a smile on their faces while everyone else tried to figure out what they had done. There was oil under this tract. From the prices that they paid, Montgomery Oil must have known that from the start. What all of the other companies wanted to know was how Montgomery Oil knew there was oil here. Montgomery Oil's discovery was a fluke, but the only ones who knew that worked for Monty-O. That was partly the reason they were smiling.

Ferryman knew there was oil here too. His professional acumen told him that, as well as the many positive core samples he had helped drill. He let his thoughts wander as he tried to piece together a theory that would explain what was going on.

"*Assume*," thought Ferryman, "*That in a fraternity as tight as the oil industry, you knew something that no one else did.*" Oil is selling at between forty five and sixty dollars a barrel. It didn't take much to make a fortune.

One hundred million barrels a day was the amount of oil used each day to feed a petroleum-hungry world. Yet a man who discovered a field that large would instantly be a billionaire. The crazed dichotomy that dictated that the same amount of oil that would make a person filthy rich for generations to come would only provide one day's oil supply for the world was as maddening as it was true.

Ferryman continued thinking. "*Suppose one company*

discovered a huge field and brought it in alone. It would be risky. Hell, even the majors throw in on the really big projects. It cuts their earnings down, but it also cuts down on their risks." Sarcastically he added, *"Sohio could have used a few partners.* Sohio, when it was better known as Standard Oil of Ohio, had announced a few years back that one dry hole near Prudhoe Bay has cost them over 125 million dollars. Ferryman did a quick bit of figuring in his head and realized that his company had spent almost close to that figure. And they were no-where near as large as Sohio.

Thinking aloud again, Ferryman admitted that, *"The only way a company of Monty-O's size would go it alone with that kind of money involved would be if the company were run by fools or if the payday were all but guaranteed."* He remembered that last year the company had over a billion dollars in profit, and that they were projecting those kinds of profits again this year.

"No company this size could be run by a fool." Hell, old Richardson has been running this company for years. That leaves number two. That one's more in line with the old man." thought Ferryman.

Ferryman sat down on the corner of his bed and for the next thirty minutes thought long and hard. After this period of cogitation Ferryman came up with what he thought was the most logical conclusion.

"That has to be it," he thought.

Ferryman's door had been closed the whole time he started packing. Someone staring at him before he shut it stated that he heard Ferryman mumble something about ghouls staring at the dead. But behind that door he was planning the most sinister and unlawful act of his forty three years.

"For once," he said, making no effort to hide his menacing smile, "Someone else is going to pay."

The chart room is a watertight compartment deep within the bowels of the drilling platform. The purpose of this particular chartroom was more for the storage of paperwork than an area for the useful analysis of charts. But at least one hard copy of all geological testing done on the platform was stored here. The information was simply placed here until it was needed again. It was here that Ferryman came looking for the key to his goal.

Carrying an empty clothes sack, he walked the two flights of steps to the chart room level. He was careful not to be seen; twice having to hide so he wouldn't get caught. Standing near the corner of a perpendicular hallway, he peered around the corner to make sure no one was around.

After seeing that the coast was clear, he stepped into the hallway. Looking both ways again, he advanced to the door, withdrew his key, and in less than three seconds he was in the chart room. Carefully shutting the door behind him and relocking it, he rolled up the clothes bag and laid it flat against the bottom of the door. Ferryman was convinced that no light could escape only when he could see that no light was entering.

He ran his hands over the wall until he felt the light switch. Fumbling at first, and even losing it, he felt around again until he found it and turned on the light.

The light illuminated the room and showed the presence of seven file cabinets, each six feet high and roughly three feet across. Three of the gray cabinets were on the left side of the room and three were on the right. The last one was against the far wall, parallel to the door. A large table and four stools occupied the center of the room. There was nothing else in the room.

Ferryman looked around the room before taking a step. Years ago his military training had taught him to always scope out the area he was occupying so if any contingencies arose, he'd have some familiarities with his surroundings. The room was roughly twenty by fifteen feet and had no distinguishable features.

"*No place to hide,*" thought Ferryman, "*that's not good.*" It meant that if anyone opened the door and saw him, the game was over and he'd have to deal with Dixon again.

"*This time,*" thought Ferryman, "*Dixon wouldn't hold back.*"

Ferryman decided that working as quickly as possible would be his best course of action. The less time he spent in the chartroom, the less his chances of getting caught.

He quickly went over to the first file cabinet drawer and fumbled for the index/file plan. The index was always filed in the first file drawer so if it were ever needed it would be in the most accessible, and easiest to remember, location.

While he was reviewing the index, his peripheral vision caught a motion in the corner of the room. He turned his head quickly to notice a large black spider, about the size of a quarter, scurrying up the sterile white walls.

"Those damn things can live anywhere," snapped Ferryman.

Ferryman was looking through the index, trying to find the drawers that would hold the key to his next step. After nearly two minutes of scanning, he found it. In the third file cabinet, second drawer from the bottom, were the charts marked 'Geological Survey Results'

Ferryman pulled on the handle, and the drawer slid silently back until it was fully withdrawn. Neatly laid in the drawer were several maps with the coordinates of the drilling platform highlighted. Ferryman briefly looked at the maps and placed them on top of the drawer.

"I know where this damn place is," he said angrily, "what I need to know is what's under it."

Next to the map were four red folders. Ferryman rifled through these, but found that they just consisted of a collection of official looking papers and documents. They also weren't the ones Ferryman was looking for.

He crouched down to see if there was anything in the back of the drawer and while he was bending down he noticed two blue folders stuffed into the furthest reaches of the drawer. He extended his arm into the drawer and retrieved them.

Ferryman, pulling the report out of the drawer and checking the date, could scarcely believe his eyes. The date on the report was showed that it was nearly two years old. Ferryman slowly looked over the report again.

"*How can this be?*" he questioned. "*We've only had this tract since...*" Ferryman stopped and shook his head. "I don't believe it! I don't believe this at all." Ferryman was suspecting that he had found his answers.

GREGORY BELL

"The money they must have spent and the favors they had to use to ramrod this venture through," thought Ferryman, *"must be awesome. That's why they paid so much for this tract. It was a sure thing. That bastard Montgomery knew he was in the money before he even stepped into the fight."*

"If this little project turns out to be what I think it is, this little report could be worth its weight in gold," said Ferryman. *"And if I can make a few dollars off of this, and if this project could get disrupted, a lot of folks might have to answer for it."*

"And as I won't be one of them," he snarled, "I could care less."

He sat down on one of the stools and began reading the cover pages of the report. He had covered no more than the first page when he put the report down and stared aimlessly into the wall. He smiled as he thought about the information he was holding in his hands.

"You bastards will remember Richard Ferryman," he laughed out loud. "If you think that damned drill string cost you, wait till your competitors get ahold of this."

Ferryman was holding the geological reports drawn from core samples accidentally taken by the drillship CRUSTACEAN almost 24 months ago. The report, titled "Analysis of the X—Project Core Samples," was made by the Houston based Henderson-Mendoza-Rachel Geologic Survey Group. Opening the report and turning to the cover page again, Ferryman re-read the letter to make sure he had the right report. It read:

Dear Sirs.

Based on the core samples we received for testing, we submit the following. CONGRATULATIONS! Never before in our twenty-three year existence have we tested a sample as positive as yours. More core samples from different positions will be required to determine the approximate size of your discovery. We feel that you may have discovered an immense deposit. The report contained herein breaks down the results of your samples even further and...

Ferryman stopped reading. His mind was saturated with his thoughts of revenge when it suddenly occurred to him that he was still in a dangerous place; one where he shouldn't be. He turned to leave and then thought to cover his tracks.

Walking back over to the file cabinets, marked '2003', Ferryman opened the drawers containing reports of survey for that year. Finding a report that was roughly the same size as the one he intended to take, Ferryman switched the cover off of it with the report he was stealing. His plan was simple and effective.

The world of the oil industry is constantly changing. With these changes come increases in technology that allow better, or at least more refined testing capabilities. Thus, in the business of drilling for oil, only the most up to date information is useful; anything old is simply for the archives. Ferryman intended to steal the document that had led Montgomery Oil officials to believe that there was petroleum, in commercial quantities, under this spot.

The best report he could have gotten was the one that was on Dixon's desk. However he knew better than to trifle with Dixon again. But now, as he prepared to go back to his room, he possessed a document that could make him a very rich man, and one that could show Monty-O that Richard Ferryman was not a pawn to be pushed about.

He closed all of the file drawers and tried to leave the room pretty much the way he had found it. As it was a pretty nondescript room, that task wasn't too difficult. He went back over to the light switch, gave a quick last-minute check and turned out the light. Reaching down by the bottom of the door, he pulled up the laundry bag he had placed to block the light. He opened the bag and placed the report into it, drawing the string tightly around the neck of the bag so that it secured its contents.

Being extremely cautious had saved his life several times. Now it constituted the most crucial part of his plan; getting back to his room unobserved and packing his treasure away.

Ferryman placed his ear to the door trying to detect the sounds of an approaching roughneck. Nothing was heard.

"So far, so good," thought Ferryman.

He had no options left. Getting back to his room was not just the victory, but his only possible outcome. Once there, he could pack the report so far down in his personal gear that they'd never know he had it.

But if he got caught doing anything that even appeared suspicious between his room and the chart room, they would search everything he owned to insure that he wasn't trying to pull a fast one. And God have mercy on him if they found the report, because he knew Dixon damn sure wouldn't.

Beads of perspiration were forming on Ferryman's forehead, rolling down the side of his head and into his sweat-soaked collar. He found himself to be more nervous than ever before. Ferryman had performed questionable actions before and, never found himself sweating like this. This time was different. This time the fear was on him. The fear of being caught or of failing again. And worst of all the fear that his revenge would be quashed; leaving unsaid his reply to their criticism and opinions.

"It's going to happen. They aren't going to treat me like this. They can't, and I won't let them."

Clenching his fists and closing his eyes, Ferryman leaned into the wall next to the door. He was fighting his fear, holding it back and putting it back where he could control it. When he was certain that it was under control he'd leave the room. But the silent battle that was raging for control of his next actions would continue unabated for several moments. It was in the dark, while he was wrestling for control of his emotions, that the decision would be made for him.

Ferryman was lost in his inner conflict when the two men came downstairs and stopped in the hallway outside of the chart room. It was a fairly isolated part of the rig, one that doesn't get much traffic; one where a small transaction could go down unobserved.

Ferryman only became aware of them a split second before one of them spoke.

"Hey man, you got the stuff?"

"Yeah I got it. Where's the money?"

"Right here, friend. All four hundred dollars. Now

where's my package."

"Here you are, some of the finest flower tops that ever left Jamaica. Ganja, the good stuff. If Bob Marley had taken a hit of this he'd still be jammin'."

Both men in the hallway laughed at that comment before one of them added, "Yeah, if we could get some of this into Elvis, he'd jump out of the grave and start rockin' again

Ferryman stayed perfectly still inside the chart room, trying not to make a sound, while the two men outside were rolling in laughter. The irony of being caught in the commission of his crime by a dope peddler and his stooge in the middle of their crime was lost on Ferryman. He didn't want to get caught, period.

After the two gentlemen outside had finished their business, they left and went back up the staircase that they had come down.

Ferryman knew he had to leave the area immediately. If someone else came down and entered the chart room he would be discovered, and that prospect carried its own particular form of hell.

Ferryman listened to the door again and after a short period of silence, he reached down, grabbed the doorknob and slowly twisted it until a tell-tale 'click' told him it was open.

He looked down the hallway and listened to see if anyone was coming before he stepped out, pulling the door shut behind him. He was committed now; there would be no turning back. If someone turned the corner now, there would be no way or time for Ferryman to try and open the door and reenter the chart room. His moment of truth had arrived, and only his stealth and cunning could get him out safely.

After five more minutes of carefully stepping and listening, ready at each step to blend into the walls of the corridors, Ferryman found himself back in his room. He slid the report into his suitcase and leaned back onto his bed.

"Only a few more hours and these bastards won't be able to touch me," thought Ferryman. He pulled a bottle of scotch out of his suitcase under his bed, opened the top and took a long victory swig.

The chopper Ferryman flew in landed just over hour after it took off from the platform. For him the life at sea for Monty-O was over.

He was back in his apartment just over an hour later. He turned on his computer and looked for only one webpage. It was the one group of people who would like to know what he had done. And the one group who would pay him handsomely for the information he had.

Ferryman had been with Monty-O long enough to know that their main rival was Bennington Oil. He had also known enough Bennington Oil people to know who the one person in that company was whom you dealt with when in possession of information like his.

Ferryman picked up his phone and dialed the number to Bennington Oil. Following the directions of the automated phone operator led him to the office of the man he sought.

"Strategic Planning Department, How may I assist you," came the feminine voice from the receiver.

"Yes," he began, "My name is Richard Ferryman. Until recently I was a drill foreman on an offshore platform in the Gulf of Mexico doing exploratory and production drilling for Monty-O. I was calling to see if I could speak with Stan Jenkins."

She placed Ferryman on hold and contacted Jenkins, who had her place the call through his office phone. Jenkins always took these types of calls, as disgruntled oil drillers seem to almost always have something informative to say about the company they used to work for.

They talked for close to forty five minutes.

After hanging up, Ferryman went through his apartment and gathered all of the possessions that he had an interest in keeping, placing them in a box addressed to his brother in Carson City Nevada. He and Bennington Oil had come to an agreement and he was leaving tonight. He would get $250,000 in cash, a car, a three month vacation in Las Vegas and a job with Monty-O when he was ready to come back to work. All he had to do was take the Monty-O report he'd stolen and accompany it to Bennington Oil headquarters in San

Francisco.

He was more than happy to oblige.

CHAPTER 23

UNDERSTANDING AND COORDINATION

The three page memo on the Louisiana Project told Morris almost everything he needed to know. It told him where the information came from and who provided it to Jenkins and when. It told Morris what the Louisiana Project was about and why it was so important to both Bennington Oil and Monty-O. It even told him how much Bennington Oil paid Ferryman for the information.

But it also told Morris some information he didn't want to see. At the bottom of the last page of the memo was a footnote. Morris read it and stared at it for a long minute.

The footnote was a two month old newspaper article describing the fatal car crash of Richard Ferryman.

Ferryman was apparently legally drunk, with a blood alcohol content of .2, when he flipped his car outside of Las Vegas. According to the article he was killed instantly.

Morris was unnerved about this article. *"Why would that be here unless they had something to do with it"* he thought.

"It's only been two days since my beating," Morris thought, *"So I know they're capable of this."*

Morris placed all of the memos down on his desk. He now had found most of what he was looking for. After he read the memos he only had two questions left.

"What role did the tanker collision play in all of this?"

and *"How far will the company go in making sure I don't become more of a problem than I am?"*

Having read about Ferryman's untimely demise, he wondered if he had the answer to his second question.

Morris looked up at the clock, registering that it was almost 4 p.m. He had every puzzle piece but one, and he now resolved to go find that one.

He called Avey in the Bennington Oil Maritime Department and asked him if he would call on his behalf and set up a meeting with Capt. Marlowe, skipper of the Benician Guardian.

Avey called back and told Morris that Capt. Marlowe did not want to talk to him, or anyone else for that matter.

Morris asked Avey to call Capt. Marlowe back one more time and to "tell him there's more to this then he knows." He also reminded Avey to use his cell phone to call Capt. Marlowe.

Morris was being careful not to get Avey involved. He had found out with Phil that those throughout Bennington Oil helping him look for information can also be harmed, be it physical or financial. Avey's cell phone call would not be tracked by Bennington Oil's communication system and as such they shouldn't be too interested in the Chief of the Maritime Department talking to one of his captains.

Avey called back on his cell and told Morris that Capt. Marlowe would see him in ninety minutes. Morris thanked Avey and hung the phone up.

But just for a second.

He picked up the receiver again and called Bill Martin's office and spoke with his secretary. Morris tried to schedule a 1 p.m. meeting with Martin for tomorrow, but Martin had a conflict and the meeting was pushed back to 4:30 p.m.

Morris got up and started getting dressed. He was about to step out the door when he realized that he had one more call to make.

He dialed the number and waited for the party at the other end to pick up

"Hello, Nelson here."

"It's Morris," he started, "Where are you right now?"

"I'm in San Francisco," he replied, "the Embarcadero Center to be specific. Why?"

"You and I need to talk," Morris started, "You're not going to believe what I have uncovered. And I may have more after I make one more stop."

"You want to talk over dinner?" asked Nelson

"Great idea" Morris replied. "Isn't there a Mexican place down there?"

"Yeah" said Nelson, "It's pretty good. When do you want to meet?"

"Eight o'clock?"

"Eight it is," said Nelson.

While Morris was speaking to Nelson he was oblivious to the need to safeguard his communication. He might have figured since it is a felony to electronically eavesdrop on anyone without a proper search warrant, he didn't need to be safe in his communications from his house. This was not the point of view shared by the man in a nondescript van parked on the street two houses up from Morris' house. He was being paid well to make sure that Bennington Oil remained informed if Morris had called anyone on the list of phone numbers that they had provided him with. Since the Bennington Oil brain trust assumed it could handle and control any current employees, none of the numbers on the list went to actual Bennington Oil phone lines. As such, Morris' call to Avey was not tracked. But the conversation to Nelson was not only flagged, noted and heard, it was being relayed into Bennington Oil before Morris had even left his house.

After speaking with Nelson and finishing getting dressed, Morris grabbed his notepad and headed out the door. From his porch he looked down the street and all he saw was two parked vans and a small number of parked cars; none of which stood out from the others.

Save one; a red Thunderbird. He could see that there was someone in the car and they appeared to be on a cell phone.

He paid no further attention to his surroundings and got in his car, started it and drove away. He had an appointment with Capt. Marlowe in San Francisco and if he wanted the answers to the last of his questions, he knew he couldn't be late.

Morris had always fashioned himself a master of details. However, the route to the freeway was so second nature to him that he drove it without worrying too much about anything. If he had taken the slightest glance into his rearview mirror, he might have noticed the red Thunderbird following him.

CHAPTER 24

MONTY-O's RESPONSE

At about the same time that Morris was reviewing his purloined Monty-O documents, Edward Richardson sat looking at his computer screen. He didn't like what he saw.

In his plush office he had just about the best of everything. State of the art technology for running his Fortune 500 Company. The finest handmade furniture available. Rare oil and watercolors hanging on the walls valued in the millions. Twelve year old scotch in $2500 decanters just waiting to be poured in to crystal snifters. Exquisite tapestries and carpets that were actually created for royalty decades ago. He had everything.

The only thing missing from his office was peace of mind, and he would have traded everything else in it for just a little of that.

His computer was showing yet another financial news service stating the same thing that all of the other news services were.

Three of New York's biggest takeover specialists were joining together to attempt a takeover of Monty-O.

Richardson was at a loss to explain or understand why this was happening. He had a dread fear that they had found out about the Louisiana Project and that he would now have to reveal it. He had called a staff meeting together to discuss this turn of events.

The news articles Richardson had seen were painting a dire picture. The arbs had already filed their Form 13-d with the SEC, showing that they held over ten percent of the outstanding shares and that they were acquiring more imminently. They stated the sources of their funding and the made no secret that they were taking the company private.

Richardson didn't know these men, but he knew their type. If they were telling the world that they held over ten percent of Monty-0 stock, Richardson was figuring that they probably controlled twice that much and weren't yet required to file. What was lost on Richardson was their motivation. And their timing.

Richardson assumed that the Louisiana Project was the reason that his company was now in play. Here was a chance to make some big money. But no one supposedly knew about it. No company news releases had trumpeted its discovery. The collision had driven the stock prices down, but Richardson knew that they were going to go up again when the oil on the beach evaporated. They always did for an oil company after a major spill.

"*It has to be the Louisiana Project,*" Richardson thought.

In fact, nothing could be further from the truth. The reality of the situation was that the arbs had sunk a huge amount of money in Monty-O when the stock was selling for at full price for almost twice as much as the shares were worth now. Their actions were solely designed to goad Jenkins over at Bennington Oil to pay them their promised consideration. They would take Monty-O private if they had to in order to recoup their money; after all, it wasn't a bad investment. They just didn't want to if there was another option.

To make matters worse for Richardson, there were rumblings that an offshore brokerage had begun buying a substantial position in Monty-O. From London Bremerton Skye and McIntosh Financial, Ltd had bought a sizable chunk of Monty-O, and since they had no requirement to disclose their intentions under law for ten days, they didn't plan to. Richardson had no idea of who they were or their intentions. He just knew that he would need to worry about them as well.

Richardson was wondering why everything had happened

now. He had even gotten a report from his spies at Bennington Oil that they were preparing to make a massive stock buyback.

"They plan to buy back almost a billion of their own stock!" thought Richardson. That meant, at least to him, that Bennington Oil was about to do something that was going to make their stock value rise and they wanted to own as much of it as possible before that event occurred.

"What's happening?" he thought, *"What's going on that's leading to all of this?"*

He only had to look as far as Bennington Oil to find his answer.

Over at Bennington Oil Jenkins not only knew what was happening but why. Simply put, it was his plan in action. He had talked his company into using New York arbitrageurs to help purchase Monty-O stock and then he reneged on his deal with them. Jenkins knew this would antagonize them to the point of action, and that action would be drastic.

When the arbs left angry, Jenkins knew they were going to try and take over Monty-O. The fact that Bennington Oil was willing to go after it was enough for them, and they would figure out the true value of this company while they were researching it.

What almost no one knew was Jenkins' relationship with Bremerton Skye and McIntosh Financial, Ltd. He had gone to college with its CEO, and remained good friends and business partners since. He had made numerous contacts with the firm over the years, starting with his time at Jupiter Petroleum and lasting until the present. He kept them close to chest in the event that he ever needed their services, or involvement. Jenkins was using their services now.

He had laid his plan out for them months ago and they have been looking forward to this profitable endeavor ever since. Jenkins had them buy a small percentage and hold it. When the institutional investors started dumping it after the spill and its aftermath, they bought even more. Bremerton Skye and McIntosh Financial, Ltd now owned eight percent and had up to ten days to file with the SEC, which they planned to do on the tenth day. Although they planned on doing this, they weren't certain they would need to, as they were sure that this event would be over and all of their Monty-O shares cashed out before they hit the ten day requirement. Jenkins had Bremerton Skye and McIntosh Financial, Ltd hold the stock. There would be no need to file. With Bennington holding a significant portion and making hostile overtures, Jenkins knew that Monty-O would react. He figured that they'd react by announcing their most precious secret -- the Louisiana Project. When that happened the price of their stock would skyrocket. Jenkins thought that if their estimates were true, Monty-O could triple in value.

Jenkins planned his gambit carefully, forcing Monty-O's hand by making them reveal their LP discovery. Jenkins cut a deal with Bremerton Skye and McIntosh Financial, Ltd ; he would give them the information and they would make the move. Profits would be split 2 to 1.

After Monty-O announced their Louisiana Project and the market reacted, Bennington Oil wouldn't be able to afford a takeover Monty-O. Additionally, the Louisiana Project disclosure would tell Bennington Oil senior execs that the process of taking over Monty-O was now beyond their capabilities, as Monty-O would be at least twice as large as Bennington Oil. More importantly, it also signaled that within a year Monty-O would be coming after them -- mainly for their resources and not for their people. This fact had never been lost on Jenkins. He knew when he hung up the phone after talking to Ferryman that if the Louisiana Project ever came on line it was over for Bennington Oil. He knew he would be out of a job if Monty-O ever brought the Louisiana Project in. The only question was when?

That day was here and now, and for Bennington Oil the beginning of the end was underway. It will never be known how many Bennington Oil employees suspected that this ending was drawing near, but what was certain was that at least one Bennington Oil exec took the threat seriously and began plotting his own course of action. Once Monty-O grew enough they would take Bennington Oil and end a corporate conflict that began before World War II. At that time all traces of Bennington Oil's existence will have been erased, the same fate Bennington Oil had in store for Monty-O.

Jenkins either had to be on the winning team or suffer the same fate as Bennington Oil would -- oblivion. He could have chosen between those two options, but he decided a different path. He chose the third option -- his option. He wouldn't rely on a golden parachute. He would invent a golden intervention -- a situation created by him to insure that he would benefit in case of Monty-O's or Bennington Oil's demise. That was when he called Bremerton Skye and McIntosh Financial, Ltd.

But the collision allowed him a greater opportunity. He called it his golden destiny. With Monty-O prices dropping and Jenkins with the ability to affect the prices downward even more, a once in a lifetime score presented itself. Jenkins quit thinking about the takeover altogether and planned on simply making the biggest gamble of his life. By manipulating the crew he let people think Monty-O was at fault for the collision. The bad press and articles he commissioned affected the stock prices even more. His actions, including the lawsuits drove Monty-O prices to record lows. If and when Monty-O was forced to reveal their Louisiana Project, their share value would skyrocket. Jenkins knew they would do what they had to do to keep from becoming a Bennington Oil subsidiary. He was playing both sides against the middle, and he was in a position where he couldn't lose.

Edward Richardson looked out over his assembled staffers. Their concern was evident in the worried expressions that they were failing to suppress. Richardson could see that his employees were scared.

But he could also see that they were his people and that they were ready to do whatever he felt was needed to resist the threat. He was working on that as he stared out amongst them.

"First the good news," he began. "Our share prices have finally stopped sliding, so I think the free fall is over." He left out that it was nearly down 50% from the spill and that Monty-O retirement and pension funds had been savaged.

"You all know now that our company is in play," Richardson stated. "The arbs trying to take us over are dangerous and must be dealt with. The British firm is an unknown commodity. We all know that Bennington Oil is waiting to strike. I'll admit it myself, our situation looks grim."

"Grim?" said Charles Gerard, the head of Public Affairs. "We're about to be hit with a three-pronged attack. How can we survive it?" We can't fight off two legitimate and one potential takeover specialists. We can invoke our poison pill provisions and counter-attack, but we won't stand long. We need a miracle."

Richardson looked deeply at Gerard and smiled. The delivery of that statement was just as they had practiced, not too fast, not too slow but with enough deliberate tension that it conveyed the sense of dread he wanted it to.

Before Richardson could even answer the question, his cell phone rang. He looked at the phone and told the staff that this call was important and that he had to take it. He told the staff that the call was from the oil platform "Elizabeth" in the Gulf of Mexico. Few staffers knew the names of the oil platforms operated by Monty-O but they all knew about this one. It was named after Richardson's mother, who was rather insulted that a piece of technology as ugly as an offshore oil platform would be his monument to her. Her attitude changed when her son told her that the ugly piece of technology he named after her was valued at over $800 million. It turned out that she thought that phrase "$800 million dollars" sounded pretty, and that none of her friends had anything named after them valued in the same ballpark.

The call was from the Platform Superintendent Dixon, and was short and to the point. Another test well was showing very positive results.

Richardson hung up his cell phone and prepared to speak. Only two other people knew what he was going to say. One was Gerard and the other was Dixon, both of whom had just played their roles in Richardson's little theater.

"I've got our miracle," Richardson announced. For the first time he told the entire staff about the progress of the Louisiana Project.

"We were holding out on advertising the Louisiana Project until we knew it was solid, that it would produce and that there were no problems with ownership," he began. He also withheld that info because he wanted to use it to forge the financial clout to attempt to takeover Bennington Oil. Right now, survival was paramount.

He looked over to Gerard.

"Put out a news release focusing on the Louisiana Project. Tell the press that we estimate it contains one billion barrels of crude and the estimates for natural gas have not been completed."

"Sir," Gerard objected, "we don't have a crude oil estimate yet over 400 million barrels. Being that the difference could mean adding billions to our stock price and...

The staff caught on

"I guess" Gerard continued, "we can always revise our estimates later, after things have slowed a bit.."

"But," he added, "The exchange won't take too kindly to this."

"So what," said Richardson, "I heard that this find would bring in as much as 600 million barrels. It's speculative, but it's not lying, per se. What it does is buy us time. We'll make it up to the exchange later."

"How does it buy us time?" asked a staffer.

"Simple," said Gerard, "at say $40 a barrel, one billion barrels would be worth over forty billion dollars. Minus the royalties and taxes and other expenses and at least half of that is profit. Add twenty billion to the cost of this company and a takeover attempt goes from $7 billion dollars to $27 billion dollars. We conservatively thought the value of the company would at least double upon the release of this info, and that's when it was trading at $48. Collectively, I don't think our assembled adversaries could ante up $27 billion in today's market.

Uncertainty in what the Louisiana Project is worth will keep them from wanting to pay too much. They won't want to pay some massive sum and then find out their investment isn't as large as they thought. Also, the sudden, and I'll bet meteoric rise in price will put this company out of their price range. We get time and right now that's what we need. Their takeover rage will have to abate for at least a couple of weeks."

"Weeks, I should add," said Richardson, "that will see us gain in strength."

"But unfortunately," Gerard added, "the bastards trying to take us over will still profit handsomely when this news comes out."

"Whoever holds our stock will profit handsomely when this comes out," Richardson added. "They may even like what they see and stay on as satisfied investors."

"But what of all the people who sold their stock while it was freefalling?" Gerard asked.

"That," said Richardson brusquely, "is the price they'll pay for not being loyal."

"Seems kind of harsh, doesn't it?" said Gerard.

"My job is to make the shareholders, as a whole, happy," Richardson stated, "I don't really give a damn about them individually."

"What about 10b-5 violations?" asked another staffer. "The SEC won't take too kindly to us not revealing this info before now."

"What about them," said Richardson casually, "we're only under a duty to disclose factual information when we disclose. But we're under no duty to disclose information whatsoever. All we have to do is make sure whatever we say is true. But we don't have to say anything unless we want to."

"And secondly," he added for emphasis, "If we're around in a couple of weeks to deal with a pissed off SEC, that will actually be a good day for us."

For the first time today he saw smiling faces in his company boardroom. He knew that within three hours the word would spread to Bennington Oil employees in the field as well.

In less than an hour he signed off on the news release telling the world about the Louisiana Project. He also approved the proper filings to the SEC discussing material changes to the value of the company. The speed of electronic filings meant that everyone found out about the news at the same time, which was just moments after the information was sent.

The markets were caught off guard by the news and were stunned. Monty-O shares skyrocketed so high and so fast that, for the second time in just weeks, the exchanges suspended all trading in Monty-O for the rest of the day.

In the US Department of the Interior members of the Mineral Management Service were realizing that they had been had. A young Congressman representing the San Francisco area was realizing that a friend had just become way more powerful than before, based on help he provided. Three arbs in New York City screamed with glee when they found out that their Monty-O shares would double or triple in just weeks. Crewmen from the Benician Guardian would have probably wondered about the company's run of bad luck, first with the spill and then with their major rival's massive expansion, if they weren't about to begin a period of mourning for a respected ship captain. At Bennington Oil, almost all the upper management now realized that the takeover was still possible, but more difficult and expensive.

One Bennington Oil exec simply smiled and bided his time. Jenkins knew this step was coming. He had only to rid himself of one loose end and his work was done. He thought that he had already taken care of this problem but it seems that the person, David Morris, was persistent. As such, Jenkins made other plans; plans that were more intense and direct.

CHAPTER 25

A CAPTAIN'S CONFESSION

Morris parked his car and looked at the address on the stately Victorian before him. The house had been a staple of the neighborhood for over eighty years, and the impressive stained glass doors could be seen from the street. Morris marveled at how beautiful this house was, and how well maintained it was, before he remembered that he had a job to do.

He walked up the manicured path from the street and knocked on the door. He waited for a few seconds and was about to knock again when the door opened. Standing before Morris was Capt. Benjamin Marlowe.

Morris had never met Marlowe, but he could tell from his first glance that he looked tired, the type of fatigue that comes more from not sleeping than any serious physical exertion.

"Can I help you?" Marlowe asked.

"It's me, Morris," he began, "I had Fred Avey call and ask if I could speak to you."

"Yes," Marlowe replied, "Come in." Morris stepped into the entry foyer and realized that the house was as beautiful inside as it was outside. Once again he had to bring himself back to the task at hand.

"I'll make it quick and dirty," Morris started. "What happened out there-outside the Golden Gate?"

"It's in the papers-don't you read them?" Marlowe

started. "After all you put it out there."

"What do you mean by that?" Morris asked, "You guys told the press-we didn't."

"I didn't tell the press," Marlowe stammered, I, I didn't tell anyone. Anyone! Not the press. Not the Coast Guard. Nobody!" He paused.

"And because I wouldn't talk they revoked my Master's Certificate," he said flinchingly. "All because I wouldn't lie."

"Why didn't you testify at the inquest," said Morris. "Were you afraid of incriminating yourself? You didn't have to be. The Constitution.."

"Damn the Constitution. It won't protect me now. What you're looking at right now, right this minute, is a scared, cowardly old bastard that..." Marlowe's voice tailed off into almost a whisper.

"You're being too hard on yourself," said Morris, "It wasn't your fault. It was an accident, a terrible accident. But nothing more."

"You're so wrong," Marlowe replied. "It was our fault."

"We," he continued, "I killed all those men."

"Capt. Marlowe, tell me please, what happened out there?" Morris asked.

"I'll tell you what, how, why when and anything else," Marlowe answered.

"We left Benicia with a cargo of roughly 50,000 tons of oil on board. The harbor pilot took us under the Golden Gate and then left us. Around that time you remember a moderate to heavy fog had set in, but it was actually clearing up a bit. With visibility under a half mile, we proceeded at one half speed forward, around eight knots. Our radar was acting up a bit and we had other problems as well but we had them under control.

"All of a sudden the collision avoidance system alarms start blaring, letting us know that we were on a collision course with another vessel. We changed our course to port thinking that would tuck us in safely behind them and give us plenty of room to spare.

"When we were close to passing the other vessel, the rudder snapped hard to starboard. That turns us, at 6-8 knots, towards whatever vessel was out there. It was the Pacific Patriarch.

"I told those people at HQ that the ship needed some major work. I told them that the radar and the rudder were suspect at best and that both of them needed to be inspected before we left again.

"I knew that this ship was ready to cause a major problem," Marlowe uttered. "But this, this was damn near murder."

"Our ship shouldn't have been out there, loaded or not. She was trouble, trouble."

"Why wouldn't they listen to me?" Marlowe implied, "Why wouldn't they dry dock her and fix her, or try to?"

"Does money mean more than human lives?"

"No" said Morris, "it doesn't."

You wouldn't know that from watching our operations," Marlowe added sarcastically."

"So that's what happened," Morris began, "our rudder went out and when they cut in front of us......."

"AND NOTHING" yelled Marlowe. "They didn't cut in front of us."

"Did they veer or what" said Morris. "I mean, how did the ships collide?

Marlowe looked at Morris and shook his head

"The ships didn't collide," Marlowe stated solemnly. "We turned into them and hit them."

"What?" was Morris' reply. "I don't think I heard you right. You said that we turned into them and hit them?"

"Your hearing is OK. The Benician Guardian was in a turning motion when it hit the Pacific Patriarch. Because we were moving in an arc instead of a straight course, I'm not even sure their collision avoidance system would have picked up our action until we were too close to miss them."

"You can't be serious?" said Morris.

"I have never been more serious in my life. Our rudder froze and put us on an arcing collision course. I threw full reverse steam on both screws, but you don't stop a tanker with 50,000 tons of crude on a dime. Our momentum carried us forward with almost no reduction in speed. All that the full reverse accomplished was to alter where we would ultimately hit the other ship."

"If we hadn't slowed we would have tagged her bow. Instead we hit her damn near dead center – then she blows up and sinks and takes the whole crew, all 37 of them with her.

Marlowe stopped for a brief moment.

Those poor men never had a chance."

"But you told the Coast Guard and the press that…"

I didn't tell anyone a damn thing," said Marlowe, and because of it they took my license. The ship malfunctioned and there was nothing we could do that we didn't"

"Nonetheless," said Morris, "You told the Coast Guard…"

"Damn it," Marlowe yelled again. "Don't you listen. I didn't tell the Coast Guard anything. Not one word!"

Morris suddenly remembered that Marlowe was the only one involved, the only one subpoenaed who didn't give a sworn statement.

"Why didn't you talk to the authorities?" asked Morris

Marlowe was standing and looked out the window at the bay for just the briefest moment. He then dropped his head and slowly turned back around to Morris. He was preparing himself to release something painful, but was at the same time fighting to hold it in.

He turned and looked out the window again and said, almost under his breath

"I didn't talk because I couldn't; I didn't want to lie."

"Going to lie?" asked Morris. "You need to slow down a bit because you're losing me."

"Don't worry," Marlowe said, "I've lost myself. Somewhere in all of these lies and fabrications I let go of the truth.

"But you didn't lie to anyone." Morris interjected

"I know," said Marlowe, But I let a lie go on and on, and now its grown too large to stop."

"Capt. Marlowe," Morris answered, "A lie is a lie. Lies are based on deception. No matter how big a lie is, it still isn't real. No lie is too big to be brought down by the truth."

"I know what the truth is, Mr. Morris" said Marlowe. "I

just don't know what to do with it. I don't know how I can make anything right."

"Give me the truth Capt. Marlowe," said Morris, I'll see it gets put where it belongs."

And talk they did, with Capt. Marlowe spending the next 90 minutes telling Morris everything he knew about the crash and the events that transpired shortly thereafter. By the time that they had finished talking, Marlowe was firmly convinced that Morris would help him clear his name.

Morris had taken his leave about thirty minutes earlier when Capt. Marlowe stood and stretched his arms out. He walked over to his writing desk pulled out a pen and several sheets of paper. He started writing and hadn't realized that over an hour had passed since he first sat down and began to write, When he finished writing he went back and proofread it twice. He made sure all of the punctuation and grammar were correct. He ensured that all of the directions, meanings and definitions were correct, as he knew there would be no chance of correcting the documents once he had finished the evening's events.

Once he had finished he stapled the sheets together and folded them neatly into an envelope. He placed the envelope in the inside pocket of his coat; in a spot that he was certain it would be easily found

He got up and walked over to a closet where he pulled out a small oaken chest and stared at its contents. Inside the chest were two chrome .38 caliber revolvers; throwbacks to the days when the .38 caliber was considered powerful. They were both loaded and perfectly functional. They were gifts to Marlowe from some far away friend who never conceived that Marlowe could one day be in such inner turmoil and pain that he would take one, place it to his temple and pull the trigger.

CHAPTER 26

ATTACKED

Morris' mind was racing nearly as fast as the car he was driving. His always impeccable driving was now being replaced with the lane to lane swerving usually demonstrated by drunken drivers or those mentally impaired drivers with cell phones stuck to their ears. And so it should be, for Morris himself would have agreed that he was driving impaired. Not by alcohol but by a cognitive overload. His mind was riveted on Marlowe's revelations, and even the California freeway traffic could not draw its full attention.

What Marlowe had relayed to Morris had shocked and surprised him. When Morris first went to Marlowe's house, he thought, or just assumed, that Marlowe was a very small cog, a bit player in this mad circus. Morris had no idea at the time just how wrong he was. After Marlowe proceeded to tell Morris what really happened during the collision and its tangled and twisted aftermath, Morris came to the realization that not only were his investigatory efforts misguided, they were also ineffectual and in vain. Morris began looking into his own company's actions only after Martin had disseminated a news release distorting the truth. It was way more than that now.

"Up till now" thought Morris, "I've been treating this as an ordinary insider trading caper. But it was more than that now. Those bastards are actually trying to...."

Morris thoughts were interrupted by a vision. Not some wraithlike, ghostly apparition with a foreboding appearance and presence, but something more common and more familiar. And more sinister.

As Morris looked into the rear view mirror he saw that a red Thunderbird was following him. He thought back a minute and recognized it as one of the cars parked near Marlowe's house. At that time he had only notice the loud red paint job and notched it up as only another parked car.

His plan was to meet Nelson for dinner at 2 Embarcadero Square. For the next ten minutes he kept driving and scanning his rear view mirror for the car that was trailing him. It was five or six car lengths behind, staying just close enough to follow but not close enough for Morris to observe the driver. Morris thought of slowing down and trying to see who was tailing him, but he had somewhere to be. He left the freeway and entered the streets of the city, winding his way around to the Embarcadero area.

Morris had just passed the 100 block of Drumm Street, just north of Sacramento Street when he saw a car pull out of a metered parking spot. Activating his turn signal, he waited for a short moment while the driver cleared the space. Morris backed into the spot and parked on his first try.

"*Touché!*" Morris thought to himself, celebrating the most miniscule of driving victories.

As Morris walked back to the intersection of Drumm and Sacramento, he looked around to see if he could find where red Thunderbird parked. It was nowhere to be seen and Morris almost chuckled at that fact.

"*I can't be so paranoid that I think every car on the freeway is following me,*" Morris thought. He looked around again to see if he could find the red Thunderbird or its driver-although he had no idea of who he was looking for.

The crowd on the street wasn't large, but it was getting dark and that combination made it too hard for one person to try and scan the immediate area.

While scanning the street to look for the red Thunderbird or its driver, Morris noticed something unusual.

There was a man, a big man, across the street staring at

him.

The man seemed familiar, but Morris couldn't place him. Morris found this unnerving and decided to walk to the next intersection and cross the street down there.

Morris started walking when he glanced over and noticed that the man across the street, who had been staring at him, had started walking down that side of the street.

Morris had crossed Davis Street and while still on Sacramento had walked nearly half way to the next intersection with Front Street when he turned and looked back at the intersection to see if the man who was staring at him was still there. He wasn't.

Morris turned around and almost started walking to the restaurant when he saw the stranger directly across the street.

Morris became concerned and fearful in one quick instant. He didn't know who this stranger was or what he wanted. Before he let his paranoia get the best of him, he even wondered if the stranger were in fact following him. He decided to check.

Morris abruptly stopped walking, turned around and began walking back the way he had come, back towards the intersection of Davis and Sacramento. He had a quicker pace working now, so that he would cover the distance back to the corner in less time than he had thus far taken.

The stranger across the street had walked on a few paces before turning to check on Morris. When he did, he noticed that Morris had retreated and was well back down the street, having retraced his steps faster than he had originally taken them.

Nelson was in the restaurant and had seen Morris coming up the street. While he nursed his beer waiting for Morris' arrival, he was staring out of the window down onto the opposite side of Sacramento Street.

He first saw Morris at the intersection and he was tracking him as he came down the street.. As he saw Morris turn back down Sacramento and walk a bit faster, he figured Morris must have left something in his car. What happened next reinforced to Nelson that Morris was in danger.

Morris had nearly made it back to the intersection when

he saw that the stranger across the street had also doubled back. Morris no longer doubted that the stranger was there on his account, and that his next few steps needed to be weighed carefully. He had made it back to the light and was waiting for it to change when the stranger made it back to the crosswalk. Morris stared at the stranger, who stared back with equal intensity.

"Where have I seen him before..."

"Damn!"

Morris suddenly remembered where he thought he had seen this stranger. His meeting with him was a brief and painful one. But the stranger was still too far away for Morris to make an accurate ID. Morris only had a second to look into the face on that occasion. But that second was enough.

"This was the man that attacked me in the garage."

Morris looked at the stranger who kept his eyes fixed on him. The light was changing and just about ready to allow the stranger to cross the street. Morris didn't want another encounter. He could only think of one course of action.

Morris turned and began sprinting down Sacramento Street. The stranger shot across Sacramento Street and took off in hot pursuit of Morris. From his above-ground vantage point, Nelson saw the whole situation develop. He saw Morris running with a large individual chasing after him, and gaining. Nelson reacted quickly, and taking his cell phone in hand, dialed 911.

Morris was running as fast as he could. It didn't occur to him to yell or scream or otherwise draw attention to his plight. He just wanted to get away from the rapidly-closing stranger. Morris had been an athlete in his younger days, but that was before a drunk driver nearly killed him and specifically tore up his knees.

Morris ran as hard as he could and took great pains to avoid running into other people along the sidewalk. His interests weren't altruistic; he knew that contact would slow him down and he didn't want to be slowed down. Going slow might have meant getting beaten again. Or far, far worse

He crossed Front Street and ran past a bar and a McDonald's and turned into an alley. Had he thought it out he would have realized that running into an alley played directly into the hands of his pursuer. Morris wasn't thinking, he was fleeing and his only intent was to get to some place of safety and regroup. Unfortunately, it wasn't about to happen that easily.

Morris was running full speed when he turned into the alley, intending to be running full speed when he left it. He wasn't counting on the large garbage truck that was nearly blocking the alley. But he didn't panic any more than he had. Morris kept sprinting towards the truck. He was banking that he could get down one side of the truck.

As Morris approached the back of the garbage truck he decided to try and ease down the left side of it. There was just enough space for him to and he was hoping his pursuer was too large to fit through the narrow aperture that he was entering. Morris had covered half the length of the truck when he saw that the front of the truck was connected to a dumpster, and that the combination blocked his way. He immediately turned around and tried to get back out and go around the other way. He knew his pursuer was close, real close, and if he didn't move fast he would find out what his pursuer's interests were-the hard way.

Morris turned around and ran towards the back of the garbage truck. He wasn't aware of how close his pursuer was, but he knew that the distance was not great. But he still thought he could make it around the back of the garbage truck and down the other side where hopefully his pursuer would have trouble getting through.

Morris turned around the back end of the truck to discover that the distance separating him from his pursuer was exactly the length of a fully extended arm with a glove encased fist.

Once Morris cleared the back of the garbage truck he caught sight of something in his peripheral vision. Instinctively, he stopped running and ducked. His little maneuver worked, as a hard thrown straight jab flew over his head by a fraction of an inch. Morris was no fighter, but for the second time in a week he either had to fight or think quickly to keep from becoming a victim. He had failed miserably in his first attempt. He knew he couldn't fail now. This attack was more blatant, more out in the open than the first. The first attack was nothing more than a message. Morris knew this was different. This attack was meant to inflict harm. A lot of it.

Morris regained his balance and turned to run back out the alley. Before taking his first step down that course he turned to see where his attacker was. The instant that he wasted with this gesture was too long. Had he run back down the alley he might have gotten away. Looking back, though it only took a brief second, still took more time that he had to spare.

If Morris had the street sense that he always bragged to Alice about, he would have high-tailed it out of that alley before turning around and seeing what his attacker was up to. Street smarts would have never led him into that alley, and once in it, would have never impeded his effort to get out of it. His very survival was at stake and Morris probably didn't realize that by turning to see his attacker he was breaking the momentum he needed to safely exit the alley. The step or two advantage he had over his assailant disappeared. Morris realized this about the time it happened.

But by then it was too late.

His attacker saw Morris try to head out the alley and he had turned to go after him. When Morris had looked back to see where his assailant was, he saw his chance. Morris recognized that his attacker was far closer than he thought and he turned to run. The attacker grabbed the back of Morris' jacket collar and yanked back hard. Morris was jerked backwards with the jacket.

While he struggled to get free and escape, his attacker jarred him with two short, but solid jabs to the head. Morris swung blindly at his attacker, hoping to land a blow that might buy him some time. He heard what he thought was laughter coming from his attacker. Morris steeled himself to make another swing at his attacker, but his time had run out. His attacker had taken a full measure of Morris and suddenly swung his fist, shifting his weight to put as much impact in the blow as he could.

Morris didn't see it coming, and its arrival was devastating.

Hitting Morris on the side of the jaw, the blow immediately took his knees out from under him. He fell to the ground like a demolished hi-rise. Morris's next recollection was that he was on his hands and knees in an alley and a huge man was approaching him to cause more agony.

Morris tried to gather his faculties to make one last defense, but he didn't seem to have control of his hands and legs. He couldn't even scream for help.

His attacker spoke.

"Give me your wallet and tell everyone it was a robbery."

Morris was barely conscious and didn't comprehend a word his attacker spoke. Morris looked at his attacker and through the fog of his battered senses noticed that his attacked had reached into his pocket and was placing something over the fingers of the hand he had struck him with. He could not yet understand what was going on.

The attacker had slipped on a pair of brass knuckles and had approached Morris again.

"My employers asked me to specifically give this to you!"

With that the attacker pulled Morris up to his knees and leaned him against the garbage truck. Holding Morris' chin in his left hand, his attacker pulled his brass-knuckled covered right hand as far back as he could. Morris was totally defenseless and this next blow would find no resistance until it came in contact with Morris's unprotected face.

"I don't know who you aggravated," said the attacker, " but know that they are paying extra for this."

With that the attacker turned to that he could again shift his weight to help drive the blow into Morris' face.

Before he could unleash the blow the alley exploded in red and white light and sound, primarily a police car loudspeaker telling the attacker to drop his fist and put his hands in the air. The attacker gave thought to hitting Morris anyway, but two things stopped him. The first was the most important—the cops were pointing their service automatics at him and just might blow him away to save his victim. The second was he didn't want the police seeing what he did. A uniformed cop makes an excellent witness for the prosecution.

Alice and Nelson ran by the police car and attended directly to Morris, who was just now regaining his full abilities.

They told him that Alice had been watching out for him all day, to the point where they had rented a car to help track his whereabouts.

"Rented a car?" Morris asked.

"Yes," Alice replied, "a red Thunderbird." Morris raised half a smile.

"I figured it was his car." Morris said, pointing to the man in the back of the squad car.

"I could see why he would want one," Nelson added, "that thing rides really smoothly."

Morris stared at Nelson for a short moment.

Morris walked over to the police car where his attacker sat. The man looked to be huge, at least six foot five and 250 pounds. Morris could attest to his attacker's strength and ability.

As this was the first time that Morris had actually seen the man without a violent outcome, Morris felt free to speak to him.

"What exactly did you mean back there that your employers wanted you to hurt me? Who sent you?"

The attacker simply sat in the back of the police car and said nothing.

The cops asked Morris a few questions and told him that the detectives would call him in the morning for his statement on the attack. He told them how they could reach him and that he would be happy to talk to them. The cops told them that the attacker had not said a word to them either, and they doubted he was going to talk to anyone without a lawyer.

After a short minute Morris gave up on trying to talk to the man and walked back to where Alice was standing. Nelson was walking back as well. He had spotted something the police overlooked and he went to see what it was. Thinking it might come in handy he picked it up and put it in his coat pocket. He made it back to Alice at the same time Morris did.

Alice's face had a curious mixture of emotions written across it. She was relieved to know that Morris was OK although slightly injured. She was glad that she was in a position to help him and stop the attacks. She was concerned that there may be more attacks. But the overriding emotion on her face was hurt. Hurt because she knew, as the three of them did, that this matter was not over and that she still was on the sidelines.

Morris looked over at Alice. Her face told him everything he needed to do. His predicament told him he needed all the help he could get.

"Alice," he began, "how much of this do you know?"

"All of it." She replied. "Why won't you tell me what's going on? Why are you keeping me out?"

"Look at me," Morris replied. "If they did this to me based on what they thought I knew, imagine what they would have done to you? These bastards are heartless. I didn't want to, mean to bring you in to this."

"I have been a part of this ever since that damned tanker blew up," Alice started, "I have been a part of this ever since I became a part of you. I am a part of you aren't I?"

"Yes," Morris replied, "God knows you are a part of me. You're the best part of me, of my life, of everything."

"But Alice," Morris asked, "how can I say I love you and not try to shield you from this madness. Even I don't know how this is going to end."

She looked him straight in the eyes.

"How could you say 'I love you' to someone that didn't want to help fight your battles? When they laid a hand on you and started all of this, it

became my war as well. I'm not staying on the sidelines and watch them come after you again."

"We're a part of each other, right!" Alice began. It was a statement and not an inquiry. Morris nodded in approval.

"Then don't ever leave me out of something this important again."

"I won't." Morris replied, smiling.

"Good." Alice added, "Let's go home and get you fixed

up."

"Hey," Nelson began, "Don't you guys still want to eat?"
Alice and Morris just looked at him.
"Just asking?"

CHAPTER 27

MARTIN'S CLARIFICATION

"Come in Dave," Martin said, "You've wanted to talk, now here's your chance."

Morris had been waiting for this 4:30 p.m. appointment with trepidation. He needed answers to questions that no one wanted to ask. He needed answers to questions he was warned against asking. He paid dearly for asking those questions. He knew about the takeover attempt, but he had also heard that Monty-O released a statement broadcasting their Louisiana Project success. If so, the markets were in for a wild ride. Events were happening fast.

"Chaos," Morris thought, *"seems to be the only constant!"*

He looked at Martin and began.

"Something crazy's going on in this company." Morris blurted. "It has been ever since the night of the tanker crash. Since then, I've been busting my butt running around this place trying to get answers to media queries and everyone I need to see is either holed up with you or Jenkins. When I started asking other questions…" His voice trailed off.

Morris' voice was still firm, but the emotion in it was rising.

"You need to be down in PR where you belong and not up here doing whatever. So what's up? Why aren't you downstairs leading this parade?"

Until he reflected upon the conversation a little later on, Morris was unsure whether he was more upset at Martin because of his absence at a critical time during this disaster, which his professional side found galling; or at his suspected complicity in the company's questionable affairs. At the time, all Morris was sure about was that Martin was neglecting his duties for some unseen corporate goal, and Morris was tired of simply standing by and watching it.

"Dave," Martin began, "nothing is going on. The brain trust that runs this company has had an idea and I've simply been..."

"Don't patronize me!" Morris snapped. "I know what you're involved in."

Martin leaned back slowly in his chair and began eyeing Morris. He was thinking how best to handle the man across from his desk when Morris spoke again.

"You can tell me what's going on," Morris stated matter-of-factly. "Or I'll tell you."

Martin, and to a greater extent Jenkins, knew that Morris was up to something and may have even been able to scratch up some information about what was going on. They had watched most of his moves for the past few days and knew everything and everyone he had talked to. Or so they thought.

As Martin looked across his desk at his defiant subordinate, the intense glare he received back told him that Morris was not being coy, that he knew something important and possibly damaging. He had to know what Morris knew. He knew that Jenkins had to know as well.

The fate of a multibillion dollar transaction rested on Martin's handling of Morris. As such, Martin decided to let Morris play his hand, to let him tell everything he knew. Martin's plan consisted of two parts: the first was to sit back and let Morris reveal just how much he knew, and the second was to allow Morris to, unknowingly, show Martin just how dangerous he might be to Bennington Oil's plans.

"Not too long ago," Morris began, "our company accepted a $5 billion dollar line of credit from a syndicate of thirty four banks. Your purpose was clear from the start. There was not going to be a company-wide upgrading of our refineries, no new oilfields to tap and no new off-shore start-ups.

"No," Morris exclaimed, "you people were after bigger game."

"You probably said to yourselves, 'Why should we spend twenty dollars a barrel bringing oil out of the ground when we can get it for less?"

"How? Easy!" he shouted in mock glee. "We buy another oil company, that's how."

"The sole purpose of that loan was to buy Montgomery Oil. Everything was set. But before your little scheme could be hatched, it was affected by a totally unforeseen chain of events."

"Two oil tankers, one full and one empty, collide some fifteen to twenty miles outside the Golden Gate. The full one, ours, T-boned the empty one, theirs. The empty one, owned by Montgomery Oil has the fumes in her empty tanks ignited by sparks and blows up like Mt. St. Helens. The blast is so powerful it's heard ninety miles away. It also killed the crew and took the bow, not to mention the structural integrity, out of our tanker, which was carrying a substantial load.

"Our tanker, just in case you didn't know, with its faulty radar, sonar engines and totally non-functioning rudder, was totally at fault. That's right, our rudder was not only non-functional, but it locked in place so that they couldn't even steer with the engines. Since they didn't have the time to try, we'll just never know will we?

"But you knew this could happen. That's right. I know that you and the rest of the staff have access to and have read the reports on the Guardian. Marlowe suspected that the rudder was acting up and he wanted to dry dock the ship and fix it. But you guys in the boardroom overwhelmed him. Then, when he really needed the rudder, it failed. That accident was not Marlowe's fault," Morris stated accusingly.

"The blame rests with you and everyone on the staff who valued profits over all else."

"The poor bastards on the Pacific Patriarch never knew what hit them."

"Then, if you can believe this, someone in our boardroom

has a brainstorm and says 'Why don't we blame their tanker. It's not like any of their witnesses will come forth!"

"Your damn right none of them will come forth!" Morris exclaimed.

"They all went down with the Pacific Patriarch. So we can do this and not get caught!" Morris stated loudly, animatedly waving his hands while he spoke.

"Yeah," he continued, "Just because we're at fault is no reason for us to take the blame!"

"All we have to do is to tell the crew what to say to the Coast Guard and the media. If they ever care to work again, they'll agree."

"After all they'd been through, you guys still send someone over to strong arm them for their testimony."

"So then you and Jenkins come up with some outright lie and you tell the crew to pass it on or else. They're scared, so they do it."

"All except Benjamin Marlowe. He refuses to lie for you, but he keeps quiet because of what you threatened to do to his crew. He couldn't live with that shame. He committed suicide rather than live with this lie. The 37 men who died in the collision were accidental. Marlowe's death is on your hands."

"Marlowe was an honest man. The collision wasn't his fault. Hell, he did what he was supposed to do. But your ship...," Morris paused briefly, ."..our faulty ship let him down."

"He knew how dangerous his predicament was during that night. After the Patriarch exploded and he gave the abandon ship order, he checked the sleeping quarters and the galley area to make sure no one else was left aboard.

Although he was decimated by the high loss of life, he could live with it. He couldn't live knowing how he allowed the desecration of the memories of those killed."

"The collision was a totally accidental occurrence," Morris continued.

"But then the boys in strategic planning, always thinking those guys, they say, 'Is it possible that if the public, outraged over the fouling of their shoreline and its effects on their livelihood, condemned Montgomery Oil, that the price of their stock could be forced lower?

"So they get you to get the public affair office to give the press a load of trash about how Montgomery Oil's environmental record is a nightmare; that their tankers are accidents waiting for a place to happen.

"That's bullshit and you know it!

"Their record is damn near the industry standard. Their tankers are environmental showcases. Twin hulls, rudders and propellers, and a 2500 ton slop tank for pumping in the sludge from cleaning their tanks rather than going outside of international waters and dumping it.

"They're what our tankers should be.

"Marlowe told me that the twin hulls on the Pacific Patriarch absorbed enough of the explosion to allow the crew of our tanker to escape. The force of the explosion went upward. The strength of their twin hulls directed the blast that way. Marlowe told me that if you put a firecracker in a paper cup, when it goes off it'll blow the paper cup all to pieces. But if you cut the top off of a tin can and put a firecracker in it, the force of the blast will go back through the opening, since the rest of the can is too strong and won't give way. A single hulled ship would have responded in the manner of the paper cup. In a double hulled vessel the blast would have gone upward, through the single layer deck plating above the tanks. While the construction of their vessel didn't do them any good, it saved the lives of our crew.

"Not that that matters to anyone in this HQ.

"Anyway, we drag Montgomery Oil through the press with lies, falsehoods and innuendo, then lo and behold, we start a shareholders panic. Their shares were dropping several points on some days.

"Then, we start taking steps that make it seem like we are actively seeking to buy a majority interest in Montgomery Oil. So you guys jump on the chance. All for what? For greed. That crap went out with the eighties. "You're figuring that with the current stock prices depressed as they are, this company will save billions.

"I thought we were just preying on their misfortune. That makes us little better than leeches. But now I know that we're the ones causing their misfortune. When not scavengers like leeches, we're predators. We've broken countless laws and we're going to get away with it. They've done everything right and they're about to pay dearly for it. Isn't there a lick of compassion in this company? You know, just a trace of plain human decency."

Martin had listened to Morris' soliloquy long enough. He learned all he wanted to about what Morris knew, and he felt now was the time to put Morris in his place.

"Compassion," Martin said coldly, ."".. is for losers. Monty-O was compassionate and they're about to become our fully owned subsidiary.

"You're right," he added, "we were going to swallow them up all along. There's nothing wrong with that. True, after the conflagration outside the Golden Gate we thought to ourselves, 'Maybe some good can come out of this'"

"Their stock would have dropped simply because they lost a $40 million dollar tanker, a partial load and bore some responsibility for an oil spill. But we saw a chance to profit even more."

"There was a large slick, a massive slick that was hitting the beaches before the crash was six hours old. Hell, it was still dark!

"When the people who live here got up and went to work and then saw the shoreline just covered with sludge, oil and all that other crap we were carrying, you can bet your ass they were going to be pissed off.

"San Francisco is based on banking, tourism, seafood and shoreline, especially this time of year. Three out of four were now threatened -- how permanently is questionable, depending on who you ask. You know the party line on that. We won't know, for months to come, the full effect of this spill.

"But what we do know now is that this slick is killing fish and other sea life, its soiled beaches for miles, it smells like hell and its affecting the commerce of this city. Conventions, honeymooners and vacationers are all going elsewhere in droves, and it's going to cost this city plenty. A lot of the public is going to want revenge. Someone is going to have to pay, and pay dearly.

"Sure, the two tankers colliding was an accident. Do you think that means anything to someone who is going to lose their job? Do you think that matters at all to the hotel owners, street vendors, store proprietors and everyone else who stands to lose millions of dollars?

"Hell no!" was Martin's sarcastic reply.

"To them, two big greedy oil companies have fouled up the bay, and they want blood. So we figured that we'd give them blood."

"Montgomery Oil's blood," stated Morris.

"Exactly," said Martin. "We decided right then and there to make Montgomery Oil look so bad that we couldn't have been responsible for the catastrophe.

"Since their ship took all hands down with it, they'd have no witnesses for their defense. The only side that could be presented with any degree of substantiation would be ours.

"You were right about me and Jenkins. We figured out what the best truth should be and we passed it on to the crew. When you saw me leave the boardroom during the night of the crash, we were going to present this to the CEO. He agreed and Jenkins and I went to the hotel where the crew was quartered.

"We only spoke to those crew members who were on duty and above deck, with a view of the crash. The rest of them were told only to talk about what they were doing at the time of the crash. At first, most of the crewmembers we talked to balked at what we were asking.

Then we told them another truth; that they would never work again if they didn't go along with it. In these days of tight employment, and shrinking employment in the American maritime arena, they saw the light, and they told the Coast Guard exactly what we told them to.

"As for Marlowe, we never thought he go as far as to do something like this. I know you don't believe this, but I am genuinely sorry. We didn't think that something like this could happen."

This statement caught Morris by surprise. He half figured that Martin and Jenkins had some involvement in Marlowe's death.

"I'm not wrong about Martin," he thought, *"he's a total bastard. But could it be that he doesn't have a choice in the role he's playing in this matter? I got caught up in this by accident. Could it be that they needed his media expertise and that his involvement is by the design of someone higher up. It never occurred to me that Martin might just be playing the cards he was dealt."*

As Morris pondered Martin's role, Martin continued.

"In short, we had our crew blame the other ship. They told the Coast Guard and the press how the other ship had cut them off and before they could react -- tragedy struck.

"Imaginative," Morris offered, "but totally false."

"I see you've done your homework," was Martin's less than courteous reply.

He continued.

"The stories I released to the press continued to berate Monty-O. We emphasized all of their problems for the last ten years. That was hard to do because there weren't that many. Anyway, our goal was to whip the public into a frenzy about how bad Monty-O was.

Martin allowed himself a smile and added, "Call it pre-emptive public relations."

"I call it fraud and deception," Morris shot back.

"I figured you would," said Martin.

"Well anyway, the pickets came out and people started protesting Monty-O stations. Here's one even you didn't know about. We've paid several, shall we call them ambitious, people to protest against Monty-O.

"This started affecting their business. Couple this up to the prevailing public attitude and their monstrous expenditures on the Louisiana Project and you have a company whose stockholders are panicking. Their own stockholders, in their panic, are driving their stock prices lower. So few people want to buy the stuff that they're accepting lower prices just to get rid of it. Like you said earlier, they're playing right into our hands.

"Last week we "commissioned" our "investment counselors" to purchase millions of Monty-O stock. Over the week we have engaged in the serious buying and corralling of Monty-O stock. Before too long we'll control Monty-O outright.

"And you know what the best part of all of this will be," Martin added, "when we announce to the world that we've assumed ownership of Monty-O in the best interest of the public."

"I can see it now," Martin said while extending his arms outward and simultaneously spreading them apart, "We'll tell the media that we're taking control of this company and we plan to shape it up."

"Hell, the only thing wrong with Monty-O is us," Morris added.

"What about your counterpart at Monty-O, Charles Gerard. Hasn't he been denying your claims to the press?"

"Yes he has," replied Martin, "rather vehemently. But once you get the press going there's just no stopping them. Rather than listening to Monty-O objectively, they've gone after them with a passion.

"Can you actually believe that the press is looking for a cover-up? Those pitiful fools couldn't see the truth if it were right in front of them. All except for one reporter, a gentleman named Larry Nelson.

"I believe you know him well."

"Before we tampered with our company's pollution record held at the state Pollution Board, which even you didn't know about that one, your reporter friend found out that Monty-O was literally the environmentalists' friend. He was going to run that fact, in a damn good story if I might add, in the East Bay Gazette, the big daily across the bay. Now that just wouldn't play into our hands.

"I called the Gazette's publisher and let them know that we did $1.35 million worth of advertising in that paper and just slightly less than that with their affiliated electronic mediums every year.

"Now you know that they're coming off of some of their worst years ever and they can't really afford to lose one of their largest advertisers. They know as well as we do that their competitors would love our account. That's why they killed the story.

"We also asked the publisher to take the precaution of pulling Nelson away from the story and giving him a nothing assignment until he cools his heels. That's the last we heard of him until he called the cops that saved your life the other night."

Upon hearing that Morris snapped back in his chair, then slowly came forward, resting his elbow deliberately on the armrest. During the whole time he never took his eyes off of Martin.

"How do you know he was there?" Morris demanded. "Unless you spoke with one of the people there you couldn't possibly have known. The only people there were Alice, Larry, the hood and the cops. I didn't tell you and you definitely haven't spoken to Alice or Larry or they would have told me about it. That leaves the hood and the cops, and somehow I don't believe you went to the police.

"You bastard," Morris said scornfully. "You sent him after me didn't you?"

"He was sent after you," Martin replied calmly, "but I was against it."

"But you didn't stop him, did you?" Morris added.

"Nothing matters to you does it? First you all but kill Marlowe and now you send some hood after me.

"You're just some heartless machine that does what your superiors program you to. You gutless ...."

The sound of Martin's fists slamming into his desk stopped Morris cold.

"That's enough," Martin yelled. I'm not somebody's little robot. There's more here than meets the eye."

"I'm ready to hear it," Morris replied.

"Shut up for a minute," Martin hissed.

"You need to understand something here. I'm in this thing up to my neck and I'm playing with people who want to win more than they want to live. Get me!"

Morris nodded as Martin continued.

"If I try to break away then they come after me like they've started coming after you."

"That's right," he restated for emphasis, "they've just

started coming after you. I don't know how long they'll keep coming after you, but you need to know this. I did know someone was coming after you but I didn't just sit there and do nothing.

"You pride yourself on the results of this little investigative caper of yours. Did you know that the guy who came after you was originally supposed to kill you? Did you?"

Morris sat stunned at that revelation.

"When he was pummeling me," said Morris, "he told me to give him my wallet so that it would look like a robbery. He told me he was only going to scare me."

"I didn't think you guys would have sunk so low."

"Well they have," said Martin, "and I don't know if they'll stop. You see, I told them that if this thug killed you, that I would go to the police because I want no part of a murder. So they told their friend to go easy on you. By the way, they call him the Priest. I guess he's good at last rites or something."

"But they have other ways of working on you. In your case, I don't think they'll be pulling any punches, no pun intended." Martin sat back down and extracted a typed piece of paper from his top desk drawer. Morris could not make out the scribbles on one side, but he knew Martin was about discuss what was written on it.

"They know everything there is to know about you. They know that the house you bought for your parents has $225,000 left on the note. They know that your car still has a $22,000 debt. They know the number of all your credit cards, and those of your lawyer friend Alice. They know that your bank and ours are one. That bank will do anything to keep its largest customer happy, including ruining another customer.

"The CEO wants me to tell him by close of business today that you'll quit this snooping of yours, or by close of business tomorrow you'll be out of a job, lose your car and possibly see your folks thrown out on the street. A job paying the kind of money you're making now won't be that easy to find, if at all. Then when they call here asking why you left, I can guarantee you won't find work around here. These people will destroy you here in San Francisco and you won't have the resources to recover anytime soon. Can your parents, in their seventies, ever recover?"

"Consider all of your options Morris, they don't look all that' good."

For a brief moment Morris stared silently at Martin. Then he dropped his chin into his up stretched palm, while resting his elbow on the arm of the chair.

Martin looked at him and knew immediately that he was staring at a beaten man. The family gambit had worked, and Martin now learned what it took to pierce Morris' armor.

Morris had made many commitments to his parents and he had always kept them. When his sister struggled for eight long years with cancer, their parent did all they could to save her. They spent their entire life savings and most of their retirement looking for a cure, and upon resigning themselves to the obvious, they did whatever it took to make her final days happy and comfortable. That was four years ago.

They had put aside a small amount that would let them survive, but just barely.

As a result of all the money they spent on their daughter's illness, their home was foreclosed and sold at auction. They were in the process of packing, in preparation of moving from the family home into a small two-bedroom apartment when he stepped in and told them that he had bought the house. Bennington offered several of its top executives a reduced interest rate home loan, and armed with one, Morris bought his parents' home. He probably would not have qualified for the house without Bennington Oil's intervention. However, since the company had him sign a promissory note for the balance and thus was not concerned about getting their money repaid, the reduced interest rate he was paying allowed him to easily afford it on his six figure salary.

But even that was being threatened now.

Morris looked back at Martin and began.

"How can you let them do this to me, to us?"

"They're not doing it to us," Martin replied coldly. "They're doing it to you. The reasoning is simple. When I was first informed about this takeover, I thought it was a good idea and I was more than happy to assist. After all, there's nothing wrong with that.

"When I found out about the crash and what the company was planning to do to Monty-O, I wanted nothing to do with that. They, the CEO and Jenkins, told me that was an option that I could not exercise. They told me what they'd do if I didn't play along and judging by your treatment, I can see they weren't joking. I knew that I'd be crushed if I balked. I then realized that I could profit handsomely if I went along. Once the purchase of Monty-O is complete, good things are going to start happening for some of us. As you have probably found out, our $5 billion dollar line of credit will be used to purchase 85% of Monty-O."

"No," questioned Morris, "I thought that $5 billion was going to be used to purchase all of Monty-O. What happens to the rest?"

Martin wasn't about to add to Morris' interpretation of the takeover, Martin abruptly changed subjects.

"We're not here to talk about what the company is going to do next," Martin began, "we're here to talk about what you're going to do next."

"You said that you changed your mind about this thing when you found out that you could profit from it. What exactly did you mean?"

"I meant," said Martin, "that early on there was a chance to make a killing. That opportunity will have passed by close of business today."

"If you had told me more about this side of it, the possibility of making money, I might have been less of a problem" said Morris.

"That possibility has passed," said Martin, and since it wasn't extended to you, I'd not worry myself about it."

"Martin," enquired Morris, "How deep are you in this thing?

"Too deep to back out or even want to," Martin said curtly.

"But enough of this chit-chat. I need to know where you stand and what you plan to do before you leave this room."

Martin had decided to end this matter once and for all. His patience had been tried and he was suspecting that Morris was trying to piece together another phase of this takeover.

Martin now knew that Morris possessed a great deal more information than either he or Jenkins suspected. Martin now realized how much of a threat Morris really was.

And yet, Martin knew he had a little time to decide what to do. The revelations about what would happen to Morris and his family would stop him from acting on what he knew, but only for a while. It was the unsaid part of the conversation that Martin knew, or at least hoped, would freeze Morris. Martin's mastery of subtlety allowed him to slip into the conversation three points that, if combined, Morris would find very disturbing. Martin had mentioned that the company would not hesitate to have Morris attacked again, that they not only knew where his parents lived but they were prepared to lash out at them and that they could destroy him professionally and financially if and when they so desired.

It worked. Morris was wondering if the company would send some thug to attack his parents, just as they had sent after him. Martin hadn't said so directly, but then he did set Morris up to be attacked. As such, Morris didn't know if what he had just heard from Martin was a threat or a warning.

All he knew was that it had to be heeded or someone close to him might pay the price. But he had to be sure.

"If I don't go along with you, exactly what's going to happen?"

"To me," Martin replied, "nothing. To you, nothing good. The CEO has already talked to the bank about you, and in a couple of days you'll be fired and with no income, you'll have violated the conditions of your loans, at which time the bank will call them all in, and the loans on your car and you house will come due. You'll be out of a job with no chance of employment in this city. And there's no guarantee that there won't be another thug in your future.

"For your own sake you should tell me that you won't do anything to harm this operation. You'll get crushed like an eggshell if you don't. You're too good a person to suffer what's about to happen to you. Throw in with us Dave. The alternative is not good, to say the least. "

"I'm not sure I can," Morris said.

Martin's look turned to pain when he heard Morris'

refusal.

"What you're proposing is wrong," Morris continued, "This is libel, stock manipulation, insider trading, conspiracy. If that got out we'd all go to jail. You people know my commitment to my parents. How am I going to help them in jail?"

"You have nothing to worry about," said Martin, "there is very little hard proof of any of this happening. You have more of this plan in your head now than even existed on paper. Getting caught by the law is the least of your worries."

"That may be," said Morris, "but I still fear the law more than I fear you guys."

"That could be a big mistake," said Martin. "Remember, there is a limit to what the law can and can't do. We have no such constraints. You've already found that out."

Martin was referring to the two attacks that Morris had already suffered at the hands of company paid hoods.

"Just because there is a tremendous profit potential," Morris added, "that doesn't make this right. What about ethics? What about the ability to look at myself in the mirror every morning and not worry about getting caught?"

"What about the ability to look at yourself in the mirror every morning with your own eyes and your face still pretty much intact? The same for your parents and your lawyer friend? This thing is bigger than you could possibly know, and if you step on the wrong side of the line you won't go far before they get you."

"Dave," Martin started, "for God's sake, put aside your petty virtues and look at the realities of your situation. You're having trouble making up your mind. I'll make it for you. I'll tell the CEO that you've agreed to stop snooping around if he agrees to call off the dogs. You will, of course, stop snooping around.

Morris looked at Martin for a moment and then lightly bowed his head in agreement.

"Good," said Martin," then I won't be lying to the boss."

CHAPTER 28

MIDNIGHT CONTEMPLATION

In the hours following his confrontation with Martin, Morris was at a crisis point.

"I'm being involved in something that I don't want to be," thought Morris. *It's larger and more complex than anything else I've ever done. If I do nothing then I am an accomplice to fraud, stock manipulation and God only knows what. By knowing and not telling the authorities I hold a share of the responsibilities of what happens next."*

"If I do tell anyone and this deal collapses, I'm ruined. And those guys will put my folks out on the street, as well as blackballing me. Martin was right; my alternatives don't look so great."

Morris sat in his car on the access entryway to Treasure Island, halfway across the San Francisco Bay, and tried to figure out his next steps.

Martin had told him, fairly accurately, of the last few days of his life. Morris had no reason to doubt Martin's view of the immediate future.

"I tried to be a hero and what did it get me? I took the high road and all it did was to get me to hell quicker. I did right and I got crushed.

"My parents, my teachers my Bible all said that the exact opposite was supposed to be happening.

Good is supposed to win, damn it! I haven't done

anything wrong and I got my ass kicked twice, my job is all but gone and my professional future is in serious doubt."

"The road to hell is truly paved with good intentions!"

Morris took a deep breath in an effort to steady himself.

"You don't believe that," he thought, *"you never did and you never will. Take stock, pull yourself together and let's see what we can salvage."*

Common sense was coming back to Morris.

"I can't influence the past. Trying to is wishful thinking at its best and a waste of time and energy at its worst. Quit feeling sorry for yourself. You're in a hellish situation and sooner or later you are going to have to find an answer. Stop feeling sorry for yourself.

But the bravado of those optimistic thoughts were always silenced by the reality of the situation

"When that man knocked me unconscious I pressed on, not because I wanted answers, but because I wanted revenge on the bastard who nailed me and on Martin for treating me like I was insignificant. It was that simple.

After I talked to Marlowe I had all of my answers. Then came the second attack. That guy got arrested. My cuts and bruises will be healed in three weeks. He's going to get years in prison. Society won't miss him.

Yet, I pity the kind of man who has to resort to hiring people like him. They're obviously cowards with big dreams and aspirations but lacking spine and conviction. What a hollow life that must be.

But now I know the truth. The Bible says the truth shall set you free. The truth will free me alright. Free me of my job, my car, my way of life, my promise to my parents

If righteousness is so right. Why am I going through hell; why am I facing a situation that will brand me "hypocrite" or "ruined?"

Whether he liked it or not, Morris knew Martin was right.

"I only have two real choices and both of them aren't very good. I've considered the alternatives. Play the game and lose my integrity or go against the grain and get destroyed.

They've threatened your lover, your parents, your friends and your job. There's no idea of what they might be capable

of. Hell, look what they've done to you and they told you that they weren't finished yet.

Everything and everyone of value in your life is now involved, whether they know it or not. Whether they want to be or not. And whether you know it or not, you got them all in. And now, you have to get them all out."

He thought about Martin's words.

"They'll never let me in. They just want me out of the picture.

"C'mon God, if you can hear me, if you're even listening, I could use some serious help. Everything is falling in and I need a miracle!"

His request was met with the same silence that preceded it.

"I can't go out like this. I won't."

He looked out across the bay again and looked at the skyscrapers. He stared at them for almost a minute before a thought came to him. The thought was a familiar one – he often had it driving over the Bay Bridge at night.

He was looking at the lit buildings when a realization broke through his pity party.

"Those buildings stand every day and their outward appearances never changes," thought Morris. *"Until night! At night, when the darkness fell, the lights left on in each building made each building individual, unique, different from all others, including itself.*

"When the darkness fell was when each building distinguished itself."

"Morris sat himself up in his seat.

"Darkness sets each of them apart. The darkness has fallen on you and then some," Morris added

"In my darkness," thought Morris, *"how can I distinguish myself, what can I do to make myself different? Individual? Unique? What can I do that they won't be expecting?"*

There was only one real answer

"Í can fight them!"

CHAPTER 29

UNSCHEDULED MEXICO

Morris had arrived home far later then Alice expected. She assumed that something big must have happened at the office and after he told her of his meeting with Martin she realized that she was right.

She felt anger when he told her that the company was behind his attacks and even more nefarious activities. Morris saw her eyes flash when he told her what Martin had told him. He also told her that they wanted him to do a business trip to Mexico City that was leaving tomorrow morning and would be gone for the next two days.

"Why you?" she started, "This isn't your job. They have courier services for stuff like this."

"They want me out of town and as far away from their news conference their having the day after tomorrow," said Morris. "I guess that's when they are going to announce their plans for Monty-O."

"Again," Alice asked matter-of-factly, "why you?"

"Pettiness," Morris responded. "Small-mindedness. They told me if I go I can keep my job. If I don't, I probably don't get to keep my job. Plain and simple!"

"To hell with this," Alice blurted, "If they think we're...

Morris cut her off.

"It's OK; I told them I'd go."

"Why?" Alice replied.

"Because I intend to use the time to plot my course. I'm not going to take this sitting down. I plan to fight them and I could use the time to think."

"Dave, I don't..."

"Alice," he stated, "I share your concerns." But in a tone of resignation he added, "I need this job-now more than ever."

He saw her look of concern and tried to allay it.

"I'll be OK, so don't worry."

It didn't work.

Almost an hour later, Morris stepped into the shower he'd been waiting for all evening. Just warm water and a chance to let the day go somewhere else for a while. It was his break from a very bad day. He welcomed the opportunity.

His stepping into the shower was also a welcomed opportunity. Alice knew she had about ten minutes as she began dialing her cell phone to talk to Nelson about this latest development.

He answered the phone and she filled him in.

"What do you know about this trip?" Nelson asked.

"Nothing" replied Alice. "It's just some short-notice, life-inconveniencing, no-value make work courier run."

"*Damn,*" Nelson thought. "*Don't hold back! Tell me what you really feel.*"

"I think they mean this trip as some sort of punishment" she added. "He thinks this will give him time to think about his next move. It's giving the Bennington Oil people time to plot their next move as well."

"Alice," Nelson began, "Do you know anyone at Bennington Oil that you trust?"

"I'm familiar with some of his co-workers, but no one I could call and drop something like this on."

She thought for a moment before continuing.

"He has mentioned a guy he was familiar with, a guy who has actually lost his job over all of this. His name was Phil something or other."

"Can you reach him?" Nelson asked.

"No, but let me check." She went over to where Morris had left his clothes and went through the pockets. She couldn't find Phil's number. It seems that the little scrap of paper that once held Nelson's and Phil's numbers was gone. Sometime during the day Nelson had discarded it.

"I don't have it but if I find it I'll text it to you. OK?" she inquired.

"OK" Nelson replied.

Alice needed to get Phil's number and didn't know where to begin looking for it. She then had a thought and took the few minutes remaining before Morris finished his shower to formulate a plan.

"Hon," Alice began as Morris re-entered the living room, "a guy named Phil called earlier today and asked if you'd call him back?

"Really," Morris replied. "Good. I've been trying to reach him and he doesn't seem to be answering his phone. I've called him at least five times this week. I need to tell him something."

"What's that?" asked Alice.

"That I'm sorry for getting him involved. And fired."

"You didn't fire him. Those other bastards did!"

"It wouldn't have happened if I had thought about what he stood to lose instead of what I stood to gain."

"It's not your fault," Alice said.

"Maybe not," Morris answered, "But it certainly feels that way, and maybe the only way I can shake this feeling is by making things right with Phil. Or at least try to make things right. It's getting late so I'll try calling him tomorrow before we go to the airport."

"You really are one of the good guys aren't you?" said Alice

"Yeah I guess," was his joking reply.

Morris had gone into the main room and started watching the evening news and hadn't noticed that Alice went into the bedroom. Their recent exchange provided Alice with exactly what she was looking for. Now, she only needed a few seconds to finish what she was planning.

She walked over to where their cell phones were charging. She picked up Morris' and with a few pressed keys came to the list of his fifteen most recent calls. She scanned the list and noticed that there were three numbers repeated on the list. She entered the number into her cell phone and dialed it.

After four rings a sleepy voice replied.

"Hello, Phil here."

"Phil," Alice started in mock surprise, "sorry, wrong number." With that she hung up the phone.

Across town an unemployed security guard stared at his cell phone, angry that one of his precious minutes had been wasted by a late night wrong number.

Alice texted the phone number to Nelson with the message. "He's awake. Call him now!"

Nelson did.

CHAPTER 30

DIRE DISCOVERY

Phil was at home, all alone and feeling upset. For all of his life he was a pushover, a nerd. He was insignificant, and he knew it. What kept him going was his vastly superior knowledge of computers, and the belief that someday, sometime in the not to distant future, in some manner, that knowledge would pay off handsomely.

But as he lay in bed there was only one daunting reality for him to face. He was fired. Whenever that special day came when his technical knowledge would pay off, his only certainty at the moment was that this wondrous day was not yet here. In fact, for most of today, he had faced the exact opposite.

"*No job means no money,*" Phil thought, "*and no money means no college.*"

"This just can't be happening," he whined. He looked over in the corner of his small cramped studio apartment and stared at the materials he was studying for his finals in the coming weeks. He wanted to bury himself in his technical manuals and textbooks in the vain hope of closing off the real world; a place he liked considerably less today than yesterday. Those thoughts quickly were erased by the cold hand of reality. He couldn't afford to stay in school without a job. He needed help and he needed it fast.

The first day after he had been fired, had gone fast.

Attempts to find work at college, or through college, had been a dismal failure. The jobs they offered were almost all minimum wage, which would allow him to either stay in school or afford an apartment and board, but not both. The newspapers were full of articles about San Francisco based corporations downsizing and Phil was now seeing firsthand how the job market was being saturated with newly laid-off workers.

Phil was trying to prioritize the remaining fragments of what had been his normal life. His choices were few and he was beginning to despair. He had not felt this bad he was stood up for his junior prom. He needed help, but he didn't know where to turn.

Phil never knew how to make friends. He had been hurt by people too many times to remember and consequently, saw no real need to have many of them in his life. Whether his lonely lifestyle was a shield against this pain, or caused by it, was an issue for therapists to decide. He had a camaraderie with many of the other security guards, and that slim contact passed for his social life. This lack of personal interaction was about to come back and haunt him.

Now that he needed friends for help, there were none there to assist him. Phil had placed his friendships in computers. He made them his friends, possibly the only real friends he wanted. Even now, though, he blamed them for part of his situation.

"If I hadn't tried to get into those computers for Mr. Morris," thought Phil, *"I would be at work now. I should have just minded my own business and let him get his answers somewhere else. I..."*

Phil stopped, knowing full well he didn't believe what he was thinking.

"Morris is cool," Phil continued, *"hell; he was one of the few people that treated me halfway decently."*

"In fact," Phil spoke aloud, "Maybe he can help me now. After all, I got in trouble because of him."

Phil made a mental note to try and contact Morris in the coming days and see if he could help him find a job.

His last few days had been fatiguing, frustrating and just plain lousy. Suicide had been an option, but he decided against it when he realized that he only had three Tylenol left and couldn't afford more.

"*With my luck, I'll just get a bad stomach ache,*" he thought.

He went to bed last night thinking that a change might be coming. He even planned on dreaming about a more positive and happy time, in the hopes that it might actually cure his dismal mood. He had barely closed his eyes and started dreaming about all of the Oakland Raider cheerleaders when his cell phone rang.

The fact that the female caller simply said "wrong number" and hung up brought Phil crashing back to reality.

"Great," he lamented. "I'm the only guy in my entire damn dream and I still can't get any..."

The phone rang again, interrupting his statement.

This time the caller introduced himself as Larry Nelson of the Eastbay Gazette. This time the caller told Phil what was happening and that his help was instrumental. This time, Phil would have to put everything on the line and hope that right would carry the day. This time, Phil realized he could make a difference and strike back at the company that struck out at him.

"*This time,*" thought Phil, "*I'm in!*"

At 4:30 a.m. Phil stepped off of the bus and stood before the Bennington Oil Building. When he left his apartment he just wanted information about what the company was trying to do, specifically to David Morris. He had agreed to meet with Nelson later today at 3:30 p.m. and he thought that Nelson would ask him what he could do to help protect Morris. Phil planned on being ahead of Nelson and decided to go to the Bennington Oil Building to see what he might be able to find out. As he stood in front of the night entrance to the building, he began to wonder if he actually knew what he was getting involved in.

As he approached the guard shack he began getting apprehensive. He didn't want trouble, and there might be some if the guard at work wasn't one of Phil's few friends. The guard shack controlled the only path to get into the night entrance of the Bennington Oil building.

As Phil approached he noticed that the security camera on top off the guard shack turning away from the area he was walking and facing an area almost 180 degrees from where he stood. Out of the guard shack stepped the night guard, Daniel Williams.

Phil had known Williams the entire time he had worked at Bennington Oil. Williams was a police officer from across the bay who worked part time at Bennington Oil as a security guard. While Phil knew that, neither of Williams' employers knew. That's how Williams wanted it and the few security guards who knew kept quiet, as they secretly enjoyed knowing that at least one of the security guards they worked with was authorized to carry arms. Williams had never been called upon to use his weapon at Bennington Oil, but the guards who worked with him knew that he would if the situation called for it. He was also known for his objectivity. In short, he was known to be fair, and accordingly, trustworthy. That made him well liked amongst the guards.

"Damn, I thought it was you," Williams began. "I figured you'd be coming back. You know we're not supposed to let you in."

"Always good to see you too," replied Phil. "You alone?"

"Yeah, since that dude got attacked in the garage we've had to move more people from the building to the garage. They pulled a lot of folks from the building and put them in the garage from about 3 p.m. to 8 p.m. Then these cheap bastards sent them home rather than pay them for the extra work they did. They figure that us guards in the building, we can lock all of the doors and increase our security, but the garage is pretty much open. Anyway, there ain't too many of us in this building, and those of us who are here are walking more floors than usual."

"Wow'" said Phil, "I always seem to miss the fun."

"Fun? Yeah, right" said Williams. Without waiting for any break in the conversation, Williams continued.

"So Phil, what are you doing here?"

"I didn't get much of a chance to collect my stuff" he

replied.

"You know I can't let you in."

"I know," said Phil, "and I understand. I don't want to cause you any trouble."

"Thanks."

"So why are you really here?" asked Williams. He broke into a grin before Phil answered him. Phil took the smile as an acknowledgement that Williams was on his side.

"I need to get some information."

"I figured that's why you were here" said Williams. "You also know I can't let you in."

"But Phil," Williams started, "you can help me with something. What happened to you? They said you were selling company secrets and stuff. I've known you for three years, and I know that there is no way you could be doing that. I mean if you were, like, all of a sudden driving around in a Porsche 911 and wearing gold around your neck I might believe it. But you barely got bus fare and food money on any given day, and while I know you play around in the company's computers; you've never taken anything before. And it don't take a genius to know that if you really want to find something valuable, you hit the CEO's database, or maybe finance. That's where the power and the money is. Word is that you were looking in Strategic Planning. There ain't no money there. What's going on?"

"I wish I knew," answered Phil. He was secretly pleased that his integrity and ethics had been recognized by someone other than himself.

"All I know is that I was helping this exec type look for some information on the computer and next thing I know, we set off some monitoring device. I don't even know what he eventually got to download."

"Why'd you help out an exec? Couldn't he access his computer on his own?"

"Nah," replied Phil, he actually needed someone who knew their way around a computer and I was the closest expert he could find."

"Who were you helping out?" asked Williams.

"Dave Morris, from up in Public Affairs."

Phil thought he heard Williams choking for a second.

Phil looked over and saw Williams staring at him.

"What?" said Phil.

Recognizing that he had somehow struck a chord with Williams, Phil walked over a little closer to him. "Are you alright?"

"Yeah," said Williams, "I'm alright. But that exec you helped, he isn't."

"What are you talking about?" asked Phil.

"Remember I told you that we got guys working the garage because someone got jacked up down there?

"Yeah," said Phil.

"Your boy Morris was the guy who got attacked."

Nelson had told this to Phil during their early morning conversation, but it was still hard news to take. Phil didn't want Williams to catch on that he knew about the attack, so he threw out a smokescreen.

He looked at Williams for some sign that he might be joking, but he saw none.

"You're serious aren't you?" was Phil's puzzled reply.

"Damn straight I am." said Williams. "From what I heard he was pretty beaten up when they got to him. Hell, he left here in an ambulance."

"An ambulance?"

"Yeah, it was an ambulance."

"Dan," began Phil, "you're one of the few people I know here that seem to like me."

"You're alright," said Williams.

"Then I need your help."

"My help," said Williams, "how can I help you?"

"Tell me what I should do next" said Phil. "If they went after an exec what do you think they'll do to a security guard?"

"Who is `they'?" said Williams.

"The people who set the trap in the computer that caught me and Morris, that's who!"

"Phil, maybe the stress of being fired has got you a little paranoid" said Williams. "If the company did this why didn't they just fire the exec like they fired you?"

"I don't know said Phil," now getting physically upset

with this turn of events. "Maybe they can't fire him because he knows too much."

"Maybe he doesn't know anything," said Williams, "and maybe he just got caught up in a robbery."

"But what if they did come after him?" said Phil. "And what happens if they come after me?"

"I don't know about you. But if they came after me, I'd try and get them first. I'd try and stop them before they took me out. That's the only way to make sure that they don't get you first."

"But how do you get to them first?" asked Phil.

"By getting them when they least expect it" said Williams. "By finding out when they are their most vulnerable and then hitting them."

"How do I do that?" asked Phil.

"Can't help you there, Phil" was Williams' response. "At some point in time you have to take whatever action you feel is best and hope that it works out for you. But you have to determine what that action will be, as you are the only one who knows what you are going through."

"In any case Phil," Williams said, "I'm stuck here at this post until my next set of rounds begins in 25 minutes. They gave me the management suite. Also, because of your firing, all of the cypher/combination locks are going to have their combinations changed--tomorrow."

Phil thanked Williams for this little tidbit and turned to walk back to the bus stop when he thought about what he had just heard.

Phil turned around and looked at Williams, who was deliberately looking away from Phil. Had Williams looked at Phil, he would have seen a quizzical look that seemed to say "Did I hear you right?"

Williams continued to look away from Phil, which was the only confirmation that he could send Phil.

"He's letting me in to look at the computers."

Phil took a step past the guard shack and towards the building and noticed that Williams was now turning to look at the spot where Phil had been standing.

A barely audible whirring noise was taking place

overhead, and Phil saw that the surveillance camera was turning back towards the way that he had come in. The path to the building was out of the camera's focal range.

Phil started planning his next steps. *"OK the cypher locks on all of the upper management offices haven't been changed yet,"* thought Phil.

"And I still know the codes!"

"Williams won't start his rounds for 25 minutes and it'll take him 10 minutes to get to the top floors," thought Phil. *"Minus the time it'll take me to get there I have roughly 30 minutes to try and find some answers,"* Phil thought again.

"Answers to questions I don't even understand myself."

Phil nearly bubbled over with glee at the opportunity to have 30 minutes alone with the company's computers. That ended when he realized how little time 30 minutes really was.

He walked into the building entrance and entered on an elevator going down to the lobby. As the doors opened up and he noticed that the guard desk covering the lobby, positioned to see everyone leaving the elevators, was not staffed.

"Why should it be," Phil thought, *"It used to be my job."*

Phil walked over to the main elevators, entered one and began his ascent to the upper floors.

Phil got off at the upper floors and took a quick glance to see if anyone else was there. This was the floor where Strategic Planning was located and this was where Phil determined his best shot for getting information in the little time he had.

"Since this was where Morris was looking, and since the company got mad at us for looking here, this is where something I can use ought to be" thought Phil.

He quickly looked at his watch and saw that his time was getting short.

Phil began walking down the foyer towards the executive suite, constantly looking for signs that others might be present. While all the offices in this section were connected to a common receptionist area, at this hour of the night it was unmanned. Phil was alone, but he knew that wouldn't be the case for long.

Of all the offices in Strategic Planning, Phil knew of only

one that would have his answers. Walking through the office suite, he looked at each of the office doors and noticed their imposing combination cypher locks on each door. When he was a security guard working the executive suite, he had been given all of the combinations and, like all of the other security guards, had memorized them. Unlike the other security guards, Phil had a penchant for numbers and hadn't forgotten the combinations when he was transferred to work the lobby. He was hoping that they hadn't been changed with his transfer.

Phil had arrived with the combinations to the locks in his head; he had all of the keys he needed. What he needed now was luck.

He walked over to one of the Strategic planning offices and entered the six-digit code and turned the door handle.

It didn't open. The codes failed, Phil was still locked out of the Strategic Planning offices and a glance at his watch showed he was down to his last seventeen minutes.

He looked over at the computer on the secretary's desk. He walked over to the secretary's desk and gave serious thought to thought to powering it up and searching the security databases, which Phil knew contained all of the cypher codes in the event someone forgot theirs. But that course led to two other problems.

The first was easy enough to see. If anyone entered the floor and saw that the terminal was on, they would search the building for the person who tried to use it. Since Phil didn't know how many other security guards were in the building, he couldn't place himself out in the open in an easily exposed position. The other problem was just as obvious. Bennington Oil tracked their computer usage, and it would be known throughout the building by 9 a.m. that someone had been engaged in the unauthorized use of a Strategic Planning computer.

"Been there, done that, got crushed," thought Phil. He wouldn't mind avoiding detection, as the last time he was discovered had turned his life on end.

"Nice try" Phil said out loud. He looked around and saw that as far as he had gotten, he could go no further without the security codes that he didn't possess.

Upset, Phil attempted to stand up without pushing the stool out from under the secretary's desk. His legs were still under the desk, and Phil felt the cold corner of a desk meet his left leg mid-thigh. The ripping sound he heard coming from his jeans reached his brain at the same time the first wave of pain hit from the deep scratch and abrasion he just had dug into his leg.

"Damn," Phil blurted. Phil was in his last good pair of jeans and was absorbing the irony that the company was still finding ways to hurt him.

He looked down at the desk and the protruding part that had caught his leg. It wasn't even a drawer, but a flat shelf that pulls out from the desk and gives the occupant a little more surface area.

Phil has lowered himself back into the secretary's chair to try and contemplate how bad one's luck must be when you're attacked and defeated by office furniture.

Phil had placed his head in his hands and rested his elbows on the surface of the desk.

"This was a big mistake" thought Phil *"What the hell was I trying to do, and how do I get out of this nightmare in one piece..?"*

Phil looked down at the shelf he had hit and had noticed that there was a name on it. He leaned down to better read the list when he saw another name.

"These are the Strategic Planning guys."

He pulled the shelf all of the way out and saw a printout of all of the Strategic Planning officers and their office locations. Behind each name was a six-digit number.

"Phil smiled so hard he had to readjust his glasses.

"Of course," snapped Phil, "we were always telling these guys not to do this. The secretary gets all of the codes and can enter any office if the staffer doesn't come in. The secretary then keeps it in an accessible location that they think is hidden and secure and then some weasel comes along and gets ahold of the codes and has access to everything he wants."

"To make it easy on themselves they made it real easy for me" said Phil, "they will come to regret this complacency."

Phil suddenly stopped his pontificating and looked at his watch.

"Eleven minutes left!"

Phil quickly wrote down the codes to the first five offices and walked over to one of the doors. He figured that if he needed information he needed to start at the top.

Looking up at the door Phil saw the name and the title he was looking for.

"Stan Jenkins, Director, Strategic Planning. Righteous!" was Phil's only comment.

Phil entered the six-digit code into the combination lock and turned the handle. This time the door opened, gliding gently until it came to the doorstop sticking out from the floorboard. Phil looked in and saw that the empty office still had its lights on.

Although he had full entry into the office, Phil still hesitated before stepping in. The Strategic Planning Chief's penchant for setting traps and capturing unwanted intruders was well known to Phil; after all he numbered amongst the captured. How easily he and Morris had been caught during their previous incursion had weighed on Phil. It was weighing heavily upon him now, as he looked into an office that he suddenly had second thoughts about entering.

Phil pulled the door closed and looked over to another office. He checked to see if he had the combination for the lock. After entering the code the door opened and Phil walked in.

He sat down behind the desk and turned on the computer. Once it was powered up, he began pecking away at the keyboard.

Phil was playing a hunch, betting that the computer system that nailed him when he was hacking into the Finance computers did not cover the Strategic Planning computers. Phil was gambling on the fact that the trap that snared him was aimed not so much at itinerant hackers like himself, but at nosy Finance Department officials who were trying to uncover the activities of the Strategic Planning Department.

The computer brought up the Windows page and Phil did a very quick scan of the monitor to see if the signs of a trap were evident. He looked at the base of the monitor for the sinister looking numerical bar that he overlooked once before. When he saw no bar running the length of the bottom of the screen, he knew that no trap was set for this computer.

"Righteous," was Phil's first comment. "That whole trap thing I fell into was designed to keep tabs on the Finance folks. These bastards are only interested in finding out who knows what they're up to."

Thinking out loud, Phil added, "This isn't security, its surveillance."

He also made a mental note to alert some of the Finance folks about this. He had a feeling that they would be interested.

Phil looked at the Windows operating system and got to work. He quickly surveyed and scrolled past all of the technical, computing and financial files. He was looking solely for text files; files with letters and written correspondence that could be quickly read.

Upon not seeing any obvious traps, Phil began his search in earnest.

Five minutes later Phil had still found nothing of value. He had checked numerous Start Plan files, including Jenkins', but had found nothing. He figured his lack of discovery was because one of two reasons. The first was his speed. He was blazing through folders as fast as he could, and this was allowing him only a cursory look at the contents. He was getting concerned that his lack of attention was leading him to overlook possibly important information. He was hoping that this was the real reason he was finding nothing, but he knew the second reason was closer to the truth. The second reason was simply that Jenkins had purged his computer's files after Phil's previous incursion.

Phil stopped and leaned back in his chair, accepting the fact that the information he wanted, that he was looking for was no longer there.

"Damn," he muttered.

"Think hard Phil, think hard! What do we need to do next!" Phil was trying to come up with his next step.

"I'm 40+ flights up in a building I've been thrown out of

once before and will be again in less than six minutes. I'm tired of getting thrown out of here like I'm nothing. I'm better than this. I won't be treated like the trash…"

Phil looked back down at the computer monitor before him. He just had a thought and only had a few minutes to act.

He went into Jenkins' files again and instead of going into his active files, he went over to the deleted folder.

"Let's see what you thought you threw away yesterday," said Phil.

Phil was banking on Jenkins assumption that deleting a file actually got rid of it, instead of sending it to a holding folder for a set period of time to allow the person deleting the luxury of restoration if the deletion was a mistake.

Phil was in Jenkins' trash folder and there were numerous documents in it. That was almost a problem in itself, as Phil only had minutes to get what he needed and get off the floor before the other security guards found him.

Phil was looking down the list of deleted messages when he discovered that one titled "Monty-O Wrap-Up."

Phil realized that he didn't have time to warm up the printers and copy anything he was about to find so he opened his note pad, grabbed his pen and opened the folder.

Phil guessed that this memo was a list of things that had to be completed soon by Jenkins. Phil knew that a takeover was underway because it was in all the papers. The memo he was looking at had twenty-four items that Phil suspected needed to be done before the takeover could happen.

It was the one titled "Morris – 14" that caught his eye.

"There couldn't possibly be 14 other notes about Morris in here could there?" thought Phil.

As he suspected, this was the only note in the folder with the name Morris in the title. He pulled it up and read it. He didn't know what it meant but he thought Nelson might, so he started writing the note verbatim.

"Priest can't do last rites as scheduled. We have called one of his associates; he'll handle matter. Unwarranted interference will be permanently excised. Today or tomorrow in MC" Phil scrawled.

Phil checked the properties of this e-mail and found that

it was addressed to a brokerage house in London. He wrote down the name and began logging off of the computer.

Phil got up and turned off the lights and headed to the elevators. When he got to there he got a shock he didn't need. Two of the six elevators were rising, and he had not yet pushed the button to summon an elevator for his downward trip. He hit the 'down' button and moved behind a pillar to see who might be getting out of the first elevator to arrive. The other elevator had stopped ten floors down and hadn't started back up yet, but the one that Phil knew was carrying Williams and other security was still rising. Although Williams was cool in Phil's eyes, he would still have to bring him in if he got caught. Phil wouldn't let his situation be imposed on another friend of his.

The elevator reached Phil's floor and when the doors opened...nothing. It was empty! Phil noticed that the other elevator was now in motion, rising again, and Phil knew this one would be occupied. He ran into the empty elevator, pushing the button to the lobby so hard he nearly jammed his finger. The doors closed and the elevator began descending just as the other elevator arrived and opened its doors.

Williams stepped out and turned to the elevator that was descending to the lobby.

"Good luck, Phil!" was his only comment. He walked over to the Strategic Planning office and gave it a quick look around to make sure that Phil didn't leave any incriminating reminders.

When Phil got to the building's night entrance, he found that the security cameras on the guard shack were facing away from him. As he left he noticed that the cameras were once again, aimed in a different direction.

"Thanks, Dan!," was Phil's parting shot. As he headed for the bus stop he smiled, knowing that he had at least one friend with the company.

As he was leaving, Phil thought he would never again step foot on Bennington Oil property. Unknown to him, he would have to make one more visit to the Bennington Oil Building, and the stakes would be even higher then.

CHAPTER 31

DESPERATE TIMES...

Nelson frantically fumbled at his phone, unable to get the good grip he needed to make the most important call of his life. That he was speeding on the freeway during the beginning rush hour didn't concern him at all. Phil, sitting next to him, had a different perspective. Phil was looking out of the window of the car, wondering when the vibrations and cracking sounds he was hearing would finally signal the end of their vehicle and their lives as they knew them.

Nelson and Phil had uncovered something that boded ill for Morris. Phil met Nelson at their scheduled 3:30 p.m. meeting and showed him what he had uncovered. Nelson was impressed that Phil had taken the initiative, but became mortified when he read Phil's notes.

"Are you sure this is what it said and who it was sent to?" Nelson asked Phil. Phil nodded his head.

"This is way worse than I thought!" was Nelson's reply. To Phil, the note he wrote was merely cryptic; he had no basis for understanding it. To Nelson, and shortly Alice, the note was the confirmation of their worst fears.

Nelson now knew that Morris wasn't simply in trouble, he was targeted. Unless he received help he didn't know he needed, Morris had already begun the last hours of his life.

Nelson knew they had to stop what was going on, but time was not on his side.

In fact, time was now their enemy.

As they flew down I-80 back to the Eastbay Gazette's headquarters, Nelson finally got a grip on the phone and dialed the number to Alice's office.

While Nelson was dialing, Phil looked down and saw that the speedometer needle was pressed over as far to the right as it could go. At exactly that time, Nelson cranked the wheel as far over as he could and the car rocketed across three lanes of traffic and onto an off-ramp. Phil was flung hard against the door. Phil, like Nelson, was worried about what might happen when Morris got off the plane in Mexico City. Unlike Nelson, Phil was questioning if either of them was going to survive the trip back to the Eastbay Gazette.

Nelson heard the phone ring twice before being answered and before the receptionist on the other end could even respond, Nelson spoke first.

"I need to speak with Alice Bradford," Nelson blurted. This is a life or death emergency—literally!"

The receptionist seemed a bit hesitant to act on a total stranger making a claim like this and replied sheepishly, "Who is this?"

Nelson held the phone in front of his face and stared at it incredulously for a second. But just for a second. During that same second Phil nearly lost his head when he saw Nelson take his eyes off the road and stare at the phone. That is usually not done at 90 miles per hour, and had never been done in front of Phil, who could have just as easily lived the rest of his life without it. His panic at this, however, was held in check by the visage of the veins in Nelson's neck and forehead starting to protrude. Phil could see that Nelson was about to explode and he only wondered if Nelson was going to keep the car in line.

"Put it this way," Nelson screamed into the phone, not even trying to mask his indignation. "Tell Alice that her lover will be dead by this time tomorrow, and rather than allowing her to prevent it you played phone tag!"

Nelson's harangue nearly cost him control of the car. His anger was such that it didn't occur to him that this poor receptionist had no idea of the events being played out, and that her question was the one that she should have rightfully asked in this situation. All Nelson knew was that his time to act was measured in minutes, maybe an hour or two, and he didn't want to spend the rest of his life wondering how he could have saved the life of a friend by just saving two minutes during this crucial time.

Phil was also internalizing his thoughts, but they were of a different ken. He looked over at Nelson and didn't know whether to try and grab the wheel from this madman or to make a jump out the door. A glance out the window showed him that the car was travelling fast, probably twice the legal speed limit. A jump would have been suicide. Phil wasn't too sure that staying in the car was going to have a different outcome. He was sure that the car was going to be wrapped around a pole or a tree in a few minutes and he was sure that he didn't want to be in it when that happened.

Phil was ready to spring into some sort of action when he noticed a change in Nelson's demeanor. Although he couldn't tell who was on the phone, the little sound he heard coming from the cell phone was distinctly feminine, and apparently friendly.

"Hello, Alice here. Who is this?"

"Alice," Nelson began, "This is Larry. We have to make sure that we get Dave off of that flight!"

"Larry that flight left San Francisco three and a half hours ago. It makes an extended stop in L.A. and then it's off to Mexico City. I don't know if it might still be in L.A., but if it is it won't be there much longer." Nelson could hear the concern rising in her voice.

"Larry, what's going on?

"Alice, something crazy is going on with that flight and it all centers around Dave." With that, Nelson handed the phone to Phil, who introduced himself and began telling her of their morning's activities. Before concluding, Phil let her know that they are going to the offices of the Eastbay Gazette and that she should meet them there.

Joe Campos had been the San Francisco supervisor at Aeromexicali Airlines for years and he had come to a not-so-startling conclusion. Air travelers are some of the rudest, most inconsiderate life-forms breathing air or standing erect. He looked over at a fellow employee to try and press his point. All the employees knew Joe and his views and while they might agree, they would never be so vocal about it.

"I tell you, Enrique," he began, "Air travelers suck."

Enrique was sorting through some paperwork, trying to be as impassive a participant as he could without offending Joe, who nonetheless continued.

"They call here all the time bitching and groaning about some flight they fooled around and missed, or about long delays on the runway. I just sell the damn tickets; I don't control the runway traffic. They should call their Congressman or Senator since they are the ones who cocked it up. They call us when they got a problem with their luggage and just about everything else. If they don't like flying, they could always take the damn train. The train is a great way to travel. Yeah it's true that the train has an equal chance of reaching its destination as it does winding up upside down in flames, with part of the car submerged in some bayou where you'll see gators and snakes long before you see rescue vehicles and..."

The ringing phone interrupted Joe.

Joe looked over at Enrique, who had already looked over to Joe to see if he was planning to answer it.

"What do you want to bet," Joe began, "that this call is somebody out there who wants to complain about air travel?"

Enrique had heard this line of questioning before. He also had a standard answer for it.

"Joe, are you going to answer that call?"

Joe looked down at the phone and replied, "I guess I have to. This is my job after all."

Enrique saw Joe reach for the phone. Enrique often wondered how someone with Joe's disposition ever received a customer service position. As Enrique looked out across the nearly empty lobby and then back at Joe, he better understood why so few people patronized his airline. He went back to his paperwork.

"Aeromexicali Airlines" said Joe.

"Excuse me please," said Alice calling from her office,

"but has the flight to Mexico City left Los Angeles?"

"Just one minute," said Joe. He checked the computer for arrivals and departures.

"It has left the terminal and has joined the taxi queue. It's on the taxiway, but it could be out there for twenty to forty-five minutes before they get permission to take off" said Joe.

"Thank you," was Alice's courteous reply to Joe.

"You're welcome," said a startled Joe.

Enrique looked up over his paperwork and looked over at Joe. "Did I hear you tell someone they were welcome?"

"Yes," said Joe. "It kind of caught me by surprise"

"It also blows your theory about air travelers. I should have taken your bet."

"Just because one person acts out of character doesn't mean my view about air travelers is inaccurate or wrong. You heard about that guy in Cleveland who broke a ticket agent's neck because his flight was late? Hell, that event alone cancels out a thousand thank you notes. And that's not even the worst case. I once read where a guy once showed up to a ticket agent's station with a chainsaw and....."

Enrique had begun droning Joe out again and went back to having pleasant thoughts, like thinking about how long it might be before the Human Resources folks at American Airlines would act on his employment application.

CHAPTER 32

...REQUIRE DESPERATE MEANS

Nelson was thinking hard. He had flashed four or five seemingly viable ideas through his mind in his attempt to get Morris off of the airplane that was speeding him to his death. He didn't have the time he needed for this, but he was desperately trying to use the time he had left in the best manner possible. Nelson had decided on one course of action that he thought would work, but he needed to bounce it off of the Alice and Phil because he not only needed their approval, he needed their assistance.

He didn't like what he was thinking. Not one iota. But he knew he didn't have time for choice. He needed to select a course of action, no matter how objectionable, and make it work. He didn't know if his plan would work, but he was certain that he knew what the next six to twelve hours of Morris' life held. Nelson acknowledged, as did Phil and Alice, that Morris' next few hours could be the last of his life, unless there was a significant intervening circumstance. Nelson knew that he was that circumstance, and he was trying his damnedest to be the savior that Morris was unaware he needed.

Nelson was about to lay out his plan to Alice and Phil when Schilling, the paper's editor came in. He didn't let that stop him.

"Nelson" started the editor, "What are you up to and

what's with the entourage?"

Nelson spent a brief moment filling Schilling in on Dave Morris, his situation, his plight and their quandary.

Schilling nodded his head when Nelson was done. He saw a huge story breaking here in his newsroom and he was about to get some other reporters to assist. But his years as an editor also trained him in reading people by their emotions, not their appearance or their words. He detected a serious problem that he was not informed about and he knew that this story hinged on the unspoken problem.

"If what you've told me about this Morris character is true," began Schilling, "you'll need him here to tell the story."

"That could be a big problem," Nelson blurted. "Once that plane leaves U.S. airspace, Dave is dead!"

Schilling stared at Nelson as his mind began grasping the enormity of the moment. "Are you sure about that?"

"We're pretty sure." said Alice. "At best we're hoping that when he gets to Mexico City he'll go to his hotel room and call me. I'll tell him what's going on and he'll get the appropriate security."

"That's if he makes it to the hotel room." said Nelson.

"If?" Alice asked.

"If," Nelson stated again. "A tourist coming from the airport is easy and fat pickings. Hell, they may even get him in his hotel room."

"When that flight takes off," Nelson added, "it will be only 20 to 30 minutes from Mexican airspace. Once they breach it, the Mexican authorities will have jurisdiction. Then that plane will land in Mexico."

"Can't we just call the cops here and ask them to get Dave off of that flight?"

"Alice," Schilling began, "that's right isn't it?"

She nodded her head in agreement.

"With that slim soup you guys call supporting evidence, you'll only lead the cops to you. Without probable cause, they are not going to divert a flight based on what you have to tell them. In fact, they'll consider you crank callers and come looking for you."

He continued. "If you want that plane down, you're

going to have to convince the authorities that putting that plane down is better than leaving it up. And from what you've told me, you got less than thirty minutes to do it."

We can call the Mexican authorities," said Alice. "They can get him as soon as he leaves the plane."

"We don't know who or what is involved down there," said Nelson. "We tip off the police and what do we do if the cops who respond are corrupt? What then?"

Nelson let that last statement hang in the air.

"We'll take that precaution as a last resort."

Nelson turned his back on the group and began keyboarding. In less than a minute he had pulled up a schematic of a DC-10. He zoomed in on a spot near where the engine pylon connected with the wing. Aeromexicali Airlines was a vacation airline operating three DC-10's from the American west coast to Mexico.

"Larry," said Schilling. "You're not doing what I think you're doing?"

"Yes I am" was Nelson's response. "In less than an half an hour a good friend is going to leave U.S. airspace and I doubt he's coming back. I'm not going to let that happen."

"I can't let you do this," said Schilling. "You'll get your name ruined, your career will go straight to hell and you'll never work in journalism again. You'll…"

Nelson cut his boss off cold.

"Boss," Nelson spun around, "He got beaten up in part because I asked him to put his nose where it didn't belong. I asked him to get me some info on a story. His turned out risking his ass for me for the sake of a byline - a damned byline!"

"I'm not going to sit here and wait for someone to kill him in a country where the crime will never be solved."

"The Mexican cops are better than you're giving them credit" said Schilling.

"Maybe they are, maybe they aren't" countered Nelson. "If Bennington Oil plans to commit murder in Mexico, I don't think they'd be above bribing the corrupt cops who would be investigating it. I have no doubt that if Morris goes to Mexico he won't be coming back."

"Boss" Nelson continued, "I got thirty minutes to try and save his life. I might be throwing everything I've ever done in the trash, but I have to try and save him. As corny as it sounds, he'd do it for me."

Alice smiled and walked over to Nelson. "What can I do to help?" she asked.

Phil had been eyeing the terminals that Nelson was working and asked Nelson to get up and let him work, as he knew he could probably work it faster.

The little team assembled on the 4th floor of the Eastbay Gazette building set about their monstrous task.

Schilling noted that all this little crew had to do was come up with a credible plan, get some authoritative body gullible enough to believe it, hope it worked and not get caught and subsequently jailed. After all, they would still need to meet Morris when he returned to plan the outing of Monty-O's plans.

They had less than twenty six minutes to develop and implement such a plan. Schilling was looking at them brainstorming away in the small office room. He figured Nelson had a plan and he had an idea of what it would be.

Schilling knew that Nelson was working on an airline safety article; he assigned it to him. He knew that Nelson would have access to the information he would need.

"But now is not the time to be backtracking, to be repeating steps or reinventing the wheel," he thought.

Schilling knew that Nelson was good at what he did. But he was only thirty four years old. Schilling had been in the newspaper business for forty years - he often joked that he'd forgotten more than the `youngsters' would ever know. To an extent, that was true.

He could plainly see that Nelson was now frantically looking for a fable, a tale that would convince hardened airline officials and possibly law enforcement officials, that the aircraft Morris was on was in such peril that it had to be diverted and put on the ground at once. He could also see that Nelson and his little band didn't have the wherewithal to make it happen. Their time was running out. Nelson's little group needed someone with a little more knowledge of the world;

someone who could put a credible story together at the drop of a dime. Someone with the respect brought on by years of experience and unquestioned integrity. Someone with sophistication, savvy and street-smarts. Traits not found in many. Schilling knew of one such man.

"What this little group needs," said Schilling, *"is me."*

With that he walked back into Nelson's office.

"Alright," Schilling began, "this is what you're going to do. First off, if any of you speak a word of what we're about to do while I'm still alive, but more importantly before the statute of limitations runs - I'll personally torment you for the rest of recorded time!"

He looked over at Nelson. "If you talk I'll see that you never work in media again." Nelson nodded his head in approval.

He looked over at Alice. "If you talk I'll see that you never practice law in this jurisdiction again." Similarly, Alice nodded her head.

He looked over at Phil. "Just who the hell are you again?" Phil looked at Schilling with that same blank stare that made everyone who knew him question how he had the intellect to be a computer genius.

"Never mind. If you talk I'll hire you and make your life a living hell."

"Understood?"

The reporter, the lawyer and the security guard all nodded in agreement.

"Good. Now what kind of airliner are we talking about and who owns it?"

"It's a DC-10," said Nelson, "Aeromexicali Airlines, a small vacation outfit that flies…"

"Whatever," snapped Schilling. Where and when the airplanes flew was unnecessary minutiae that served to only take up precious time. He didn't need or care to hear it. Schilling just wanted the facts about Morris' flight.

" It stopped in LA and is probably back in the air headed for Mexico as we speak" he said. "I take it we don't want that, right?"

The three nodded in agreement.

"I take it," Schilling began again, "that we probably don't want the guys who are pursuing him to know that he'll be back in San Francisco sooner than they thought?"

The three nodded in agreement again.

"Okay then." began Schilling. "We are going to divert this bird to..." He walked over to the map on the office wall took a quick glance and then stabbed his finger at what appeared to be the border of Texas.

"... here!"

Nelson looked at the map and shot a puzzled look back over to his boss. "That's Albuquerque. That's a two and a half-hour flight from here. We want him back here. Why there?"

"Here's why!" Schilling said as he began telling them of his plan to get Morris' plane on the ground.

Two blocks from the newspaper a badly-dressed, stocky man in his mid-thirties lifted the receiver of a pay phone and began dropping coins into the slot. The gloves on his hands impeded both his coin insertion and dialing, but the inconvenience was minor, at best. More importantly, the gloves kept his fingerprints a secret, which is how he wanted it. In light of his next actions, the gloves were a prudent requirement.

The phone rang twice before a cheerful voice at the other end spoke.

"Welcome to Aeromexicali Airlines, how may we be of assistance?"

The man in the phone booth spoke clearly and quickly and when he was finished, he placed the phone back in its cradle. He knew he had gotten his message across. He also knew that at that very moment, the Aeromexicali Airlines employee who answered the phone was pushing the crisis response button. That move was more than expected. It was intended.

He walked over to a waiting car and got in. He drove to another phone booth three blocks away and called the editor of the Eastbay Gazette with the same message he told to the Aeromexicali Airlines employee.

From the same phone booth, the man made a third call.

This call would be as calculating and precise as the earlier calls, but this call was being handled differently. The caller had received simple instructions: make this last call with the minimum in delay over the phone. This call would be traced and the person making it needed to be gone before the police, who would surely be summoned by the FBI, came by.

"Federal Bureau of Investigation, San Francisco region. How may I direct your call?"

"You can begin," said the man, "...by turning on your tape recorders because I'm only going to say this once."

The receptionist's crisis awareness training kicked in, allowing repetitive training and conditioned instinct to take over for personal choice. Depressing a foot pedal beneath the desk allowed the receptionist to both begin taping the conversation and notify superiors of the impending crisis without so much as giving the slightest hint of difficulty to others standing nearby.

"There is a bomb," began the voice on the phone, "on the Aeromexicali Airline vacation flight just leaving Los Angeles. It is located on the aircraft near the point where the engine pylon connects with the wing. There you will find a junction of hydraulic lines and other systems very important to the continued flight of that aircraft. A small explosion there will affect the aircraft's ability to climb or land. We have attached such a charge to this aircraft, and a pressure solenoid will activate the device once the aircraft climbs above 3000 feet. It will detonate once the aircraft drops below an altitude of 3,000. I will contact you in two hours with instructions and our demands."

"Wait," began the receptionist, "I want to patch you through to our agents who can handle this type of stuff." The receptionist was intentionally playing dumb in an attempt to prolong the phone call.

The caller wasn't buying it.

"The tape recording of this message will tell your special agents all they need to know."

"Wait then," started the receptionist, "Authentication. They'll want authentication from you. Who are you?"

"We are the reunited Brotherhood for Free Democracy

317

II" said the unknown caller. "As for authentication—your authentication will be spread out all over the northern Mexican desert when that plane burns in!"

"You have got to let me transfer you to...," the receptionist began but then stopped mid-sentence.

The dial-tone created by the other party hanging up let the receptionist know that the call was over. It didn't last long enough to send agents to the call initiation site.

The caller ambled over to a car parked near the phone booth. He walked over to the passenger side and got in. His disheveled appearance was in direct contrast to the attractive, well-dressed sister sitting behind the wheel of the car.

"You think they'll go for it?" said Alice.

"I don't know if they will," began Nelson as he sat in the passenger seat trying to pull his appearance together. "But you have to admit it was a better plan than we were coming up with."

"If they don't go for the part of the plan we just carried out," Nelson continued, "I'm sure they'll believe once Schilling gets through with them."

The FBI became a flurry of activity in the blink of an eye. Copies of the tape were being made and disseminated. Agents were pulling up every scrap of information that they could on the Brotherhood for Free Democracy II, Aeromexicali Airlines and the McDonnell-Douglas DC-10. The L.A. Bureau chief had been alerted and plans were being made as to how this operation would be handled.

As a first order of business, the FBI contacted LA control and had the airliner remain in U.S. airspace until they had determined the validity of the threat. If they took the threat too seriously and it turned out to be a hoax, hundreds of holiday revelers would be inconvenienced, at most. It the FBI took the threat too lightly and it turned out to be real, teams of emergency rescue workers would be spending the next few days in the Mexican heat planting flagged wooden stakes in the ground next to suspected human remains amid the charred and jagged metal edges of a destroyed airliner.

Senior Agent Stephen Halloran was the first bureau official to respond. He came up alongside the receptionist and reviewed the information she was able to get while on the phone. It wasn't much but since it was tape recorded Halloran felt that it was no big deal.

Back at the Eastbay Gazette everyone was scrambling as well. The reporter working the news desk had received the call from an unidentified party claiming that a bomb was going to blow up a flight originating from San Francisco if certain demands weren't met. The news was immediately transferred to the Schilling, who promptly assigned a team of reporters to cover the story. The reporters were anxious; both anticipating and fearing what they felt could be the biggest story of their careers. Only Schilling knew the truth, and he felt no small sense of disappointment that these reporters were clamoring to work on a story that didn't exist. But he had his role to play, and his reporters were just the first group that he had to convince.

Schilling stared at his phone and for a moment, just a moment, he vacillated over the call that he now needed to make. This call was the linchpin in his plan. It had to be made, and only he could make it. This call was the one that was going to ad credibility to the plan to get Morris off of his flight to Mexico.

Picking up his phone, Schilling dialed the number that would put him in contact with the director of the San Francisco region of the Federal Bureau of Investigation.

Special Agent Halloran was huddled in his office with his top advisors when his secretary appeared at his door, motioning for him.

"Sir," she began, "there is a called from someone stating that he is the editor of the Eastbay Gazette."

Halloran was about to tell her to dismiss the caller when she added, "They know about the bomb threat on Aeromexicali Airlines."

"Damn!," Halloran muttered under his breath.

Halloran was not ready to comment to the press about the bomb threat. A lot of work still needed to be done to determine if this threat was real or just a hoax. Agents were just beginning to pore over the Brotherhood for a Free Democracy to see if they were legitimate. Contact with airport specialists to determine if the plane was ever left in a position where an unauthorized party could have tampered with it still needed to be accomplished. Hundreds of questions needed to be asked before Halloran had a good idea of what, and possibly who, he was up against. He wasn't comfortable talking about this incident until he had more than the ten minutes that had passed since the receptionist was contacted by the BFD caller.

But Halloran was now facing a quandary. He was not planning to publicly comment about this matter; at least not now. However, the media was now informed about the incident and asking him questions. If nothing happened with this bomb threat and the plane landed safely at its appointed destination, Halloran would be a happy man. But if the plane were to blow up in flight and crash in flames into the desert, at least one newspaper editor will know of some of the events that transpired.

Halloran didn't want to involve the public in this matter just yet, but one fact bothered him. If this newspaper editor was telling the truth, then one of the members of the BFD had contacted him and talked. This was not a step that the average prankster pulled. Most bomb threats consist of one call to one source and then silence from the alleged bombers. The more that one of these members of the BFD talked, the more clues they left and the more people they involved in their illicit activity. Only two types of criminals enlarged the sphere of their illegal criminal activity. The inexperienced, and the very shrewd.

Halloran's training and instinct was leading him to believe that the BFD was shrewd. The multiple reporting of their bomb threats was intended to inform outside agencies in the hope of forcing the FBI's hands. The recorded bomb threat revealed enough information about the DC-10s construction to show that someone within the BFD had, at least, a familiarity with the airframe.

Halloran thought for a quick second and decided that he did need to talk to Schilling. He needed to know what Schilling knew about the bomb threat.

Halloran picked up the receiver and spoke.

"Halloran here," he started, "I'm in charge of the San Francisco region of the FBI."

"Schilling here, editor of the Eastbay Gazette. I got a call saying there is a bomb on an outbound SF flight. I called the airline and they told us that they would be referring any queries to you. I'm sending a reporter to the airport and I'm sending one to your office for a statement."

"Not yet!" Halloran protested. "We're just getting into this incident ourselves."

"I'm looking into this now," Schilling interjected. "Here's my phone number—call me when you get anything. I'll surely be calling you."

The call didn't go the way Halloran wanted. His intent to wrest any tidbit of information from Schilling turned into something different. Now he was racing a newspaper's deadline and the thought that in a few hours a newspaper would be printing and disseminating everything it had about this incident.

"If the plane were still flying by then it wouldn't be too much trouble," thought Halloran.

"But if it's downed..."

Halloran put the receiver down and went back into his office. "Ladies and gentlemen," he announced to the assembled advisors, "we have our afternoon's work cut out for us..."

CHAPTER 33

ALIGNING THE CHESSBOARD

The FBI had snapped into action the minute they received the bomb threat. An agent was immediately assigned to research the BFD II to make a threat assessment. They needed to know, "Was this call and this group credible?"

The research didn't take long.

The original BFD was an anti-war, counter-culture group that had made some noise in the early seventies. They were now thought to be firmly enveloped in obscurity. There was only one anti-government act of defiance attributed to them, but there was no confirmation that they had committed the act.

In 1972 the BFD threatened, in an anonymous communiqué, to blow up a government building. The San Francisco police took this threat seriously enough to place protection at numerous federal buildings and structures. Every federal building, federal courthouse and federal administrative center was watched. No one had given the merest thought to an Army recruiting center. This wasn't the police's fault; it was just that a small two-room office pales as a target in comparison with a forty story building.

The BFD was not a heartless crew, just the opposite. They stated in their communiqué that the blast would occur at 4:30 a.m., early enough as to ensure that no one would be around, but late enough to ensure that the morning rush hour would be hopelessly fouled. It wasn't however, the way things happened.

Then, one foggy San Franciscan night in 1972, while numerous police officers were working overtime to protect government buildings, a small explosion shattered the calm. It was 3:17 a.m.

The fire department had the blaze contained within fifteen minutes of the blast, but it was still too long. A badly burned body lay in the debris of the Army recruiting center. There were no clothes on the body and the identity of the man was unknown. Further investigation of the man, primarily through an autopsy and review of his teeth, showed an individual in such poor health that many in the coroner's office though the blast did him a favor by not prolonging his agony. The coroner suspected the man to be a bum who had picked an incredibly lousy spot to bunker down for the night. Shortly after the blast the city had him buried as a John Doe.

Halloran didn't know what to make of this historical view of the first BFD. He knew that any kid with an Internet access could read about the American Airlines DC-10 crash in Chicago or the Untied DC-10 crash in Iowa City to learn all that anyone could want to know about the hydraulic workings of a DC-10. That the BFD II had not delivered a more detailed bomb threat told Halloran that he might be working with a prankster. But Halloran didn't have enough information yet to take that chance.

He looked over to a subordinate and said, "Get L.A. control and have them spin that bird until we get a rough idea of what's going on."

Less than two minutes after Halloran stated those words, the Aeromexicali Airlines DC-10 was diverted and ordered to fly in a huge circle until further notice. At no time were they allowed to leave American airspace. The pilot protested this action, but airline officials filled him in on the situation and he concurred.

"A pressure solenoid is a small device that acknowledges the changes in air pressure, mainly due to altitude, and then reacts based upon a programmed instruction once the prescribed altitude or air pressure, has been achieved."

The voice emanating from the conference call speaker in

the middle of the table was that of the FBI's most senior explosives expert in Washington D.C. It was also information that Halloran was already aware.

"Since it is a pressure solenoid and not a timer, we have until the plane needs to land to work with." The voice continued. "However..."

"However?" asked Halloran.

"Yes," the expert replied, "However."

"If we believe what we know up to now to be true, then the pressure solenoid will engage if the plane drops below 3000 feet. There are very few airports at 3000 feet above sea level that can handle a DC-10."

Halloran walked over to a map of the United States. Turning to look back over his shoulder he spoke back into the conference call receiver.

"Which ones?"

"Denver, Salt Lake City and Albuquerque. There may be others, but these have the runways, the altitude and the FBI resources to handle this situation."

Halloran looked at the map and traced the distances involved. Albuquerque was over 800 miles from Los Angeles. Denver was over 1000. Salt Lake City was only 700 miles away.

"*I would have thought that this was a crank call,*" thought Halloran, "*but they have made some moves that a prankster would not have. They wanted someone else to know about the bomb so they called the press. They wanted someone else to know about this so that there could be no cover up or spin applied if this plane blows up. They are either jokers or they want to humiliate the government's best law enforcement agency. Your average prankster would not have done that— they would have read about their exploits in the morning paper. They would not risk an unnecessary telephone call and another clue, another chance to expose themselves. Calling us with their message requires gall and a steady touch.*"

Halloran was discovering that the caller had in fact covered his tracks. The call was traced to a phone booth in Oakland. They had known enough about this plane and its schedule to call after it had taken off from Los Angeles

International.

Halloran was in a quandary. Mexico City was higher than 3000 feet above sea level, so there shouldn't be a problem with the alleged bomb going off due to a drop in altitude. He was more concerned over whether this threat was real and if the Mexican authorities could handle the situation. He had no idea whether they could handle it or not – but he didn't want to take chances either.

Turning back to the conference call phone he announced his intention.

"I'm going to have L.A. control divert this bird to Albuquerque."

Halloran hung up the phone and sat back in his seat. The next few hours were going to be excruciating for him. He would wonder he had made the right decision until such time that he either received a call from someone relieving his anxiety or confirming his worst fears.

Like any good law enforcement official he wasn't planning to sit around waiting. Other clues might be available in the communications received by his office, the newspaper and the airline. He had begun reviewing the events of the day to try and uncover some of them. He needed to know what kind of bomb was involved? Where was it located? How? Why? The questions kept mounting up the more he thought about them.

He started by having an agent contact AeroMexicali Airlines to see if anybody had inquired about flight information on this particular flight. What he would find out over the next twelve hours would open his eyes unlike any other case he ever handled.

CHAPTER 34

THE ATTACK
- PART 2 -

Human nature is such that an individual can sit for long periods of time reviewing a past event of their life, over and over again, at the expense of all other human activity. The world around them is relegated to the realm of later, a place where they promise to devote their full attention, just as soon as they finish paying their full attention considering and reconsidering this past event; an event that they cannot change or alter, just relive. It carries with it the same happiness, the same pain, the same consternation and the same emotion. The only difference is that in review, the hope and excitement are gone, and all that is really left is the damning reality of facing that which they cannot change.

Once the DC-10 had taken off, Morris had plenty of time to think about his predicament. He knew now that he had badly misplayed his hand and now he was paying for it. Sitting in his cramped coach seat, he was wondering how things had gotten so bad and where he had lost control. He thought about how this whole thing got started when he tried to discover the whereabouts of his boss during the company's worst catastrophe. What he discovered, and more importantly, what he would come to learn about the company's future had pretty much come to mean the end of his future with the company.

"The truth will, in fact, shall set you free..." Morris said under his breath.

Morris had been staring out of the window for the past 30 minutes; ever since the plane had taken off from LAX. It was nearly dark outside as nightfall was close to enveloping the West Coast. Morris didn't notice the change. In fact, he was beyond noticing the change of day to night. When trouble interfered with the organized life of David Morris, he retreated to his thoughts. While he might not find a friend there, he knew he would find no enemies. He was going over everything he could remember about this mess and trying to fashion a redemption.

He was so enmeshed in his thoughts that he hadn't heard, let alone listened to, the last two messages that were broadcast over the cabin intercom. He was oblivious to the hushed murmurs that his fellow passengers were creating. He seemed not to have any interest in what was going on with the rest of the passengers.

That, however, changed in an instant.

"Excuse me sir," began one of the flight attendants. "The captain has requested that we ask all passengers if they had any questions about our flight diversion."

"Flight diversion?" said Morris. "Where are we being diverted to?"

"You haven't been listening to the Captain," started the attendant. "We've been diverted to Albuquerque."

The plane touched down at 1:30 a.m. in Albuquerque New Mexico. It stopped at the end of the taxiway and was then escorted by a small armada of safety vehicles to a secured ramp hundreds of yards from the terminal. The crew advised the passengers to be calm and follow their directions. After deplaning the passengers were led to a lighted area on the tarmac about 200 yards from the plane. Those that turned around and looked saw a sea of people approaching the plane and begin looking up into it as if there was something extraordinary that they were supposed to see.

Within twenty minutes all of the corralled passengers were on shuttles heading to the terminal buildings. As the bomb threat was not initiated from the plane none of the passengers were considered suspects. Accordingly they were all free to go. Therein was the problem.

Where to go?

All of the passengers of the Aeromexicali Airlines flight to Mexico City were stranded. It was too late to leave the airport and look for lodging. Yet there was a lot of night still left to sit through.

As Aeromexicali Airlines only operated on the west coast, there was no one with any corporate heft in Albuquerque who could help the passengers. They were on their own until they made other arrangements or the FBI cleared their plane. The flight's captain was with the FBI at the airplane and the crew members did their best to try and calm the passengers.

Morris figured they were stuck as a group until tomorrow morning. As he only traveled with a small suit bag that he carried onboard with him, he was allowed to take it with him when he deplaned. He was happy for this small bit of forethought because he could now roll the suit bag up and use it as a pillow once he stretched out. That was his immediate plan right after he called Alice and let her know of the change in his travel itinerary.

He took his cell phone out of his pocket and began dialing. He smiled when he heard the voice at the other end. Her message erased his smile as quickly as it came.

In a three minute call she had told him everything that had transpired in her previous twenty-four hours. He knew about the cryptic message as to his fate in Mexico; he knew why his plane was diverted to Albuquerque and he knew, now, that he had to get to San Francisco on the first plane out tomorrow. They meant to silence him and unless he struck first, they were going to finish him off, once and for all.

Alice added one more thing that Morris was unaware of. The FBI had asked the East Bay Gazette not to run their story on the airline diversion, at least not yet. They were concerned that this revelation would result in a rash of copy-cats. They offered the paper a full exclusive if anything were found on the plane. Schilling, in a rare moment of editorial conciliation, agreed.

Before hanging up, Morris asked Alice to purchase an online ticket for him on the first airline leaving for San Francisco. He knew it could take a while, but he wasn't going anywhere. No airline counter was open at this time and Morris figured that since he hadn't heard any aircraft take off in the time he'd been there, that some sort of noise restrictions applied. In short, nothing was leaving for three to four hours, until whatever passed for the morning arrived.

Morris had tried to sleep for the past two hours, but soon discovered that airport seats were not conducive to that. It was nearly 4:30 a.m. when he looked at his phone and saw that there was a voicemail from Alice. He accessed his voicemail and found that Alice had him booked on a 6 a.m. flight back to San Francisco. He took out his pen and wrote the flight and the confirmation number down on a scrap of paper. He gave a quick thought to calling her back, but then realized it was even earlier in San Francisco, and that she needed her sleep too.

"I'll call her at 6 a.m. her time," thought Morris.

"As always, thanks love!," he added under his breath.

He looked around to try and find something to wrap his mind into. It was 5 a.m. local, and while still early, Morris was seeing the first signs of airport life.

He started noticing food scents, he saw custodial staffers finishing their jobs, retail gift and magazine counters opening up. He even saw representatives of the airline he was ticketed on beginning to open their counter.

He got up from the seat and walked over to the counter and checked the departure/arrival board for information on his flight. He was booked on a 6 a.m. flight and it was good to go at 6 a.m.; just under one hour from now.

As he finished up with the representatives he turned around and saw eighteen other travelers behind him in line, all going back to SF. More were expected, as well.

"I guess great minds do think alike," Morris thought to himself.

Morris next walked over to the area where Aeromexicali Airlines was using as a staging area to assemble their passengers. Their staff was trying to get as many of the passengers back towards this area so that the re-boarding of their Mexico City flight could take place. Rather than wait for the FBI to search the whole plane before releasing it, the airline chartered another one. They had contacted an airline operating out of Albuquerque to handle the loading of passengers and cargo and their plan was to be one of the first flights out.

Morris went up to one of the representatives and volunteered that he wouldn't be going on to Mexico City and that he had booked a flight to return to San Francisco with another airline.

They asked, and stopped just short of pleading with, him to reconsider and continue his flight, but they understood. The flight diversion and flurry of activity upon landing had unnerved some passengers, and all the reassurances in the world couldn't convince some of them to fly this airline again.

The representative asked him if he would need his luggage removed and he told them that he only had his overnight bag, and it was with him.

He walked back over to the seating area and sat down again. He was awake for good now, and that meant it was time for him to start thinking about his immediate future.

Things were changing too fast for him. He planned on using the two days in Mexico City to think, to formulate, to plan an attack. Now, the events of his life had gone from bad to nightmarish. He assumed it was going to get worse.

The stunt to get him off the plane was bad enough. Knowing that his death was waiting for him in Mexico City showed him that he had to act now, today, or else he might not get the chance to stop what Bennington Oil was trying to do. He now knew that Jenkins, Martin and others were now accessories to what was intended to be his murder. There could be no holding back on his part now. Plan or not, when he got to San Francisco he had to strike first and decisively. There might not be a second chance.

"It's all or nothing for them," Morris thought, *"They don't plan to hold anything back. It's now me, or them."*

Morris's biggest problem was that he had only the length of his flight back to San Francisco to plan his strategy. He had a rough plan sketched out in his mind, but he would need to do a few things first. One was try to disrupt Bennington Oil's scheduled press conference. Another was to stop Jenkins and Martin cold. The third was the most immediate.

He needed to go to the restroom.

Morris left his bag on the chair and headed to the first restroom. It was only about 50 yards away, but it was closed for cleaning. He looked inside and saw two men cleaning the Men's Room. He didn't look into the Ladies Room to see if it was still open as he had no intent on using it even if it were. If it turned out open and some half-dressed woman looked up and saw him looking in...it might be a hard problem to explain to Alice.

He headed off to the next restroom further down the concourse. Even before he got to it he saw the yellow tape marked "Caution" stretching across the restroom's entrance. It was closed for repairs.

Morris heard what sounded like a drill and plaster tiles breaking. The dusty look of the entrance told him that this construction work had been going on for some while, and that this restroom would also be out of commission.

"Man they start construction early in New Mexico," was his joking retort.

Morris looked back and barely saw the restroom he had just left. Since the janitorial cart was still in front of it he figured they were still cleaning it.

Morris looked down the concourse and saw another restroom. He checked his watch and realized he could make use that restroom and still make his flight.

Morris turned to walk to the distant restroom, but in doing so he didn't notice the man that had gotten up from the assembled Aeromexicali Airlines passengers. The man was walking to the restroom that Morris had just left. Rather than see if it were available to use, he simply walked over to the construction cart and gave it a quick review.

After he saw what he was looking for he stepped back a pace and looked around. Morris had not yet reached the other restroom and all of the other passengers were still assembled a distance away. The man walked back to the cart and leaned over to the far side of it, deftly reaching down and pulling up a long screwdriver and a half roll of the same yellow "Caution" tape that stretched across the restroom opening.

He found the beginning of the tape roll while he was walking towards the restroom that Morris just entered, and pulled a length of it out. He'd been scanning the restroom for a few minutes, so he knew only Morris was in it. When he reached it he stuck one end of the tape on the restroom entrance edge and pulled a length of it long enough to reach across and effectively close the restroom. He stuck his head into the ladies side of the restroom and turned off the lights, giving it the appearance of being out of order.

Like Morris, this man's plans were adversely affected by the plane's sudden diversion to Albuquerque. Just like Morris, he now had to fashion a whole new comprehensive plan of action quickly. Unlike Morris', his plans didn't have to be tactical, multi-faceted or thorough. They just had to be brutally, and mercilessly, efficient.

Morris had finished using one of the urinals and was washing his hands. He's was nearly finished when he noticed that the man who had just entered was standing there doing nothing more than rubbing his hands and staring at him.

Then suddenly, he advanced towards Morris.

Morris finished quickly and as he did the other man spoke.

"You should have known that we'd be prepared" He took one step and then swung at Morris. Morris ducked and stepped aside as the closed hand flew over his head.

Morris recovered quickly enough to see that his opponent was wearing leather gloves

"*He wasn't rubbing his hands,*" Morris thought, "*He was putting those damned things on.*"

The gloves would allow the attacker to deliver high impact blows without leaving tell-tale cuts and bruises.

They were now standing four paces apart. Morris was looking at his enemy and trying to piece together an attack.

Morris thought of screaming for help, but he didn't. In a flash he knows that while calling for help will bring an end to this attack, he'll also be kept by the authorities past his flight. He had to be on the San Francisco bound plane regardless of what happens now. He looked at his opponent and realized for the first time today, but probably not the last time today, it's all or nothing.

His opponent stood there soundlessly thinking of a way to silently, and quickly, end this matter. This action was not supposed to take place on American soil. He may have doubted that he would have been caught committing murder in Mexico, but he damn sure didn't want to get caught in America.

While Morris was trying to stare down his attacker, he was formulating his next plan of action.

"I've taken all kinds of crap from you and those like you," Morris started. "That ends here and now, starting with you. I thought if I ran you people would figure that I was afraid and leave me the hell alone. But no, you bastards figured if I didn't fight back I would be an even easier mark. Well you're wrong. I'm fighting back now. The company that hired you will find that out later today. But you, you asshole, you're about to find out now!"

Morris snatched a plastic tissue dispenser off of the counter and threw it at his assailant. He ducked underneath it easily, as Morris intended for him to do. But it set him up for Morris' next move.

Interlocking his fingers, Morris came down as hard as he could with his combined fist on the back of his assailant's neck. He fell hard to the ground and when he hit Morris heard a strangely metallic sound, like a piece of steel sliding across tile. Morris looked and thought he saw a knife or other long pointed object, but he didn't have time to focus. His attacker quickly rose up and started closing in again.

He swung at Morris, who easily evaded the blow and threw one of his own, catching his attacker just under his right eye. Morris saw the man's head snap with the blow, but realized that it didn't do much harm.

At that moment, the hood realized that he had held the advantage all along. The words and the new found confidence of his opponent could not be backed up – at least not physically. He saw Morris throw that last punch and he knew that Morris had put everything he had behind it. Although it stung, it wasn't hard enough to cause serious injury.

He now approached Morris with the knowledge that Morris' greatest punches were not going to stop him.

Morris swung, but his attacker raised his left arm to block it and countered with a right to the temple. The blow dropped Morris to one knee.

The attacker turned around and scanned the ground and then saw what he was looking for. He walked across the bathroom to where his weapon had skittered and slowly bent over to pick it up. After he picked it up he straightened and then started turning towards Morris.

Morris was already up to one knee when he saw his attacker bending down to pick something up. He stood and began running as fast as he could towards his attacker. He crouched low to the ground and bent at the waist with his back almost straight with the floor.

He caught his attacker around the waist and in less than two steps slammed him against the hard tiled wall.

Morris fell backwards and landed on the floor, barely hearing the anguished hiss being made by his attacker. Morris noticed that the man was having trouble breathing and that his feet were two to three inches off of the floor. He knew that he must have lifted the man from the floor when they first impacted but Morris didn't comprehend why he was still in the air.

Morris looked back at his adversary's face and saw a mask of twisted pain. It just took a slight glance to each side for Morris to realize what happened.

As he looked at the wall he saw a continuous row of metal coat hangers. These were those mass produced coat racks that stick out about three inches and have a lower, curved hook.

The only spot were Morris couldn't see the coat hangers was the spot were his attacker was. What he did see was a small pool of blood under the man, a small pool that was growing.

When Morris picked up his attacker and slammed him into the wall, he inadvertently drove him onto one of these. The top prong of the coat rack pierced the attacker's back, broke a rib and punctured a lung. He was still impaled on the rack, but he was trying his best to lift himself off of it. Unfortunately for him he was failing miserably.

Morris took another look at his attacker and saw this as his big chance to get away. He turned to the door and took two steps when he stopped and turned around.

He didn't give the slightest damn about the man hanging on the hook. *"Hell,"* thought Morris, *"whatever happens to him, he deserved it big-time."* But he still couldn't reconcile the fact that he had been reduced to the point where he might leave a man to die.

"That's not who I am."

Morris walked over to his former attacker. When Morris first noticed that his attacker was somehow impaled on the wall, he saw that the man was trying hard to get himself down. It was as though he was trying to pull himself off of the object penetrating his back. Now he was just coughing up blood and having trouble keeping his eyes open. Morris grabbed him under his arms and gently pulled him backwards till he could feel he was free and then lowered him down onto the floor. Morris rolled him onto his back and moved up over his face.

"Look" he began, "I'm not a doctor but you have a deep hole in your back and I think you've got a major internal problem, judging by your blood flow. I put you on your back so that the injury would drain blood outside of you rather than into you. I think your coughing means that you were drowning on your own blood. You won't now."

Morris looked up the wall at the streak of blood from just under the coat rack to the floor.

Before he could turn back he felt a hand grab his arm.

The man had reached out and grabbed Morris, as if asking him to stay until help arrived. Morris looked at him and then gently pried his arm free

"I'll send help back here for you. But I'll be gone before it gets here. It'll be in your best interest not to tell them about me because if you do, you'll have to explain what you were trying to do. My self-defense argument will work so much better than a discussion about your conspiracy to commit murder."

The man stared at Morris, and after staring back at him for a second, Morris rose and headed out of the restroom. Morris would later state that even through the pain and agony from his injury, the attacker's glare showed that he understood Morris' implication.

CHAPTER 35

PREPARATION

The plane bringing Morris back to San Francisco landed at a little before 7 a.m. Alice and Nelson were at San Francisco International, awaiting his arrival. They had quite a story to tell him, and he had one for them. But both sides knew that their war stories would have to wait. Their battle had not yet been fought, and they still needed to prepare for the events to come.

Schilling was now fully informed as to what Morris and Nelson knew about the Bennington Oil/Monty-O takeover attempt, and he was saving the front page of tomorrow's newspaper to cover the events scheduled for later today. He was the only newspaper editor in the Bay Area in possession of the information he had, and he was planning a grand spread. It was not lost upon him that he was now getting his own back from the company that had caused him to pull a story against his wishes just days ago. He almost wished Jack Abbs from advertising were here to see this.

"Let's see you protect their sorry asses now!"

While Schilling was not above gloating, his professionalism instinctively reminded him that there was a time and a place for everything, and that right now the time was for putting together a great front page on his exclusive. All he was waiting for was the outcome of the Bennington Oil press conference.

They started heading back towards the doors, and down to the cars that would take them back to the Bennington Oil Building. Schilling made sure that his best photographer, criminal writer and business writer were going to be in attendance. He had briefed them on what to expect and they were ready.

As they were getting into their cars, Morris looked over and said, "Before we go to the press conference I have some stops to make."

The first stop is the federal building and the FBI. This stop was expected, as Morris had some information that he felt Special Agent Halloran might want. The next stop caught the entire group by surprise. Except Morris.

"This is the San Francisco police department, or at least one of their precincts, Nelson began, "Dave we're dealing with federal issues here. What could you possibly want with these guys?"

"Help" said Dave, "The kind of help we'll need but that we'll never be able to get. Up till now we couldn't even think like the people who get the kind of help I'm looking for here."

Nelson looked at Morris and looked back at the police building. At that time, a light came on in his cognitive process. Alice simultaneously came to the same conclusion. She spoke first.

"You're not possibly thinking about?"

"Yes" said Dave, "I need a Priest."

Forty five minutes later Morris came out of the police station with a tall hulking figure. They all recognized the Priest as the assailant who attacked Morris in the alley. The tall figure walking next to Morris maintained a menacing stance even when he wasn't on the attack. Yet Morris did not seem to fear him. He almost seemed like he was in control; in control of a man who recently pummeled him and tried to kill him. Yet here they were, and the man known as the Priest made no effort to harm or move away from Morris. He seemed like he was being controlled, and he wasn't fighting it.

"Dave, are you crazy?" blurted Nelson.

"Yeah" said Morris, "I'm crazy. That's my only advantage. They don't think I can be like them. They think I'm in Mexico City about to be served up by their assassin. Instead I'm coming back at them when they are going to be exposed the most-during their press conference. And this time I'll be armed with their number one weapon."

Morris nodded towards the Priest. Alice and Nelson looked over at the Priest, who smiled and nodded back at them.

This is too damn hard to believe," said Nelson.

"Look," Morris began, "this is almost too crazy for me to believe," he said stopping to ponder before finishing, "but the rest of my life hinges on what I do today."

He looked back over to Alice.

"One way or another Alice, this will be over today. I promise."

She saw the determination in his face and she knew that today would be a turning point for him. One way or another.

CHAPTER 36

OPENING GAMBIT

The public relations executive, the lawyer, the reporter and the former security guard got out of their vehicles and met at the entrance of the Bennington Oil building. With them was another figure whose height and stature dwarfed his erstwhile companions. The man they simply knew as the Priest unnerved every member of the group except Morris. For reasons of his own, Morris knew that not only was the Priest of no danger to this group, but in fact he was in their debt in a manner that none of them could begin to understand. He was their trump card.

At the entrance of the Bennington Building Morris stopped and looked upward. The shining glass spire reflected the sunlight off its face. One of the reflected beams was shining directly on Morris and his group, and while he didn't consider himself overly spiritual, he saw this as a good sign.

He turned and looked back at Alice, who was also looking up at the building's facade in an effort to steel herself for the role that she would be playing in just a few minutes.

Morris walked the two steps over to her and gently touched her on the elbow. She looked down from the building and smiled at him.

Morris wanted to say a million things to her. He wanted to thank her for being his rock, for helping and believing him when only a few would; for being there for him when it seemed as though life couldn't get any worse. He knew he was looking into the eyes of a special person, but he also recognized that he was looking into the eyes of a person he brought into this mess. He could see the fear in her eyes that she was masking so well with every other part of her presence.

He had wanted to speak to her about what was going on and to tell her how much her support meant, but he also wanted to reassure her that this nightmare was concluding today.

"Alice," he began, "I..." he stopped

"Yes, Dave" she inquired.

"I'm sorry about what's been going on. You were never meant to be a part of this. I didn't want you to...."

Alice stopped him cold

"Dave, we're a team, remember? I got involved with this the minute those two tankers collided and you got pulled into it."

She smiled at Dave and added, "Let's end this now! As you like to say, `They called down the thunder..."

"...now here it comes." Morris finished.

As they looked each other in the eyes for just the briefest second, Morris noticed that the fear he saw earlier was gone and her trademark resolution was replacing it. He also knew that he was looking into the eyes of his best friend, trusted confidant and, in short, the love of his life. Somehow, he knew she felt the same thing.

Nelson walked over to the Priest and was just out of earshot when he spoke.

"Look," Nelson began, "now that you're on our side this might come in handy." Nelson pulled a small metal expandable baton from his coat and gave it to the Priest.

"I figured you dropped it in the alley the other night."

The Priest nodded and put the baton in his waistband.

Morris turned and looked at his assembled group. It wasn't much to be going up against a Fortune 500 company, but he had surprise and right on his side. He was hoping that would be enough.

"Let's go do it." he courageously offered.

At that, they turned into the building and separated.

Fifteen minutes before the press conference was to begin Alice and Nelson entered the fourteenth floor conference room. Forty five other journalists were already there and the best positions for pictures and interviews were already taken. This was exactly what Nelson wanted, as now they would have to blend in and mingle as opposed to being easily identified. While Nelson started getting set up, Alice scanned the room, looking for the furthest point from the podium where a visiting journalist could actually be positioned. It was where she needed to be in less than twelve minutes. She had also scanned the crowd in the most discreet manner possible, as someone looking around for suspicious people tend to get labeled as suspicious themselves. She wanted to know where the security was without drawing her attention to them.

"In just a few minutes I'll let them know where I am" she thought. *"But that minute isn't here yet."*

In scanning the room she saw Martin and Jenkins talking. She had never met them personally, and only pictures from the company's most recent annual statement provided her with an idea of what they looked like. Her scanning had also discovered three good-sized men in business suits who were too well dressed to be media reporters; their lack of camera equipment or support personnel led her to suspect that they were not on-air broadcast reporters as well. They were not milling about or engaging in conversation. They seemed to be on guard for something.

This was a problem for Alice. She was about to play her part in this drama and getting caught as she started would doom everything to failure.

She needed to know if these gentlemen were security. She had to know where they would be standing before she started. And as she has done in every other part of her life, Alice took the initiative.

She walked over to the closest of the three men she suspected to be guards.

"Excuse me," she began while offering her widest smile, "but do you know where the ladies' rooms are?"

"I'm sorry," came the deep-throated reply, "But I can't

help you with that. You might try the folks at the table where you signed in."

"Thank you," Alice replied. While standing before the guard she also noticed a feint wire leading into some kind of earpiece and a peculiar bulging in the upper left quadrant of the man's jacket. She didn't need to see or ask more to know that this was not an executive with Bennington, or a member of the Bennington Building's hospitality staff

"*That was easy enough,*" she thought. "*Since any usher would know where the customer comfort stations were, he isn't an usher. The jacket and earpiece say both security and connected to some sort of control facility or the other security guards.*"

She walked back to her seat next to Nelson and filled him in on her suspected guards were and that they may have a faster backup response than they considered. Nelson nodded and leaned over and whispered something in her ear. She nodded before breaking into a smile that barely hid her enjoyment of what he was saying.

Looking back at Nelson, she asked, "Do you think this will work?"

"I don't know," he began, "But regardless of how this turns out, it starts now."

Alice looked at her watch. The press conference was due to start in three minutes and her role was to start now.

She looked back at Nelson and smiled.

"Here goes!" was her resolute salutation.

The assembled media had placed their microphones in position and had performed their sound checks. Camera lenses and light meters had the speaker's podium properly sighted. Jenkins and Martin stood by the door waiting for a lower level public relations official to welcome the assembled media and give a brief overview of the purpose behind the press conference. The public relations official was looking to Martin for a sign to begin. All that was left was the silent, awkward moment that takes place before a major announcement.

In an instant, that moment was mightily disturbed.

"BENNINGTON OIL WAS RESPONSIBLE FOR THE TANKER CRASH!' yelled a well-dressed black woman from the very back of the conference room.

Like everyone else in the room, Nelson turned around to see the commotion. Unlike everyone else in the room, Nelson knew who was causing the commotion.

"THEIR   CRIMINALLY   NEGLIGENT MAINTENANCE ALLOWED..." Alice was cut short as the first of the security guards reached her and commanded her to be quiet. She thought about not complying with this request, but she was told in advance not to resist because the security contingent might use force. The three guards brusquely led her to the door.

"What the hell was that all about?" Martin asked.

"Nothing much," replied Jenkins. "Just a little situation that I had anticipated."

Jenkins had figured that an environmentalist or two might intrude and cause a scene, which is why he hired professional security over the buildings' normal security to watch over the crowd.

The guards were going to take her downstairs and turn her over to building security until the police, who would soon be summoned, arrived.

The media was still staring at the demonstrator, known only to one of them, as she was being led out. Jenkins and Martin were staring at them as well as they left the conference room and headed downstairs.

Jenkins had prepared for this distraction, but as he looked across the room he noticed that there was no more security present. His background and experience led him to process this situation quickly.

"It's a trap!' he muttered

Jenkins quickly stepped into the corridor to use the closed circuit security phone to either recall the security contingent or to try and get replacements. His cell phone in the conference room would have meant speaking loudly enough for others to hear. Especially the gathered media host.

Martin was just a step behind Jenkins, preparing to ask why he needed to leave the conference room.

Jenkins had barely stepped to the phone when a large man stepped between him and the wall. Jenkins looked up and stared into the face of the Priest.

The Priest motioned for Jenkins to step away from the phone, and reinforced his order by opening his coat and showing Jenkins the merest tip of the metal baton hidden in his waistband. Jenkins then looked around the corridor before realizing that no additional security was arriving.

My orders," began the Priest, "are to keep you quiet, by any means necessary."

"Whose orders are those?" Jenkins said contemptuously.

"Mine," said Morris, coming up behind Jenkins and Martin.

"Those orders are mine."

The hired security guards escorted the female demonstrator into a service elevator. In a not to gentle manner the guards pushed her to the back of the elevator and closed the door. The elevator took its passengers to the basement level of the Montgomery Oil Building, where they would turn the demonstrator over to the building's security force to await the police. The foreman of the Monty-O security force greeted the elevator when its doors opened.

"I'm Daniel Williams," he began. He looked at Alice and added, "So this is our troublemaker."

"Yeah," answered one of the guards from the elevator. "You guys need to call the cops and hold her until the cops get here. Think you can handle it?"

Since they worked for a private firm and not Monty-O's security force, the guards in the elevator didn't know the guards about to take their demonstrator.

Williams didn't like the last barb thrown at him by the contract security guard, but he let it slip. He figured that they weren't about to like what he was up to as well.

"We can handle her." Williams responded. "You guys need to get back upstairs."

The contract security guard didn't even acknowledge Williams' last statement as he turned back into the freight elevator with his two companions.

As the doors closed on the elevator, Williams turned around and took the few steps separating him from Alice. He let a sly smile come to his face and spoke to her.

"I don't believe you guys tried a stunt like that." Williams said. "They didn't hurt you did they?"

"I'm O.K.," Alice replied. "They seriously lacked interpersonal skills, but they didn't hurt me."

"Good," Williams replied. "Hey Phil, are you done with that computer yet?"

Phil looked up from a laptop that he was working with in the security guard shack. He had been working it for about three minutes before the contract security guards came down.

"Yeah, I'm done," was Phil's reply.

Williams took Alice's hand and led her over to where Phil was finishing up.

"Now remember Phil," Williams began sarcastically, "I'm expecting you to turn her over to the cops."

Phil smiled back at Williams.

"I will," he replied. "Dan thanks for helping me. Are you going to get into a lot of trouble over this?"

"Don't sweat it Phil," Williams replied. "I got a feeling they are going to have worse than me to worry about. By the way, how long did you program the building's computers to hold those guards up there for?"

"It'll take them twenty minutes to get where they are going. They're going to be pissed off when they get out and..."

"I wouldn't worry too much about them," Williams replied matter-of-factly. "Remember I get to carry a gun and they don't. Don't get me wrong, I mean I'll let them rant and rave, if only to vent. But only to a point."

"And when they cross that point?" asked Alice.

"Then they have the right to be silent." Williams stated. "They'll have the right to know that everything they say can and will be used against them in a court of law."

Phil and Alice both smiled, as they both knew the rest of the standard Miranda warnings that all police officers give to those whom they have arrested.

"You guys better head out, before anyone else comes around."

"And Phil," Williams continued, "thanks for the helping me clear up my credit report and get the home loan. We couldn't have done it without you."

"That's alright," Phil started.

"Hey Dan," Phil added.

Williams turned and looked at Phil.

"Keep in touch, O.K."

"I will," Williams replied.

"Fixing up credit reports Phil?" Alice inquired. "Phil, as a lawyer, should I have heard that?"

"Heard what?" was Phil's answer.

"Oh, nothing" Alice said, thinking of her equally audacious airline foray of less than 24 hours ago.

"Thanks" said Phil.

"The thanks is all mine," Alice replied.

Three minutes earlier the leader of the contract security guards got in and pushed the button to go back to the 14th floor conference room. The elevator began ascending and when it got to the seventh floor promptly stopped. The guards began pushing buttons in a futile attempt to get the elevator moving. It didn't budge. One of the guards opened the compartment containing the emergency phone, but found that the line was dead. In the same compartment however was a typewritten note. One of the guards withdrew the note and began reading it aloud.

"Dear Friends" the note began, *"by now you will realize that the elevator is not working. This is due to it being programmed to remain here for twenty minutes. After that it will operate smoothly. At no time will you be in any danger because in the event of a fire or other natural disaster the elevators automatically go to the bottom floor. But until such occurrence, or the remainder of twenty minutes, you will be contained within this elevator. Also, it is stopped on a floor where the building's own concrete and steel framework will compromise the reception to your cell phones. In short gentlemen just sit back and enjoy it, because you have no other options. The Management.*

The guards sat down on the floor of the elevator and wondered aloud about what kind of scheme was going on that involved the sequestering of security.

CHAPTER 37

COUNTER OFFENSIVE

"Your calling this press conference together was, shall we say, advantageous," Morris started. "I have a complete and totally receptive audience ready to hear what I have to say."

"Morris," Jenkins began, "You're crazy if you think I'll just stand here and let you commandeer my press conference."

Morris could feel the anger seething in each of Jenkins' words. He enjoyed it because it meant he was getting to Jenkins.

"I don't think you'll stand there and let me take over your press conference" Morris said. "But if you try to stop me, or you too, for that fact," said Morris while looking at Martin, "neither of you will be standing for long."

"He'll see to that," said Morris, motioning his head towards the Priest.

Morris leaned over closer to Jenkins.

"He's pretty damn good at it – take it from me personally."

Jenkins looked contemptuously at Morris before turning to face the Priest.

"Whatever he's paying you," Jenkins seethed, "I'll triple it. Just shut him up and get him out of here!"

Jenkins turned and almost took a step back towards the conference room when a large hand lowered onto his shoulder and stopped him.

"You can't top his bid," the Priest said to Jenkins.

Jenkins was taken aback, almost as much as by the Priest's refusal to accept his offer as by the large hand holding him in place.

"Why not?" Jenkins enquired.

"Because," Morris started, "California is three strikes and you're never going to get out of prison state. With two prior felony convictions, his next one means an automatic life sentence with no chance at parole. As you can see he's a healthy, strapping lad..."

"Thanks" interjected the Priest.

"Forget it," Morris replied.

"Anyway, his life expectancy is at least thirty five years beyond where he is today. So I made a deal with him. He helps me commandeer your press conference and I'll drop the felony assault charges. He jumped on that chance like a cannibal on a missionary. What could you possibly offer him to top that—his freedom for the rest of his life."

Jenkins looked over at the Priest.

"I know countless different felonious acts that you've committed. Crush this insect now or I'll turn you in myself!"

"Nice try," countered Morris. Morris looked over at the Priest as well.

"Didn't I tell you that he'd try that?"

The Priest nodded in the affirmative.

"Just try that," Morris added. "But remember, in every felonious act that you talk about, either you commissioned it or you had knowledge of it. A high ranking corporate exec or a paid thug – who do you think the feds will give immunity to? Under immunity he can tell everything he knows about you activities -- regardless of his complicity."

"In short" said Morris, "he gets off scot-free and you get indicted for the things he did under your direction."

Jenkins quickly surveyed the room one more time, in preparation of making a mad dash and screaming for help.

The Priest noticed Jenkins' subtle review of the conference room and took a step over to block the move.

"Don't even think it," said the Priest. "I was told that if I only get one of you, it would be you." He again pulled back his jacket and revealed the butt of a small metal baton.

"I'll get you before you go two steps. And I guarantee that you won't wake up before this time tomorrow. I'm not doing life; not for you people."

Jenkins realized that the trap was closing around him, but he remained combative.

"With all the media assembled here, you won't get away with assaulting me" he said.

"Picture this," Morris began, "He'll beat you to a pulp and then turn states evidence on you if you decide to press charges. You'll get the beating of your life, shown on national television and you won't be able to do a damn thing about it."

"Actually" said the Priest, "if either of you tries to run I'll take both of you out."

"He is that good." Morris added, somewhat facetiously.

"Alright" said Jenkins, "you have the podium. Just what is it that you plan to say?"

Morris looked at Jenkins and met his gaze with matched intensity.

"I'm going to tell the truth."

"The truth," Jenkins snickered, "you have no idea of what the truth really is."

"Here's the truth Jenkins," Morris started, "I know about the tanker collision and how you and Martin here had the crew lie about what actually happened. I know about the Louisiana Project, Monty-O's expenditures, Ferryman's part in this and his subsequent death outside of Vegas..."

"Ferryman's dead?" Martin blurted. He looked over to Jenkins with the shocked look of a man who had just found out that his problems had just multiplied ten-fold.

In a barely audible voice, Martin said, "My God, Jenkins just what have you done?"

"What have we done," Jenkins added with emphasis on the word `we', "What have we done?"

"Anyway" Jenkins continued. "We didn't kill Ferryman. He drank a lot and he liked his women like his cars – fast and unique. He was the kind of man whose ego would always be in turbo, if he only had the money. You don't have to kill some people. You just set up the proper scenario and they'll kill themselves. Make them careless and place them in an arena where they can show off and they'll blow it every time. We gave him the alcohol and we gave him the cash and set him up in Vegas. The rest he did on his own."

Morris continued.

I'll also talk how you used some of Wall Street's biggest investors to force a takeover to try and buy Monty-O on the cheap, especially and right up to the crash.

Each part of this bizarre puzzle was laid out in such a manner as to make it seem that Bennington Oil was taking over Monty-O. Even forcing Monty-O to reveal its discovery of a gas giant in the Gulf of Mexico was just a ruse for the real gambit – eh, Jenkins.

Jenkins simply glowered at Morris.

Morris paused for a second, but just so he could turn towards Martin.

"Bill," Morris started, "you got played right along with the rest of us. You were going to go out there and announce that Bennington Oil was going to break off its takeover.

"After all," Morris continued, "once Monty-O disclosed the new major discovery their stock price has nearly tripled. It'll go up even more in the coming weeks if the figures I read about the discovery were correct."

"Anyway," he went on, "Jenkins played us all for fools. He got Bennington Oil to go after Monty-O once he found out about the Louisiana Project. He got the Wall Street investors to tie up huge chunks of Monty-O stock—he even got Bennington Oil to buy up huge chunks of our own stock in anticipation of the windfall that would come when we assumed control of Monty-O.

"This all gave the impression that someone was trying to buy Monty-O. The tanker collision was a true accident, but it played perfectly into Jenkins hands. For a short while the investors and Bennington Oil were fighting together for Monty-O. The cost of cleaning the oil slick and numerous lawsuits simply added to the forces driving down the price of Monty-O stock. And while the stock was free falling, there stood Bennington Oil and the investors, waiting for the stock price plummet to stop and to pounce on the cheapened stock.

Then Jenkins here went and pissed off the investors, telling them Bennington Oil couldn't pay them the agreed upon price for their stock because the price free fall had driven the price too low to pay what he had promised. The investors had spent so much money based on Jenkins assertions that they were now in a financial position where they had to take over Monty-O themselves just to get their money back."

"But even while this was happening," Morris continued, shifting his gaze to Jenkins again, "this bastard sold Bennington Oil out."

"What do you mean?" Martin inquired.

"Martin," Morris began, "Have you ever heard of Bremerton Skye and McIntosh Financial, Ltd in London?"

"Why would I?" Martin replied.

"Because while everyone else was waiting for Monty-O stocks to stop free falling, Bremerton Skye and McIntosh bought over $500 million in Monty-O stock. Since that was less than 5% of the stock and since this company doesn't have the wherewithal to pull off this takeover—they positioned themselves to benefit and make a serious strike."

"Now follow me," Morris said.

"The collision," Morris continued, "and all of the other collateral acts have driven down Monty-O stock prices. While once allies, the investors and Bennington Oil are now fighting to carve up Monty-O. A third party then starts buying up Monty-O shares, giving the impression that another suitor has entered the battle. But the third party isn't interested in taking over Monty-O, in fact they are too small to do it. The have another goal. They wanted to hold onto a significant stock position when Monty-O revealed the Louisiana Project. They knew that Monty-O was damn near working in secret about the Louisiana Project. They knew that if the Louisiana Project was announced that Monty-O stock would skyrocket. All that was needed was an external stimulus that would make Monty-O feel threatened enough to reveal its most sensitive secret. That's where Jenkins came in."

"Jenkins was the one who needed to craft this mosaic so that Monty-O would react as expected. I doubt that Bennington Oil was ever really going to take over Monty-O.

But Jenkins gets all of us here at Bennington Oil all juiced up about taking over Monty-O. Bremerton Skye and McIntosh buy their shares and waits for Jenkins to lead us to an attempted takeover. Monty-O reveals their massive new petroleum discovery to prevent them from being taken over and their shares skyrocket. They've tripled already in just a few days. The investors who were trying to take over Monty-O are happy because the stock is now over their break-even point. In London, champagne corks are popping at a certain investment firm. Monty-O is breathing easier because their survival is ensured, at least for the short term. The only people who are going to get left behind are the workers and shareholders of Bennington Oil. Once Monty-O brings the Louisiana Project on-line they will be so flush with cash that they will have the tools to take Bennington Oil over and reduce it to its component parts. The hard assets will get sold and the soft assets will get fired. There won't be a Bennington Oil in two years, but you really don't give a damn about that do you Jenkins?"

Jenkins didn't say a word and continued his harsh stare at Morris. It showed Morris that he was striking a chord with Jenkins.

"Bremerton Skye and McIntosh's shares in Monty-O have already tripled and may go higher before long, as the stock is still rising rapidly. The total price of their holdings could reach $1.5 billion - a $1 billion dollars profit on a $500 million investment in just days. And I'll bet Jenkins here will be sharing in that windfall and everyone else at Bennington Oil be damned."

"Think about it Martin," Morris continued, "if he only got a 20% slice of the profit for running this menagerie he could be in for over $200 million—all of it offshore."

Jenkins looked at Morris and Martin.

"Pretty good Hercule Poirot" Jenkins said sarcastically. "You pieced together a very complex puzzle."

Jenkins was as stern faced as ever, still trying to stare down his adversary. But this time his adversary was different. The recent experiences that Morris had endured had hardened him, and he had no intention of being beaten down again, physically or mentally.

Jenkins spoke up.

"I put this plan together and I mean for it to work. I won't let you stop me. Besides, you're already too late. Bremerton Skye and McIntosh will have already cashed out by now and they are adept at covering their tracks. You'll tell an interesting story to the press, but one you won't be able to back up."

Jenkins was playing his last card and he knew it. He was trying to figure out how to deal with this last change in plans. He looked contemptuously at Martin, thinking *"If only you had handled him like I told you too!"*

Jenkins smiled and looked at Morris.

"It's too late; you see I've already won."

Martin was beside himself with rage and made no attempt to hold his anger back.

"Why you double-crossing bastard," Martin blurted, "you were selling all of us down the river for a small piece of the action...."

"That small piece of the action," Jenkins shot back, "will ensure that my great grandchildren won't have to work."

"I trusted you," Martin added, "the board, the front office and the CEO, we all trusted you!"

"And I trusted no one," Jenkins added smugly. "And guess who got screwed?"

Jenkins was getting cocky; he was almost enjoying this banter.

"My money is in an offshore account and I got 33%, not 20%. That's just above $330 million. I don't suppose your paltry stock options and employee stock option program contributions will pay you as well."

"Do you really think that you'll get away with?" Morris asked.

"I know I will," Jenkins replied triumphantly. "You can get mad, but you can't get even. I've already won, so go out there and host your damn press conference."

"But know this." Jenkins seethed, "You'll pay for this intrusion. I swear it!"

Morris looked at the Priest and nodded his head towards an open conference room down the hall. Martin could barely lift his feet as he walked while Jenkins's steps were as light as the air.

The Priest noticed this difference in steps and kept a closer eye on Jenkins than Martin. It was a precaution that no one present felt was needed. Jenkins knew what the Priest was capable of. No one thought he had intentions of finding out how effective he was on a first-hand basis. He walked down the hall and turned into the conference room.

A few feet behind and traveling significantly slower was a visibly affected Martin. He was trying to figure out how to salvage the rest of his career.

The Priest had turned around to Martin and spoke.

"Let's hurry it up, I don't have all day."

Even though they were only a few feet behind, Jenkins was putting the few seconds he had before the Priest entered the room to good use. He quickly scanned the room and noticed a small metal fire extinguisher on the wall.

"Perfect" Jenkins thought.

Jenkins quickly took the extinguisher off of its hook and held it over his head with both hands. He figured to immediately render the Priest useless and then get to Morris before he had a chance to speak.

Hiding behind the open door, Jenkins spoke.

"You two coming in here or what?"

"We're coming so just shut up," was the Priest's reply.

Judging from the sound of the reply Jenkins determined that the Priest was first. He tightened his grip on the fire extinguisher, making sure that he held it securely enough to make sure that the first blow counted. There might not be a second swing.

Jenkins saw the first figure come through the door and swung. Jenkins had anticipated that the blow would strike the Priest on the bridge of his nose; potentially a fatal blow. He was counting on it either killing the Priest or rendering his useless. He then figured in the following confusion that he could also get to Morris with the extinguisher, or at least disrupt the assembled media in the hope that his security could respond and apprehend Morris. His calculation took many variables into consideration. There was just one slight problem that he hadn't considered.

He didn't figure on Martin being the first one through the door.

Jenkins swing grazed Martin's forehead and nothing more.

"I figured as much," said the Priest. "He withdrew the metal baton from the front of his clothing and extended it to its full length.

Morris had watched the trio go into the conference and was ready to go to the press conference when he heard five quick sounds that sounded like someone punching a pillow.

"They couldn't have been stupid enough to try and test that guy's abilities?" he thought.

Morris turned to go to the conference room when he decided that he didn't want to know what had just happened with Martin and Jenkins. He turned and went into the main conference room, where the assembled press awaited a press conference.

Morris was intending to see that they got one.

CHAPTER 38

CHECKMATE

It was his moment.

He had been through much to be where he was. He looked at all of the media assembled in the room and he knew the culmination of his battle with Bennington Oil was now.

He looked at his watch, realized that everyone there had come for a press conference, and as he strode to the podium he realized that in just a few seconds he would begin a speech that would change his life.

"Ladies and gentlemen of the media," he began, "I have a story to tell you about greed, about dishonesty and about how the truth can never stay hidden."

Morris began telling the whole story of Bennington Oil's attempts to acquire Monty-O. He told the whole story as he came to know it, in excruciating and agonizingly real detail. He spoke about the illegal deals, the attacks upon him, the lies spread by other corporate officials and the greed that led otherwise noble men to perform so egregiously. He spoke about the accidental ship collision and how its consequences were manipulated for Bennington Oil's needs. He spoke of a ship's master who was so agonized over the role he played that he ended his own life, and he spoke how others gleefully engaged in felonious securities activities. He spoke about the irony of watching people who knew better behaving in a manner beneath contempt, all for greed.

He spoke for almost an hour to an assembled news media that could not believe what it was hearing. The questions would take almost another hour longer.

All Morris wanted to do was to make sure that the truth got out. It wasn't just to set him free, it was to restore the order of his life. People like Jenkins were taking corporations to the cleaners for the better part of the last generation. Waiting for them to change and engage ethics, or waiting for the government to act in the interest of the people, were fools' choices. Morris had to not only find the truth but he had to tell it to everyone. Otherwise when would be no better than the type of people he loathed. He couldn't change the entire corporate world, but he could impact the part of it he touched.

Morris wanted to be sure that he stayed true to his teachings, his beliefs, his parents and himself. Morals, ethics, truth, professionalism and conviction weren't just easily discarded buzz words for him. He didn't just do his job; he believed in it. He didn't believe that he had to change for his job. He believed in the truth.

His belief was not misplaced; the truth was the only thing that saved him. That and a small cadre of friends and strangers who were willing to risk much for a man who was daring to risk all.

There's a story out there about a storm that had such powerful waves that thousands of small crabs got washed far up on the beach. After the storm one man ran out and started throwing the crabs back into the surf. Even though some pinched him out of fear, he continued to throw the crabs back into the surf. A bystander approached and saw the thousands of beached crabs and yelled at the man throwing them back, "What are you doing? You aren't going to make much of a difference on this beach." The man yelled back, "I know." He said, picking up another crab. "But I can make a difference for this crab." And as he reached for another, "And I can make a difference for this crab."

This was the integrity's plight Morris had confronted. He had faced the biggest crisis of his life and won by refusing to abandon the rules and the laws that guided him. He won because he chose to get involved rather than abdicate his responsibilities and just complain from the margins.

He managed to stand tall by just standing up.

This was all a part of Morris' truth, and that was why only he could tell it. But the truth he was exposing wasn't everything. He would come to find even more truth than he could handle or comprehend. Even as he was speaking from the podium, the truth kept unfolding.

Upset at being on the sidelines for so long, Alice took the offensive herself. While Morris was in Albuquerque, she had called a friend of hers at the Security and Exchange Commission in New York. He gave her a contact and number at the Ministry of the Exchequer in London. She called them while Morris was flying back and they spoke for over an hour. She told them that they would be very interested in what would be happening at the press conference. She also told them that Bremerton Skye and McIntosh Financial, Ltd held a substantial block of the shares in the company involved and that they were acquired through insider trading.

The Exchequer contacted the FBI and upon being given the whole story from Special Agent Halloran himself, the Ministry became very interested and took the unusual step of blocking all transactions in Monty-O until further investigation could be undertaken.

At almost the same time that the press conference was beginning and Morris was taking the podium, Bremerton Skye and McIntosh Financial, Ltd was finding itself frozen out— unable to market their shares and the British government watchdogs beginning to close in on them with some very uncomfortable questions.

Both Jenkins and Morris were unaware that this was occurring. One man was crowing that he had won, while another feared that he had lost. Both of them were wrong.

During the press conference, Alice made another call. While driving with Phil back to the Eastbay Gazette, Alice contacted the Security and Exchange Commission one more time. This call, however, was to their Enforcement Division. She had asked them about a little known law called the Bounty Provision, which was aimed at promoting and enhancing whistle blowing against insider trading. The law allowed whistle blowers to receive a percentage of the money recovered from exposing insider trading. She broke into a mile wide grin when she was told that it applied here.

She couldn't wait to tell Morris that by bringing this $7 billion dollar insider trading scam to light, he might be eligible for 3-5%.

CHAPTER 39

A SIGN OF HOPE IN THE RUINS

Morris was in his office clearing out his desk when he noticed that Martin was in his office-pretty much doing the same thing. While their particular circumstances were different, the outcome was the same. They had both been fired. Morris was fired for leading the efforts to end Bennington Oil's takeover of Monty-O, and Martin for allegedly committing, or assisting in the commission of, numerous felonies.

Morris chuckled at that thought. They would both be leaving the company by the end of the day, but they would be leaving to face different realities. Morris would need to find a job. He had some savings that would allow him to support himself, Alice and his parents, but not enough for a long term endeavor. He was not thrilled with that proposition, especially since his name had been splayed over all of the newspapers and media throughout the Bay Area. But he knew, deep down, that he had done the right thing and as simplistic a notion as that was, he still felt it had to count for something somewhere. He also felt that no matter how bad he had it, it was going to be worse for Martin

Martin was probably facing a criminal trial, a civil trial, the freezing of his assets, the withholding of his corporate stock options and other corporate compensation, and the even more daunting prospect of trying to find a corporate job at 50+

years old with a criminal record on his resume. He had gambled big and had lost. It was just now sinking in to him exactly how much he lost. Still, he fared better than Jenkins, who had already been arrested and charged.

Morris stared at Martin packing and was about to turn back to packing his own office when he thought of a question that had been on his mind for a while. He was standing in his office with a stack of books he had just taken down when he decided he would have one final conversation with Martin. He put the books down and walked over to Martin's office.

"Bill," Morris began, "I am probably the last person you want to talk to right now, but I need to know the answer to a question that has been bothering me."

Martin looked over at Morris and said nothing. His first thought was to let whatever question had been bothering Morris continue gnawing away at him for the rest of his life. Morris was right; Martin didn't want to talk to him.

Morris could see that Martin wasn't in a mood to talk, and after everything he had been through, he wasn't planning on being the target of a misplaced outburst by Martin. He turned to go back to his office when Martin spoke.

"Dave," Martin began, "don't go. What did you want to know?"

Morris didn't think that Martin was going to talk to him and as such, was a little taken aback. He recovered so quickly that Martin never noticed his reaction.

"Bill, when this started and I began looking for answers, why didn't you just fire me? It would have gotten me off of your backs?"

"You're wrong Dave," Martin replied, "It would not have gotten you off of our backs."

Martin continued. "From the time that you looked at what we had on the Strategic Planning offices databases, you knew too much. You managed to piece it together and all you needed was some small element of proof to validate whatever hypothesis you arrived at."

Martin stopped and looked at Morris. His normally hard eyes had a softened look now. He, and all of Bennington Oil, had been beaten by the man he was looking at. As conflicted as he was emotionally, that thought registered.

"I guess you found your proof."

"Anyway, we didn't fire you for a couple of reasons. First, Jenkins thought he could control you better if he knew your every move. Because of your financial commitment to your parents, we knew you couldn't afford to just up and quit, so you were here until we felt otherwise. Secondly, you did a very good job dealing with the slick. Since the slick took up most of your time, Jenkins only had to have you watched during the times you weren't working. Cutting you free would have required a greater effort on all of our parts to keep you in line. Jenkins thought that if he knew all of your whereabouts and what you were up to, that he could pull your reins in at any time he'd like. Or so he thought."

"I'll never say this again, but seeing Jenkins being led off in handcuffs was almost worth all this." Martin managed a weak smile and looked at Morris. Even though he had lost greatly, Martin took solace in the only victory that he could claim from the outcome of this matter. He came out ahead of Jenkins, and while that was very little consolation indeed, it would have to be enough. After all, that was the only bright point in this matter for Martin.

Without saying another word, Martin turned back to packing his office. Morris knew then that his conversation, and his acquaintance, with Martin was over. Morris would have preferred something different, a more collegial parting, but that call was not his to make.

CHAPTER 40

LAST ACT

In a small chartered boat twenty seven miles outside of the Golden Gate, a young man carried out the last request of a tormented, yet noble man. Morris was the only one attending this somber ceremony, yet he knew this was how Marlowe would have wanted it.

The small boat moved over to the orange and yellow buoy that was bobbing in the waves and current. Its happy colors contradicted the seriousness of its task. It marked the spot where the accommodation area of the Pacific Patriarch went down with its entire crew.

It was here that Marlowe had chosen as his final resting spot.

"We're here, Mr. Morris," a voice from the ship's bridge called out.

Morris was startled at how close they were still to the shore.

"That didn't take long," he thought.

After looking around for a quick moment he started thinking about what his next action should be.

After committing suicide, Marlowe had wished for his remains to be scattered at sea. This was just one of the instructions he left.

An envelope found on his body gave detailed instructions on what was to happen to his estate. The personal belongings would be donated to any maritime museum or home that wanted them. As he had no family that anyone knew about, what would happen with the remainder of his estate was still to be determined. The oil company carried a $1,000,000 life insurance policy on him as well as a $750,000 Master's Policy given him when he was promoted to captain all those years ago. He took another $500,000 term life policy and placed an old friend as the beneficiary. A subsequent falling out with that friend resulted in the beneficiary of his policy being his personal estate. The Victorian he had purchased and lived in since 1961 had been paid off years ago. Those who knew him would talk about he constantly griped about the $238 a month note for the entire thirty years he carried the mortgage.

Now, the contents of an envelope given to the Pieter and Feldstein law firm would determine what would happen to all of Marlowe's possessions. The same envelope carried the final request that found David Morris miles outside the Golden Gate. Marlowe had once asked Morris to make sure the truth was told. He was now asking another request of Morris; to see that his remains were taken care of. Morris agreed instantly.

Now, he walked over to the railing at the stern of the boat and looked at the buoy. He was just a touch wobbly after the journey—the sign of a slight case of seasickness. He'd later make jokes about it, "Hell, I'm Air Force, not Navy!"

He took the urn containing Marlowe's remains and looked back at the buoy.

"Like it was just a few days ago, Captain Marlowe, it's just you and me. I asked you for the truth and you gave it to me. I told you I'd put it where it belonged and I did. I paid a price, but it was nothing compared to yours. You're the only real tragedy in this whole mess. Of everything that happened, only yours was so preventable and unnecessary."

Morris found himself getting angry and moved to stop it.

"You told us everything we needed to set things rights with everybody but yourself. Why didn't you tell us what was happening inside you. We could have helped you. You didn't need to ...."

Morris suddenly realized he was just talking to the waves. No one else was within earshot and if Marlowe wasn't beyond hearing, he was beyond responding. And as they have for millions of years, the waves continued to move to and fro, gently rocking the boat as they did. As always, they never gave the slightest inclination if the heard the voices of those upon it. They offered continuity, contemplation and stability. Solace and forgiveness would have to be found elsewhere.

"You didn't do anything anyone else wouldn't have done. The world now knows what you were up against. In light of all of this it makes your last act look…"

Morris paused and looked around the railing again.

"Oh, well. It's not up to me to pass judgment. Not now. And not on you."

"You stated that this is where you wanted your remains to be placed. Nothing out here but waves." Morris smiled. "But then, this is where you've spent your life isn't it?"

"So be it, friend," Morris started. "Here you shall stay. With the winds and the waves. You'll have eternity out here in the one place you really ever called home. Farewell Captain. Marlowe. And thank you, for everything you did."

With that, Morris turned the urn over and emptied it into the Pacific. The ashes floated on the waves and then sank, taking down the last vestiges of an honorable soul who was caught in the center of man's greed, and who found it tragically incompatible with his way of life.

Morris said a silent prayer for Marlowe and then dropped the urn into the water. When he was done he waved to the boat captain. The captain nodded and started the engines. Two hours later Morris would be back in San Francisco.

The boat had barely turned to head back when Morris' cell phone rang. It was Charles Gerard from Monty-O. He had called Morris' home number and Alice gave him the cell phone number. The fight was over and Monty-O had won. Morris wondered why Gerard was calling and why it couldn't wait.

"How are you, Dave?"

"OK I guess," Morris responded, "Just trying to come to grips with all of the changes going on in my life."

"You're still out to sea aren't you?" asked Gerard. "He must have thought highly of you to ask you to carry out his last request. He knew you'd do it. Just as you did with the press conference."

"Thanks Charles," Morris stated, "I was wondering when I was going to hear something positive from anyone from the corporate world. My company couldn't fire me fast enough."

"Well Monty-O appreciates everything you've done for us" Gerard added.

"I just told the truth," Morris started, "I can't tell you how surprised I am to see people impressed by that."

"Well, there's one man in particular that you really impressed..." Gerard started.

Morris was about to thank Gerard in advance for the compliment he thought was coming.

"The old man thought that someone with your integrity, guts and smarts should be working for us" Gerard began. "I asked the boss if I could hire you to work for PR here at Monty-O"

"Are you serious?" Morris asked.

"Certainly" Gerard answered. "Richardson himself wanted your answer hours ago. When we found out where you were and what you were doing he was even more impressed. Anyhow, he figures Monty-O is going to expand significantly in the next twelve months and he wants good people to help with it. That means he's going to raid Bennington Oil until such time he plans to take it over. He suspects that you know the kind of qualified and quality people we should keep over there so he wants you on board as soon as possible."

"You interested?" asked Gerard.

"When do I start?" answered Morris.

"I'll let you know later today," said Gerard. "Before you start with us you might want to take a short vacation. Spend a week or two in Monterey. Richardson's house there is damn near a palace. One phone call and it'll be ready for you."

"You can make a call like that?" Morris asked skeptically.

"I can't" said Gerard, "but Richardson will if you want him to. Like I said earlier, you really impressed him. You have no idea what it means to have someone like him on your side. You didn't hear this from me, but with a phone call he could make your lady friend a senior partner in any firm in San Francisco. Imagine what he could do if he put some thought into it."

"Get yourself back to shore and we'll talk later. And Dave," Gerard continued, " thanks. That's from me."

Morris was puzzled but happy when he hung up the phone.

"I didn't see that coming," he added.

He dialed Alice's number and after two rings she answered.

"Dave" she said, "you won't believe who I just spoke with. He's a friend at Pieter and Feldstein. That's Captain Marlowe's law firm."

He smiled a bit upon hearing her refer to Captain Marlowe by his proper rank and title.

"Dave," she continued, "he left instructions that you were to receive everything. His house, cash, property and apparently everything else. The estate is also the beneficiary of three life insurance policies. They said that all told it's over $2 million dollars. He left you everything."

"Dave," she paused, "why would he do that?'

"He had lost hope that there was anyone out there who cared about what happened. Marlowe didn't give a damn about corporate shenanigans. He cared about those other men and his crew. He wanted to make sure the truth was told to insure that their memories wouldn't be tainted. That's all that a lot of families have left from this madness, the memories of husbands and sons lost. Protecting those memories for those families meant more to Marlowe than his life itself."

"But" Alice continued, "why did he leave it all to you?"

"I think that he believed that I would get to the truth and tell it." Morris started. "He must have suspected that it would come at some price and all I can think of is that he wanted to make sure that when it was all said and done that I was somehow taken care of, at least financially."

"Amazing" said Alice, "After all that you went through you'll be the only one at Monty-O to come out ahead."

"Yeah" said Morris, "But if I had it all to do over again I'd just as soon not have it happen."

"I hear you," Alice responded.

"Dave," she added, "You know you are, and you have always been my hero."

"Alice" Morris began, "I'm no hero. I couldn't have done all of this without you. You make me whatever hero you feel I am. You shared this nightmare with me and your only complaint was that I didn't let you do more."

"Well" Alice replied, "that's what this love stuff is about. Helping each other shoulder their problems and such. Dave...."

Morris abruptly cut her off.

Alice, I've asked you to help share the burden when all hell was breaking loose. I guess that's what love is. It's also sharing everything you have with someone with the knowledge that their happiness is your happiness."

"Is there something in particular you want to share with me?" Alice asked.

"Yes" said Morris, "All my tomorrows. All of my dreams. All of my life."

"Dave, are you asking me to......

"I'll be back on shore in less than three hours," Morris said. "Let's discuss this face to face."

"Vertically" she said with her most sultry voice, "or horizontally?

"You decide," he laughingly replied, "but you only have two hours to make a choice. I'll see you then."

"Alice," he added just before hanging up, "I've always loved you and I know that I always will."

As he looked out over the waves, Morris smiled again. He was just starting to recognize that in less than three hours he would be starting a life far different than the one he had when he left San Francisco.

He couldn't wait to begin.

GREGORY BELL

ABOUT THE AUTHOR

Gregory is the third of six siblings born to Marcus and Doris Bell. His father served twenty two years in the US Air Force before retiring in 1972. His main reason for leaving the Air Force was to ensure that all of his children could receive a quality education in one location; a location that both he and Doris could personally supervise. Their active involvement in their children's education is why five out of their six children graduated from college and all five have advanced degrees. Gregory was accepted to and attended the California State University at Hayward in Hayward California, graduating in 1979 with a B.A in Mass Communication.

Following his father's military footsteps, Bell participated in the Air Force Reserve Officer Training Corp at U.C. Berkeley. Commissioned in the U.S. Air Force as a Second Lieutenant, he began his career as a Public Affairs Officer at Beale Air Force Base in Marysville California. He would later be stationed in San Antonio, Texas; RAF Lakenheath, United Kingdom and lastly in Dallas Texas. He would also go on to earn a Master's in Public Administration from Troy State University, Alabama, in 1989. Bell left the Air Force to attend the University of Washington School Of Law, graduating in June 1995 and becoming a member of the Washington State Bar Association in February 1996.

GREGORY BELL

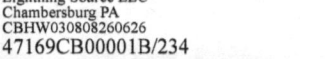